CW00821210

Mary J. Holmes

The English Orphans

Mary J. Holmes

The English Orphans

1st Edition | ISBN: 978-3-75236-185-8

Place of Publication: Frankfurt am Main, Germany

Year of Publication: 2020

Outlook Verlag GmbH, Germany.

Reproduction of the original.

THE ENGLISH ORPHANS

BY

MRS. MARY J. HOLMES

CHAPTER I.

THE EMIGRANTS.

"What makes you keep that big blue sun-bonnet drawn so closely over your face? are you afraid of having it seen?"

The person addressed was a pale, sickly-looking child about nine years of age, who, on the deck of the vessel Windermere, was gazing intently towards the distant shores of old England, which were fast receding from view. Near her a fine-looking boy of fourteen was standing, and trying in vain to gain a look at the features so securely shaded from view by the gingham bonnet.

At the sound of his voice the little girl started, and without turning her head, replied, "Nobody wants to see me, I am so ugly and disagreeable."

"Ugly are you?" repeated the boy, and at the same time lifting her up and forcibly holding her hands, he succeeded in looking her fully in the face, "Well, you are not very handsome, that's a fact," said he, after satisfying his curiosity, "but I wouldn't be sullen about it. Ugly people are always smart, and perhaps you are. Any way, I like little girls, so just let me sit here and get acquainted."

Mary Howard, the child thus introduced to our readers, was certainly not very handsome. Her features, though tolerably regular, were small and thin, her complexion sallow, and her eyes, though bright and expressive, seemed too large for her face. She had naturally a fine set of teeth, but their beauty was impaired by two larger ones, which, on each side of her mouth, grew directly over the others, giving to the lower portion of her face a peculiar and rather disagreeable expression. She had frequently been told that she was homely, and often when alone had wept, and wondered why she, too, was not handsome like her sister Ella, on whose cheek the softest rose was blooming, while her rich brown hair fell in wavy masses about her white neck and shoulders. But if Ella was more beautiful than Mary, there was far less in her character to admire. She knew that she was pretty, and this made her proud and selfish, expecting attention from all, and growing sullen and angry if it was withheld.

Mrs. Howard, the mother of these children, had incurred the displeasure of her father, a wealthy Englishman, by marrying her music teacher, whose dark eyes had played the *mischief* with her heart, while his fingers played its accompaniment on the guitar. Humbly at her father's feet she had knelt and sued for pardon, but the old man was inexorable, and turned her from his house, cursing the fate which had now deprived him, as it were, of his only remaining daughter. Late in life he had married a youthful widow who after the lapse of a few years died, leaving three little girls, Sarah, Ella, and Jane, two of them his own, and one a step-daughter and a child of his wife's first marriage.

As a last request Mrs. Temple had asked that her baby Jane should be given to the care of her sister, Mrs. Morris who was on the eve of embarking for America, and who within four weeks after her sister's death sailed with her; young niece for Boston. Sarah, too, was adopted by her father's brother; and thus Mr. Temple was left alone with his eldest daughter, Ella. Occasionally he heard from Jane, but time and distance gradually weakened the tie of parental affection, which wound itself more closely around Ella; and now, when she, too, left him, and worse than all, married a poor music teacher, the old man's wrath knew no bounds.

"But, we'll see," said he, as with his hands behind him, and his head bent forward, he strode up and down the room—"we'll see how they'll get on. I'll use all my influence against the dog, and when Miss Ella's right cold and hungry, she'll be glad to come back and leave him."

But he was mistaken, for though right cold and hungry Ella ofttimes was, she only clung the closer to her husband, happy to share his fortune, whatever it might be. Two years after her marriage, hearing that her father was dangerously ill, she went to him, but the forgiveness she so ardently desired was never gained, for the old man's reason was gone. Faithfully she watched until the end, and then when she heard read his will (made in a fit of anger), and knew that his property was all bequeathed to her sister in America, she crushed the tears from her long eyelashes and went back to her humble home prepared to meet the worst.

In course of time three children, Frank, Mary, and Ella were added to their number, and though their presence brought sunshine and gladness, it brought also an increase of toil and care. Year after year Mr. Howard struggled on, while each day rumors reached him of the plenty to be had in the land beyond the sea; and at last, when hope seemed dying out, and even his brave-hearted Ella smiled less cheerfully than was her wont to do he resolved to try his fortune in the far-famed home of the weary emigrant. This resolution he communicated to his wife, who gladly consented to accompany him, for England now held nothing dear to her save the graves of her parents, and in the western world she knew she had two sisters, Sarah having some years before gone with her uncle to New York.

Accordingly the necessary preparations for their voyage were made as soon as possible, and when the Windermere left the harbor of Liverpool, they stood upon her deck waving a last adieu to the few kind friends, who on shore were bidding them "God speed."

Among the passengers was George Moreland, whose parents had died some months before, leaving him and a large fortune to the guardianship of his uncle, a wealthy merchant residing in Boston. This uncle, Mr. Selden, had written for his nephew to join him in America, and it was for this purpose that George had taken passage in the Windermere. He was a frank, generous-hearted boy, and though sometimes a little too much inclined to tease, he was usually a favorite with all who knew him. He was a passionate admirer of beauty, and the moment the Howards came on board and he caught a sight of Ella, he felt irresistibly attracted towards her, and ere long had completely won her heart by coaxing her into his lap and praising her glossy curls. Mary, whose sensitive nature shrank from the observation of strangers, and who felt that one as handsome as George Moreland must necessarily laugh at her, kept aloof, and successfully eluded all his efforts to look under her bonnet. This aroused his curiosity, and when he saw her move away to a distant part of the vessel, he followed her, addressing to her the remark with which we commenced this chapter. As George had said he liked little girls, though he greatly preferred talking to pretty ones. On this occasion, however, he resolved to make himself agreeable, and in ten minutes' time he had so far succeeded in gaining Mary's friendship, that she allowed him to untie the blue bonnet, which he carefully removed, and then when she did not know it, he scanned her features attentively as if trying to discover all the beauty there was in them.

At last gently smoothing back her hair, which was really bright and glossy, he said, "Who told you that you were so ugly looking?" The tears started to Mary's eyes, and her chin quivered, as she replied, "Father says so, Ella says so, and every body says so, but mother and Franky."

"Every body doesn't always tell the truth," said George, wishing to administer as much comfort as possible. "You've got pretty blue eyes, nice brown hair, and your forehead, too, is broad and high; now if you hadn't such a muddy complexion, bony cheeks, little nose, big ears and awful teeth, you wouldn't be such a fright!"

George's propensity to tease had come upon him, and in enumerating the defects in Mary's face, he purposely magnified them; but he regretted it, when he saw the effect his words produced. Hiding her face in her hands, Mary burst into a passionate fit of weeping, then snatching the bonnet from George's lap, she threw it on her head and was hurrying away, when George caught her and pulling her back, said, "Forgive me, Mary. I couldn't help plaguing you a little, but I'll try and not do it again."

For a time George kept this resolution, but he could not conceal the preference which he felt for Ella, whose doll-like face, and childish ways were far more in keeping with his taste, than Mary's old look and still older manner. Whenever he noticed her at all, he spoke kindly to her; but she knew there was a great difference between his treatment of her and Ella, and oftentimes, when saying her evening prayer she prayed that George Moreland might love her a little just a little.

Two weeks had passed since the last vestige of land had disappeared from view, and then George was taken dangerously ill with fever. Mrs. Howard herself visited him frequently, but she commanded her children to keep away, lest they, too, should take the disease. For a day or two Mary obeyed her mother, and then curiosity led her near George's berth. For several minutes she lingered, and was about turning away when a low moan fell on her ear and arrested her footsteps. Her mother's commands were forgotten, and in a moment she stood by George's bedside. Tenderly she smoothed his tumbled pillow, moistened his parched lips, and bathed his feverish brow, and when, an hour afterward, the physician entered, he found his patient calmly sleeping, with one hand clasped in that of Mary, who with the other fanned the sick boy with the same blue gingham sun-bonnet, of which he had once made fun, saying it looked like its owner, "rather skim-milky."

"Mary! Mary Howard!" said the physician, "this is no place for you," and he endeavored to lead her away.

This aroused George, who begged so hard for her to remain, that the physician went in quest of Mrs. Howard, who rather unwillingly consented, and Mary was duly installed as nurse in the sick room. Perfectly delighted with her new vocation, she would sit for hours by her charge, watching each change in his features and anticipating as far as possible his wants. She possessed a very sweet, clear voice; and frequently, when all other means had failed to quiet him, she would bend her face near his and taking his hands in hers, would sing to him some simple song of home, until lulled by the soft music he would fall away to sleep. Such unwearied kindness was not without its effect upon George, and one day when Mary as usual was sitting near him, he called her to his side, and taking her face between his hands, kissed her forehead and lips, saying, "What can I ever do to pay my little nurse for her kindness?"

Mary hesitated a moment, and then replied, "Love me as well as you do Ella!"

"As well as I do Ella!" he repeated, "I love you a great deal better. She has not been to see me once. What is the reason?"

Frank, who a moment before had stolen to Mary's side, answered for her, saying, "some one had told Ella that if she should have the fever, her curls would all drop off; and so," said he, "she won't come near you!"

Just then Mrs. Howard appeared, and this time she was accompanied by Ella, who clung closely to her mother's skirt, looking cautiously out from its thick folds. George did not as usual caress her, but he asked her mockingly, "if her hair had commenced coming out!" while Ella only answered by grasping at her long curls, as if to assure herself of their safety.

In a few days George was able to go on deck, and though he still petted and played with Ella, he never again slighted Mary, or forgot that she was present. More than once, too, a kind word, or affectionate look from him, sent such a glow to her cheek and sparkle to her eye, that Frank, who always loved her best, declared, "she was as pretty as Ella any day if she'd break herself of putting her hand to her mouth whenever she saw one looking at her," a habit which she had acquired from being so frequently told of her uneven teeth.

At last after many weary days at sea, there came the joyful news that land was in sight; and next morning, when the children awoke, the motion of the vessel had ceased, and Boston, with its numerous domes and spires, was before them. Towards noon a pleasant-looking, middle-aged man came on board, inquiring for George Moreland, and announcing himself as Mr. Selden. George immediately stepped forward, and after greeting his uncle, introduced Mr. and Mrs. Howard, speaking at the same time of their kindness to him during his illness.

All was now confusion, but in the hurry and bustle of going ashore, George did not forget Mary. Taking her aside, he threw round her neck a small golden chain, to which was attached a locket containing a miniature likeness of himself painted a year before.

"Keep it," said he, "to remember me by, or if you get tired of it, give it to Ella for a plaything."

"I wish I had one for you," said Mary; and George replied, "Never mind, I can remember your looks without a likeness. I've only to shut my eyes, and a little forlorn, sallow-faced, old-looking girl, with crooked teeth—"

He was prevented from finishing his speech by a low cry from Mary, who, pressing his hands in hers, looked beseechingly in his face, and said, "Oh, don't, George!—don't talk so."

He had not teased her about her looks for a long time, and now just as he was leaving her, 'twas more than she could bear. Instantly regretting his thoughtless words, George took her in his arms, and wiping away her tears, said, "Forgive me, Mary. I don't know what made me say so, for I do love you dearly, and always will. You have been kind to me, and I shall remember it, and some time, perhaps, repay it." Then putting her down, and bidding adieu to Mr. and Mrs. Howard, Frank, and Ella, he sprang into his uncle's carriage, and was rapidly driven away.

Mary looked after him as long as the heads of the white horses were in sight, and then taking Frank's hand, followed her parents to the hotel, where for a few days they had determined to stop while Mrs. Howard made inquiries for her sister.

Meantime, from the richly curtained windows of a large handsome building a little girl looked out, impatiently waiting her father's return, wondering why he was gone so long and if she should like her cousin George, or whether he was a bearish looking fellow, with warty hands, who would tease her pet kitten and ink the faces of her doll babies. In the centre of the room the dinner table was standing, and Ida Selden had twice changed the location of her cousin's plate, once placing it at her side, and lastly putting it directly in front, so she could have a fair view of his face.

"Why don't they come?" she had said for the twentieth time, when the sound of carriage wheels in the yard below made her start up, and running down stairs, she was soon shaking the hands of her cousin, whom she decided to be handsome, though she felt puzzled to know whether her kitten and dolls were in any immediate danger or not!

Placing her arm affectionately around him, she led him into the parlor, saying, "I am so glad that you have come to live with me and be my brother. We'll have real nice times, but perhaps you dislike little girls. Did you ever see one that you loved?"

"Yes, two," was the answer. "My cousin Ida, and one other."

"Oh, who is she?" asked Ida. "Tell me all about her How does she look? Is she pretty?"

Instantly as George had predicted, there came before his vision the image of "a forlorn-looking, sallow-faced child," whom he did not care about describing to Ida. She, however, insisted upon a description, and that evening when tea was over, the lamps lighted, and Mr. Selden reading the paper, George told her of Mary, who had watched so kindly over him during the weary days of his illness. Contrary to his expectations, she did not laugh at the picture which he drew of Mary's face, but simply said, "I know I should like her." Then after a moment's pause, she continued; "They are poor, you say, and Mr. Howard is a music teacher. Monsieur Duprês has just left me, and who knows but papa can get Mr. Howard to fill his place."

When the subject was referred to her father, he said that he had liked the appearance of Mr. Howard, and would if possible find him on the morrow and engage his services. The next morning Ida awoke with an uncomfortable impression that something was the matter with the weather. Raising herself on her elbow, and pushing back the heavy curtains, she looked out and saw that the sky was dark with angry clouds, from which the rain was steadily falling, —not in drizzly showers, but in large round drops, which beat against the casement and then bounded off upon the pavement below.

All thoughts of Mr. Howard were given up for that day and as every moment of Mr. Selden's time was employed for several successive ones, it was nearly a week after George's arrival before any inquiries were made for the family. The hotel at which they had stopped was then found, but Mr. Selden was told that the persons whom he was seeking had left the day before for one of the inland towns, though which one he could not ascertain.

"I knew 'twould be so," said Ida rather fretfully, "father might have gone that rainy day as well as not. Now we shall never see nor hear from them again, and George will be so disappointed." But George's disappointment was soon forgotten in the pleasures and excitements of school, and if occasionally thoughts of Mary Howard came over him, they were generally dispelled by the lively sallies of his sprightly little cousin, who often declared that "she should be dreadfully jealous of George's travelling companion, were it not that he was a great admirer of beauty and that Mary was terribly ugly."

CHAPTER II.

CHICOPEE.

It was the afternoon for the regular meeting of the Ladies Sewing Society in the little village of Chicopee, and at the usual hour groups of ladies were seen wending their way towards the stately mansion of Mrs. Campbell, the wealthiest and proudest lady in town.

Many, who for months had absented themselves from the society, came this afternoon with the expectation of gaining a look at the costly marble and rosewood furniture with which Mrs. Campbell's parlors were said to be adorned. But they were disappointed, for Mrs. Campbell had no idea of turning a sewing society into her richly furnished drawing-rooms. The spacious sitting-room, the music-room adjoining, and the wide cool hall beyond, were thrown open to all, and by three o'clock they were nearly filled.

At first there was almost perfect silence, broken only by a whisper or under tone, but gradually the restraint wore way, and the woman near the door, who had come "because she was a mind to, but didn't expect to be noticed any way," and who, every time she was addressed, gave a nervous hitch backward with her chair, had finally hitched herself into the hall, where with unbending back and pursed up lips she sat, highly indignant at the ill-concealed mirth of the young girls, who on the stairs were watching her retrograde movements. The hum of voices increased, until at last there was a great deal more talking than working. The Unitarian minister's bride, Lilly Martin's stepmother, the new clerk at Drury's, Dr. Lay's wife's new hat and its probable cost, and the city boarders at the hotel, were all duly discussed, and then for a time there was again silence while Mrs. Johnson, president of the society, told of the extreme destitution in which she had that morning found a poor English family, who had moved into the village two or three years before.

They had managed to earn a comfortable living until the husband and father suddenly died, since which time the wife's health had been very rapidly failing, until now she was no longer able to work, but was wholly dependent for subsistence upon the exertions of her oldest child Frank, and the charity of the villagers, who sometimes supplied her with far more than was necessary, and again thoughtlessly neglected her for many days. Her chief dependence, too, had now failed her, for the day before the sewing society, Frank had been taken seriously ill with what threatened to be scarlet fever.

"Dear me," said the elegant Mrs. Campbell, smoothing the folds of her rich India muslin—"dear me, I did not know that we had such poverty among us. What will they do?"

"They'll have to go to the poor-house, won't they?"

"To the poor-house!" repeated Mrs. Lincoln, who spent her winters in Boston, and whose summer residence was in the neighborhood of the pauper's home, "pray don't send any more low, vicious children to the poor-house. My Jenny has a perfect passion for them, and it is with difficulty I can keep her away."

"They are English, I believe," continued Mrs. Campbell. "I do wonder why so many of those horridly miserable creatures will come to this country."

"Forgets, mebby, that she's English," muttered the woman at the door; and Mrs. Johnson added, "It would draw tears from your eyes, to see that little pale-faced Mary trying to wait upon her mother and brother, and carrying that sickly baby in her arms so that it may not disturb them."

"What does Ella do?" asked one, and Mrs. Johnson replied, "She merely fixes her curls in the broken looking-glass, and cries because she is hungry."

"She is pretty, I believe?" said Mrs. Campbell, and Rosa Pond, who sat by the window, and had not spoken before, immediately answered, "Oh, yes, she is perfectly beautiful; and do you know, Mrs. Campbell, that when she is dressed clean and nice, I think she looks almost exactly like your little Ella!"

A haughty frown was Mrs. Campbell's only answer, and Rosa did not venture another remark, although several whispered to her that they, too, had frequently observed the strong resemblance between Ella Howard and Ella Campbell.

From what has been said, the reader will readily understand that the sick woman in whom Mrs. Johnson was so much interested, was our old acquaintance Mrs. Howard.

All inquiries for her sisters had been fruitless, and after stopping for a time in Worcester, they had removed to Chicopee, where recently Mr. Howard had died. Their only source of maintenance was thus cut off, and now they were reduced to the utmost poverty. Since we last saw them a sickly baby had been added to their number. With motherly care little Mary each day washed and dressed it, and then hour after hour carried it in her arms, trying to still its feeble moans, which fell so sadly on the ear of her invalid mother.

It was a small, low building which they inhabited, containing but one room and a bedroom, which last they had ceased to occupy, for one by one each article of furniture had been sold, until at last Mrs. Howard lay upon a rude lounge, which Frank had made from some rough boards. Until midnight the little fellow toiled, and then when his work was done crept softly to the cupboard, there lay one slice of bread, the only article of food which the house contained. Long and wistfully he looked at it, thinking how good it would taste; but a glance at the pale faces near decided him. "They need it more than I," said he, and turning resolutely away, he prayed that he "might sleep pretty soon and forget how hungry he was."

Day after day he worked on, and though his cheek occasionally flushed with anger when of his ragged clothes and naked feet the village boys made fun, he never returned them any answer, but sometimes when alone the memory of their thoughtless jeers would cause the tears to start, and then wiping them away, he would wonder if it was wicked to be poor and ragged. One morning when he attempted to rise, he felt oppressed with a languor he had never before experienced, and turning on his trundlebed, and adjusting his blue cotton jacket, his only pillow, he again slept so soundly that Mary was obliged to call him twice ere she aroused him.

That night he came home wild with delight,—he had earned a whole dollar, and knew how he could earn another half dollar to-morrow. "Oh, I wish it would come quick," said he, as he related his success to his mother.

But, alas, the morrow found him burning with fever and when he attempted to stand, he found it impossible to do so. A case of scarlet fever had appeared in the village and it soon became evident that the disease had fastened upon Frank. The morning following the sewing society Ella Campbell and several other children showed symptoms of the same disease, and in the season of general sickness which followed, few were left to care for the poor widow. Daily little Frank grew worse. The dollar he had earned was gone, the basket of provisions Mrs. Johnson had sent was gone, and when for milk the baby Alice cried, there was none to give her.

At last Frank, pulling the old blue jacket from under his head, and passing it to Mary, said, "Take it to Bill Bender,—he offered me a shilling for it, and a shilling will buy milk for Allie and crackers for mother,—take it."

"No, Franky," answered Mary, "you would have no pillow, besides, I've got something more valuable, which I can sell. I've kept it long, but it must go to keep us from starving;"—and she held to view the golden locket, which George Moreland had thrown around her neck.

"You shan't sell that," said Frank. "You must keep it to remember George, and then, too, you may want it more some other time."

Mary finally yielded the point, and gathering up the crumpled jacket, started in quest of Billy Bender. He was a kind-hearted boy, two years older than Frank, whom he had often befriended, and shielded from the jeers of their companions. He did not want the jacket, for it was a vast deal too small; and it was only in reply to a proposal from Frank that he should buy it that he had casually offered him a shilling. But now, when he saw the garment, and learned why it was sent he immediately drew from his old leather wallet a quarter, all the money he had in the world and giving it to Mary bade her keep it, as she would need it all.

Half an hour after a cooling orange was held to Frank's parched lips, and Mary said, "Drink it, brother, I've got two more, besides some milk and bread," but the ear she addressed was deaf and the eye dim with the fast falling shadow of death. "Mother, mother!" cried the little girl, "Franky won't drink and his forehead is all sweat. Can't I hold you up while you come to him?"

Mrs. Howard had been much worse that day, but she did not need the support of those feeble arms. She felt, rather than saw that her darling boy was dying, and agony made her strong. Springing to his side she wiped from his brow the cold moisture which had so alarmed her daughter chafed his hands and feet, and bathed his head, until he seemed better and fell asleep.

"Now, if the doctor would only come," said Mary; but the doctor was hurrying from house to house, for more than one that night lay dying in Chicopee. But on no hearthstone fell the gloom of death so darkly as upon that low, brown house, where a trembling woman and a frail young child watched and wept over the dying Frank. Fast the shades of night came on, and when all was dark in the sick room, Mary sobbed out, "We have no candle, mother, and if I go for one, and he should die—"

The sound of her voice aroused Frank, and feeling for his sister's hand, he said, "Don't go, Mary:—don't leave me,—the moon is shining bright, and I guess I can find my way to God just as well."

Nine;—ten;—eleven;—and then through the dingy windows the silvery moonlight fell, as if indeed to light the way of the early lost to heaven. Mary had drawn her mother's lounge to the side of the trundlebed, and in a state of almost perfect exhaustion, Mrs. Howard lay gasping for breath while Mary, as if conscious of the dread reality about to occur, knelt by her side, occasionally caressing her pale cheek and asking if she were better. Once Mrs. Howard laid her hands on Mary's head, and prayed that she might be preserved and kept from harm by the God of the orphan, and that the sin of disobedience resting upon her own head might not be visited upon her child.

After a time a troubled sleep came upon her, and she slept, until roused by a low sob. Raising herself up, she looked anxiously towards her children. The moonbeams fell full upon the white, placid face of Frank, who seemed calmly sleeping, while over him Mary bent, pushing back from his forehead the thick, clustering curls, and striving hard to smother her sobs, so they might not disturb her mother.

"Does he sleep?" asked Mrs. Howard, and Mary, covering with her hands the face of him who slept, answered, "Turn away, mother;—don't look at him. Franky is dead. He died with his arms around my neck, and told me not to wake you."

Mrs. Howard was in the last stages of consumption, and now after weeping over her only boy until her tears seemed dried, she lay back half fainting upon her pillow. Towards daylight a violent coughing fit ensued, during which an ulcer was broken, and she knew that she was dying. Beckoning Mary to her side, she whispered, "I am leaving you alone, in the wide world. Be kind to Ella, and our dear little Allie, and go with her where she goes. May God keep and bless my precious children,—and reward you as you deserve, my darling —"

The sentence was unfinished, and in unspeakable awe the orphan girl knelt between her mother and brother, shuddering in the presence of death, and then weeping to think she was alone.

CHAPTER III.

BILLY BENDER.

Just on the corner of Chicopee Common, and under the shadow of the century-old elms which skirt the borders of the grass plat called by the villagers the "Mall," stands the small red cottage of widow Bender, who in her way was quite a curiosity. All the "ills which flesh is heir to," seemed by some strange fatality to fall upon her, and never did a new disease appear in any quarter of the globe, which widow Bender, if by any means she could ascertain the symptoms, was not sure to have it in its most aggravated form.

On the morning following the events narrated in the last chapter, Billy, whose dreams had been disturbed by thoughts of Frank, arose early, determined to call at Mrs. Howard's, and see if they were in want of any thing. But his mother, who had heard rumors of the scarlet fever, was up before him, and on descending to the kitchen, which with all her sickness Mrs. Bender kept in perfect order, Billy found her sitting before a blazing fire, —her feet in hot water, and her head thrown back in a manner plainly showing that something new had taken hold of her in good earnest. Billy was accustomed to her freaks, and not feeling at all frightened, stepped briskly forward, saying, "Well, mother, what's the matter now? Got a cramp in your foot, or what?"

"Oh, William," said she, "I've lived through a sight but my time has come at last. Such a pain in my head and stomach. I do believe I've got the scarlet fever, and you must run for the doctor quick."

"Scarlet fever!" repeated Billy, "why, you've had it once, and you can't have it again, can you?"

"Oh, I don't know,—I never was like anybody else, and can have any thing a dozen times. Now be spry and fetch the doctor but before you go, hand me my snuff-box and put the canister top heapin' full of tea into the tea-pot."

Billy obeyed, and then, knowing that the green tea would remove his mother's ailment quite as soon as the physician, he hurried away towards Mrs. Howard's. The sun was just rising, and its red rays looked in at the window, through which the moonlight had shone the night before. Beneath the window a single rose-tree was blooming, and on it a robin was pouring out its morning song. Within the cottage there was no sound or token of life, and thinking its inmates were asleep, Billy paused several minutes upon the threshold, fearing that he should disturb their slumbers. At last with a vague presentiment that all was not right, he raised the latch and entered, but instantly started back in astonishment at the scene before him. On the little trundlebed lay Frank, cold and dead, and near him in the same long dreamless sleep was his mother, while between them, with one arm thrown lovingly across her brother's neck, and her cheek pressed against his, lay Mary—her eyelids moist with the tears which, though sleeping she still shed. On the other side of Frank and nestled so closely to him that her warm breath lifted the brown curls from his brow, was Ella. But there were no tear stains on her face, for she did not yet know how bereaved she was.

For a moment Billy stood irresolute, and then as Mary moved uneasily in her slumbers, he advanced a step or two towards her. The noise aroused her, and instantly remembering and comprehending the whole, she threw herself with a bitter cry into Billy's extended arms, as if he alone were all the protector she now had in the wide, wide world. Ere long Ella too awoke, and the noisy outburst which followed the knowledge of her loss, made Mary still the agony of her own heart in order to soothe the more violent grief of her excitable sister.

There was a stir in the cradle, and with a faint cry the baby Alice awoke and stretched her hands towards Mary who, with all a mother's care took the child upon her lap and fed her from the milk which was still standing in the broken pitcher. With a baby's playfulness Alice dipped her small fingers into the milk, and shaking them in her sister's face, laughed aloud as the white drops fell upon her hair. This was too much for poor Mary, and folding the child closer to her bosom she sobbed passionately.

"Oh, Allie, dear little Allie, what will you do? What shall we all do? Mother's dead, mother's dead!"

Ella was not accustomed to see her sister thus moved, and her tears now flowed faster while she entreated Mary to stop. "Don't do so, Mary," she said. "Don't do so. You make me cry harder. Tell her to stop, Billy. Tell her to stop."

But Billy's tears were flowing too, and he could only answer the little girl by affectionately smoothing her tangled curls, which for once in her life she had forgotten to arrange At length rising up, he said to Mary, "Something must be done. The villagers must know of it, and I shall have to leave you alone while I tell them."

In half an hour from that time the cottage was nearly filled with people, some of whom came out of idle curiosity, and after seeing all that was to be seen, started for home, telling the first woman who put her head out the chamber window for particulars, that "'twas a dreadful thing, and such a pity, too, that Ella should have to go to the poor-house, with her pretty face and handsome curls."

But there were others who went there for the sake of comforting the orphans and attending to the dead, and by noon the bodies were decently arranged for burial. Mrs. Johnson's Irish girl Margaret was cleaning the room, and in the bedroom adjoining, Mrs. Johnson herself, with two or three other ladies, were busily at work upon some plain, neat shrouds, and as they worked they talked of the orphan children who were now left friendless.

"There will be no trouble," said one, "in finding a place for Ella, she is so bright and handsome, but as for Mary, I am afraid she'll have to go to the poor-house."

"Were I in a condition to take either," replied Mrs. Johnson, "I should prefer Mary to her sister, for in my estimation she is much the best girl; but there is the baby, who must go wherever Mary does, unless she can be persuaded to leave her."

Before any one could reply to this remark, Mary, who had overheard every word, came forward, and laying her face on Mrs. Johnson's lap, sobbed out, "Let me go with Alice, I told mother I would."

Billy Bender, who all this while had been standing by the door, now gave a peculiar whistle, which with him was ominous of some new idea, and turning on his heel started for home, never once thinking, until he reached it, that his mother more than six hours before had sent him in great haste for the physician. On entering the house, he found her, as we expected, rolled up in bed, apparently in the last stage of scarlet fever; but before she could reproach him, he said "Mother, have you heard the news?"

Mrs. Bender had a particular love for news, and now for getting "how near to death's door" she had been, she eagerly demanded, "What news? What has happened?"

When Billy told her of the sudden death of Mrs. Howard and Frank, an expression of "What? That all?" passed over her face, and she said, "Dear me, and so the poor critter's gone? Hand me my snuff, Billy. Both died last night, did they? Hain't you nothin' else to tell?"

"Yes, Mary Judson and Ella Campbell, too, are dead."

Mrs. Bender, who like many others, courted the favor of the wealthy, and tried to fancy herself on intimate terms with them, no sooner heard of Mrs. Campbell's affliction, than her own dangerous symptoms were forgotten, and springing up she exclaimed, "Ella Campbell dead! What'll her mother do? I must go to her right away. Hand me my double gown there in the closet, and give me my lace cap in the lower draw, and mind you have the tea-kettle biled agin I get back."

"But, mother," said Billy, as he prepared to obey her, "Mrs. Campbell is rich, and there are enough who will pity her. If you go any where, suppose you stop at Mrs. Howard's, and comfort poor Mary, who cries all the time because she and Alice have got to go to the poor-house."

"Of course they'll go there, and they orto be thankful they've got so good a place—Get away.—That ain't my double gown;—that's a cloak. Don't you know a cloak from a double gown?"

"Yes, yes," said Billy, whose mind was not upon his mother's toilet—"but," he continued, "I want to ask you, can't we,—couldn't you take them for a few days, and perhaps something may turn up."

"William Bender," said the highly astonished lady what can you mean? A poor sick woman like me, with one foot in the grave, take the charge of three pauper children! I shan't do it, and you needn't think of it."

"But, mother," persisted Billy, who could generally coax her to do as he liked, "it's only for a few days, and they'll not be much trouble or expense, for I'll work enough harder to make it up."

"I have said *no* once, William Bender, and when *I* say no, I mean no," was the answer.

Billy knew she would be less decided the next time the subject was broached, so for the present, he dropped it, and taking his cap he returned to Mrs. Howard's, while his mother started for Mrs. Campbell's.

Next morning between the hours of nine and ten, the tolling bell sent forth its sad summons, and ere long a few of the villagers were moving towards the brown cottage, where in the same plain coffin slept the mother and her only boy. Near them sat Ella, occasionally looking with childish curiosity at the strangers around her, or leaning forward to peep at the tips of the new morocco shoes which Mrs. Johnson had kindly given her; then, when her eye fell upon the coffin, she would burst into such an agony of weeping that many of the villagers also wept in sympathy, and as they stroked her soft hair, thought, "how much more she loved her mother than did Mary," who, without a tear upon her cheek, sat there immovable, gazing fixedly upon the marble face of her mother. Alice was not present, for Billy had not only succeeded in winning his mother's consent to take the children for a few days, but he had also coaxed her to say that Alice might come before the funeral, on condition that he would remain at home and take care of her. This he did willingly, for Alice, who had been accustomed to see him would now go to no one else except Mary.

Billy was rather awkward at baby tending, but by dint of emptying his mother's cupboard, blowing a tin horn, rattling a pewter platter with an iron spoon, and whistling Yankee Doodle, he managed to keep her tolerably quiet until he saw the humble procession approaching the house. Then, hurrying with his little charge to the open window, he looked out. Side by side walked Mary and Ella, and as Alice's eyes fell upon the former, she uttered a cry of joy, and almost sprang from Billy's arms. But Mary could not come; and for the next half hour Mrs. Bender corked her ears with cotton, while Billy, half distracted, walked the floor, singing at the top of his voice every tune he had ever heard, from "Easter Anthem" down to "the baby whose father had gone a hunting," and for whom the baby in question did not care two straws.

Meantime the bodies were about to be lowered into the newly made grave, when Mrs. Johnson felt her dress nervously grasped, and looking down she saw Mary's thin, white face uplifted towards hers with so earnest an expression, that she gently laid her hand upon her head, and said, "What is it, dear?"

"Oh, if I can,—if they only would let me look at them once more. I couldn't see them at the house, my eyes were so dark."

Mrs. Johnson immediately communicated Mary's request to the sexton, who rather unwillingly opened the coffin lid. The road over which they had come, was rough and stony and the jolt had disturbed the position of Frank, who no lay partly upon his mother's shoulder, with his cheek resting against hers. Tenderly Mary laid him back upon his own pillow, and then kneeling down and burying her face in her mother's bosom, she for a time remained perfectly silent, although the quivering of her frame plainly told the anguish of that parting. At length Mrs. Johnson gently whispered "Come, darling, you must come away now;" but Mary did not move; and when at last they lifted her up, they saw that she had fainted. In a few moments she recovered, and with her arms across her sister's neck, stood by until the wide grave was filled, and the bystanders were moving away.

As they walked homeward together, two women, who had been present at the funeral, discussed the matter as follows:—

"They took it hard, poor things, particularly the oldest."

"Yes, though I didn't think she cared as much as t'other one, until she fainted, but it's no wonder, for she's old enough to dread the poor-house. Did you say they were staying at widder Bender's?"

"Yes, and how in this world widder Bender, as poor as she pretends to be, can afford to do it, is more than I can tell."

"Are you going to the other funeral this afternoon?"

"I guess I am. I wouldn't miss it for a good deal. Why as true as you live, I have never set my foot in Mrs. Campbell's house yet, and know no more what is in it than the dead."

"Well, I do, for my girl Nancy Ray used to live there, and she's told me sights. She says they've got a big looking-glass that cost three hundred dollars."

"So I've heard, and I s'pose there'll be great doin's this afternoon. The coffin, they say, came from Worcester, and cost fifty dollars."

"Now, that's what I call wicked. Sposin' her money did come from England, she needn't spend it so foolishly; but then money didn't save Ella's life, and they say her mother's done nothing but screech and go on like a mad woman since she died. You'll go early, won't you?"

"Yes, I mean to be there in season to get into the parlor if I can."

And now, having reached the corner, where their path diverged, with a mutual "good day" they parted.

CHAPTER IV.

ELLA CAMPBELL.

Scarcely three hours had passed since the dark, moist earth was heaped upon the humble grave of the widow and her son, when again, over the village of Chicopee floated the notes of the tolling bell, and immediately crowds of persons with seemingly eager haste, hurried towards the Campbell mansion, which was soon nearly filled. Among the first arrivals were our acquaintances of the last chapter, who were fortunate enough to secure a position near the drawing-room, which contained the "big looking-glass."

On a marble table in the same room, lay the handsome coffin, and in it slept young Ella. Gracefully her small waxen hands were folded one over the other, while white, half-opened rose buds were wreathed among the curls of her hair, which fell over her neck and shoulders, and covered the purple spots, which the disease had left upon her flesh. "She is too beautiful to die, and the only child too," thought more than one, as they looked first at the sleeping clay and then at the stricken mother, who, draped in deepest black, sobbed convulsively and leaned for support upon the arm of the sofa. What now to her were wealth and station? What did she care for the elegance which had so often excited the envy of her neighbors? That little coffin, which had cost so many dollars and caused so much remark, contained what to her was far dearer than all. And yet she was not one half so desolate as was the orphan Mary, who in Mrs. Bender's kitchen sat weeping over her sister Alice, and striving to form words of prayer which should reach the God of the fatherless.

But few of the villagers thought of her this afternoon. Their sympathies were all with Mrs. Campbell; and when at the close of the services she approached to take a last look of her darling, they closed around her with exclamations of grief and tears of pity, though even then some did not fail to note and afterwards comment upon the great length of her costly veil, and the width of its hem! It was a long procession which followed Ella Campbell to the grave, and with bowed heads and hats uplifted, the spectators stood by while the coffin was lowered to the earth; and then, as the Campbell carriage drove slowly away, they dispersed to their homes, speaking, it may be, more tenderly to their own little ones, and shuddering to think how easily it might have been themselves who were bereaved.

Dark and dreary was the house to which Mrs. Campbell returned. On the stairs there was no patter of childish feet. In the halls there was no sound of a merry voice, and on her bosom rested no little golden head, for the weeping mother was childless. Close the shutters and drop the rich damask curtains, so that no ray of sunlight, or fragrance of summer flowers may find entrance there to mock her grief. In all Chicopee was there a heart so crushed and bleeding as hers? Yes, on the grass-plat at the foot of Mrs. Bender's garden an orphan girl was pouring out her sorrow in tears which almost blistered her eyelids as they fell.

Alice at last was sleeping, and Mary had come out to weep alone where there were none to see or hear. For her the future was dark and cheerless as midnight. No friends, no money, and no home, except the poor-house, from which young as she was, she instinctively shrank.

"My mother, oh, my mother," she cried, as she stretched her hands towards the clear blue sky, now that mother's home, "Why didn't I die too?"

There was a step upon the grass, and looking up Mary saw standing near her, Mrs. Campbell's English girl, Hannah. She had always evinced a liking for Mrs. Howard's family, and now after finishing her dishes, and trying in vain to speak a word of consolation to her mistress, who refused to be comforted, she had stolen away to Mrs. Bender's, ostensibly to see all the orphans, but, in reality to see Ella, who had always been her favorite. She had entered through the garden gate, and came upon Mary just as she uttered the words, "Why didn't I die too?"

The sight of her grief touched Hannah's heart, and sitting down by the little girl, she tried to comfort her. Mary felt that her words and manner were prompted by real sympathy, and after a time she grew calm, and listened, while Hannah told her that "as soon as her mistress got so any body could go near her, she meant to ask her to take Ella Howard to fill the place of her own daughter."

"They look as much alike as two beans," said she, "and sposin' Ella Howard ain't exactly her own flesh and blood, she would grow into liking her, I know."

Mary was not selfish, and the faint possibility that her sister might not be obliged to go to the poor-house, gave her comfort, though she knew that in all probability she herself must go. After a few more words Hannah entered the cottage, but she wisely chose to keep from Ella a knowledge of her plan, which very likely might not succeed. That night after her return home Hannah lingered for a long time about the parlor door, glancing wistfully towards her mistress, who reclined upon the sofa with her face entirely hidden by her cambric handkerchief.

"It's most too soon, I guess," thought Hannah, "I'll wait till to-morrow."

Accordingly next morning, when, as she had expected, she was told to carry her mistress's toast and coffee to her room, she lingered for a while, and seemed so desirous of speaking that Mrs. Campbell asked what she wanted.

"Why, you see, ma'am, I was going to say a word about,—about that youngest Howard girl." (She dared not say Ella.) "She's got to go to the poor-house, and it's a pity, she's so handsome. Why couldn't she come here and live? I'll take care of her, and 'twouldn't be nigh so lonesome."

At this allusion to her bereavement Mrs. Campbell burst into tears, and motioned Hannah from the room.

"I'll keep at her till I fetch it about," thought Hannah, as she obeyed the lady's order. But further persuasion from her was rendered unnecessary, for Mrs. Lincoln, whom we have once before mentioned, called that afternoon, and after assuring her friend that she never before saw one who was so terribly afflicted, or who stood so much in need of sympathy, she casually mentioned the Howards, and the extreme poverty to which they were reduced. This reminded Mrs. Campbell of Hannah's suggestion, which she repeated to her visitor, who answered, "It would unquestionably be a good idea to take her, for she is large enough to be useful in the kitchen in various ways."

Mrs. Campbell, who had more of real kindness in her nature than Mrs. Lincoln, replied, "If I take her, I shall treat her as my own, for they say she looks like her, and her name, too, is the same."

Here Mrs. Campbell commenced weeping and as Mrs. Lincoln soon took her leave, she was left alone for several hours. At the end of that time, impelled by something she could not resist, she rang the bell and ordered Hannah to go to Mrs. Bender's and bring Ella to her room as she wished to see how she appeared.

With the utmost care, Ella arranged her long curls, and then tying over her black dress the only white apron which she possessed, she started for Mrs. Campbell's. The resemblance between herself and Ella Campbell was indeed so striking, that but for the dress the mother might easily have believed it to have been her own child. As it was, she started up when the little girl appeared, and drawing her to her side, involuntarily kissed her; then causing her to sit down by her side, she minutely examined her features, questioning her meantime concerning her mother and her home in England. Of the latter Ella could only tell her that they lived in a city, and that her mother had once taken her to a large, handsome house in the country, which she said was her old home.

"There were sights of trees, and flowers, and vines, and fountains, and little deer," said the child, "and when I asked ma why she did not live there now, she cried, and pa put his arm tight 'round her,—so."

From this Mrs. Campbell inferred that Ella's family must have been superior to most of the English who emigrate to this country, and after a few more questions she decided to take her for a time, at least; so with another kiss she dismissed her, telling her she would come for her soon. Meantime arrangements were making for Mary and Alice and on the same day in which Mrs. Campbell was to call for Ella, Mr. Knight, one of the "Selectmen," whose business it was to look after the town's poor,[In Massachusetts each town has its own poor-house.] also came to the cottage. After learning that Ella was provided for, he turned to Mary, asking "how old she was, and what she could do," saying, that his wife was in want of just such a girl to do "chores," and if she was willing to be separated from Alice, he would give her a home with him. But Mary only hugged her sister closer to her bosom as she replied "I'd rather go with Alice. I promised mother to take care of her."

"Very well," said the man, "I'm going to North Chicopee, but shall be back in two hours, so you must have your things all ready."

"Don't cry so, Mary," whispered Billy, when he saw how fast her tears were falling. "I'll come to see you every week, and when I am older, and have money, I will take you from the poor-house, and Alice too."

Just then, Mrs. Campbell's carriage drove up. She had been taking her afternoon ride, and now, on her way home, had stopped for Ella, who in her delight at going with so handsome a woman, forgot the dreary home which awaited her sister, and which, but for Mrs. Campbell's fancy, would have been hers also. While she was getting ready, Mr. Knight returned, and driving his old-fashioned yellow wagon, with its square box-seat up by the side of Mrs. Campbell's stylish carriage, he entered the house, saying, "Come, gal, you're ready, I hope. The old mare don't want to stand, and I'm in a desput hurry, too. I orto be to hum this minute, instead of driving over that stony Portupog road. I hope you don't mean to carry that are thing," he continued, pointing with his whip towards Alice's cradle, which stood near Mary's box of clothes.

The tears came into Mary's eyes, and she answered "Alice has always slept in it, and I didn't know but—"

Here she stopped, and running up to Ella, hid her face in her lap, and sobbed, "I don't want to go. Oh, I don't want to go, can't I stay with you?"

Billy's yellow handkerchief was suddenly brought into requisition, and Mrs. Bender, who, with all her imaginary aches and pains, was a kind-hearted woman, made vigorous attacks upon her snuff-box, while Mrs. Campbell patted Mary's head, saying, "Poor child. I can't take you both, but you shall see your sister often."

Ella was too much pleased with Mrs. Campbell, and the thoughts of the fine home to which she was going, to weep but her chin quivered, when Mary held up the baby for her to kiss, and said, "Perhaps you will never see little Allie again."

When all was ready, Mr. Knight walked around his wagon, and after trying to adjust the numerous articles it contained, said, "I don't see how in the world I can carry that cradle, my wagon is chuck full now. Here is a case of shoes for the gals to stitch, and a piller case of flour for Miss Smith, and forty 'leven other traps, so I guess you'll have to leave it. Mebby you can find one there, and if not, why, she'll soon get used to going without it."

Before Mary could reply, Billy whispered in her ear "Never mind, Mary; you know that little cart that I draw mother's wood in, the cradle will just fit it, and to-morrow afternoon I'll bring it to you, if it doesn't rain."

Mary knew that he meant what he said, and smiling on him through her tears, climbed into the rickety wagon, which was minus a step, and taking Alice in her arms, she was soon moving away. In striking contrast to this, Ella, about five minutes afterwards, was carefully lifted into Mrs. Campbells handsome carriage, and reclining upon soft cushions, was driven rapidly towards her new home.

Will their paths in life always continue thus different? Who can tell?

CHAPTER V.

THE POOR-HOUSE.

How long and tiresome that ride was with no one for a companion except Mr. Knight, who, though a kind-hearted man knew nothing about making himself agreeable to little girls, so he remained perfectly taciturn, whipping at every cow or pig which he passed, and occasionally screaming to his horse, "Git up, old Charlotte. What are you 'bout?"

Mary, who had seldom been out of the village, and who knew but little of the surrounding country, for a time enjoyed looking about her very much. First they went down the long hill which leads from the village to the depot. Then they crossed the winding Chicopee river, and Mary thought how much she should love to play in that bright green meadow and gather the flowers which grew so near to the water's edge. The causeway was next crossed, and turning to the right they came upon a road where Mary had never been before, and which grew more rough and stony as they advanced.

On the top of a steep hill Mary looked back to see if Chicopee were yet, visible, but nothing was to be seen except the spire of the Unitarian Meeting-House. About a quarter of a mile to the west, however, the graveyard was plainly discernible, and she looked until her eyes were dim with tears at the spot where she knew her parents and brother were lying. By this time Alice was asleep, and though the little arms which held her ached sadly, there was no complaint, but she wished Mr. Knight would speak to her once, if it were only to ask her how she did!

At last, concluding there would be no impropriety in making the first advances herself, she said timidly, "Is it such a very bad place at the poor-house?"

"Why, no, not so dreadful. There's places enough, sight worse, and then agin there's them, a good deal better But you needn't be afeard. They'll take good care of you."

"I wasn't thinking of myself," said Mary.

"Who was you thinkin' of, then?"

"Of Alice; she's always been sick and is not used to strangers, and among so many I am afraid she will be frightened."

"Oh, she'll soon get used to 'em. Nothin' like, habit. Weakly, is she? Wall, the poor-house ain't much of a place to get well in, that's a fact. But she'd be better off to die and go to her mother, and then you could get a good place at some farmer's."

Mary wondered how he could speak thus carelessly of what would cause her so much sorrow. Gently lifting the old faded shawl, she looked down upon Alice as she slept. There was a smile upon her face. She was dreaming, and as her lips moved, Mary caught the word, "Ma," which the child had applied indiscriminately both to herself and her mother. Instantly the tears gushed forth, and falling upon the baby's face awoke her. Her nap was not half out, and setting up a loud cry, she continued screaming until they drove up to the very door of the poor-house.

"For the land's sake," said Mr. Knight, as he helped Mary from the wagon, "what a racket; can't you contrive to stop it? you'll have Sal Furbush in your hair, for she don't like a noise."

Mary glanced nervously round in quest of the goblin Sal, but she saw nothing save an idiotic face with bushy tangled hair; and nose flattened against the window pane. In terror Mary clung to Mr. Knight, and whispered, as she pointed towards the figure, which was now laughing hideously, "What is it? Are there many such here?"

"Don't be afeard," said Mr. Knight, "that's nobody but foolish Patsy; she never hurt any body in her life. Come, now, let me show you to the overseer."

Mary looked towards the woods which skirted the borders of the meadow opposite, and for half a moment felt inclined to flee thither, and hide herself in the bushes; but Mr. Knight's hand was upon her shoulder, and he led her towards a red-whiskered man, who stood in the door.

"Here, Parker," said he, "I've brought them children I was tellin' you about. You've room for 'em, I s'pose."

"Why, ye-es, we can work it so's to make room. Guess we shall have rain to-morrow."

Mary remembered that Billy would not come if it rained, and with a sigh she noticed that the clouds were dark and threatening. They now entered the kitchen, which was a long, low, narrow room, with a fireplace on the right, and two windows opposite, looking towards the west. The floor was painted and very clean, but the walls were unfinished, and the brown rafters were festooned with cobwebs. In the middle of the room, the supper table was standing, but there was nothing homelike in the arrangement of the many colored dishes and broken knives and forks, neither was there any thing tempting to one's appetite in the coarse brown bread and white-looking butter. Mary was very tired with holding Alice so long, and sinking into a chair near the window, she would have cried; but there was a tightness in her throat, and a pressure about her head and eyes, which kept the tears from flowing. She had felt so once before. Twas when she stood at her mother's grave; and now as the room grew dark, and the objects around began to turn in circles, she pressed her hands tightly to her forehead, and said, 'Oh, I hope I shan't faint."

"To be sure you won't," said a loud, harsh voice, and instantly large drops of water were thrown in her face, while the same voice continued: "You don't have such spells often, I hope, for Lord knows I don't want any more fitty ones here."

"No, ma'am," said Mary, meekly; and looking up, she saw before her a tall, square-backed, masculine-looking woman, who wore a very short dress, and a very high-crowned cap, fastened under her chin with bows of sky-blue ribbon.

Mary knew she was indebted to this personage for the shower bath, for the water was still trickling from her fingers, which were now engaged in picking her teeth with a large pin. There was something exceedingly cross and forbidding in her looks, and Mary secretly hoped she would not prove to be Mrs. Parker, the wife of the overseer. She was soon relieved of her fears by the overseer himself, who came forward and said, "Polly, I don't see any other way but you'll have to take these children into the room next to yourn. The baby worries a good deal, and such things trouble my wife, now she's sick."

The person addressed as "Polly," gave her shoulders an angry jerk, and sticking the pin on the waist of her dress, replied, "So I s'pose it's no matter if I'm kept awake all night, and worried to death. But I guess you'd find there'd be queer doins here if I should be taken away. I wish the British would stay to hum, and not lug their young ones here for us to take care of."

This was said with a lowering frown, and movement towards Mary, who shrank back into the corner and covered her mouth with her hand, as if that were the cause of offence.

"But you can take an extra nap after dinner," said Mr. Parker, in a conciliatory manner. "And then you are so good at managing children, that I thought they would be better off near you."

This speech, while it mollified Polly, made Mary shudder, as she thought of Alice's being "managed" by such a woman. But she had no time for thought, for Polly, who was very rapid in her movements, and always in a hurry, said, "Come, child, I will show you where you are going to sleep;" at the same time she caught up Alice, who, not liking her handling, kicked so vigorously that she was soon dropped; Polly remarking, that "she was mighty strong in her

27

legs for a sick baby."

After passing up a dark stairway they came to a door, which opened under the garret stairs, and Mary was startled by a voice which seemed to be almost over her head, and which, between a sneer and a hiss, called out, "See where the immaculate Miss Grundy comes!"

This was followed by a wild, insane chuckle, which made Mary spring in terror to Polly's side.

"Oh, who is it?" said she. "Is it Patsy?"

"Patsy!" was the tart reply. "She never is saucy like that. It's Sal Furbush."

Mary longed to ask who Sal Furbush was; but as her guide did not seem, at all inclined to be communicative, she followed on in silence until they came to a longer and lighter hall, or "spaceway," as it is frequently called in New England. On each side of this there were doors opening into small sleeping rooms, and into one of these Polly led her companion, saying, as she did so, "This is your room, and it's a great favor to you to be so near me. But mind, that child mustn't cry and keep me awake nights, for if she does, may-be you'll have to move into that other space, where we heard the laugh."

Mary thought she would rather do any thing than that. She also felt a great curiosity to know who her companion was, so she at last ventured to ask, "Do you live here, Miss Polly?"

"Why, yes, I'm staying here for a spell now:—kind of seeing to things. My name isn't Polly. It's Mrs. Mary Grundy, and somehow folks have got to nicknaming me Polly, but it'll look more mannerly in you to call me Mrs. Grundy; but what am I thinking of? The folks must have their supper. So you'd better come down now."

"If you please," said Mary, who knew she could not eat a mouthful, "If you please, I'd rather stay here and rest me if I can have some milk for Alice by and by."

"Mercy sakes, ain't that child weaned?" asked Mrs. Grundy.

"Ma'am?" said Mary, not exactly understanding her.

"Ain't Ellis weaned, or must we break into the cream a dozen times a day for her?"

"She has never eaten any thing but milk," said Mary, weeping to think how different Mrs. Grundy's manner was from her own dear mother's.

"Wall, there's no use blubberin' so. If she must have milk, why she must, and that's the end on't. But what I want to know is, how folks as poor as yourn, could afford to buy milk for so big a child."

Mary could have told of many hungry nights which she and Frank had passed in order that Ella and Alice might be fed, but she made no remark, and Mrs. Grundy soon left the room saying, "Come down when you get ready for the milk I s'pose *skim* will do."

Half an hour after Alice began to cry; and Mary, knowing she was hungry, laid her upon the bed and started for the milk. She trembled as she drew near the garret stairs, and trod softly that she might not be heard, but as she was passing the mysterious door, a voice entirely different in its tone from the one assumed towards Mrs. Grundy, called out, "Come here, little dear, and see your Aunty."

Mary's circle of acquaintances was quite as large as she cared to have it, and quickening her steps, she was soon in the kitchen, where she found several old ladies still lingering over cups of very weak and very red looking tea. As she entered the room they all suspended their operations, and looking hard at her, asked if she were the little English girl. On being told that she was, three of them returned to their cups, while one shook her head, saying. "Poor child, I pity you."

Mary had heard that remark many times, but she knew that the words now conveyed other meaning than what referred to her face or teeth.

"Where can I find Mrs. Grundy?" she at last ventured to ask.

"Where can you find who?" asked a spiteful looking woman. "Did she tell you to call her so?"

"She told me that was her name,—yes, ma'am," said Mary.

"Well, *Mrs.* Grundy is in the but'ry," indicating with her elbow the direction.

Mary had no trouble in finding "the but'ry," but on trying the door, she found it fastened inside. In answer to her gentle knock a harsh voice replied, "Who's there?"

"It's I. I've come after the milk for Alice."

With a jerk Mrs. Grundy opened the door, and putting a pint cup two thirds full of blue milk in Mary's hand, she hastily shut and fastened it again. Quick as her movements were, Mary caught a smell of strong green tea, and the sight of a sugar bowl and a slice of white bread. She knew now why the door was buttoned, but thinking it was none of her business, she started to return to the kitchen. As she passed the outer door, an old gray-haired man, with a face perfectly simple and foolish in its expression, stepped towards her, stretching out his hands as if to reach her. With a loud cry she rushed headlong into the kitchen, where one of the women was still sitting.

"What's broke loose now?" asked the woman, to which Mary replied, "Look at him!" at the same time pointing to the man, who with his hand thrust out was still advancing towards her.

"Don't be scared," said the woman. "It's uncle Peter. Let him touch you and he'll go off;" but Mary didn't choose to be touched, and retreating towards the chamber door, she fled rapidly up the stairs.

This time she was not accosted by any one, but as she passed the dark closet, she was surprised to hear a musical voice singing the national air of her own country, and she wondered, too, at the taste of the singer in finishing every verse with "God save Miss Grundy."

That night Alice, who missed her cradle, was unusually restless, and Mary, remembering Mrs. Grundy's threat, carried her in her arms until after midnight. Then without undressing she threw herself upon the bed, and, for the first time in many weeks, dreamed of George and his parting promise to see her again. The next morning when she awoke she found Mr. Parker's prediction verified, for the clouds were pouring rain. "Billy won't come to-day," was her first thought, and throwing herself upon the floor she burst into tears, wishing as she had once done before that she had died with her mother.

In the midst of her grief the door was pushed hastily open, and Mrs. Grundy's harsh voice exclaimed, "Wall, so you are up at last, hey? I didn't know but you was goin' to take it upon you to sleep over, but that don't answer here."

"Is it after breakfast time?" asked Mary.

"After breakfast time," repeated Mrs. Grundy. "No, but I guess you'll find there's something to do before breakfast, or did you think we's goin' to support you in idleness?"

Here, touched perhaps by the pale, tearful face uplifted to hers, Mrs. Grundy's voice softened, and in a milder tone she added, "We won't mind about it, seein' it's the first morning, but come, you must be hungry by this time."

Although so poor, Mrs. Howard had been extremely neat and as she said "cold water cost nothing," she had insisted upon her children's being very nice and particular in their morning toilet. Mary remembered this, and now casting a rueful glance around the room she said, "I wonder where I am going to wash me."

The loud, scornful laugh which followed this remark made her look up amazed at Mrs. Grundy, who replied, "In the back room sink, of course. Maybe you expected to have a china bowl and pitcher in your room, and somebody to empty your slop. I wonder what *airs* paupers won't take on themselves next."

"I didn't mean to take airs," said Mary; "I don't care where I wash myself, but Alice is sick, and mother had me bathe her every morning. While we were at Mrs. Bender's, though, I didn't do it, and I don't think she seems as well."

"Pride and poverty," muttered Mrs. Grundy. "She won't get many baths here, I can tell you, nor you either, unless it is a dishwater one. Know how to wash dishes hey?"

"Yes, ma'am," said Mary meekly.

"Then I'll give you a chance to try your hand after breakfast, but come, I'm in a hurry."

Mary glanced at Alice. She was sleeping sweetly, and though there seemed to be no reason, she still lingered.

"What are you waiting for?" asked Mrs. Grundy, and Mary, with some hesitation, answered, "I haven't said my prayers yet."

A change passed suddenly over Mrs. Grundy's face, and she turned away without a word. When she was gone Mary fell on her knees, and though the words she uttered were addressed more to her mother than to God, she felt comforted, and rising up started for the kitchen. It was a motley group which she found assembled around the breakfast table, and as she entered the room, the man called Uncle Peter smiled on her, saying, "Come here, little daughter, and let me touch you with the tip of my fourth finger."

Shrinking to nearly half her usual size, she managed to pass him without coming in contact with said finger, which was merely a stump, the first joint having been amputated. On reaching the back room she readily found the place where she with all the rest was to wash. For this she did not care, as the water was as cold and pure, and seemed as refreshing as when dipped from her mother's tin wash-basin. But when she came to the wiping part, and tried in vain to find a clean corner' on the long towel, which hung upon a roller, she felt that she was indeed a pauper.

"I should think we might have a decent towel," thought she. "Mother used to say it cost nothing to be clean;" then looking round to be sure that no one saw her, she caught up the skirt of her dress and drying her face with it, went back to the kitchen.

31

She would greatly have preferred a seat by a pleasant looking old lady who looked kindly on her, but Mrs. Grundy bade her sit down by her and help herself. She did not exactly fancy the looks of the thick fried pork, swimming in grease, so she took a potato and a slice of bread, to get which she reached so far that the lower hook on her dress which for a day or two had been uncertain whether to come off or stay on, now decided the matter by dropping on the floor. As she was proceeding with her breakfast, Uncle Peter suddenly dropping his knife and fork, exclaimed, "Little daughter's teeth are awry, ain't they?"

Mary had hoped that at the poor-house her mouth would not be a subject of comment, but she was disappointed, and bursting into tears would have risen from the table, had not the kind looking woman said, "Shame on you, Peter, to plague a little girl."

Uncle Peter, too, who was fond of children, seemed distressed, and passing towards her the bowl of milk which was standing by him, he said, "Drink it, daughter;—milk for babes, and meat for strong men."

There was so much of real kindness in his manner that Mary's fear of him diminished, and taking the offered milk she thanked him so kindly that Uncle Peter, who was quite an orator, considered it his duty to make a speech. Pushing back his chair, he commenced with a bow which required do many changes of his legs that Mary wondered they were not entirely twisted up.

"Ladies and gentlemen, one and all," said he, "but particularly ladies, what I have to say is this, that henceforth and for ever I am the champion of this unprotected female, who from parts unknown has come among us.—God bless her. I will also announce formally that I still hold myself in readiness to teach the polite accomplishment of dancing in my room, No. 41, Pauper's Hotel."

Having finished this speech he resumed his breakfast, after which with another of his wonderful bows he quitted the room. Mary was about following his example when Mrs. Grundy said. "Come, catch hold now and see how spry you can clear the table, and you, Rind," speaking to a simple looking girl with crooked feet, "do you go to your shoes. Be quick now, for it's goin' on seven o'clock."

At this moment Mary caught sight of Mr. Parker, who was standing just without the door, and his mischievous look as Mrs. Grundy gave out her orders made Mary a little suspicious of that lady's real position among them. But she had no time for thought, for just then through all the closed doors and the long hall there came to her ears the sound of a scream. Alice was crying, and instantly dropping the plate she held in her hand, Mary was hurrying away, when Mrs. Grundy called her back, saying "Let her cry a spell. 'Twill strengthen her lungs."

Mary had more spirit than her face indicated, and in her mind she was revolving the propriety of obeying, when Mr. Parker, who was still standing by the door, said, "If that baby is crying, go to her by all means."

The look of gratitude which Mary's eyes flashed upon him, more than compensated for the frown which darkened Mrs. Grundy's brow as she slammed the doors together, muttering about "hen-hussies minding their own business."

Mary was not called down to finish the dishes, and when at last she went to the kitchen for milk, she found them all washed and put away. Mrs. Grundy was up to her elbow in cheese curd, and near her, tied into an arm chair, sat Patsy, nodding her head and smiling as usual. The pleasant looking woman was mopping the kitchen floor, and Mary, for the first time, noticed that she was very lame.

"Go out doors and come round. Don't you see you'll track the floor all up?" said Mrs. Grundy, and the lame woman replied, "Never mind, Polly, I can easy wipe up her tracks, and it's a pity to send her out in the rain."

Mary chose to obey Mrs. Grundy, who wiped the crumbs of curd and drops of whey from her arms and took the cup, saying, "More milk? Seems to me she eats a cart load! I wonder where the butter's to come from, if we dip into the cream this way."

Had Mary been a little older, she might have doubted whether the blue looking stuff Mrs. Grundy poured into her cup ever saw any cream, but she was only too thankful to get it on any terms, and hurried with it back to her room. About noon the clouds broke away, while here and there a patch of bright blue sky was to be seen. But the roads were so muddy that Mary had no hope of Billy's coming, and this it was, perhaps, which made the dinner dishes so hard to wash, and which made her cry when told that all the knives and forks must be scoured, the tea-kettle wiped, and set with its nose to the north, in what Mrs. Grundy called the "Pout Hole," and which proved to be a place under the stairs, where pots, kettles and iron ware generally were kept.

All things have an end, and so did the scouring, in spite of Mary's fears to the contrary, and then watching a time when Mrs. Grundy did not see her, she stole away up stairs. Taking Alice on her lap she sat down by the open window where the damp air cooled and moistened her flushed face. The rain was over, and across the meadow the sun was shining through the tall trees, making the drops of water which hung upon the leaves sparkle and flash in the sunlight like so many tiny rainbows. Mary watched them for a time, and then looking upward at the thin white clouds which chased each other so rapidly across the blue sky, wondered if her mother's home were there, and if she ever thought of her children, so sad and lonely without her.

A movement of Alice aroused her from her reverie, and looking into the road, she saw directly opposite the house Billy Bender, and with him, Alice's cradle. In a moment Mary's arms were thrown about his neck as tightly as if she thought he had the power and was come to take her away.

"Oh, Billy, Billy," she said, "I was afraid you would not come, and it made me so unhappy. Can't you take me home with you?"

Billy had expected as much, and had tried hard to make his mother say that if Mary and Alice were very homesick he might bring them home. But this was Mrs. Bender's sick day, and Billy's entreaties only increased the dangerous symptoms of *palsy* from which she was now suffering, the scarlet fever having been given up until another time.

"If the *s'lect* men pay me well for it," said she, "I will take them what little time I have to live, but not without."

Billy knew the town could support them much cheaper where they were, so he gave up his project, and bought Mary a pound of seed cakes and Alice a stick of candy. Then, the moment the rain had ceased he got himself in readiness to start, for he knew how long the day would seem to Mary, and how much Alice would miss her cradle. Three times before he got outside the gate his mother called him back—once to find her snuff-box;—once to see if there was not more color in her face than there ought to be, and lastly to inquire if her mouth hadn't commenced turning a little towards the right ear! After finding her box, assuring her that her color was natural and her mouth all straight, he at last got started. The road was long and the hills were steep, but patiently Billy toiled on, thinking how surprised and pleased Mary would be; and when he saw how joyfully she received him, he felt more than paid for his trouble. Some boys would have rudely shaken her off, ashamed to be caressed by a little girl, but Billy's heart was full of kindly sympathy, and he returned her caresses as a brother would have done.

As he released her, he was startled at hearing some one call out, "Bravo! That, I conclude, is a country hug. I hope she won't try it on me!"

Turning about he saw before him a white-faced boy, nearly of his own age, whose dress and appearance indicated that he belonged to a higher grade, as far as wealth was concerned. It was Henry Lincoln, notorious both for pride and insolence. Billy, who had worked for Mr. Lincoln, had been insulted by Henry many a time, and now he longed to avenge it, but native politeness taught him that in the presence of Mary 'twould not be proper, so without a word to Henry he whispered to the little girl, "That fellow lives near here, and if he ever gives you trouble, just let me know."

"Kissed her then, didn't you?" sneeringly asked Henry, retreating at the same time, for there was something in Billy's eye, which he feared.

"Come into the house," said Mary, "where he can't see us," and leading the way she conducted him up to her own room, where there was no fear of being interrupted.

Alice was first carefully fixed in her cradle, and then kneeling down at Billy's side, and laying her arms across his lap, Mary told him of every thing which had happened, and finished by asking, "how long she must stay there."

Had Billy's purse been as large as his heart, that question would have been easily answered. Now he could only shake his head in reply, while Mary next asked if he had seen Ella.

"I have not seen her," returned he, "but I've heard that rainy as it was this morning, Mrs. Campbell's maid was out selecting muslins and jaconets for her, and they say she is not to wear black, as Mrs. Campbell thinks her too young."

Mary did not speak for some time, but her head dropped on Billy's knee and she seemed to be intently thinking. At last, brushing aside the hair which had fallen over her forehead, Billy said, "What are you thinking about?"

"I was wondering if Ella wouldn't forget me and Allie now she is rich and going to be a lady."

Billy had thought the same thing, and lifting the little girl in his lap, he replied, "If *she* does, I never will;"—and then he told her again how, when he was older, and had money, he would take her from the poor-house and send her to school, and that she should some time be as much of a lady as Ella.

By this time Mrs. Grundy's work in the kitchen was done. Patsy had been shaken for stealing a ginger cake; the lame woman had been scolded because her floor had dried in streaks, which was nothing remarkable considering how muddy it was. Uncle Peter had been driven from the pantry for asking for milk, and now the lady herself had come up to change her morning apparel and don the high-crowned cap with the sky-blue ribbons. Greatly was she surprised at the sound of voices in the room adjoining, and while Mary was still in Billy's lap the door opened, and Mrs. Grundy appeared, with her hands thrown up and the wide border of her morning cap, which also did night service for its fair owner, flying straight back.

"Mary Howard!" said she; "a *man* up in this hall where no male is ever permitted to come! What does it mean? I shall be ruined!"

"No danger, madam, I assure you," said Billy. "I came to bring Alice's cradle, and did not suppose there was any thing improper in coming up here."

"It's nobody but Billy Bender," said Mary, frightened at Mrs. Grundy's wrathful looks.

"And who is Billy Bender? A beau? 'Pears to me you are beginning young, and getting on fast, too, a settin' in his lap. S'posin' I should do so—wouldn't it be a town's talk?"

Mary tried to get down, but Billy, greatly amused at the highly scandalized lady's distress, held her tightly, and Mrs. Grundy, slamming the door together, declared "she'd tell Mr. Parker, and that's the end on't."

But no Mr. Parker made his appearance, and as the sun was getting towards the west, Billy ere long started up, saying, he must go now, but would come again next week. Mary followed him down stairs, and then returning to her room cried herself into so sound a sleep that Mrs. Grundy was obliged to scream to her at least a dozen times to come down and set the supper table, adding as a finale, that "she wondered if she thought she was a lady boarder or what."

CHAPTER VI

SAL FURBUSH.

The next morning between nine and ten, as Mary sat by Alice's cradle rocking her to sleep, she was sensible of an unusual commotion in and around the house. First there was the sound as of some one dancing in the dark passage. Then there was the same noise in the kitchen below, and a merry voice was heard singing snatches of wild songs, while occasionally peals of laughter were heard mingled with Mrs. Grundy's harsher tones. Mary's curiosity was roused, and as soon as Alice was fairly asleep, she resolved to go down and ascertain the cause of the disturbance, which had now subsided.

As she opened her door, she saw advancing towards her from the farthest extremity of the hall, a little, shrivelled up woman, with wild flashing eyes, and hair hanging loosely over her shoulders. She was shaking her fist in a very threatening manner, and as she drew nearer Mary saw that her face was going through a great variety of changes, being at first perfectly hideous in its expression, and then instantly changing into something equally ridiculous, though not quite so frightful. Quickly divining that this must be Sal Furbush, Mary sprang back, but had not time to fasten her door ere the wild woman was there. In a tremor of terror Mary ran under the bed as the only hiding-place the room afforded, but her heart almost ceased beating as she saw her pursuer about to follow her. Springing out with a bound she would perhaps have made her egress through the open window, had not Sally prevented her by seizing her arm, at the same time saying, "Don't be alarmed, duckey, I shan't hurt you; I'm Sal. Don't you know Sal?"

The voice was low and musical, and there was something in its tones which in a measure quieted Mary's fears, but she took good care to keep at a respectful distance. After a while Sally asked, "Have you come here to board?"

"I have come here to live," answered Mary, "I have no other home."

"Well, for your sake I hope there'll be an improvement in the fare, for if there isn't I declare *I* won't stay much longer, though to be sure you don't look as if you'd been used to any thing better than skim-milk. What ails your teeth, child?"

Involuntarily Mary's hand went up to her mouth, and Sally, who if she expected an answer, forgot to wait for it, continued. "Do you know grammar, child?"

Mary replied that she had studied it a few months in Worcester, and a few weeks in Chicopee.

"Oh, I am so glad," said Sal, "for now I shall have an associate. Why, the greatest objection I have to the kind of people one meets with here, is that they are so horribly vulgar in their conversation and murder the Queen's English so dreadfully. But won't you and I have good times saying the rules in concert?"

Unfortunately Mary's knowledge of grammar was rather limited, and as she did not exactly fancy Sal's proposition, she answered that she had nearly forgotten all she ever knew of grammar.

"Oh, that's nothing, child that's nothing," said Sal. "It will return to you gradually. Why, things that happened forty years ago and were forgotten twenty years ago come back to me every day, but then I always did forget more in one night than some people, Miss Grundy, for instance, ever knew in all their life."

"Have you lived here long?" asked Mary.

"Yes, a great while," and the expression of Sally's face grew graver, as she added, "Perhaps you don't know that I lost little Willie, and then Willie's father died too, and left me all alone. Their graves are away on the great western prairies, beneath the buckeye trees, and one night when the winter wind was howling fearfully, I fancied I heard little Willie's voice calling to me from out the raging storm. So I lay down on the turf above my lost darling, and slept so long, that when I awoke my hair had all turned gray and I was in Chicopee, where Willie's father used to live. After a while they brought me here and said I was crazy, but I wasn't. My head was clear as a bell, and I knew as much as I ever did, only I couldn't tell it, because, you see, the right words wouldn't come. But I don't care now I've found some one who knows grammar. How many *genders* are there, child?"

"Four," answered Mary, who had been studying Smith.

Instantly Sal seized Mary's hands, and nearly wrenching them off in her joy, capered and danced about the room, leaping over the cradle, and finally exclaiming, "Capital! You think just as I do, don't you? And have the same opinion of her? What are the genders, dear? Repeat them"

"Masculine, Feminine, Neuter and Common," said Mary

"O, get out with your *common* gender," screamed Sal. "*My* grammar don't read so. It says Masculine, Feminine Neuter and *Grundy* gender, to which last but one thing in the world belongs, and that is the lady below with the cast iron back and India-rubber tongue."

"Do you mean Mrs. Grundy?" asked Mary, and Sal replied, "*Mrs. Grundy*? and who may Mrs. Grundy be? Oh, I understand, she's been stuffing you."

"Been what?" said Mary.

"Excuse me," answered Sal. "That's a slang term I've picked up since I've been here. It's so easy to get contaminated, when one is constantly associated with such low people. I mean that during my temporary seclusion Miss Grundy has probably given you erroneous impressions which I take pleasure in correcting. She has no more right to order us boarders around, and say when we shall breathe and when we shan't, than I have. She's nothing more nor less than a town pauper herself, and has to work at that."

"So do we all," interrupted Mary, and Sal continued. "On that point you are slightly mistaken, my dear. I don't have to. I didn't come here to work. They tried it once."

Here pushing her tangled hair back from her brow, she pointed to a long scar, saying, "Do you see that?" Mary nodded, and Sal continued: "When I first came here, the overseer was a bad man, not at all like Mr. Parker. One day he told me to wash the dinner dishes, and to use more than a pint of water, too, so I gathered them up and threw them into the well; but this method of washing did not suit the overseer's ideas of housekeeping, so he took a raw hide, and said he would either 'break my will,' or 'break my neck,' and because he could not break my will, and dared not break my neck, he contented himself with breaking my head. Every blow that he struck me was like melted lead poured into my brains, which puffed out like sausages, and have never recovered their wonted dimensions. The town took the matter up, but I don't remember much about it, for I went to sleep again, and when I woke the overseer was gone, and Mr. Parker was here in his place. I was chained like a wild beast under the garret stairs, and Miss Grundy's broad, stiff back was hung there for a door. Nobody asks me to work now, but occasionally, just for pastime, I go into Mrs. Parker's room and read to her, and tell her about my Willie, who went away."

"How long has Mrs. Parker been sick?" asked Mary.

"I'm no judge of time," answered Sal, "but it seems a great while, for since her illness Miss Grundy has been at the helm in the kitchen, and perhaps it is all right that she should be, for somebody must manage, and, as I had declared I would not work, 'twould hardly have been consistent to change my mind. And then, too, Miss Grundy seems admirably suited for the place. Her *forte* is among pots and kettles, and she will get the most work out of the boarders, keep them on the least fare, and put more money into Mr. Parker's pocket at the end of a year, than any one he could hire, and this is the secret of his bearing so much from her."

"But why does she want to fill his pockets with money?"

Sal gave a knowing wink and replied, "You are not old enough to see into every thing, so I dare say you wouldn't understand me if I should hint that Mrs. Parker has the consumption, and can't live always." Mary's looks plainly told that this remark had given her no idea whatever, and Sal continued, "I knew you wouldn't understand, for you haven't my discernment to begin with, and then you were never sent away to school, were you?"

"No, ma'am, was you?" asked Mary.

"Say '*were you*,' if you please, it is more euphonious Yes, I was at school in Leicester two years, and was called the best grammarian there, but since I've sojourned with this kind of people, I've nearly lost my refinement. To be sure I aim at exclusiveness, and now you've come I shall cut them all, with the exception of Uncle Peter, who would be rather genteel if he knew more of grammar."

Just then Alice awoke, and Sally, who had not observed her before, sprang forward with a scream of joy, and seizing the child in her arms, threw her up towards the ceiling, catching her as she came down as easily as she would a feather. Strange to say Alice neither manifested any fear of the woman, nor dislike of the play, but laid her head on Sally's shoulder as naturally as if it had been her mother.

"Dear little fellow," said Sal, "he looks like Willie, only not half so handsome."

"She isn't a boy," quickly interrupted Mary. "Her name is Alice."

"No consequence," said Sally, "he's Willie to me;" and ever after, in spite of Mary's remonstrance, she persisted in speaking of Alice as "he," and "the little boy."

Mary soon found that the poor-house with Sal Furbush shut up, and the poor-house with Sal at liberty, were quite different affairs. Now it was no longer lonely, for Sal's fertile imagination was constantly suggesting something new, either by way of pastime or mischief. Towards Miss Grundy, she and the other paupers evinced a strong dislike, owing, in a great measure, to the air of superiority which that lady thought proper to assume, and which was hardly more than natural considering the position which she occupied. She was a capital housekeeper, and to one unacquainted with the circumstances it seemed strange, why a person, apparently so strong and healthy, should be in the Alms-House. Unfortunately, however, she was subject to fits, which made her presence so unpleasant to the people with whom she lived that at last, no one was willing to hire her. About that time, too, she was taken very ill, and as she had no relatives, she was removed to the poor-house, where she had remained ever since.

When Mrs. Parker became too feeble to work, Miss Grundy immediately stepped into her place, filling it so well, that as Sal had said, Mr. Parker bore a great deal from her, knowing that no one whom he could hire would do as well, or save as much as she did. Sal Furbush she could neither manage nor make work, and she vented her spite towards her by getting her shut up on the slightest pretexts. Sal knew very well to whom she was indebted for her "temporary seclusions," as she called them, and she exerted herself to repay the debt with interest. Sometimes on a sultry summer morning, when the perspiration stood thickly on Miss Grundy's face as she bent over a red-hot cook-stove in the kitchen, Sal with her, feet in the brook, which ran through the back yard, and a big palm-leaf fan in her hand, would call out from some shady spot, "Hallo, Miss Grundy, don't you wish you were a lady boarder, and could be as cool and as comfortable as I am?" Occasionally, too, when safely fastened in the pantry enjoying her green tea and Boston crackers, she would be startled with the words, "That must have an excellent relish!" and looking up, she would spy Sal, cosily seated on the top shelf, eyeing her movements complacently, and offering, perhaps, to assist her if she found the tea too strong!

Miss Grundy wore a wig, and as she seemed disturbed whenever the fact was mentioned, the walls of the house both inside and out were frequently ornamented with ludicrous pictures of herself, in which she was sometimes represented as entirely bald-headed, while with spectacles on the end of her nose, she appeared to be peering hither and thither in quest of her wig. On these occasions Miss Grundy's wrath knew no bounds, and going to Mr. Parker she would lay the case before him in so aggravated a form, that at last to get rid of her, he would promise that, for the next offence, Sal should be shut up. In this way the poor woman, to use her own words, "was secluded from the visible world nearly half the time."

With the other inmates of the house, however, she was a special favorite, and many were the kind turns which she had done for the lame woman, whom Miss Grundy took delight in reminding that "she didn't half earn the salt to her porridge."

Next to the wig, nothing more annoyed Miss Grundy than to see Sal, with grammar in hand, perched upon the window sill or table, and repeating at the top of her voice the "rules," of which every fourth one seemed to have been made with direct reference to herself. But it was of no use for Miss Grundy to complain of this, for as Sal said, "Mr. Parker merely winked at it as the vagaries of a disordered mind," and she was free to quote her grammar from morning till night. Whenever she was crazier than usual, her command of language was proportionately greater, and her references to her grammar more frequent, while no one in the house could venture a remark without being immediately corrected for some impropriety of speech.

Uncle Peter, who had a high opinion of Sally's abilities, always did his best to converse as she directed, but in her "inspired days" even he became utterly confounded, and once when in one of her lofty strains, she had labored hard to impress upon him the all-important fact that *adjectives* are frequently changed into *adverbs* by the suffix "ly," the old man, quite out of his wits with his efforts to understand and profit by her teachings, was guilty of a laughable blunder.

"Uncle Peter," said she, "did you notice how unusually funnily Miss Grundy's wig was arranged at dinner to-day?"

Thinking that he fully understood the reply which he was expected to make, and anxious to make amends for his former stupidity, Uncle Peter promptly replied, "No, madam I did not-*ly*.'"

The look of horror which Sally's face assumed, convinced Uncle Peter that he had failed in his attempts at speaking grammatically, and with a sudden determination never again to try, he precipitately left the house, and for the next two hours amused himself by playing "Bruce's Address" upon his old cracked fiddle. From that time Sal gave up all hopes of educating Uncle Peter, and confined herself mostly to literary efforts, of which we shall speak hereafter.

The night following Sal's first acquaintance with Mary, Alice cried until nearly day dawn. The milk which Miss Grundy's stinginess allowed her, was not particularly conducive to her health, and besides that, she missed the invigorating bath to which she had been accustomed during her mother's lifetime. Mary had spoken of it two or three times, but Miss Grundy only jerked her shoulders, saying, "she guessed she wasn't going to have such a slush around the house. You can bring her down," said she, "to the sink, and pump as much water on her as you like;" so Mary said no more about it until the night of which we have spoken, and then she determined on making one more effort. But her heart almost failed her, when, on entering the kitchen, she saw how the chairs and Miss Grundy's shoulders danced round. She well knew that something was wrong, and attributing it to Alice's crying, she awaited in silence for the storm to burst.

"Rind," said Miss Grundy to the girl with crooked feet, who was washing the milk-pail, "ain't there nary spare room in the dark passage?"

"None but the wool room, as I know on," was Rind's sullen response.

"Well, wool room 'tis then,—for, as for my being kep' awake night after night, by a good for nothin' young one, that hain't no business here, any way, I shan't do it. So (speaking to Mary) you may just pick up your duds and move this very morning."

"Going to put 'em in with the wool?" asked Rind, suspending operations, and holding up the pail so that the water ran out of the spout.

"You shet up," said Miss Grundy, "and wait until you're invited to speak. Goodness alive, look at that slop! Tip up the pail, quick."

By this time Mary had found courage to say she thought Alice would be better if she could have her usual bath every morning. This only increased Miss Grundy's wrath, and she whirled round so swiftly, that her forehead came in contact with the sharp edge of the cellar door, which chanced to be open.

"Good," softly whispered Rind, while the shuffling motion of her club feet showed how pleased she was.

Mary, on the contrary, was really distressed, for she knew the bumped head would be charged to her, and felt sure that she was further than ever from the attainment of her object. Still, after Miss Grundy's forehead was duly bathed in cold water, and bound up in a blue cotton handkerchief (the lady's favorite color), she again ventured to say, "Miss Grundy, if you will only let me wash Alice in my room, I'll promise she shan't disturb you again."

After a great deal of scolding and fretting about whims stuck-up notions, and paupers trying to be somebody, Miss Grundy, who really did not care a copper where Alice was washed, consented, and Mary ran joyfully up stairs with the bucket of clear, cold water, which was so soothing in its effects upon the feeble child, that in a short time she fell into a deep slumber. Mary gently laid her down, and then smoothing back the few silken curls which grew around her forehead, and kissing her white cheek, she returned to the kitchen, determined to please Miss Grundy that day, if possible.

But Miss Grundy was in the worst of humors, and the moment Mary appeared she called out, "Go straight back, and fetch that young one down here. Nobody's a goin' to have you racin' up stairs every ten minutes to see whether or no she sleeps with her eyes open or shet. She can stay here as well as not, and if she begins to stir, Patsy can jog the cradle."

Mary cast a fearful glance at Patsy, who nodded and smiled as if in approbation of Miss Grundy's command. She dared not disobey, so Alice and her cradle were transferred to the kitchen, which was all day long kept at nearly boiling heat from the stove room adjoining. Twice Mary attempted to shut the door between, but Miss Grundy bade her open it so she could "keep an eye on all that was going on." The new sights and faces round her, and more than all, Patsy's strange appearance, frightened Alice, who set up such loud screams that Miss Grundy shook her lustily, and then cuffed Patsy, who cried because the baby did, and pulling Mary's hair because she "most knew she felt gritty," she went back to the cheese-tub, muttering something about "Cain's being raised the hull time."

At last, wholly exhausted and overcome with the heat Alice ceased screaming, and with her eyes partly closed, she lay panting for breath, while Mary, half out of her senses tipped over the dishwater, broke the yellow pitcher, and spilled a pan of morning's milk.

"If there's a stick on the premises, I'll use it, or my name isn't Grundy," said the enraged woman, at the same time starting for a clump of alders which grew near the brook.

At this stage of affairs, Sal Furbush came dancing in curtseying, making faces, and asking Mary if she thought "the temperature of the kitchen conducive to health."

Mary instinctively drew nearer to her, as to a friend, and grasping her dress, whispered, "Oh, Sally, Aunt Sally, don't let her whip me for nothing," at the same time pointing towards Miss Grundy, who was returning with an alder switch, stripping off its leaves as she came.

"Whip you? I guess she won't," said Sal, and planting herself in the doorway as Miss Grundy came up, she asked, "Come you with hostile intentions?"

"Out of my way," said Miss Grundy. "I'll teach, that upstart to break things when she's mad." Pushing Sal aside, she entered the kitchen.

Mary retreated behind the cupboard door, and Miss Grundy was about to follow her, when Sal, with a nimble bound, sprang upon her back, and pulling her almost to the floor, snatched the whip from her hand, and broke it in twenty pieces. How the matter would have ended is uncertain, for at that moment Mr. Parker himself appeared, and to him Miss Grundy and Sal detailed their grievances, both in the same breath.

"I can't get at a word," said he, and turning to the pleasant-looking woman, who was quietly paring apples, he asked what it meant.

In a plain, straightforward manner, she told all, beginning from the time when Alice was first brought into the kitchen, and adding, as an opinion of her own, that the child was suffering from heat. Mr Parker was a good-natured, though rather weak man, and in reality slightly feared Miss Grundy. On this occasion, however, he did not take sides with her but said, "It was ridiculous to have such works, and that if Mary wanted whipping, he would do it himself."

"But Sal Furbush," said Miss Grundy, as she adjusted her head-gear, which was slightly displaced, "can't she be shut up? There's bedlam to pay the whole durin' time when she's loose."

Mr. Parker knew this very well, but before he had time to answer, Mary looked pleadingly in his face, and said, "if you please, don't shut her up. She was not to blame, for I asked her to help me."

"Wall, wall, we'll let her off this time, I guess," said he; and as Uncle Peter just then put his head into the window, saying that "the lord of the manor was wanted without," Mr. Parker left, glad to get out of the muss so easily. No sooner was he gone, than Sal, catching up the cradle, sorted for the stairs, saying, "I won't work, but I can, and will take care of little Willie, and I choose to do it in a more congenial atmosphere." Then, as Mary looked a little startled, she added, "Never you fear, dearie, Sal knows what she's about, and she won't make the little boy the least bit of a face."

From that time there was no more trouble with Alice during the day, for she seemed to cling naturally to Sally, who hour after hour rocked and took care of her, while Mary, in the kitchen below, was busy with the thousand things which Miss Grundy found for her to do.

CHAPTER VII.

THE LINCOLNS

Mary had been at the poor-house about three weeks, when Miss Grundy one day ordered her to tie on her sun-bonnet, and run across the meadow and through the woods until she came to a rye stubble, then follow the footpath along the fence until she came to another strip of woods, with a brook running through it. "And just on the fur edge of them woods," said she, "you'll see the men folks to work; and do you tell 'em to come to their dinner quick."

Mary tied her sun-bonnet and hurried off, glad to escape for a few moments from the hot kitchen, with its endless round of washing dishes, scouring knives, wiping door-sills, and dusting chairs. She had no difficulty in finding the way and she almost screamed for joy, when she came suddenly upon the sparkling brook, which danced so merrily beneath the shadow of the tall woods.

"What a nice place this would be to sit and read," was her first exclamation, and then she sighed as she thought how small were her chances for reading now.

Quickly her thoughts traversed the past, and her tears mingled with the clear water which flowed at her feet, as she recalled the time when, blessed with a father's and mother's love, she could go to school and learn as other children did. She was roused from her sad reverie by the sound of voices, which she supposed proceeded from the men, whose tones, she fancied, were softer than usual. "If I can hear them, they can hear me," thought she, and shouting as loud as she could, she soon heard Mr. Parker's voice in answer, saying he would come directly.

It was a mild September day, and as Mary knew that Sal would take care of Alice, she determined not to hurry, but to follow the course of the stream, fancying she should find it to be the same which ran through the clothes-yard at home. She had not gone far, when she came suddenly upon a boy and two little girls, who seemed to be playing near the brook. In the features of the boy she recognized Henry Lincoln, and remembering what Billy had said of him, she was about turning away, when the smallest of the girls espied her, and called out, "Look here, Rose, I reckon that's Mary Howard. I'm going to speak to her."

"Jenny Lincoln, you mustn't do any such thing. Mother won't like it," answered the girl called Rose.

But whether "mother would like it," or not, Jenny did not stop to think, and going towards Mary she said, "Have you come to play in the woods?"

"No," was Mary's reply. "I came to call the folks to dinner."

"Oh, that was you that screamed so loud. I couldn't think who it was, but it can't be dinner time?"

"Yes 'tis; it's noon."

"Well we don't have dinner until two, and we can stay here till that time. Won't you play with us?"

"No, I can't, I must go back and work," said Mary.

"Work!" repeated Jenny. "I think it's bad enough to have to live in that old house without working, but come and see our fish-pond;" and taking Mary's hand, she led her to a wide part of the stream where the water had been dammed up until it was nearly two feet deep and clear as crystal. Looking in, Mary could see the pebbles on the bottom, while a fish occasionally darted out and then disappeared.

"I made this almost all myself," said Jenny. "Henry wouldn't help me because he's so ugly, and Rose was afraid of blacking her fingers. But I don't care Mother says I'm a great,—great,—I've forgotten the word, but it means dirty and careless, and I guess I do look like a fright, don't I?"

Mary now for the first time noticed the appearance of her companion, and readily guessed that the word which she could not remember, was "slattern." She was a fat, chubby little girl, with a round, sunny face and laughing blue eyes, while her brown hair hung around her forehead in short, tangled curls. The front breadth of her pink gingham dress was plastered with mud. One of her shoe strings was untied, and the other one gone. The bottom of one pantalet was entirely torn off, and the other rolled nearly to the knee disclosing a pair of ankles of no Liliputian dimensions. The strings of her white sun-bonnet were twisted into a hard knot, and the bonnet itself hung down her back, partially hiding the chasm made by the absence of three or four hooks and eyes. Altogether she was just the kind of little girl which one often finds in the country swinging on gates and making mud pies.

Mary was naturally very neat; and in reply to Jenny's question as to whether she looked like a fright, she answered, "I like your face better than I do your dress, because it is clean."

"Why, so was my dress this morning," said Jenny, "but here can't any body play in the mud and not get dirty. My pantalet hung by a few threads, and as I wanted a rag to wash my earthens with, I tore it off. Why don't you wear pantalets?"

Mary blushed painfully, as she tried to hide her bare feet with her dress, but she answered, "When mother died I had only two pair, and Miss Grundy says I sha'nt wear them every day. It makes too much washing."

"Miss Grundy! She's a spiteful old thing. She shook me once because I laughed at that droll picture Sal Furbush drew of her on the front door. I am afraid of Sal, ain't you?"

"I was at first, but she's very kind to me, and I like her now."

"Well, I always run when I see her. She makes such faces and shakes her fist so. But if she's kind to you, I'll like her too. You go away (speaking to Henry), and not come here to bother us."

Henry gave a contemptuous whistle, and pointing to Mary's feet, said, "Ain't they delicate? Most as small as her teeth!"

The tears came into Mary's eyes, and Jenny, throwing a stick at her brother, exclaimed, "For shame, Henry Lincoln! You always was the meanest boy. Her feet ain't any bigger than mine. See," and she stuck up her little dumpy foot, about twice as thick as Mary's.

"Cracky!" said Henry, with another whistle. "They may be, too, and not be so very small, for yours are as big as stone boats, any day, and your ankles are just the size of the piano legs." So saying, he threw a large stone into the water, spattering both the girls, but wetting Jenny the most. After this he walked away apparently well pleased with his performance.

"Isn't he hateful?" said Jenny, wiping the water from her neck and shoulders; "but grandma says all boys are so until they do something with the oats,—I've forgot what. But there's one boy who isn't ugly. Do you know Billy Bender?"

"Billy Bender? Oh, yes," said Mary quickly, "he is all the friend I've got in the world except Sal Furbush."

"Well, he worked for my pa last summer, and oh, I liked him *so* much. I think he's the *bestest* boy in the world. And isn't his face beautiful?"

"I never thought of it," said Mary. "What makes you think him so handsome?"

"Oh, I don't know unless it's because he makes such nice popple whistles!" and as if the argument were conclusive, Jenny unrolled her pantalet, and tried to wipe some of the mud from her dress, at the same time glancing towards her sister, who at some little distance was reclining against an old oak tree, and poring intently over "Fairy Tales for Children."

Seeing that she was not observed, Jenny drew nearer to Mary and said, "If you'll never tell any body as long as you live and breathe, I'll tell you something."

Mary gave the required promise, and Jenny continued: "I shouldn't like to have my mother know it, for she scolds all the time now about my 'vulgar tastes,' though I'm sure Rose likes the same things that I do, except Billy Bender, and it's about him I was going to tell you. He was so pleasant I couldn't help loving him, if mother did say I mustn't. He used to talk to me about keeping clean, and once I tried a whole week, and I only dirtied four dresses and three pair of pantalets in all that time. Oh, how handsome and funny his eyes looked when I told him about it. He took me in his lap, and said that was more than he thought a little girl ought to dirty. Did you ever see any boy you loved as well as you do Billy Bender?"

Mary hesitated a moment, for much as she liked Billy, there was another whom she loved better, though he had never been one half as kind to her as Billy had. After a time she answered, "Yes, I like, or I did like George Moreland, but I shall never see him again;" and then she told Jenny of her home in England, of the long, dreary voyage to America, and of her father's death; but when she came to the sad night when her mother and Franky died, she could not go on, and laying her face in Jenny's lap, she cried for a long time. Jenny's tears flowed, too, but she tried to restrain them, for she saw that Rose had shut her book and was watching her movements.

Ere long, however, she resumed her reading, and then Jenny, softly caressing Mary, said, "Don't cry so, for I'll love you, and we'll have good times together too. We live in Boston every winter, but it will be most six weeks before we go and I mean to see you every day."

"In Boston?" said Mary, inquiringly. "*George* lives in Boston."

Jenny was silent a moment, and then suddenly clapping her hands together, she exclaimed. "I know George Moreland. He lives just opposite our house, and is Ida Selden's cousin. Why he's most as handsome as Billy Bender, only he teases you more. I'll tell him about you, for mother says he's got lots of money, and perhaps he'll give you some."

Mary felt that she wouldn't for the world have George know she was in the poor-house, and she quickly answered, "No, no, you mustn't tell him a word about me. I don't want you to. Promise that you won't."

Loth as Jenny was to make such a promise, she finally did, adding, "I guess

I won't tell Rose either, for she and Ida are great friends. George says he don't know which he likes best, though he thinks Rose the handsomest. He like handsome girls, and so do I."

Mary knew she had no beauty of which to boast, but Ella had, so she very naturally mentioned her sister, saying how much she wished to see her.

"Why, you can see her at church," answered Jenny. "Why don't you ever go?"

"I am going next Sunday, Sally and I," was Mary's reply. "Billy told me the last time he was here that he would come and stay with Alice."

"Oh, I'm glad, and I hope they'll put you in my Sabbath school class, for Ella is in it, but if they do I'll contrive to have Rose sit off a good ways because,—because—"

Here Jenny paused, but seeing that Mary was waiting for her to finish the sentence, she added, "She's proud, and sometimes laughs at poor girls."

"Thank you, Miss Jenny Lincoln," said Rose, coming forward. "I'll tell mother of this new intimacy, and she'll put a stop to it, I'll assure you. But come along, I'm going home."

Jenny arose to obey, but whispered to Mary, "You'll find me most any time in these woods. I'd ask you to come to our house, only mother wouldn't let you sit in the parlor. I shall see you Sunday,—Good-bye."

Mary watched her until she disappeared among the bushes and then she too started for home, with a lighter heart than she had known before for many a day. She had found a new friend, and though Miss Grundy scolded because she had been gone so long, and threatened to shut her up in Sal Furbush's cage, she did not mind it and actually commenced humming a tune while Miss Grundy was storming about a bowl of sour milk which she had found in the cupboard. A sharp box on her ears brought her song to an end and the tears into her eyes, but she thought of Jenny, and the fact that she too knew George made him seem nearer, and when Miss Grundy did not see her she hastily drew the golden locket from her bosom, and glancing at the handsome, boyish face it revealed, quickly thrust it back as she heard a quick step in the passage.

She had no opportunity of seeing Jenny again that week, for she was kept busy from morning till night, running here and there, first after eggs, then after water, next for potatoes, and then after wood. And still Miss Grundy told her fifty times a day that "she didn't half pay her way, to say nothing about the young one."

"Bolt at once," said Sal. "Bolt, and say you didn't come here to work: that's the way I did."

Mary was willing to do whatever she could, but she often wished Mrs. Parker were able to be round, for then she was sure she would not have to work so hard. She had several times been sent of errands to Mrs. Parker's room, and that lady had always spoken kindly to her, asking her if she was tired, or what made her look so pale. It was through Mrs Parker's influence, too, that she had obtained permission to attend church the following Sabbath. Mrs. Parker was a professor of religion, and before her illness, some of the family had attended church every Sunday. But since she had been sick, her husband had thought it hardly worth while to harness up his horses, though he said any one might go who chose to walk. Few, however, were able to walk; so they remained at home, and Sunday was usually the noisiest day in the week. Sal Furbush generally took the lead, and mounting the kitchen table, sung camp meeting hymns as loud as she could scream. Uncle Peter fiddled, Patsy nodded and laughed, the girl with crooked feet by way of increasing the bedlam would sometimes draw a file across the stove-pipe, while Miss Grundy scolded, and declared "she could not and would not have such a noise."

"Shut your head, madam, and there'll be less," was Sal's ready rejoinder, as at the end of a verse she paused for breath.

The first Sabbath Mary looked on in perfect amazement, but the next one she spent in her own room, and after a deal of trouble, succeeded in coaxing Sal to stay there too, listening while she read to her from her little Bible. But the reading was perplexing business, for Sal constantly corrected her pronunciation, or stopped her while she expounded Scripture, and at last in a fit of impatience Mary tossed the book into the crazy creature's lap, asking her to read her self.

This was exactly what Sal wanted, and taking the foot of Mary's bed for her rostrum, she read and preached so furiously, that Mary felt almost glad when Miss Grundy came up to stop the racket, and locked Sal in her own room.

CHAPTER VIII.

AT CHURCH.

The Sabbath following Mary's first acquaintance with Jenny was the one on which she was to go to church. Billy Bender promised that if his mother were not suffering from any new disease, he would come to stay with Alice, and in case he failed, the pleasant-looking woman was to take his place. Mary would have preferred going alone, but Sally begged so hard, and promised so fairly "not to make a speck of a face at the preacher, provided he used good grammar," that Mary finally asked Mr. Parker to let her go.

He consented willingly, saying he hoped the house would be peaceable for once. And now, it was hard telling which looked forward to the next Sunday with the most impatience, Mary or Sal, the latter of whom was anxious to see the fashions, as she fancied her wardrobe was getting out of date. To Mary's happiness there was one drawback. A few weeks before her mother's death she had given to Ella her straw hat, which she had outgrown, and now the only bonnet she possessed was the veritable blue one of which George Moreland had made fun, and which by this time was nearly worn out. Mrs. Campbell, who tried to do right and thought that she did, had noticed Mary's absence from church, and once on speaking of the subject before Hannah, the latter suggested that probably she had no bonnet, saying that the one which she wore at her mother's funeral was borrowed Mrs. Campbell immediately looked over her things, and selecting a straw which she herself had worn three years before, she tied a black ribbon across it, and sent it as a present to Mary.

The bonnet had been rather large for Mrs. Campbell, and was of course a world too big for Mary, whose face looked bit, as Sal expressed it, "like a yellow pippin stuck into the far end of a firkin." Miss Grundy, however, said "it was plenty good enough for a pauper," reminding Mary that "beggars shouldn't be choosers."

"So it is good enough for paupers like you," returned Sal, "but people who understand grammar always have a keen sense of the ridiculous."

Mary made no remark whatever, but she secretly wondered if Ella wore such a hat. Still her desire to see her sister and to visit her mother's grave, prevailed over all other feelings, and on Sunday morning it was a very happy child which at about nine o'clock bounded down the stairway, tidily dressed in a ten cent black lawn and a pair of clean white pantalets.

There was another circumstance, too, aside from the prospect of seeing Ella, which made her eyes sparkle until they were almost black. The night before, in looking over the articles of dress which she would need, she discovered that there was not a decent pair of stockings in her wardrobe. Mrs. Grundy, to whom she mentioned the fact, replied with a violent shoulder jerk, "For the land's sake! ain't you big enough to go to meetin' barefoot, or did you think we kept silk stockin's for our quality to wear?"

Before the kitchen looking-glass, Sal was practising a courtesy which she intended making to any one who chanced to notice her next day; but after overhearing Miss Grundy's remark, she suddenly brought her exercises to a close and left the kitchen. Arrived at her room, she commenced tumbling over a basket containing her wearing apparel, selecting from it a pair of fine cotton stockings which she had long preserved, because they were the last thing Willie's father ever gave her. "They are not much too large for her now," thought she, "but I guess I'll take a small seam clear through them." This being done, she waited until all around the house was still, and then creeping stealthily to Mary's room, she pinned the stockings to the pantalets, hanging the whole before the curtainless window, where the little girl could see them the moment she opened her eyes! Mary well knew to whom she was indebted for this unexpected pleasure, and in her accustomed prayer that morning she remembered the poor old crazy woman, asking that the light of reason might again dawn upon her darkened mind.

On descending to the kitchen, Mary found Sal waiting for her, and, as she had expected, rigged out in a somewhat fantastic style. Her dress, which was an old plum-colored silk, was altogether too short-waisted and too narrow for the prevailing fashion. A gauze handkerchief was thrown across her neck, and fastened to her belt in front by a large yellow bow. Her bonnet, which was really a decent one, was almost entirely covered by a thick green veil, and notwithstanding the sun was shining brightly, she carried in her hand a large blue cotton umbrella, for fear it would rain!

"Come, child," said she, the moment Mary appeared, "put on your *tea-kettle* (referring to the bonnet which Mary held in her hand), and let us start."

There was no looking-glass in Mary's room, and she stepped before the one in the kitchen while she adjusted her hat, but her courage almost failed her as she saw the queer-looking image reflected by the mirror. She was unusually thin, and it seemed to her that her teeth were never so prominent before. Her eyes, always large, now looked unnaturally so and as she placed what Sal had termed a "tea-kettle" upon her head, she half determined not to go. But Sal caught her hand, saying, "Come, child, it's time we were off. They'll all know it's Mrs. Campbell's old bonnet, and will laugh at her for giving it to you."

Billy had not come, but the pleasant-looking woman had succeeded in making friends with Alice, and as Mary passed out of the yard she saw her little sister spatting the window sill, and apparently well pleased with her new nurse. Scarcely were they out of sight of the house, when Sal, seating herself upon a large stone, commenced divesting her feet of her shoes and stockings.

"What are you doing?" asked Mary, in great surprise.

"I guess I know better than to wear out my kid slippers when I've got no Willie's father to buy me any more," answered Sal. "I'm going barefoot until I reach the river bridge, and then I shall put them on again."

The shoes and stockings being carefully rolled up in a paper which Sal produced from her pocket, they walked briskly forward, and reached the village some time before the first bell rang for church.

"Come down this street, please," said Mary to her companion, who with slippers readjusted and umbrella hoisted was mincing along, courtesying to every one she met, and asking them how they did—"Come down this street; I want to see my old home."

Sal readily complied, saying as they drew near the low brown house, in which a strange family were now living, "There is nothing very elegant in the architecture of this dwelling."

Mary made no reply. With her head resting upon the garden fence, and one hand clasped around a shrub which Franky had set out, she was sobbing as though her heart would break. Very gently Sal laid her hand on Mary's shoulder, and led her away, saying, "What would I not have given for such a command of tears when Willie's father died. But I could not weep; and my tears all turned to burning coals, which set my brain on fire."

The next time Mary raised her head they were opposite Mrs. Bender's, where Sal declared it her intention to stop. As they were passing up to the side door, Billy, who heard their footsteps, came out, and shaking hands with Mary, and trying hard to keep from laughing at the wonderful courtesy, which Sal Furbush made him. On entering the house they found Mrs. Bender flat on her back, the pillow pulled out from under her head, and the bed clothes tucked closely up under her chin.

"Mother was so sick I couldn't come," said Billy to Mary, while Sal, walking up to the bedside, asked, "Is your sickness unto death, my good woman?"

"Oh, I am afeard not," was the feeble response. "Folks with my difficulty suffer for years."

Mary looked inquiringly at Billy, and a smile but little according with his mother's seeming distress parted his lips as he whispered, "She was reading yesterday about a woman that had been bed-ridden with a spinal difficulty, and now she declares that she too 'has got a spine in her back,' though I fancy she would be in a pretty predicament without one. But where did you get that fright of a bonnet?" he continued. "It's like looking down a narrow lane to see your face."

Mary knew that Billy was very observing of dress, and she blushed painfully as she replied, that Mrs. Campbell gave it to her.

"Well, she ought to be ashamed," said he, "with all her money to give you a corn-basket of a thing like that. Ella doesn't wear such a one, I can tell you."

Just then the first bell rang, and Sal, who had mischievously recommended a mustard poultice, as being the most likely to draw Mrs. Bender's spine to a head, started to go saying, "she wanted to be there in season, so as to see the folks come in."

Accordingly they again set forward, attracting more attention, and causing more remarks, than any two who had passed through Chicopee for a long time. On reaching the church, Sal requested the sexton to give her a seat which would command a view of the greater part of the congregation, and he accordingly led them to the farthest extremity of one of the side galleries. Mary had been there at church before, but as she had always sat near the door, she did not know in what part of the building Mrs. Campbell's pew was located. As she leaned over the railing, however, she concluded that the large square one with crimson velvet cushions must be hers. Erelong the bell began to toll, and soon a lady dressed in deep mourning appeared, and passing up the middle aisle, entered the richly cushioned pew. She was accompanied by a little girl, tastefully dressed in a frock of light-blue silk tissue. A handsome French straw hat was set jauntily on one side of her head, and her long curls hung over her white neck and shoulders. Mary knew that this was Ella, and involuntarily starting up, she leaned forward far enough to bring her bonnet directly in sight of some thoughtless girls, who immediately commenced tittering, and pointing her out to those near them.

Blushing scarlet, the poor girl sank back into the seat, saying half aloud, "O, I wish I hadn't come."

"What's the matter?" said Sal. "Has somebody laughed at you? I'll warrant there has;" and leaning over the railing herself, she shook her fist threateningly at the girls, whose eyes were still directed that way.

Mary felt instinctively that her companion was attracting more attention than her bonnet; and twitching her dress bade her sit down. Sal obeyed; but she had no opportunity that morning of deciding whether the sermon were grammatical or not, for she was constantly on the look out, and whenever she saw any one scrutinizing Mary or herself more closely than they ought, a shake of her fist and a horrid face warned them to desist. Twice during church time Mary thought, nay felt sure that she caught her sister's eye, but it was quickly withdrawn, as if unwilling to be recognized.

When church was out, Sal insisted upon going down immediately; so they descended together to the porch below, reaching it just as Mrs. Campbell appeared in the doorway. Had she chosen, Mary could have touched the lady's dress as she passed; but she rather shrank from being seen, and would probably not have been observed at all, had not Sal planted herself directly in front of Mrs. Campbell, saying loudly enough for all near her to hear, "Madam, do you not recognize your munificent gift of charity in yonder amazing bonnet?" at the same time pointing towards Mary, who nervously grasped the strings of her hat, as if to remove the offensive article.

Mrs. Campbell haughtily pushed Sal aside, and advancing towards the child, said, "I am glad to see you at church Mary, and hope you will now come regularly. You can accompany Ella home after the Sabbath school, if you like."

The words and manner were so cold and formal, that Mary was obliged to force down her tears before she replied, that she was going to her mother's grave, and wanted Ella to go with her.

"It is pretty warm to walk so far, but if Ella wishes it she has my permission. Only tell her not to get red and heated," said Mrs. Campbell; and gathering up the folds of her rich silk, the texture of which Sal Furbush had been examining, and comparing with her own plum-color, she walked away.

Scarcely was she gone, when Jenny Lincoln came tripping up, and seizing both Mary's hands, exclaimed, "I am real glad you are here. I thought you hadn't come, until I heard them talking about a crazy woman. But let's go to my class, and you'll have a chance to see Ella while the scholars are getting their seats."

Mary accompanied her young friend to a pew, at the door of which she met her sister face to face. There was a sudden exclamation of joy on Mary's part, and an attempt to throw her arms around Ella's neck, but the little girl drew back, and merely offering her hand, said, "Oh, it's you, isn't it? I didn't know you, you looked so queer."

"Heavens! what a head-dress! Big as our carriage top any day!" was the next exclamation which reached Mary's ear, as Rose Lincoln brushed past. Glancing from her sister to Rose, Mary half determined to tear the bonnet from her head and trample it under her feet, but Jenny softly squeezed her hand, and whispered, "Don't mind what Rose says; I love you, and so does Billy Bender. I saw him in the village yesterday, and asked him if he didn't, and he said he did."

It required more than Billy Bender's love to soothe Mary then. Her sister's cool reception, so different from what she had anticipated, had stung her heart; and sitting down near the door, she burst into a passionate fit of tears. Jenny, who was really distressed, occasionally pressed her hand in token of sympathy, at the same time offering her cloves, peanuts and sugar-plums. There was a brighter flush, too, than usual, on Ella's cheek, for she knew that she had done wrong, and she so jumbled together the words of her lesson, that the teacher made her repeat it twice, asking her what was the matter.

By the time Sabbath school was over, Mary had dried her tears; and determining to make one more advance towards her sister, she said, "Won't you go to mother's grave with me? I want to tell you about little Allie. I have taught her to call your name most as plain as *I* can."

Ella looked down at her embroidered pantalets, and hanging her head on one side, said, "Oh, it's so dusty. I'm afraid I'll get all dirt,—and hot, too. Mamma doesn't like to have me get hot."

"Why not?" asked Jenny, who always wished to know the reason of things.

"'Cause it makes folks' skin rough, and break out," was Ella's reply.

"Oh, pshaw!" returned Jenny, with a vain attempt to turn up her little bit of a nose. "I play every day till I am most roasted, and my skin ain't half as rough as yours. But say, will you go with Mary? for if you don't I shall!"

"I guess I won't," said Ella, and then, anxious to make Mary feel a little comfortable, she added, "Mamma says Mary's coming to see me before long, and then we'll have a real good time. I've lots of pretty things—two silk dresses, and I wear French gaiters like these every day."

Glancing first at Mary, and then at Ella, Jenny replied, "Pho, that's nothing; Mary knows more than you do, any way. Why, she can say every speck of the multiplication table, and you only know the 10's!"

When Ella was angry, or felt annoyed, she generally cried; and now declaring that she knew more than the 10's she began to cry; and announcing her intention of never speaking to Jenny again "as long as she lived and breathed," she walked away, while Mary and Jenny proceeded together towards the burying ground. With a bitter cry Mary threw herself upon her mother's grave, and wept for a long, long time.

"It would not be so bad," said Mary, "if there was any body left, but I am all alone in the world. Ella does not love me—nobody loves me."

It was in vain that Jenny told her of Billy Bender's love, of her own, and George Moreland's too. Mary only wept the more, wishing that she had died, and Allie too. At last remembering that she had left Sal Furbush behind her, and knowing that it was time for her to go, she arose, and leaning on Jenny, whose arm was passed lovingly about her, she started to return.

Afternoon service had commenced ere they reached the church, and as Mary had no desire of again subjecting her bonnet to the ridicule of Rose Lincoln, and as Jenny had much rather stay out doors in the shade, they sat down upon the steps, wondering where Sal Furbush had taken herself. "I mean to look in and see if she is here," said Jenny, and advancing on tiptoe to the open door, she cast her eye over the people within; then clapping her hand over her mouth to keep back a laugh, she returned to Mary, saying, "Oh, if it isn't the funniest thing in the world. There sits Sal in Mrs. Campbell's pew, fanning herself with that great palm-leaf, and shaking her fist at Ella every time she stirs!"

It seems that Sal had amused herself during the intermission by examining and trying the different pews, and taking a fancy to Mrs. Campbell's, she had snugly ensconced herself in one corner of it, greatly to the fear and mortification of Ella, who chanced to be the only one of the family present. When service was out, Sal gathered up her umbrella and courtesying her way through the crowd, soon found Mary and started for home, declaring the clergyman to be "a well-read grammarian, only a trifle too emphatic in his delivery."

As they were descending the long hill which led to the river bridge, Mr. Lincoln's carriage passed them, and Jenny, who was inside, seized the reins, saying, "Please, pa, stop and let them ride—there's nobody but Rose and me in here, and it is so hot and so far."

Mr. Lincoln might possibly have complied with his daughter's request, had not Rose chirrupped to the spirited horses, and said, "Don't, father, for mercy's sake! ask those paupers to ride."

So the carriage dashed on, but Mary forgot the long walk by remembering the glance of affection which Jenny gave her as she looked back from the window. Sal seemed unusually silent, and even forgot to take off her shoes and stockings when she reached the river bridge. Mary saw there was something weighing upon her mind, but she forbore asking any questions, knowing that Sal would in her own good time make her thoughts known. They had nearly reached home, when Sal suddenly turned aside, and seating herself upon a rock under a white beech-tree, said, "Miss Howard, I've been thinking what a splendid minister was spoiled when they put dresses on me! Oh how hard I had to hold myself to-day to keep from extemporizing to the congregation. I reckon there wouldn't have been quite so many nodding as there were."

In the excitement of the moment Sal arose, and throwing out her eyes, gesticulated in a manner rather alarming to Mary, who had never before seen so wild a look in the crazy woman's eyes. Soon, however, her mood changed, and resuming her seat, she continued in a milder tone, "Did you ever hear that I was an authoress?"

"An authoress!" repeated Mary—"an authoress! Why no; are you?"

"To be sure I am," answered Sal. "What's to hinder. Haven't I told you repeatedly, that I once possessed an unusually large amount of judgment; and this, added to my knowledge of grammar, and uncommon powers of imagination, enabled me to produce a work which, but for an unaccountable freak of the publisher, would have rendered my name immortal."

"I don't understand," said Mary, and Sally continued: "You see, I wrote about six hundred pages of foolscap, which the publisher to whom it was sent for examination was impolite enough to return, together with a note, containing, as I suppose, his reasons for rejection; but if he thinks I read it he's mistaken. I merely glanced at the words, 'Dear Madam—We regret—' and then threw it aside. It was a terrible disappointment, and came near turning my brain; but there are other publishing houses in the world, and one of these days I shall astonish mankind. But come, we must hasten on, or the gormandizers will eat up those custard pies which I found in the cellar with the brass-kettle covered over them."

Accordingly they started for home, but found, as Sal had predicted, that supper was over and the pies all gone. By a little dexterous management, however, she managed to find half of one, which Miss Grundy had tucked away under an empty candle-box for her own future eating.

CHAPTER IX.

THE NEW BONNET.

The next morning, for a wonder. Jenny Lincoln was up before the sun, and in the large dark closet which adjoined her sleeping room, she rummaged through band-boxes and on the top shelves until she found and brought to light a straw hat, which was new the fall before, but which her mother had decided unfit to appear again in the city. Jenny had heard the unkind remarks which Mary's odd-looking bonnet elicited, and she now determined to give her this one, though she did not dare to do so without her mother's consent. So after breakfast, when her mother was seated at her work in the parlor, Jenny drew near, making known her request, and asking permission to carry the bonnet to Mary herself.

"Mercy on me!" said Mrs. Lincoln, "what won't you think of next, and where did you get such vulgar taste. It must have been from your father, for I am sure you never took it from me. I dare say, now, you had rather play with that town pauper than with the richest child in Boston."

For a moment Jenny was silent, and then as a new idea came into her head, she said, "Ma, if you should die, and pa should die, and every body should die, and we hadn't any money, wouldn't I have to be a town pauper?"

"What absurd questions you ask," said Mrs. Lincoln, overturning a work-box to find a spool of cotton, which lay directly on top. "Do what you please with the bonnet, which I fancy you'll find as much too small for Mary as the one she now has is too large."

Jenny felt fearful of this, but "where there's a will there's a way;" and after considering a moment, she went in quest of her sister, who had one just like it. Rose did not care a fig for the bonnet, and after a while she agreed to part with it on condition that Jenny would give her a coral bracelet, with gold clasps, which she had long coveted. This fanciful little ornament was a birthday present from Billy and at first Jenny thought that nothing would tempt her to part with it, but as Rose was decided, she finally yielded the point, brushing away a tear as she placed the bracelet in her sister's hand. Then putting the bonnet in a basket, and covering it with a newspaper, she started for the poorhouse.

"Good morning, Miss Grundy," said she, as she appeared in the doorway.

"May I see Mary, just a little minute? I've got something for her."

Miss Grundy was crosser than usual this morning on account of a sudden illness which had come upon Patsy, so she jerked her shoulders, and without turning her head, replied, "It's Monday mornin', and Mary ain't goin' to be hindered by big bugs nor nobody else. Here 'tis goin' on nine o'clock, and them dishes not done yet! If you want to see her, you can go into the back room where she is."

Nothing daunted by this ungracious reception, Jenny advanced towards the "back room," where she found Mary at the "sink," her arms immersed in dishwater, and a formidable pile of plates, platters and bowls all ready to be wiped, standing near her. Throwing aside her bonnet and seizing the coarse dish towel, Jenny exclaimed, "I'm going to wipe dishes Mary, I know how, and when they are done, if Miss Grundy won't let you go up stairs a minute, I'll ask Mr. Parker. I saw him under the woodshed grinding an axe."

It was a rare thing to see Jenny Lincoln in the kitchen at the poor-house, and now the fact that she was there, and wiping dishes too, circulated rapidly, bringing to the spot the sour-faced woman, the pleasant-looking woman, the girl with the crooked feet, and half a dozen others, each of whom commented upon the phenomenon after her own fashion.

"Do see the little thing," said one; "handles the wiping rag just like any body!"

"And look there," cried a second; "setting them up in the cupboard! Did you ever!" While a third remarked that she wore silk stockings, wondering whether they were bought on purpose for her, or had been cut over from a pair of her mother's.

Thus noticed and flattered Jenny worked away, assisting in scouring knives and washing spiders, until her dress was splashed with dishwater, and her white apron crocked by the kettles.

"Won't your marm scold you for getting so dirty?' asked the girl with the crooked feet.

"I s'pose so," said Jenny, carelessly; "but then she scolds most all the time, so I don't mind it!"

The dishes being done, and Miss Grundy making no objections, Mary accompanied Jenny up stairs, where the latter, opening her basket, held to view a neat-looking straw hat, far prettier than the one which Mrs. Campbell had presented.

"See," said she, placing it upon Mary's head; "this is for you. I wanted to give you mine, but 'twasn't big enough, so Rose let you have hers. It's real becoming, too."

The tears which fell from Mary's eyes were caused not less by Jenny's kindness, than by the thought that the haughty Rose Lincoln had given her a bonnet! She did not know of the sacrifice which the noble-hearted Jenny had made to obtain it, and it was well she did not, for it would have spoiled all the happiness she experienced in wearing it.

"Thank you, Jenny, and Rose too," said she. "I am so glad, for I love to go to church, and I surely would never have gone again and wore that other bonnet."

"I wouldn't either," returned Jenny. "I think it was ridiculous for Mrs. Campbell to give you such an old dud of a thing, and I know mother thinks so too, for she laughed hard for her, when I described it, though she said nothing except that 'beggars shouldn't be choosers.' I wonder what that means. Do you know?"

Mary felt that she was beginning to know, but she did not care to enlighten Jenny, who soon sprang up, saying she must go home, or her mother would be sending Henry after her. "And I don't want him to come here," said she, "for I know you don't like him, and there don't hardly any body, he's so stuck up and kind of—I don't know what."

In passing through the hall, the girls met Miss Grundy, who had just come from Patsy's room. As soon as she saw Mary, she said, "Clap on your bonnet quick, and run as fast as ever you can to Miss Thornfield's. Dr. Gilbert has gone there, and do you tell him to come here right away, for Patsy is dreadful sick, and has fits all the time."

There was a tremor in her voice, and she seemed much excited, which surprised the girls, who fancied she would not care even if Patsy died. Mrs. Thornfield's was soon reached, the message given, and then they hurried back.

"Is Patsy worse?" asked Mary, as she saw the bedroom door open, and two or three women standing near the bed.

Miss Grundy did not answer, and when next her face was visible, the girls saw that her eyes were red, as if she had been weeping.

"Funny, isn't it?" said Jenny, as she started for home. "I didn't suppose any thing would make her cry, and I guess now the tears are sort of *sour!*"

Dr. Gilbert came, but his skill could not save the poor idiot girl, and at about four that afternoon she died. Around the bed of death there were no tears or lamentations, for those who stood by and watched the lamp of life as it went out, felt that the spirit which was leaving them would be happier far in another world, for never in this had a ray of reason shone upon poor Patsy's darkened mind. We have said there were no tears, and yet, although the waters came not to the surface, there was one heart which wept, as with unflinching nerve the cold, stern woman arrayed the dead girl for the grave.

That night Mary was aroused from sleep, by some one whispering her name in her ear, and starting up, she saw Sally bending over her.

"Come with me," said she softly, "and I'll show you the queerest sight you ever saw."

Trembling in every joint, Mary arose and followed Sal, who led her towards the room where Patsy lay. As she drew near the door they paused, and by the light of the autumn moon, which streamed through the curtained window Mary saw Miss Grundy kneeling by the cold body, and sobbing bitterly. Once she spoke, and Mary caught the words, "My child, my poor child."

Wonderingly she looked up to Sally for an explanation; but the crazy woman only replied, as they returned to their rooms, "Yes,—there's been queer doings some time or other, it's very evident; but I know one thing, I'll never draw her profile again, and I'll call her *Mrs.* Grundy after this!"

It was hardly worth while, as the neighbors thought, to be at all the trouble and expense of carrying a foolish girl without friends or relatives to the graveyard, so they buried her beneath the shadow of a wide-spreading maple, in a little inclosure where several other unfortunate ones lay sleeping At the funeral many wondered at the ghastly whiteness of Miss Grundy's face, and why she grasped at the coffin lid, as if to keep from falling, when with others she gazed upon the pale face which, in its dreamless slumber, looked calm and placid as that of a child.

There were but few who knew of Miss Grundy's sin, and her secret was buried in Patsy's grave, where often a mother's form was bending and a mother's tears were shed, when the world was dark and still, and there was no eye to see, save that of Him who said, "Go and sin no more."

CHAPTER X

WINTER AT THE POOR-HOUSE.

One afternoon about the middle of October, Mary sat under an apple-tree in the orchard, weeping bitterly. It was in vain that Alice, who was with her, and who by this time was able to stand alone, climbed up to her side, patting her cheeks, and trying various ways to win her attention. She still wept on, unmindful of the sound of rapid footsteps upon the grass, nor until twice repeated did she hear the words, "Why, Mary, what is the matter? What's happened?"—then looking up she saw Billy Bender, who raised her in his arms, and insisted upon knowing what was the matter.

Laying her head on his shoulder, she sobbed out, "She's gone,—she's gone, and there's nobody left but Sally. Oh dear, oh dear!"

"Gone! Who's gone?" asked Billy.

"Jenny," was Mary's reply. "She's gone to Boston, and won't come back till next May; and I loved her so much."

"Oh, yes, I know," returned Billy. "I met them all on their way to the depot; but I wouldn't feel so badly. Jenny will come again, and besides that, I've got some real good news to tell you."

"About Ella?" said Mary.

"No, not about Ella, but about myself; I'm coming here to live with you."

"Coming here to live!" repeated Mary with astonishment. "What for? Are your folks all dead?"

Billy smiled and answered, "Not quite so bad as that. I went to school here two years ago, and I know I learned more than I ever did at home in two seasons. The boys, when Henry Lincoln is away, don't act half as badly as they do in the village; and then they usually have a lady teacher, because it's cheaper I suppose, for they don't pay them half as much as they do gentlemen, and I think they are a great deal the best. Any way, I can learn the most when I go to a woman."

"But what makes you come here, and what will your mother do?" asked Mary.

"She's got a sister come from the West to stay with her, and as I shall go home every Saturday night, she'll get along well enough. I heard Mr. Parker in the store one day inquiring for a boy to do chores. So after consulting mother, I offered my services, and was accepted. Won't we have real nice times going to school together, and then I've brought a plaything for you. Are you afraid of dogs?"

So saying he gave a whistle, and a large Newfoundland dog came bounding through the orchard. At first Mary drew back in alarm, for the dog, though young, was unusually large; but her fears soon vanished when she saw how affectionate he was, licking her own and Alice's hands, and bounding playfully upon his master's shoulders.

"He is a nice fellow," said she, stroking his shaggy sides. What do you call him?"

"Tasso," answered Billy; and then seeing Mr. Parker at a distance, and wishing to speak to him, he walked away.

Three weeks from that time the winter school commenced; and Billy took up his abode at the poor-house, greatly to the satisfaction of Sally and Mary, and greatly to the annoyance of Miss Grundy, who, since Patsy's death, was crosser and more fault-finding than ever.

"Smart idea!" said she, "to have that great lummux around to be waited on!" and when she saw how happy his presence seemed to make Mary, she vented her displeasure upon her in various ways, conjuring up all sorts of reasons why she should stay out of school as often as possible, and wondering "what the world was a coming to, when young ones hardly out of the cradle begun to court! It wasn't so in her younger days, goodness knew!"

"I wouldn't venture a great many remarks about my younger days, if I were you, *Mrs.* Grundy," said Sal, who had adhered to her resolution of always addressing her old enemy as *Mrs.*, though she whispered it to Mary as her opinion that the woman didn't fancy her new title.

Much as Mary had learned to prize Sally's friendship, before winter was over she had cause to value it still more highly. Wretched and destitute as the poor crazed creature now was, she showed plainly that at some period or other of her life, she had had rare advantages for education, which she now brought into use for Mary's benefit. When Mary first commenced attending school, Miss Grundy insisted that she should knit every evening, and thus she found no opportunity for studying at home. One evening when, as usual, a part of the family were assembled around a blazing fire in the kitchen, Sal Furbush suddenly exclaimed, "Mary, why don't you bring your books home at night, just as Mr. Bender does."

She had conceived a great respect for Billy, and always called him *Mr.* Mary cast a rueful glance at the coarse sock, which certainly was not growing fast, and replied, "I should like to, but I have to knit all the time."

"Fudge on your everlasting knitting," said Sal, snatching the sock from Mary's hands and making the needles fly nimbly. "I'm going to be very magnanimous, and every time you'll bring your books home I'll knit for you —I beg Mrs. Grundy, that you'll not throw the fire all over the floor," she added, as that lady gave the forestick a violent kick.

"The Lord save us!" was Miss Grundy's exclamation when after supper the next evening she saw the three-legged stand loaded down with Billy's and Mary's school books.

But as no one made her any reply, she quietly resumed her work, appropriating to her own use the only tallow candle there was burning, and leaving Billy and Mary to see as best they could by the firelight. For some time Mary pored over her lesson in Colburn, but coming to the question, "24 is 3/5 of how many times 10?" she stopped, unable to proceed farther. Again and again she read it over, without gathering a single idea, and was on the point of asking Billy to assist her, when Sal, who had been watching her, said, "Let me take your book, child."

Mary did so, and then, as if conscious for the first time of Miss Grundy's monopoly of the candle, Sal seized a large newspaper lying near, and twisting it up, said, "Let there be light;" then thrusting one end of it into the flames and drawing it out again, added, "and there is light."

After tumbling over the leaves awhile, she continued, "No, they didn't study this when I was young; but tell me what 'tis that troubles you."

Mary pointed to the problem, and after looking at it attentively a moment, Sal said, "The answer to it is 4; and if you will give me some little inkling of the manner in which you are taught to explain them at school, perhaps I can tell you about that."

"It begins in this way," said Mary. "If 24 is 3/5 of some number, 1/5 of that number must be something or other, I don't know what."

"One third of 24 of course," said Sal.

"Oh, yes, that's it," exclaimed Mary, who began to understand it herself. "Now, I guess I know. You find what one third of 24 is, and if that is *one* fifth, *five* fifths would be five times that, and then see how many times 10 will go in it."

"Exactly so," said Sal. "You'll make an arithmetic yet, and have it out just about the time I do my grammar. But," she added in another tone, "I've concluded to leave out the Grundy gender!"

Each night after this Mary brought home her books, and the rapid improvement which she made in her studies was as much owing to Sally's useful hints and assistance as to her own untiring perseverance. One day when she returned from school Sally saw there was something the matter, for her eyes were red and her cheeks flushed as if with weeping. On inquiring of Billy, she learned that some of the girls had been teasing Mary about her teeth, calling them "tushes," &c.

As it happened one of the paupers was sick, and Dr. Gilbert was at that time in the house. To him Sal immediately went, and after laying the case before him, asked him to extract the offending teeth. Sally was quite a favorite with the doctor, who readily consented, on condition that Mary was willing, which he much doubted, as such teeth came hard.

"Willing or not, she shall have them out. It's all that makes her so homely," said Sal; and going in quest of Mary, she led her to the doctor, who asked to look in her mouth.

There was a fierce struggle, a scream, and then one of the teeth was lying upon the floor.

"Stand still," said Sal, more sternly than she had ever before spoken to Mary, who, half frightened out of her wits stood still while the other one was extracted.

"There," said Sal, when the operation was finished, "you look a hundred per cent. better."

For a time Mary cried and spit, hardly knowing whether the relished the joke or not; but when Billy praised her improved looks, telling her that "her mouth was real pretty," and when she herself dried her eyes enough to see that it was a great improvement, she felt better, and wondered why she had never thought to have them out before.

Rapidly and pleasantly to Mary that winter passed away, for the presence of Billy was in itself a sufficient reason why she should be happy. He was so affectionate and brother-like in his deportment towards her, that she began questioning whether she did not love him as well, if not better, than she did her sister Ella, whom she seldom saw, though she heard that she had a governess from Worcester, and was taking music lessons on a grand piano which had been bought a year before. Occasionally Billy called at Mrs. Campbell's, but Ella seemed shy and unwilling to speak of her sister.

"Why is there this difference?" he thought more than once, as he contrasted

67

the situation, of the two girls,—the one petted, caressed, and surrounded by every luxury, and the other forlorn, desolate, and the inmate of a poor-house; and then he built castles of a future, when, by the labor of his own head or hands, Mary, too, should be rich and happy.

CHAPTER XI.

ALICE.

As spring advanced, Alice began to droop, and Sally's quick eye detected in her infallible signs of decay. But she would not tell it to Mary, whose life now seemed a comparatively happy one. Mr. and Mrs. Parker were kind to her,— the pleasant-looking woman and the girl with crooked feet were kind to her. Uncle Peter petted her, and even Miss Grundy had more than once admitted that "she was about as good as young ones would average." Billy, too, had promised to remain and work for Mr. Parker during the summer, intending with the money thus earned to go the next fall and winter to the Academy in Wilbraham. Jenny was coming back ere long, and Mary's step was light and buoyant as she tripped singing about the house, unmindful of Miss Grundy's oft-expressed wish that "she would stop that clack," or of the anxious, pitying eyes Sal Furbush bent upon her, as day after day the faithful old creature rocked and tended little Alice.

"No," said she, "I cannot tell her. She'll have tears enough to shed by and by, but I'll double my diligence, and watch little Willie more closely." So night after night, when Mary was sleeping the deep sleep of childhood, Sally would steal noiselessly to her room, and bending over the little wasting figure at her side, would wipe the cold sweat from her face, and whisper in the unconscious baby's ear messages of love for "the other little Willie, now waiting for her in Heaven."

At last Mary could no longer be deceived, and one day when Alice lay gasping in Sally's lap she said, "Aunt Sally isn't Alice growing worse? She doesn't play now, nor try to walk."

Sally laid her hand on Mary's face and replied, "Poor child, you'll soon be all alone, for Willie's going to find his mother."

There was no outcry,—no sudden gush of tears, but nervously clasping her hands upon her heart, as if the shock had entered there, Mary sat down upon her bed, and burying her face in the pillow, sat there for a long time. But she said nothing, and a careless observer might have thought that she cared nothing, as it became each day more and more evident that Alice was dying. But these knew not of the long nights when with untiring love she sat by her sister's cradle, listening to her irregular breathing, pressing her clammy hands, and praying to be forgiven if ever, in thought or deed, she had wronged the little one now leaving her.

And all this time there came no kind word or message of love from Ella, who knew that Alice was dying, for Billy had told her so. "Oh, if she would only come and see her;" said Mary, "it wouldn't seem half so bad."

"Write to her," said Sal; "peradventure that may bring her."

Mary had not thought of this before, and now tearing a leaf from her writing-book, and taking her pen, she wrote hurriedly, "Ella, dear Ella, won't you come and see little Alice once before she dies? You used to love her, and you would now, if you could see how white and beautiful she looks. Oh, do come. Mrs. Campbell will let you, I know."

This note, which was blurred and blotted with tears was carried by Billy, who was going to the village, and delivered to Mrs. Campbell herself. Perhaps the proud woman remembered the time when her own darling died, or it may be that conscience upbraided her for caring so much for one orphan and utterly neglecting the other two. Be that as it may, her tears fell upon the paper and mingled with Mary's as she replied, "Ella shall come this afternoon."

But before afternoon a drizzling shower came on, and Mary watched and wept in vain, for Ella did not come. The next morning was bright and beautiful as April mornings often are, and at as early an hour as was consistent with Mrs. Campbell's habits, her carriage was before the door, and herself and Ella seated within it. The little lady was not in the best of humors, for she and her maid had quarrelled about her dress; Ella insisting upon a light-blue merino, and the maid proposing a plain delaine, which Ella declared she would not wear. Mrs. Campbell, to whom the matter was referred, decided upon the delaine, consequently Ella cried and pouted, saying she wouldn't go, wondering what Alice wanted to be sick for, or any way why they should send for her.

Meantime in and around the poor-house there was for once perfect silence. Sal Furbush had been invisible for hours,—the girl with crooked feet trod softly as she passed up and down the stairs,—Uncle Peter's fiddle was unstrung, and, securely locked in his fiddle box, was stowed away at the bottom of his old red chest,—and twice that morning when no one saw her, Miss Grundy had stolen out to Patsy's grave. Mary was not called to wash the dishes, but up in her own room she sat with her head resting upon the window sill, while the sweet, fresh air of the morning swept over her face, lifting the hair from her flushed brow. Billy Bender was standing near her, his arm thrown around her, and his lips occasionally pressing her forehead.

Suddenly there was the sound of carriage wheels, and he whispered in her ear, "Ella is coming."

Hastily running down the stairs, Mary met her sister in the doorway, and throwing her arms around her neck, burst into tears. Ella would gladly have shaken her off, for she felt that her curls were in danger of being mussed, and she had besides hardly recovered from her pet. But Mary firmly held her hand, and led her on through the long hall, into a room which they usually denominated "the best room."

There, upon the table, lay a little stiffened form. The blue eyes were closed, and the long eyelashes rested upon the marble cheek, and in the waxen hands, folded so carefully over the other, there was a single snow-drop. No one knew who placed it there, or whence it came. Gently Mary laid back the thin muslin covering, saying as she did so, "Allie is dead. I've got no sister left but you!" and again her arms closed convulsively about Ella's neck.

"You kind of choke me!" said Ella, trying to get free, and it was not until Mrs. Campbell, thoroughly ashamed of her want of feeling, took her hand and placed it on Alice's cold cheek, asking her if she were not sorry her little sister was dead, that she manifested any emotion whatever. Then, as if something of her better nature were roused, her lip trembled for a moment, and she burst into a violent fit of weeping.

"It is hardly natural that she should feel it as deeply as Mary," said Mrs. Campbell to Billy Bender, who was present.

He made no reply, but he never forgot that scene; and when years after he met with Ella on terms of perfect equality,—when he saw her petted, flattered, and admired, he turned away from the fawning multitude, remembering only the April morning when she stood by the dead body of her sister.

During all this time no trace of Sal Furbush had been seen, and at last a strict search was instituted but to no effect, until Billy, who chanced to be passing the dark closet under the garret stairs, heard her whispering to herself, "Yes, little Willie's dead, and Sally's got *three* in Heaven now."

Entering the place, he found her crouched in one corner, her hair hanging down her back, and her eyes flashing with unusual brightness.

"Why, Sally," said he, "what are you here for?"

"To save the credit of the house," was her ready reply. "When the other Willie died, they chained me in this dungeon, and thinking they might do so again, I concluded to come here quietly wishing to save all trouble and confusion, for the utmost decorum should be preserved in the house of death."

"Poor woman," said Billy kindly, "no one wishes you to stay here. Come with me,"—and he took her hand to lead her forth.

But she resisted him, saying, that "fasting and solitude were nature's great restoratives."

"She has showed her good sense for once," said Miss Grundy, on hearing of Sally's whereabouts, "but' ain't the critter hungry?" and owing to some newly touched chord of kindness, a slice of toast and a cup of hot tea erelong found entrance into the darksome cell.

Strange to say, too, the hand which brought it was not repulsed, though very demurely and in seeming earnestness was the question asked, "Mrs. Grundy, haven't you met with a change?"

The next day was the funeral. At first there was some talk of burying the child in the same inclosure with Patsy; but Mary plead so earnestly to have her laid by her mother, that her request was granted, and that night when the young spring moon came out, it looked quietly down upon the grave of little Alice, who by her mother's side was sweetly sleeping.

CHAPTER XII.

A NEW FRIEND.

Three weeks had passed away since Alice's death, and affairs at the poor-house were beginning to glide on as usual. Sal Furbush, having satisfied her own ideas of propriety by remaining secluded for two or three days, had once more appeared in society; but now that Alice was no longer there to be watched, time hung wearily upon her hands, and she was again seized with her old desire for authorship. Accordingly, a grammar was commenced, which she said would contain Nine Hundred and Ninety Nine rules for speaking the English language correctly!

Mary, who had resumed her post as dish washer in the kitchen, was almost daily expecting Jenny; and one day when Billy came in to dinner, he gave her the joyful intelligence that Jenny had returned, and had been in the field to see him, bidding him tell Mary to meet her that afternoon in the woods by the brook.

"Oh, I do hope Miss Grundy will let me go," said Mary, "and I guess she will, for since Allie died, she hasn't been near so cross."

"If she don't, I will," answered Mr. Parker, who chanced to be standing near, and who had learned to regard the little orphan girl with more than usual interest.

But Miss Grundy made no objections, and when the last dishcloth was wrung dry, and the last iron spoon put in its place, Mary bounded joyfully away to the woods, where she found Jenny, who embraced her in a manner which showed that she had not been forgotten.

"Oh," said she, "I've got so much to tell you, and so much to hear, though I know all about dear little Allie' death,—didn't you feel dreadfully?"

Mary's tears were a sufficient answer, and Jenny, as if suddenly discovering something new, exclaimed, "Why, what have you been doing? Who pulled your teeth?"

Mary explained the circumstance of the tooth-pulling, and Jenny continued: "You look a great deal better, and if your cheeks were only a little fatter and your skin not quite so yellow, you'd be real handsome; but no matter about that. I saw George Moreland in Boston, and I wanted to tell him about you, but I'd promised not to; and then at first I felt afraid of him, for you can't think what a great big fellow he's got to be. Why, he's awful tall! and handsome, too. Rose likes him, and so do lots of the girls, but I don't believe he cares a bit for any of them except his cousin Ida, and I guess he does like her;—any way, he looks at her as though he did."

Mary wondered *how* he looked at her, and would perhaps have asked, had she not been prevented by the sudden appearance of Henry Lincoln, who directly in front of her leaped across the brook. He was evidently not much improved in his manners, for the moment he was safely landed on terra firma, he approached her, and seizing her round the waist, exclaimed, "Hallo, little pauper! You're glad to see me back, I dare say."

Then drawing her head over so that he could look into her face, he continued, "Had your tusks out, haven't you! Well, it's quite an improvement, so much so that I'll venture to kiss you."

Mary struggled, and Jenny scolded, while Henry said "Don't kick and flounce so, my little beauty. If there's any thing I hate, it's seeing girls make believe they're modest. That clodhopper Bill kisses you every day, I'll warrant."

Here Jenny's wrath exploded; and going up to her brother, she attempted to pull him away, until bethinking her of the brook, she commenced sprinkling him with water, but observing that more of it fell upon Mary than her brother, she desisted, while Henry, having accomplished his purpose, began spitting and making wry faces, assuring Mary that "she needn't be afraid of his ever troubling her again, for her lips were musty, and tasted of the poor-house!"

Meanwhile Tasso, who had become a great favorite with Mary, and who, on this occasion, had accompanied her to the woods, was standing on the other side of the brook, eyeing Henry's movements, and apparently trying to make up his mind whether his interference was necessary or not. A low growl showed that he was evidently deciding the matter, when Henry desisted, and walked leisurely off.

Erelong, however, he returned, and called out, "See, girls, I've got an elegant necklace for you."

Looking up, they saw him advancing towards them, with a small water snake, which he held in his hand; and, readily divining his purpose, they started and ran, while he pursued them, threatening to wind the snake around the neck of the first one he caught. Jenny, who was too chubby to be very swift-footed, took refuge behind a clump of alder bushes but Mary kept on, and just as she reached a point where the brook turned, Henry overtook her, and would perhaps have carried his threat into execution, had not help arrived from an unexpected quarter. Tasso, who had watched, and felt sure that this time all was not right, suddenly pounced upon Henry, throwing him down, and then planting himself upon his prostrate form, in such a manner that he dared not move.

"Oh, good, good," said Jenny, coming out from her concealment; "make Tasso keep him there ever so long; and," she continued, patting the dog, "if you won't hurt him much, you may shake him just a little."

"No, no," said Henry, writhing with fear, "call him off, do call him off. Oh, mercy!" he added, as Tasso, who did not particularly care to have the case reasoned, showed two rows of very white teeth.

Mary could not help laughing at the figure which Henry cut; but thinking him sufficiently punished, she called off the dog, who obeyed rather unwillingly, and ever after manifested his dislike to Henry by growling angrily whenever he appeared.

One morning about two weeks afterwards, Mary was in the meadow gathering cowslips for dinner, when she heard some one calling her name; and looking up, she saw Jenny hurrying towards her, her sun-bonnet hanging down her back as usual, and her cheeks flushed with violent exercise. As soon as she came up, she began with, "Oh my, ain't I hot and tired, and I can't stay a minute either, for I run away. But I had such good news to tell you, that I would come. You are going to have a great deal better home than this. You know where Rice Corner is, the district over east?"

Mary replied that she did, and Jenny continued: "We all went over there yesterday to see Mrs. Mason. She's a real nice lady, who used to live in Boston, and be intimate with ma, until three or four years ago, when Mr. Mason died. We didn't go there any more then, and I asked Rose what the reason was, and she said Mrs. Mason was poor now, and ma had 'cut her;' and when I asked her what she *cut* her with, she only laughed, and said she believed I didn't know any thing. But since then I've learned what it means."

"What does it?" asked Mary, and Jenny replied: "If a person dies and leaves no money, no matter how good his folks are, or how much you like them, you mustn't know them when you meet them in the street, or you must cross over the other side if you see them coming; and then when ladies call and speak about them, you must draw a great long breath, and wonder 'how the poor thing will get along, she was so dreadful extravagant.' I positively heard mother say those very words about Mrs. Mason; and what is so funny, the washwoman the same day spoke of her, and cried when she told how kind she was, and how she would go without things herself for the sake of giving to the poor. It's queer, isn't it?"

Ah, Jenny, Jenny, you've much of life yet to learn!

After a moment's pause, Jenny proceeded: "This Mrs. Mason came into the country, and bought the prettiest little cottage you ever saw. She has lots of nice fruit, and for all mother pretends in Boston that she don't visit her, just as soon as the fruit is ripe, she always goes there. Pa says it's real mean, and he should think Mrs. Mason would see through it."

"Did you go there for fruit yesterday?" asked Mary.

"Oh, no," returned Jenny. "Mother said she was tired to death with staying at home. Besides that, she heard something in Boston about a large estate in England, which possibly would fall to Mrs. Mason, and she thought it would be real kind to go and tell her. Mrs. Mason has poor health, and while we were there, she asked mother if she knew of any good little girl she could get to come and live with her; 'one,' she said, 'who could be quiet when her head ached, and who would read to her and wait on her at other times.' Mother said she did not know of any; but when Mrs. Mason went out to get tea, I followed and told her of you, and the tears came into her eyes when I said your folks were all dead, and you were alone and sorry. She said right off that she would come round and see you soon, and if she liked you, you should live with her. But I must run back, for I suppose you know mother brought our governess with us, and it's time I was turning my toes out and my elbows in. Ugh! how I do hate such works. If I ever have a house, there shan't be a fashionable thing about it. I'll have it full of cats, dogs, and poor children, with a swing and a 'teater' in every room, and Billy Bender shall live with me, and drive the horses!"

So saying, she ran off; and Mary, having gathered her cowslips, sat down to think of Mrs. Mason, and wonder if she should ever see her. Since Alice's death she had been in the daily habit of learning a short lesson, which she recited to Sally, and this afternoon, when the dishes were all washed, she had as usual stolen away to her books. She had not been long occupied, ere Rind called her, saying Mr. Knight, who, it will be remembered, had brought her to the poor-house, was down stairs and wanted to see her, and that there was a lady with him, too.

Mary readily guessed that the lady must be Mrs. Mason and carefully brushing her hair, and tying on a clean apron, she descended to the kitchen, where she was met by Mr. Knight, who called out, "Hallo, my child, how do you do? 'Pears to me you've grown handsome. It agrees with you to live here I reckon, but I'll venture you'll be glad enough to leave, and go and live with her, won't you?" pointing towards a lady, who was just coming from Mrs. Parker's room, and towards whom Mary's heart instantly warmed.

"You see," continued Mr. Knight, "one of the Lincoln girls has taken a mighty shine to you, and it's queer, too, for they're dreadful stuck-up folks."

"If you please, sir," said Mary, interrupting him, "Jenny isn't a bit stuck up."

"Umph!" returned Mr. Knight. "She don't belong to the Lincoln race then, I guess. I know them, root and branch. Lincoln's wife used to work in the factory at Southbridge, but she's forgot all about that, and holds her head dreadful high whenever she sees me. But that's neither here nor there. This woman wants you to live with her. Miss Mason, this is Mary. Mary, this is Miss Mason."

The introduction being thus happily over, Mrs. Mason proceeded to ask Mary a variety of questions, and ended by saying she thought she would take her, although she would rather not have her come for a few days, as she was going to be absent. Miss Grundy was now interrogated concerning her knowledge of work, and with quite a consequential air, she replied, "Perhaps, ma'am, it looks too much like praising myself, considerin' that I've had the managin' of her mostly, but I must confess that she's lived with me so long and got my ways so well, that she's as pleasant a mannered, good-tempered child, and will scour as bright a knife as you could wish to see!"

Mary saw that Mrs. Mason could hardly repress a smile as she replied, "I am glad about the temper and manners, but the scouring of knives is of little consequence, for Judith always does that."

Sal Furbush, who had courtesied herself into the room, now asked to say a word concerning Mary. "She is," said she, "the very apple of my eye, and can parse a sentence containing three double relatives, two subjunctive moods and four nominatives absolute, perfectly easily."

"I see you are a favorite here," said Mrs. Mason, laying her hand gently on Mary's head, "and I think that in time you will be quite as much of one with me, so one week from Saturday you may expect me."

There was something so very affectionate in Mrs. Mason's manner of speaking, that Mary could not keep her tears back; and when Sally, chancing to be in a poetic mood, said to her, "Maiden, wherefore weepest thou?" she replied, "I can't help it. She speaks so kind, and makes me think of mother."

"Speaks so *kindly*, you mean," returned Sal, while Mrs. Mason, brushing a tear from her own eye, whispered to the little girl, "I will be a mother to you, my child;" then, as Mr. Knight had finished discussing the weather with Mr. Parker, she stepped into his buggy, and was driven away.

"That's what I call a thoroughly grammatical lady," said Sal, looking after her until a turn in the road hid her from view, "and I shall try to be resigned, though the vital spark leaves this house when Mary goes."

Not long after, Rind asked Miss Grundy if William Bender was going away.

"Not as I know on," answered Miss Grundy. "What made you think of that?"

"'Cause," returned Rind, "I heard Sal Furbush having over a mess of stuff about the *spark's* leaving when Mary did, and I thought mebby he was going, as you say he's her spark!"

The next afternoon Jenny, managing to elude the watchful eyes of her mother and governess, came over to the poor-house.

"I'm so glad you are going," said she, when she heard of Mrs. Mason's visit. "I shall be lonesome without you, but you'll have such a happy home, and when you get there mayn't I tell George Moreland about you the next time I see him?"

"I'd rather you wouldn't," said Mary, "for I don't believe he remembers me at all."

"Perhaps not," returned Jenny, "and I guess you wouldn't know him; for besides being so tall, he has begun to *shave*, and Ida thinks he's trying to raise whiskers!"

That night, when Mary was alone, she drew from its hiding-place the golden locket, but the charm was broken, and the pleasure she had before experienced in looking at it, now faded away with Jenny's picture of a whiskered young man, six feet high! Very rapidly indeed did Mary's last week at the poor-house pass away, and for some reason or other, every thing went on, as Rind said, "wrong end up." Miss Grundy was crosser than usual, though all observed that her voice grew milder in its tone whenever she addressed Mary, and once she went so far as to say, by way of a general remark, that she "never yet treated any body, particularly a child, badly, without feeling sorry for it."

Sal Furbush was uncommonly wild, dancing on her toes, making faces, repeating her nine hundred and ninety-nine rules of grammar, and quoting Scripture, especially the passage, "The Lord gave, and the Lord taketh away, &c." Uncle Peter, too, labored assiduously at "Delia's Dirge," which he intended playing as Mary was leaving the yard.

Saturday came at last, and long before the sun peeped over the eastern hills, Mary was up and dressed. Just as she was ready to leave her room, she heard Sally singing in a low tone, "Oh, there'll be mourning,—mourning,—mourning,—mourning, Oh, there'll be mourning when Mary's gone away."

Hastily opening her own door, she knocked at Sal's, and was bidden to enter. She found her friend seated in the middle of the floor, while scattered around her were the entire contents of the old barrel and box which contained her wearing apparel.

"Good morning, little deary," said she, "I am looking over my somewhat limited wardrobe, in quest of something wherewith to make your young heart happy, but my search is vain. I can find nothing except the original MS. of my first novel. I do not need it now, for I shall make enough out of my grammar. So take it, and when you are rich and influential, you'll have no trouble in getting it published,—none at all."

So saying, she thrust into Mary's hand a large package, carefully wrapped in half a dozen newspapers, and the whole enveloped in a snuff-colored silk handkerchief, which "Willie's father used to wear." Here Rind came up the stairs saying breakfast was ready, and after putting her present aside, Mary descended to the kitchen, where she found the table arranged with more than usual care. An old red waiter, which was only used on special occasions, was placed near Miss Grundy, and on it stood the phenomenon of a hissing coffee-pot: and what was stranger, still, in the place of the tin basin from which Mary had recently been accustomed to eat her bread and milk, there was now a cup and saucer, which surely must have been intended for her. Her wonder was at its height when Miss Grundy entered from the back room, bearing a plate filled with snowy white biscuit, which she placed upon the table with an air of "There! what do you think of that?"—then seating herself, she skimmed all the cream from the bowl of milk, and preparing a delicious cup of coffee, passed it to Mary, before helping the rest.

"Is the Millennium about to be ushered in?" asked Sal in amazement; while Uncle Peter, reverently rising, said, Fellow-citizens, and ladies, for these extras let us thank the Lord, remembering to ask a continuation of the same!"

"Do let your victuals stop your mouth," said Miss Grundy, "and don't act as though we never had coffee and biscuit for breakfast before."

"My memory has failed wonderfully, if we ever did," was Uncle Peter's reply.

Breakfast being over, Mary as usual commenced clearing the table, but Miss Grundy bade her "sit down and *rest* her," and Mary obeyed, wondering what she had done to tire herself. About 9 o'clock, Mr. Knight drove up alone, Mrs. Mason being sick with nervous headache. "I should have been here sooner," said he, "but the roads is awful rough and old Charlotte has got a stub or somethin' in her foot But where's the gal? Ain't she ready?"

He was answered by Mary herself, who made her appearance, followed by

Billy bearing the box. And now commenced the leave-takings, Miss Grundy's turn coming first.

"May I kiss you, Miss Grundy?" said Mary, while Sal exclaimed aside, "What! kiss those sole-leather lips?" at the same time indicating by a guttural sound the probable effect such a process would have upon her stomach!

Miss 'Grundy bent down and received the child's kiss, and then darting off into the pantry, went to skimming pans of milk already skimmed! Rind and the pleasant-looking woman cried outright, and Uncle Peter, between times, kept ejaculating, "Oh, Lord!—oh, massy sake!—oh, for land!" while he industriously plied his fiddle bow in the execution of "Delia's Dirge," which really sounded unearthly, and dirgelike enough. Billy knew it would be lonely without Mary, but he was glad to have her go to a better home, go he tried to be cheerful; telling her he would take good care of Tasso, and that whenever she chose she must claim her property.

Aside from him, Sally was the only composed one. It is true, her eyes were very bright, and there was a compression about her mouth seldom seen, except just before one of her frenzied attacks. Occasionally, too, she pressed her hands upon her head, and walking to the sink, bathed it in water, as if to cool its inward heat; but she said nothing until Mary was about stepping into the buggy, when she whispered in her ear, "If that novel should have an unprecedented run, and of course it will, you would not mind sharing the profits with me, would you?"

80

CHAPTER XIII.

A NEW HOME IN RICE CORNER.

Very different this time was Mary's ride with Mr. Knight from what it had been some months before, and after brushing away a few natural tears, and sending back a few heart-sighs to the loved ones left behind, her spirits rallied, and by the time they reached the borders of Rice Corner, there was such a look of quiet happiness on her face that even Mr. Knight noticed it.

"I'll be hanged if I know what to make of it," said he. "When you rid with me afore, I thought you was about as ugly favored a child as I ever see, and now you look full as well as they'll average. What you been doin'?"

"Perhaps it's because I've had my teeth out," suggested Mary, and Mr. Knight, with another scrutinizing look in her face, replied, "Wall, I guess 'tis that. Teeth is good is their place, but when they git to achin', why, yank 'em out."

So saying, he again relapsed into silence, and commenced whipping at the thistle tops and dandelions. As they rode on, Mary fancied that the country looked pleasanter and the houses better, than in the region of the poor-house; and when a sudden turn of the road brought into view a beautiful blue sheet of water, embosomed by bright green hills, her delight knew no bounds. Springing up and pointing towards it, she exclaimed, "Oh, please stop a moment and look. Isn't it lovely! What is it?"

"That? Oh, that's nothing but 'Pordunk Pond, or as folks most generally call 'em, seem' there's two, North and South Pond."

"But it's big enough to be a lake, isn't it?" asked Mary.

"Why, yes," returned her companion. "It's better than five miles long, and a mile or so wide, and in York State I s'pose they'd call it a lake, but here in old Massachusetts we stick to fust principles, and call all things by their right names."

"How far is the pond from Mrs. Mason's?" asked Mary, casting longing glances towards the distant sandy beach, and the graceful trees which drooped over the water's edge.

"It's farther back than 'tis there, 'cause it's up bill all the way," said Mr. Knight, "but here we be at Miss Mason's,—this house right here," and he pointed to a neat, handsome cottage, almost hidden from view by the dense foliage which surrounded it.

There was a long lawn in front, and into the carriage road on the right of it Mr. Knight turned, and driving up to a side door; said to Mary, "Come, jump down, for my foot is so lame I don't believe I'll get out. But there's your chest. You can't lift that. Hallo, Judith, come 'ere."

In answer to this call, a fat, pleasant-looking colored woman appeared in the doorway, and as if fresh from the regions of cookdom, wiped the drops of perspiration from her round jolly face.

"Here, Judith," said Mr Knight, "help this gal lift her traps out."

Judith complied, and then bidding old Charlotte to "get up," Mr. Knight drove away, leaving Mary standing by the kitchen door.

"Come in and sit down," said Judith, pushing a chair towards Mary with her foot. "It's as hot here as oven, but I had crambry sass and ginger snaps, and massy knows what to make this morning, and I got belated; but set down and make yourself to home."

Mary took the proffered seat, and then Judith left the room for a few moments, saying when she returned, that as Mrs. Mason was still suffering from a headache, she could not see Mary until after dinner. "And," continued Judith "she told me to entertain you, but I don't know what to say, nor do first. Harry died just a week to a day before he was to be married, and so I never had any little girls to talk to. Can't you think of something to talk about? What have you been used to doing?"

"Washing dishes," was Mary's reply, after glancing about the room, and making sure that on this occasion there were none to wash.

"Wall," answered Judith, "I guess you won't have that to do here; for one night when some of the neighbors were in, I heard Miss Mason tell 'em that she got you to read to her and wait on her. And then she said something about your not having an equal chance with your sister. You hain't but one, now t'other's dead, have you?"

Mary replied in the negative, and Judith continued: "Wall, now, you've got over the first on't, I reckon you'se glad the baby's dead, for she must have been kind of a bother, wasn't she?"

Instantly Mary's thoughts flew back to an empty cradle, and again a little golden head was pillowed upon her breast, as often in times past it had been, and as it would never be again. Covering her face with her hands, she sobbed, "Oh, Allie, Allie! I wish she hadn't died."

Judith looked on in amazement, and for want of something better to do, placed a fresh stick of wood in the stove, muttering to herself. "Now I never! I might of knew I didn't know what to say. What a pity Harry died. I'll give her that big ginger snap the minute it's baked. See if I don't."

Accordingly, when the snap was done, Judith placed it in Mary's hands, bidding her eat it quick, and then go up and see the nice chamber Mrs. Mason had arranged for her.

"If you please," said Mary, rapidly shifting the hot cake from one hand to the other,—"if you please, I had rather go up now, and eat the cake when it is cool."

"Come, then," said Judith; and leading the way, she conducted Mary up the staircase, and through a light, airy hall to the door of a small room, which she opened, saying "Look, ain't it pretty?"

But Mary's heart was too full to speak, and for several minutes she stood silent. With the exception of her mother's pleasant parlor in Old England, she had never before seen any thing which seemed to her so cosy and cheerful as did that little room, with its single bed, snowy counterpane, muslin curtains, clean matting, convenient toilet table, and what to her was fairer than all the rest, upon the mantel-piece there stood two small vases, filled with sweet spring flowers, whose fragrance filled the apartment with delicious perfume. All this was so different from the bare walls, uncovered floors, and rickety furniture of the poor-house, that Mary trembled lest it should prove a dream, from which erelong she would awake.

"Oh, why is Mrs. Mason so kind to me?" was her mental exclamation; and as some of our readers may ask the same question, we will explain to them that Mrs. Mason was one of the few who "do to others as they would others should do to them."

Years before our story opens, she, too, was a lonely orphan, weeping in a dreary garret, as ofttimes Mary had wept in the poor-house, and it was the memory of those dark hours, which so warmed her heart towards the little girl she had taken under her charge. From Jenny we have learned something of her history. Once a happy, loving wife, surrounded by wealth and friends, she had thought the world all bright and beautiful. But a change came over the spirit of her dream. Her noble husband died,—and the day succeeding his burial, she was told that their fortune, too, was gone. One by one, as misfortune came upon her, did her fashionable friends desert her, until she was left alone, with none to lean upon except the God of the widow and fatherless, and in Him she found a strong help for her dark hour of need. Bravely she withstood the storm, and when it was over, retired with the small remnant of her once large fortune to the obscure neighborhood of Rice Corner, where with careful economy she managed to live comfortably, besides saving a portion for the poor and destitute. She had taken a particular fancy to Mary, and in giving her a home, she had thought more of the good she could do the child, than of any benefit she would receive from her services as waiting maid. She had fully intended to go for Mary herself; but as we already know, was prevented by a severe headache, and it was not until three o'clock in the afternoon, that she was even able to see her at all. Then, calling Judith, she bade her bring the little girl to her room, and leave them alone.

Judith obeyed, charging Mary to "tread on tiptoe, and keep as still as a mouse, for Miss Mason's head ached fit to split."

This caution was unnecessary, for Mary had been so much accustomed to sick persons that she knew intuitively just what to do and when to do it and her step was so light, her voice so low, and the hand which bathed the aching head so soft and gentle in its touch, that Mrs. Mason involuntarily drew her to her bosom, and kissing her lips, called her her child, and said she should never leave her then laying back in her easy chair, she remained perfectly still, while Mary alternately fixed her hair, and smoothed her forehead until she fell into a quiet slumber, from which she did not awake until Judith rang the bell for supper, which was neatly laid out in a little dining parlor, opening into the flower garden. There was something so very social and cheering in the appearance of the room, and the arrangement of the table, with its glossy white cloth, and dishes of the same hue, that Mary felt almost as much like weeping as she did on the night of her arrival at the poor-house. But Mrs. Mason seemed to know exactly how to entertain her; and by the time that first tea was over, there was hardly a happier child in the world than was Mary.

As soon as Mrs. Mason arose from the table, she, too, sprang up, and taking hold of the dishes, removed them to the kitchen in a much shorter space of time than was usually occupied by Judith. "Git away now," said that lady as she saw Mary making preparations to wash the cups and saucers. "I never want any body putterin' round under my feet. I always wash and wipe and scour my own things, and then I know they are done."

Accordingly, she returned to Mrs. Mason, who, wishing to retire early, soon dismissed her to her own room, where she for some time amused herself with watching the daylight as it gradually disappeared from the hills which lay beyond the pond. Then when it all was gone, and the stars began to come out, she turned her eyes towards one, which had always seemed to her to be her mother's soul, looking down upon her from the windows of heaven. Now, to-night there shone beside it a smaller, feebler one, and in the fleecy cloud which floated around it, she fancied she could define the face of her baby sister. Involuntarily stretching out her hands, she cried, "Oh, mother, Allie, I am so happy now;" and to the child's imagination the stars smiled lovingly upon her, while the evening wind, as it gently moved the boughs of the tall elm trees, seemed like the rustle of angels' wings. Who shall say the mother's spirit was not there to rejoice with her daughter over the glad future opening so brightly before her?

CHAPTER XIV.

VISITORS.

The Tuesday following Mary's arrival at Mrs. Mason's, there was a social gathering at the house of Mr. Knight. This gathering could hardly be called a tea party, but came more directly under the head of an "afternoon's visit," for by two o'clock every guest had arrived, and the "north room" was filled with ladies, whose tongues, like their hands, were in full play. Leathern reticules, delicate embroidery, and gold thimbles were not then in vogue in Rice Corner; but on the contrary, some of Mrs. Knight's visitors brought with them large, old-fashioned work-bags, from which the ends of the polished knitting-needles were discernible; while another apologized for the magnitude of her work, saying that "her man had fretted about his trousers until she herself began to think it was time to finish them; and so when she found Miss Mason wasn't to be there, she had just brought them along."

In spite of her uniform kindness, Mrs. Mason was regarded by some of her neighbors as a bugbear, and this allusion to her immediately turned the conversation in that direction.

"Now, do tell," said Widow Perkins, vigorously rapping her snuff-box and passing it around. "Now, do tell if it's true that Miss Mason has took a girl from the town-house?"

On being assured that such was the fact, she continued "Now I *will* give up. Plagued as she is for things, what could have possessed her?"

"I was not aware that she was very much troubled to live," said Mrs. Knight, whose way of thinking, and manner of expressing herself, was entirely unlike Mrs. Perkins.

"Wall, she is," was Mrs. Perkins's reply; and then hitching her chair closer to the group near her, and sinking her voice to a whisper, she added, "You mustn't speak of it on any account, for I wouldn't have it go from me, but my Sally Ann was over there t'other day, and neither Miss Mason nor Judy was to home. Sally Ann has a sight of curiosity,—I don't know nothing under the sun where she gets it, for I hain't a mite,—Wall, as I was tellin' you, there was nobody to home, and Sally Ann she slips down cellar and peeks into the pork barrel, and as true as you live, there warn't a piece there. Now, when country folks get out of salt pork, they are what I call middlin' poor."

And Mrs. Perkins finished her speech with the largest pinch of maccaboy she could possibly hold between her thumb and forefinger.

"Miss Perkins," said an old lady who was famous for occasionally rubbing the widow down, "Miss Perkins, that's just as folks think. It's no worse to be out of pork than 'tis to eat codfish the whole durin' time."

This was a home thrust, for Mrs. Perkins, who always kept one or two boarders, and among them the school-teacher was notorious for feeding them on codfish.

Bridling up in a twinkling, her little gray eyes flashed fire as she replied, "I s'pose it's me you mean, Miss Bates; but I guess I've a right to eat what I'm a mind to. I only ask a dollar and ninepence a week for boarding the school marm—"

"And makes money at that," whispered a rosy-cheeked girlish-looking woman, who the summer before had been the "school-marm," and who now bore the name of a thrifty young farmer.

Mrs. Perkins, however, did not notice this interruption but proceeded with, "Yes, a dollar and ninepence is all I ever ask, and if I kept them so dreadful slim, I guess the committee man wouldn't always come to me the first one."

"Mrs. Perkins, here's the pint," said Mrs. Bates, dropping a stitch in her zeal to explain matters; "you see the cheaper they get the school-ma'am boarded, the further the money goes, and the longer school they have. Don't you understand it?"

Mrs. Knight, fancying that affairs were assuming altogether too formidable an aspect, adroitly turned the conversation upon the heroine of our story, saying how glad she was that Mary had at last found so good a home.

"So am I," said Mrs. Bates; "for we all know that Mrs. Mason will take just as good care of her, as though she were her own; and she's had a mighty hard time of it, knocked around there at the poor-house under Polly Grundy's thumb."

"They do say," said Mrs. Perkins, whose anger had somewhat cooled, "They do say that Miss Grundy is mowing a wide swath over there, and really expects to have Mr. Parker, if his wife happens to die."

In her girlhood Mrs. Perkins had herself fancied Mr. Parker, and now in her widowhood, she felt an unusual interest in the failing health of his wife. No one replied to her remark, and Mrs. Bates continued: "It really used to make my heart ache to see the little forlorn thing sit there in the gallery, fixed up so old and fussy, and then to see her sister prinked out like a milliner's show window, a puckerin' and twistin', and if she happens to catch her sister's eye, I have actually seen her turn up her nose at her,—so—" and Mrs. Bates's nasal organ went up towards her eyebrows in imitation of the look which Ella sometimes gave Mary. "It's wicked in me, perhaps," said Mrs. Bates, "but pride must have a fall, and I do hope I shall live to see the day when Ella Campbell won't be half as well off as her sister."

"I think Mrs. Campbell is answerable for some of Ella's conduct," said Mrs. Knight, "for I believe she suffered her to visit the poor-house but once while Mary was there."

"I guess she'll come oftener now she's living with a city bug," rejoined Mrs. Perkins.

Just then there was the sound of carriage wheels, and a woman near the door exclaimed, "If you'll believe it there she is now, going right straight into Mrs. Mason's yard."

"Well, if that don't beat me," said Mrs. Perkins. "Seems to me I'd have waited a little longer for look's sake. Can you see what she's got on from here?" and the lady made a rush for the window to ascertain if possible that important fact.

Meantime the carriage steps were let down and Mrs. Campbell alighted. As Mrs. Knight's guests had surmised, she was far more ready to visit Mary now than heretofore. Ella, too, had been duly informed by her waiting-maid that she needn't mind denying that she had a sister to the Boston girls who were spending a summer in Chicopee.

"To be sure," said Sarah, "she'll never be a fine lady like you and live in the city; but then Mrs. Mason is a very respectable woman, and will no doubt put her to a trade, which is better than being a town pauper; so you mustn't feel above her any more, for it's wicked, and Mrs. Campbell wouldn't like it, for you know she and I are trying to bring you up in the fear of the Lord."

Accordingly Ella was prepared to greet her sister more cordially than she had done before in a long time, and Mary that day took her first lesson in learning that too often friends come and go with prosperity. But she did not think of it then. She only knew that her sister's arm was around her neck, and her sister's kiss upon her cheek. With a cry of joy, she exclaimed, "Oh, Ella, I knew you'd be glad to find me so happy."

But Ella wasn't particularly glad. She was too thoroughly heartless to care for any one except herself, and her reception of her sister was more the result of Sarah's lesson, and of a wish expressed by Mrs. Campbell, that she would "try and behave as well as she could towards Mary." Mrs. Campbell, too, kissed the little girl, and expressed her pleasure at finding her so pleasantly situated; and then dropping languidly upon the sofa, asked for Mrs. Mason, who soon appeared, and received her visitor with her accustomed politeness.

"And so you, too, have cared for the orphan," said Mrs. Campbell. "Well, you will find it a task to rear her as she should be reared, but a consciousness of doing right makes every thing seem easy. My dear, (speaking to Ella,) run out and play awhile with your sister, I wish to see Mrs. Mason alone."

"You may go into the garden," said Mrs. Mason to Mary, who arose to obey; but Ella hung back, saying she 'didn't want to go,—the garden was all nasty, and she should dirty her clothes."

"But, my child," said Mrs. Campbell, "I wish to have you go, and you love to obey me, do you not?"

Still Ella hesitated, and when Mary took hold of her hand, she jerked it away, saying, "Let me be."

At last she was persuaded to leave the room, but on reaching the hall she stopped, and to Mary's amazement applied her ear to the keyhole.

"I guess I know how to cheat her," said she in a whisper. "I've been sent off before, but I listened and heard her talk about me."

"Talk about you!" repeated Mary. "What did she say?"

"Oh, 'set me up,' as Sarah says," returned Ella; and Mary, who had never had the advantage of a waiting maid, and who consequently was not so well posted on "slang terms," asked what "setting up" meant.

"Why," returned Ella, "she tells them how handsome and smart I am, and repeats some cunning thing I've said or done; and sometimes she tells it right before me, and that's why I didn't want to come out."

This time, however, Mrs. Campbell's conversation related more particularly to Mary.

"My dear Mrs. Mason," she began, "you do not know how great a load you have removed from my mind by taking Mary from the poor-house."

"I can readily understand," said Mrs. Mason, "why you should feel more than a passing interest in the sister of your adopted daughter, and I assure you I shall endeavor to treat her just as I would wish a child of mine treated, were it thrown upon the wide world."

"Of course you will," returned Mrs. Campbell, "and I only wish you had it in your power to do more for her, and in this perhaps I am selfish. I felt badly about her being in the poor-house, but truth compels me to say, that it was more on Ella's account than her own. I shall give Ella every advantage which money can purchase, and I am excusable I think for saying that she is admirably fitted to adorn any station in life; therefore it cannot but be exceedingly mortifying to her to know that one sister died a pauper and the other was one for a length of time. This, however, can not be helped, and now, as I said before I only wish it were in your power to do more for Mary. I, of course, know that you are poor, but I do not think less of you for that—"

Mrs. Mason's body became slightly more erect, but she made no reply, and Mrs. Campbell continued.

"Still I hope you will make every exertion in your power to educate and polish Mary as much as possible, so that if by chance Ella in after years should come in contact with her, she would not feel,—ahem,—would not,— would not be—"

"Ashamed to own her sister, I suppose you would say," interrupted Mrs. Mason. "Ashamed to acknowledge that the same blood flowed in her veins, that the same roof once sheltered them, and that the same mother bent lovingly over their pillows, calling them her children."

"Why, not exactly that," said Mrs. Campbell, fidgeting in her chair and growing very red. "I think there is a difference between feeling mortified and ashamed. Now you must know that Ella would not be particularly pleased to have a homely, stupid, rawboned country girl pointed out as her sister to a circle of fashionable acquaintances in Boston, where I intend taking her as soon as her education is finished; and I think it well enough for Mary to understand, that with the best you can do for her there will still be a great difference between her own and her sister's position."

"Excuse me, madam," again interrupted Mrs. Mason, "a stupid, awkward country girl Mary is not, and never will be. In point of intellect she is far superior to her sister, and possesses more graceful and lady-like manners. Instead of Ella's being ashamed of her, I fancy it will be just the reverse, unless your daughter's foolish vanity and utter selfishness is soon checked. Pardon me for being thus plain, but in the short time Mary has been with me, I have learned to love her, and my heart already warms towards her as towards a daughter, and I cannot calmly hear her spoken of so contemptuously."

During this conversation, Ella had remained listening at the keyhole, and as the voices grew louder and more earnest, Mary, too, distinguished what they said. She was too young to appreciate it fully, but she understood enough to wound her deeply; and as she just then heard Ella say there was a carriage coming, she sprang up the stairs, and entering her own room, threw herself upon the bed and burst into tears. Erelong a little chubby face looked in at the door, and a voice which went to Mary's heart, exclaimed, "Why-ee,—Mary, —crying the first time I come to see you!"

It was Jenny, and in a moment the girls were in each other's arms.

"Rose has gone to the garden with Ella," said Jenny, "but she told me where to find you, and I came right up here. Oh, what a nice little room, so different from mine with my things scattered every where. But what is the matter? Don't you like to live with Mrs. Mason?"

"Yes, very much," answered Mary. "It isn't that," and then she told what she had overheard.

"It's perfectly ridiculous and out of character for Mrs. Campbell to talk so," said Jenny, looking very wise. "And it's all, false, too. You are not stupid, nor awkward, nor very homely either; Billy Bender says so, and he knows. I saw him this morning, and he talked ever so much about you. Next fall he's going to Wilbraham to study Latin and Chinese too, I believe, I don't know though. Henry laughs and says, 'a plough-jogger study Latin!' But I guess Billy will some day be a bigger man than Henry don't you?"

Mary was sure of it; and then Jenny proceeded to open her budget of news concerning the inmates of the poor-house. "Sal Furbush," said she, "is raving crazy now you are gone, and they had to shut her up, but yesterday she broke away and came over to our house. Tasso was with her, and growled so at Henry that he ran up garret, and then, like a great hateful, threw bricks at the dog. I told Sally I was coming to see you, and she said, 'Ask her if she has taken the first step towards the publication of my novel. Tell her, too, that the Glory of Israel has departed, and that I would drown myself if it were not for my clothes, which I fear Mrs. Grundy would wear out!'"

Here Rose called to her sister to come down, and accordingly the two girls descended together to the parlor, where they found Mrs. Lincoln. She was riding out, she said, and had just stopped a moment to inquire after Mrs. Mason's health and to ask for a *very few* flowers,—they did look so tempting! She was of course perfectly delighted to meet Mrs. Campbell, and Mrs. Campbell was perfectly delighted to meet her; and drawing their chairs together, they conversed for a long time about Mrs. So and So, who either had come, or was coming from Boston to spend the summer.

"I am so glad," said Mrs. Lincoln, "for we need some thing to keep us alive. I don't see, Mrs. Campbell, how you manage to live here through the winter, no society nor any thing."

Here Mrs. Mason ventured to ask if there were not some very pleasant and intelligent ladies in the village.

"Oh, ye-es," said Mrs. Lincoln, with a peculiar twist to her mouth, which Jenny said she always used when she was "putting on." "They are well enough, but they are not the kind of folks we would recognize at home. At least they don't belong to 'our set,'" speaking to Mrs. Campbell who replied, "Oh, certainly not." It was plain even to a casual observer that Mrs. Lincoln's was the ruling spirit to which Mrs. Campbell readily yielded, thinking that so perfect a model of gentility could not err. Mr. Knight possibly might have enlightened her a little with regard to her friend's pedigree, but he was not present, and for half an hour more the two ladies talked together of their city acquaintances, without once seeming to remember that Mrs. Mason, too, had formerly known them all intimately. At last Mrs. Lincoln arose, saying she must go, as she had already stopped much longer than she intended, "but when I get with you," said she, turning to Mrs. Campbell, "I never know when to leave."

Mrs. Mason invited her to remain to tea, saying it was nearly ready. Mrs. Campbell, who had also arisen, waited for Mrs. Lincoln to decide, which she soon did by reseating herself and saying, laughingly, "I don't know but I'll stay for a taste of those delicious looking strawberries I saw your servant carry past the window."

Erelong the little tea-bell rang, and Mrs. Lincoln, who had not before spoken to Mary, now turned haughtily towards her, requesting her to watch while they were at supper and see if the coachman did not drive off with the horses as he sometimes did. Mary could not trust herself to reply for she had agreed to sit next Jenny at table, and had in her own mind decided to give her little friend her share of berries. She glanced once at Mrs. Mason, who apparently did not notice her, and then gulping down her tears, took her station by the window, where she could see the coachman who, instead of meditating a drive around the neighborhood was fast asleep upon the box. Jenny did not miss her companion until she was sitting down to the table, and then noticing an empty plate between herself and her mother, who managed to take up as much room as possible, she rather impolitely called out, "Here, mother, sit along and make room for Mary. That's her place. Why, where is she? Mrs. Mason, may I call her?"

Mrs. Mason, who had seen and heard more than Mary fancied, and who in seating her guests had contrived to bring Mary's plate next to Mrs. Lincoln, nodded, and Jenny springing up ran to the parlor, where Mary stood counting flies, looking up at the ceiling, and trying various other ways to keep from crying. Seizing both her hands Jenny almost dragged her into the dining-room, where she found it rather difficult squeezing in between her mother and

Rose, whose elbows took up much more room than was necessary. A timely *pinch*, however, duly administered, sent the young lady along an inch or so, and Jenny and Mary were at last fairly seated.

Mrs. Lincoln reddened,—Mrs. Campbell looked concerned,—Mrs. Mason amused,—Rose angry,—Mary mortified,—while Ella, who was not quick enough to understand, did not look at all except at her strawberries, which disappeared rapidly. Then in order to attract attention, she scraped her saucer as loudly as possible; but for once Mrs. Mason was very obtuse, not even taking the hint when Mrs. Campbell removed a portion of her own fruit to the plate of the pouting child, bidding her "eat something besides berries."

After a time Mrs. Lincoln thought proper to break the silence which she had preserved, and taking up her fork said, "You have been buying some new silver, haven't you?"

"They were a present to me from my friend, Miss Martha Selden," was Mrs. Mason's reply.

"Possible!" said Mrs. Campbell.

"Indeed!" said Mrs. Lincoln, and again closely examining the fork, she continued, "Aunt Martha is really getting liberal in her old age. But then I suppose she thinks Ida is provided for, and there'll be no particular need of her money in that quarter."

"Provided for? How?" asked Mrs. Mason, and Mrs Lincoln answered, "Why didn't you know that Mr. Selden's orphan nephew, George Moreland, had come over from England to live with him? He is heir to a large fortune, and it is said that both Mr. Selden and Aunt Martha are straining every nerve to eventually bring about a match between George and Ida."

There was no reason why Mary should blush at the mention of George Moreland, still she did do so, while Jenny slyly stepped upon her toes. But her embarrassment was unobserved, for what did she, a pauper girl, know or care about one whose future destiny, and wife too, were even then the subject of more than one scheming mother's speculations. Mrs. Mason smiled, and said she thought it very much like child's play, for if she remembered rightly Ida couldn't be more than thirteen or fourteen.

"About that," returned Mrs. Lincoln; "but the young man is older,— eighteen or nineteen, I think."

"No, mother," interrupted Jenny, who was as good at keeping ages as some old women, "he isn't but seventeen."

"Really," rejoined Mrs. Campbell, "I wouldn't wonder if our little Jenny had some designs on him herself, she is so anxious to make him out young."

"Oh, fy," returned Jenny. "He can't begin with Billy Bender!"

Mrs. Lincoln frowned, and turning to her daughter, said 'I have repeatedly requested, and now I command you not to bring up Billy Bender in comparison with every thing and every body."

"And pray, who is Billy Bender?" asked Mrs. Mason, and Mrs. Lincoln replied, "Why, he's a great rough, over grown country boy, who used to work for Mr. Lincoln, and now he's on the town farm, I believe."

"But he's *working* there," said Jenny, "and he's going to get money enough to go to school next fall at Wilbraham; and I heard father say he deserved a great deal of credit for it and that men that made themselves, or else men that didn't, I've forgot which, were always the smartest."

Here the older portion of the company laughed, and Mrs. Lincoln, bidding her daughter not to try to tell any thing unless she could get it straight, again resumed the subject of the silver forks, saying to Mrs. Mason, "I should think you'd be so glad. For my part I'm perfectly wedded to a silver fork, and positively I could not eat without one."

"But, mother," interrupted Jenny, "Grandma Howland hasn't any, and I don't believe she ever had, for once when we were there and you carried yours to eat with, don't you remember she showed you a little two tined one, and asked if the victuals didn't taste just as good when you lived at home and worked in the,—that great big noisy building,—I forget the name of it?"

It was fortunate for Jenny's after happiness that Mrs. Campbell was just then listening intently for something which Ella was whispering in her ear, consequently she did not hear the remark, which possibly might have enlightened her a little with regard to her friend's early days. Tea being over, the ladies announced their intention of leaving, and Mrs. Mason, recollecting Mrs. Lincoln's request for flowers, invited them into the garden, where she bade them help themselves. It required, however, almost a martyr's patience for her to stand quietly by, while her choicest flowers were torn from their stalks, and it was with a sigh of relief that she finally listened to the roll of the wheels which bore her guests away.

Could she have listened to their remarks, as on a piece of wide road their carriages kept side by side for a mile or more, she would probably have felt amply repaid for her flowers and trouble too.

"Dear me," said Mrs. Campbell, "I never could live in such a lonely out of the way place."

"Nor I either," returned Mrs. Lincoln, "but I think Mrs. Mason appears more at home here than in the city. I suppose you know she was a poor girl when Mr. Mason married her, and such people almost always show their breeding. Still she is a good sort of a woman, and it is well enough to have some such nice place to visit and get fruit. Weren't those delicious berries, and ain't these splendid rosebuds?"

"I guess, though," said Jenny, glancing at her mother's huge bouquet, "Mrs. Mason didn't expect you to gather quite so many. And Rose, too, trampled down a beautiful lily without ever apologizing."

"And what if I did?" retorted Rose. "She and that girl have nothing to do but fix it up."

This allusion to Mary, reminded Mrs. Campbell of her conversation with Mrs. Mason, and laughingly she repeated it. "I never knew before," said she, "that Mrs. Mason had so much spirit. Why, she really seemed quite angry, and tried hard to make Mary out beautiful, and graceful, and all that."

"And," chimed in Ella, who was angry at Mrs. Mason for defending her sister, and angry at her sister for being defended, "don't you think she said that Mary ought to be ashamed of me."

"Is it possible she was so impudent!" said Mrs. Lincoln; "I wish I had been present, I would have spoken my mind freely, but so much one gets for patronizing such creatures."

Here the road became narrow, and as the western sky showed indications of a storm, the coachmen were told to drive home as soon as possible.

Mrs. Campbell's advice with regard to Mary, made no difference whatever with Mrs. Mason's plans. She had always intended doing for her whatever she could, and knowing that a good education was of far more value than money, she determined to give her every advantage which lay in her power. There was that summer a most excellent school in Rice Corner, and as Mrs. Mason had fortunately no prejudices against a district school, where so many of our best and greatest men have been educated, she resolved to send her little protegé, as soon as her wardrobe should be in a suitable condition. Accordingly in a few days Mary became a regular attendant at the old brown school-house, where for a time we will leave her, and passing silently over a period of several years, again in another chapter open the scene in the metropolis of the "Old Bay State."

CHAPTER XV.

THE THREE YOUNG MEN

It was beginning to be daylight in the city of Boston; and as the gray east gradually brightened and grew red in the coming of day, a young man looked out upon the busy world around him, with that feeling of utter loneliness which one so often feels in a great city where all is new and strange to him. Scarcely four weeks had passed since the notes of a tolling bell had fallen sadly upon his ear, and he had looked into a grave where they laid his mother to her last dreamless rest. A prevailing fever had effected what the fancied ailments of years had failed to do, and Billy Bender was now an orphan, and alone in the wide world. He knew that he had his own fortune to make, and after settling his mother's affairs and finding there was nothing left for him, he had come to the city, and on the morning which we have mentioned went forth alone to look for employment, with no other recommendation than the frank, honest expression of his handsome face. It was rather discouraging, wearisome work, and Billy's heart began to misgive him as one after another refused his request.

"It was foolish in me to attempt it," thought he, as he stopped once more in front of a large wholesale establishment on M—— street.

Just then his eye caught the sign on which was lettered, "R.J. Selden & Co." The name sounded familiar, and something whispered to him to enter. He did so, and meeting in the doorway a tall, elegant-looking young man, he asked for Mr. Selden.

"My uncle," returned the gentleman, who was none other than George Moreland, "has not yet come down, but perhaps I can answer your purpose just as well. Do you wish to purchase goods?"

Billy, thinking that every one must know his poverty, fancied there was something satirical in the question, but he was mistaken; the manner was natural to the speaker, who, as Billy made no direct reply, again asked. "What would you like, sir?"

"Something to do, for I have neither money nor home," was Billy's prompt answer.

"Will you give me your name?" asked George.

Billy complied, and when he spoke of his native town, George repeated it after him, saying, "I have some acquaintances who spend the summer in Chicopee; but you probably have never known them."

Immediately Billy thought of the Lincolns, and now knew why the name of Selden seemed so familiar. He had heard Jenny speak of Ida, and felt certain that R.J. Selden was her father.

For a moment George regarded him intently, and then said, "We seldom employ strangers without a recommendation; still I do not believe you need any. My uncle is wanting a young man, but the work may hardly suit you," he added, naming the duties he would be expected to perform, which certainly were rather menial. Still, as the wages were liberal, and he would have considerable leisure, Billy, for want of a better, accepted the situation, and was immediately introduced to his business. For some time he only saw George at a distance, but was told by one of the clerks that he was just graduated at Yale, and was now a junior partner in his uncle's establishment. "We all like him very much," said the clerk, "he is so pleasant and kind, though a little proud, I guess."

This was all that Billy knew of him until he had been in Mr. Selden's employment nearly three weeks; then, as he was one day poring over a volume of Horace which he had brought with him, George, who chanced to pass by, looked over his shoulder, exclaiming, "Why, Bender, can you read Latin? Really this is a novelty. Are you fond of books?"

"Yes, very," said Billy, "though I have but a few of my own."

"Fortunately then I can accommodate you," returned George, "for I have a tolerably good library, to which you can at any time have access. Suppose you come round to my uncle's to-night. Never mind about thanking me," he added, as he saw Billy about to speak; "I hate to be thanked, so to-night at eight o'clock I shall expect you."

Accordingly that evening Billy started for Mr. Selden's. George, who wished to save him from any embarrassment, answered his ring himself, and immediately conducted him to his room, where for an hour or so they discussed their favorite books and authors. At, last, George, astonished at Billy's general knowledge of men and things, exclaimed, "Why, Bender. I do believe you are almost as good a scholar as I, who have been through college. Pray how does it happen?"

In a few words Billy explained that he had been in the habit of working summers, and going to school at Wilbraham winters; and then, as it was nearly ten, he hastily gathered up the books which George had kindly loaned him, and took his leave. As he was descending the broad stairway he met a young girl fashionably dressed, who stared at him in some surprise and then passed on, wondering no doubt how one of his evident caste came to be in the front part of the house. In the upper hall she encountered George, and asked of him who the stranger was.

"His name is Bender, and he came from Chicopee," answered George.

"Bender from Chicopee," repeated Ida. "Why I wonder if it isn't the Billy Bender about whom Jenny Lincoln has gone almost mad."

"I think not," returned her cousin, "for Mrs. Lincoln would hardly suffer her daughter to *mention* a poor boy's name, much less to go mad about him."

"But," answered Ida, "he worked on Mr. Lincoln's farm when Jenny was a little girl; and now that she is older she talks of him nearly all the time, and Rose says it would not surprise her if she should some day run off with him."

"Possibly it is the same," returned George. "Any way, he is very fine-looking, and a fine fellow too, besides being an excellent scholar."

The next day, when Billy chanced to be alone, George approached him, and after making some casual remarks about the books he had borrowed, &c., he said, "Did you ever see Jenny Lincoln in Chicopee?"

"Oh, yes," answered Billy, brightening up, for Jenny had always been and still was a great favorite with him; "Oh, yes, I know Jenny very well. I worked for her father some years ago, and became greatly interested in her."

"Indeed? Then you must know Henry Lincoln?"

"Yes, I know him," said Billy; while George continued, "And think but little of him of course?"

On this subject Billy was noncommittal. He had no cause for liking Henry, but would not say so to a comparative stranger, and at last he succeeded in changing the conversation. George was about moving away, when observing a little old-fashioned looking book lying upon one of the boxes, he took it up and turning to the fly-leaf read the name of "Frank Howard."

"Frank Howard! Frank Howard!" he repeated; "where have I heard that name? Who is he, Bender?"

"He was a little English boy I once, loved very much; but he is dead now," answered Billy; and George, with a suddenly awakened curiosity, said, "Tell me about him and his family, will you?"

Without dreaming that George had ever seen them, Billy told the story of Frank's sickness and death,—of the noble conduct of his little sister, who, when there was no other alternative, went cheerfully to the poor-house, winning by her gentle ways the love of those unused to love, and taming the wild mood of a maniac until she was harmless as a child. As he proceeded with his story, George became each moment more and more interested, and when at last there was a pause, he asked, "And is Mary in the poor-house now?"

"I have not mentioned her name, and pray how came you to know it?" said Billy in some surprise.

In a few words George related the particulars of his acquaintance with the Howards, and then again asked where both Mary and Ella were.

Billy replied that for a few years back Mary had lived with a Mrs. Mason, while Ella, at the time of her mother's death had been adopted by Mrs. Campbell. "But," said he, "I never think of Ella in connection with Mary, they are so unlike; Ella is proud and vain and silly, and treats her sister with the utmost rudeness, though Mary is far more agreeable and intelligent, and as I think the best looking."

"She must have changed very much," answered George; "for if I remember rightly, she was not remarkable for personal beauty."

"She hasn't a silly, doll baby's face, but there isn't a finer looking girl in Chicopee, no, nor in Boston either," returned Billy, with so much warmth and earnestness that George laughed aloud, saying, "Why, really, Bender, you are more eloquent on the subject of female beauty than I supposed you to be; but go on; tell me more of her. Is she at all refined or polished?"

"I dare say she would not meet with *your* ideas of a lady," answered Billy; "but she does mine exactly, for she possesses more natural refinement and delicacy than two thirds of the city belles."

"Really, I am getting quite interested in her," said George. "How is her education?"

"Good, very good," returned Billy, adding that she was now teaching in Rice Corner, hoping to earn money enough to attend some seminary in the fall.

"Teaching!" repeated George; "why she can't be over sixteen."

He was going to say more, when some one slapped him rudely on the shoulder, calling out, "How are you, old feller, and what is there in Boston to interest such a scapegrace as I am?"

Looking up, Billy saw before him Henry Lincoln, exquisitely dressed, but bearing in his appearance evident marks of dissipation.

"Why, Henry," exclaimed George, "how came you here? I supposed you were drawing lampblack caricatures of some one of the tutors in old Yale. What's the matter? What have you been doing?"

"Why you see," answered Henry, drawing his cigar from his mouth and squirting, by accident of course, a quantity of spittle over Billy's nicely blacked shoes; "Why you see one of the sophs got his arm broken in a row, and as I am so tender-hearted and couldn't bear to hear him groan, to say nothing of his swearing, the faculty kindly advised me to leave, and sent on before me a recommendation to the old man. But, egad I fixed 'em. I told 'em he was in Boston, whereas he's in Chicopee, so I just took the letter from the office myself. It reads beautifully. Do you understand?"

All this time, in spite of the tobacco juice, Henry had apparently taken no notice of Billy, whom George now introduced, saying, he believed they were old acquaintances. With the coolest effrontery Henry took from his pocket a quizzing glass and applying it to his eye, said, "I've absolutely studied until I'm near-sighted, but I don't think I ever met this chap before."

"Perhaps, sir," said Billy haughtily, "it may refresh your memory a little to know that I was once the owner of Tasso!"

"Blast the brute," muttered Henry, meaning Billy quite as much as the dog; then turning to George, he asked, "how long the *old folks* had been in Chicopee."

"Several weeks, I think," answered George; and then, either because he wanted to hear what Henry would say, or because of a re-awakened interest in Mary Howard, he continued, "By the way, Henry, when you came so unceremoniously upon us, we were speaking of a young girl in Chicopee whom you have perhaps ferreted out ere this, as Bender says she is fine looking."

Henry stroked his whiskers, which had received far more cultivation than his brains, stuck his hat on one side, and answered. "Why, yes, I suppose that in my way I am some thing of a b'hoy with the fair sex, but really I do not now think of more than one handsome girl in Chicopee, and that is Ella Campbell, but she is young yet, not as old as Jenny—altogether too small fry for Henry Lincoln, Esq. But who is the girl?"

Billy frowned, for he held Mary's name as too sacred to be breathed by a young man of Henry Lincoln's character; while George replied, "Her name is Mary Howard."

"What, the pauper?" asked Henry, looking significantly at Billy, who replied, "The same, sir."

"Whew-ew," whistled Henry, prolonging the diphthong to an unusual

100

length. "Why, she's got two teeth at least a foot long, and her face looks as though she had just been in the vinegar barrel, and didn't like the taste of it."

"But without joking, though, how does she look?" asked George; while Billy made a movement as if he would help the insolent puppy to find his level.

"Well, now, old boy," returned Henry, "I'll tell you honestly, that the last time I saw her, I was surprised to find how much she was improved. She has swallowed those abominable teeth, or done something with them, and is really quite decent looking. In short," he continued, with a malicious leer at Billy, which made the blood tingle to his finger's end, "In short, she'll do very well for a city buck like me to play the mischief with for a summer or so, and then cast off like an old coat."

There was a look in Billy's eye as Henry finished this speech which decided that young man to make no further remarks concerning Mary, and swaggering towards the door he added, "Well, Moreland, when will you come round and take a horn of brandy? Let me know, and I'll have in some of the bloods."

"Thank you," said George, "I never use the article."

"I beg your pardon," returned Henry, in a tone of mock humility. "I remember now that you've taken to carrying a Prayer Book as big as an old woman's moulding board, and manage to come out behind in the service about three or four lines so as to be distinctly heard; but I suppose you think it pleases the old gent your uncle, and that furthers your cause with the daughter. By the way, present my compliments to Miss Selden, and ask her if she has any word to send to Chicopee, for I'll have to go there by and by, though I hate to mightily, for it'll be just like the old man to put me through in the hay field; and if there's any thing I abominate, it's work."

So saying, he took his leave. Just then there was a call for Mr, Moreland, who also departed, leaving Billy alone.

"It is very strange that she never told me she knew him," thought he; and then taking from his pocket a neatly folded letter, he again read it through. But there was nothing in it about George, except the simple words, "I am glad you have found a friend in Mr. Moreland. I am sure I should like him, just because he is kind to you."

"Yes, she's forgotten him," said Billy, and that belief gave him secret satisfaction. He had known Mary long and the interest he had felt in her when a homely, neglected child, had not in the least decreased as the lapse of time gradually ripened her into a fine, intelligent-looking girl. He was to her a brother still, but she to him was dearer far than a sister; and though in his letters he always addressed her as such, in his heart he claimed her as something nearer, and yet he had never breathed in her ear a word of love, or hinted that it was for her sake he toiled both early and late, hoarding up his earnings with almost a miser's care that she might be educated.

Regularly each week she wrote to him, and it was the receipt of these letters, and the thoughts of her that kept his heart so brave and cheerful, as, alone and unappreciated, except by George, he worked on, dreaming of a bright future, when the one great object of his life should be realized.

CHAPTER XVI.

THE SCHOOL-MISTRESS.

In the old brown school-house, overshadowed by apple-trees and sheltered on the west by a long steep hill, where the acorns and wild grapes grew, Mary Howard taught her little flock of twenty-five, coaxing some, urging others, and teaching them all by her kind words and winsome ways to love her as they had never before loved an instructor.

When first she was proposed as a teacher in Rice Corner, Widow Perkins, and a few others who had no children to send, held up their hands in amazement, wondering "what the world was comin' to, and if the committee man, Mr. Knight, s'posed they was goin' to be rid over rough-shod by a town pauper; but she couldn't get a *stifficut*, for the Orthodox minister wouldn't give her one; and if he did, the Unitarian minister wouldn't!"

Accordingly, when it was known that the ordeal had been passed, and that Mary had in her possession a piece of paper about three inches square, authorizing her to teach a common district school, this worthy conclave concluded that "either every body had lost their senses, or else Miss Mason, who was present at the examination, had sat by and whispered in her ear the answers to all hard questions." "In all my born days I never seen any thing like it," said the widow, as she distributed her green tea, sweetened with brown sugar, to a party of ladies, which she was entertaining "But you'll see, she won't keep her time more'n half out.—Sally Ann, pass them nutcakes.—Nobody's goin' to send their children to a pauper. There's Miss Bradley says she'll take her'n out the first time they get licked.—Have some more sass, Miss Dodge. I want it eat up, for I believe it's a workin',—but I told her that warn't the trouble; Mary's too softly to hurt a miskeeter. And so young too. It's government she'll lack in.—If any body'll have a piece of this dried apple pie, I'll cut it."

Of course, nobody wanted a piece, and one of the ladies, continuing the conversation, said she supposed Mary would of course board with Mrs. Mason. The tea-pot lid, which chanced to be off, went on with a jerk, and with the air of a much injured woman the widow replied: "Wall, I can tell her this much, it's no desirable job to board the school-marm, though any body can see that's all made her so anxious for Mary to have the school. She's short on't, and wants a little money. Do any on you know how much she charges?"

Nobody knew, but a good many "guessed she didn't charge any thing," and the widow, rising from the table and telling Sally Ann to "rense the sass dishes, and pour it in the vinegar bottle," led her guests back to the best room, saying, "a dollar and ninepence (her usual price) was next to nothing, but she'd warrant Miss Mason had more'n that"

Fortunately, Mary knew nothing of Mrs. Perkins's displeasure, and never dreamed that any feeling existed towards her, save that of perfect friendship. Since we last saw her, she had grown into a fine, healthy-looking girl. Her face and figure were round and full, and her complexion, though still rather pale, was clear as marble, contrasting well with her dark brown hair and eyes, which no longer seemed unnaturally large. Still she was not beautiful, it is true, and yet Billy was not far from right when he called her the finest looking girl in Chicopee; and it was for this reason, perhaps, that Mrs. Campbell watched her with so much jealousy.

Every possible pains had been taken with Ella's education. The best teachers had been hired to instruct her, and she was now at a fashionable seminary, but still she did not possess one half the ease and gracefulness of manner, which seemed natural to her sister. Since the day of that memorable visit, the two girls had seen but little of each other. Ella would not forgive Mrs. Mason for praising Mary, nor forgive Mary for being praised; and as Mrs. Campbell, too pretended to feel insulted, the intercourse between the families gradually ceased; and oftentimes when Ella met her sister, she merely acknowledged her presence by a nod, or a simple "how d'ye do?"

When she heard that Mary was to be a teacher, she said "she was glad, for it was more respectable than going into a factory, or working out." Mrs. Campbell, too, felt in duty bound to express her pleasure, adding, that "she hoped Mary would give satisfaction, but 'twas extremely doubtful, she was *so* young, and possessed of so little dignity!"

Unfortunately, Widow Perkins's red cottage stood directly opposite the school-house; and as the widow belonged to that stirring few who always "wash the breakfast dishes, and make the beds before any one is up in the house," she had ample leisure to watch and report the proceedings of the new teacher. Now Mrs. Perkins's clock was like its mistress, always half an hour in advance of the true time and Mary had scarcely taught a week ere Mr. Knight, "the committee man," was duly hailed in the street, and told that the 'school-marm wanted lookin' to, for she didn't begin no mornin' till half-past nine, nor no afternoon till half past one! "Besides that," she added, "I think she gives 'em too long a play spell. Any ways, seem's ef some on em was out o'door the hull time."

Mr. Knight had too much good sense to heed the widow's complaints, and he merely replied, "I'm glad on't. Five hours is enough to keep little shavers cramped up in the house,—glad on't."

The widow, thus foiled in her attempts at making disturbance, finally gave up the strife, contenting herself with quizzing the older girls, and asking them if Mary could do all the hard sums in Arithmetic, or whether she took them home for Mrs. Mason to solve! Old leathern-bound Daboll, too, was brought to light, and its most difficult problems selected and sent to Mary, who, being an excellent mathematician, worked them all out to the widow's astonishment. But when it was known that quill pens had been discarded, and steel ones substituted in their place, Mrs. Perkins again looked askance, declaring that Mary couldn't make a quill pen, and by way of testing the matter, Sally Ann was sent across the road with a huge bunch of goose quills, which "Miss Howard" was politely requested "to fix, as ma wanted to write some letters."

Mary candidly confessed her ignorance, saying she had never made a pen in her life; and the next Sabbath the widow's leghorn was missed from its accustomed pew in the Unitarian church, and upon inquiry, it was ascertained that "she couldn't in conscience hear a man preach who would give a 'stifficut' to a girl that didn't know how to make a pen!"

In spite, however, of these little annoyances, Mary was contented and happy. She knew that her pupils loved her and that the greater part of the district were satisfied, so she greeted the widow with her pleasantest smile, and by always being particularly polite to Sally Ann, finally overcame their prejudices to a considerable extent.

One afternoon about the middle of July, as Mrs. Perkins was seated by her front window engaged in "stitching shoes," a very common employment in some parts of New England, her attention was suddenly diverted by a tall, stylish-looking young man, who, driving his handsome horse and buggy under the shadow of the apple-trees, alighted and entered into conversation with a group of little girls who were taking their usual recess. Mrs. Perkins's curiosity was roused, and Sally Ann was called to see who the stranger was. But for a wonder, Sally Ann didn't know, though she "guessed the hoss was one of the East Chicopee livery."

"He's talkin' to Liddy Knight," said she, at the same time holding back the curtain, and stepping aside so as not to be visible herself.

"Try if you can hear what he's sayin," whispered Mrs. Perkins; but a class of boys in the school-house just then struck into the multiplication table, thus effectually drowning any thing which Sally Ann might otherwise have heard.

"I know them children will split their throats. Can't they hold up a minute," exclaimed Mrs. Perkins, greatly annoyed at being thus prevented from overhearing a conversation, the nature of which she could not even guess.

But as some other Widow Perkins may read this story we will for her benefit repeat what the young man was saying to Lydia Knight, who being nearest to him was the first one addressed.

"You have a nice place for your school-house and play-grounds."

"Yes, sir," answered Lydia, twirling her sun-bonnet and taking up a small round stone between her naked toes.

"Do you like to go to school?"

"Yes, sir."

"Have you a good teacher?"

"Yes, sir."

"What is her name?"

"Miss Howard,—Mary Howard, and she lives with Miss Mason."

"Mary Howard,—that's a pretty name,—is she pretty too?"

"Not so dreadful," chimed in Susan Bradley. "She licked brother Tim to-day, and I don't think she's much pretty."

This speech quickly called out the opinion of the other girls as follows:

"He ought to be licked, for he stole a knife and then lied about it; and Miss Howard is real pretty, and you needn't say she ain't, Susan Bradley."

"Yes, indeed, she's pretty," rejoined a second. "Such handsome eyes, and little white hands."

"What color are her eyes?" asked the stranger, to which two replied, "blue," and three more said "black;" while Lydia Knight, who was the oldest of the group, finally settled the question by saying, that "they sometimes looked blue; but if she was real pleased, or sorry either, they turned black!"

The stranger smiled and said, "Tell me more about her. Does she ever scold, or has she too pretty a mouth for that?"

"No, she never scolds," said Delia Frost, "and she's got the nicest, whitest teeth, and I guess she knows it, too for she shows them a great deal."

"She's real white, too," rejoined Lydia Knight, "though pa says she used to be yaller as saffron."

Here there was a gentle rap upon the window, and the girls starting off, exclaimed, "There, we must go in."

"May I go too?" asked the stranger, following them to the door.

The girls looked at each other, then at him, then at each other again, and at last Lydia said, "I don't care, but I guess Miss Howard will be ashamed, for 'twas Suke Bradley's turn to sweep the school-house this noon-time, and she wouldn't do it, 'cause Tim got licked."

"Never mind the school-house," returned the stranger, "but introduce me as Mr. Stuart."

Lydia had never introduced any body in her life, and following her companions to her seat, she left Mr. Stuart standing in the doorway. With her usual politeness, Mary came forward and received the stranger, who gave his name as Mr. Stuart, saying, "he felt much interested in common schools, and therefore had ventured to call."

Offering the seat of honor, viz., the splint-bottomed chair, Mary resumed her usual duties, occasionally casting a look of curiosity at the stranger, whose eyes seemed constantly upon her. It was rather warm that day, and when Mary returned from her dinner, Widow Perkins was greatly shocked at seeing her attired in a light pink muslin dress, the short sleeves of which showed to good advantage her round white arms. A narrow velvet ribbon confined by a small brooch, and a black silk apron, completed her toilet, with the exception of a tiny locket, which was suspended from her neck by a slender gold chain. This last ornament, immediately riveted Mr. Stuart's attention, and from some strange cause sent the color quickly to his face. After a time, as if to ascertain whether it were really a locket, or a watch, he asked "if Miss Howard could tell him the hour."

"Certainly sir," said she, and stepping to the desk and consulting a silver time-piece about the size of a dining plate, she told him that it was half-past three.

He nodded, and seemed very much interested in two little boys who sat near him, engaged in the laudable employment of seeing which could snap spittle the farthest and the best.

Just then there was a movement at the door, and a new visitor appeared in the person of Mrs. Perkins, who, with her large feather fan and flounced gingham dress, entered smiling and bowing, and saying "she had been trying all summer to visit the school."

Mr. Stuart immediately arose and offered his chair, but there was something in his manner which led Mary to suppose that an introduction was not at all desired, so she omitted it, greatly to the chagrin of the widow, who, declining the proffered seat, squeezed herself between Lydia Knight and another girl, upsetting the inkstand of the one, and causing the other to make a curious character out of the letter "X" she chanced to be writing.

"Liddy, Liddy," she whispered, "who is that man?"

But Lydia was too much engrossed with her spoiled apron to answer this question, and she replied with, "Marm may I g'wout; I've spilt the ink all over my apron."

Permission, of course, was granted, and as the girl who sat next knew nothing of the stranger, Mrs. Perkins began to think she might just as well have staid at home and finished her shoes. "But," thought she, "may-be I shall find out after school."

Fortune, however, was against the widow, for scarcely was her feather fan in full play, when Sally Ann came under the window, and punching her back with a long stick, told her in a loud whisper, that "she must come right home, for Uncle Jim and Aunt Dolly had just come from the cars."

Accordingly, Mrs. Perkins, smoothing down her gingham flounces, and drawing on her cotton gloves, arose to go, asking Mary as she passed, "if that was an acquaintance of hers."

Mary shook her head, and the widow, more puzzled than ever, took her leave.

When school was out, Mr. Stuart, who seemed in no haste whatever, entered into a lively discussion with Mary concerning schools and books, adroitly managing to draw her out upon all the leading topics of the day. At last the conversation turned upon flowers; and when Mary chanced to mention Mrs. Mason's beautiful garden, he instantly expressed a great desire to see it, and finally offered to accompany Mary home, provided she had no objections. She could not, of course, say no, and the Widow Perkins, who, besides attending to "Uncle Jim" and "Aunt Dolly," still found time to watch the school-house, came very near letting her buttermilk biscuit burn to a cinder, when she saw the young man walking down the road with Mary. Arrived at Mrs. Mason's, the stranger managed to make himself so agreeable, that Mrs. Mason invited him to stay to tea,—an invitation which he readily accepted. Whoever he was, he seemed to understand exactly how to find out whatever he wished to know; and before tea was over, he had learned of Mary's intention to attend the academy in Wilbraham, the next autumn.

"Excuse me for making a suggestion," said he, "but why not go to Mt. Holyoke? Do you not think the system of education there a most excellent one?"

Mary glanced at Mrs. Mason, who replied, that "she believed they did not care to take a pupil at South Hadley for a less period than a year; and as Mary was entirely dependent upon herself, she could not at present afford that length of time."

"That does make a difference," returned Mr. Stuart "but I hope she will not give up Mt. Holyoke entirely, as I should prefer it to Wilbraham."

Tea being over, Mr. Stuart arose to go; and Mary, as she accompanied him to the door, could not forbear asking how he liked Mrs. Mason's garden, which he had forgotten even to look at!

Blushing deeply, he replied, "I suppose Miss Howard has learned ere this, that there are in the world things fairer and more attractive than flowers, but I will look at them when I come again;" then politely bidding her good night, be walked away, leaving Mary and Mrs. Mason to wonder,—the one what he came there for, and the other whether he would ever come again. The widow, too, wondered and fidgeted, as the sun went down behind the long hill, and still under the apple-tree the gray pony stood.

"It beats all nater what's kept him so long," said she, when he at last appeared, and, unfastening, his horse, drove off at a furious rate; "but if I live I'll know all about it to-morrow;" and with this consolatory remark she returned to the best room, and for the remainder of the evening devoted herself to the entertainment of Uncle Jim and his wife Aunt Dolly.

That evening, Mr. Knight, who had been to the Post Office, called at Mrs. Mason's, bringing with him a letter which bore the Boston postmark. Passing it to Mary, he winked at Mrs. Mason, saying, "I kinder guess how all this writin' works will end; but hain't there been a young chap to see the school?"

"Yes; how did you know it," returned Mrs. Mason, while Mary blushed more deeply than she did when Billy's letter was handed her.

"Why, you see," answered Mr. Knight, "I was about at the foot of the Blanchard hill, when I see a buggy comin' like Jehu. Just as it got agin me it kinder slackened, and the fore wheel ran off smack and scissors."

"Was he hurt?" quickly asked Mary.

"Not a bit on't," said Mr. Knight, "but he was scared some, I guess. I got out and helped him, and when he heard I's from Rice Corner, he said he'd been into school. Then he asked forty-'leven questions about you, and jest as I was settin' you up high, who should come a canterin' up with their long-tailed gowns, and hats like men, but Ella Campbell, and a great white-eyed pucker that came home with her from school. Either Ella's horse was scary, or she did it a purpose, for the minit she got near, it began to rare and she would have fell off, if that man hadn't catched it by the bit, and held her on with t'other hand. I allus was the most sanguinary of men, (Mr. Knight was never so far wrong in his life,) and I was buildin' castles about him, and our little school-marm, when Ella came along, and I gin it up, for I see that he was took, and she did look handsome with her curls a flyin'. Wall, as I wasn't of no more use, I whipped up old Charlotte and come on."

"When did Ella return?" asked Mary, who had not before heard of her sister's arrival.

"I don't know," said Mr. Knight. "The first I see of her she was cuttin' through the streets on the dead run; but I mustn't stay here, gabbin', so good night, Miss Mason,—good night, Mary, hope you've got good news in that are letter."

The moment he was gone, Mary ran up to her room, to read her letter, from which we give the following extract.

"You must have forgotten George Moreland, or you would have mentioned him to me. I like him very much indeed, and yet I could not help feeling a little jealous, when he manifested so much interest in you. Sometimes, Mary, I think that for a brother I am getting too selfish, and do not wish any one to like you except myself, but I surely need not feel so towards George, the best friend I have in Boston. He is very kind, lending me books, and has even offered to use his influence in getting me a situation in one of the best law offices in the city."

After reading this letter, Mary sat for a long time, thinking of George Moreland,—of the time when she first knew him,—of all that William Bender had been to her since,—and wondering, as girls sometimes will, which she liked the best. Billy, unquestionably, had the strongest claim to her love, but could he have known how much satisfaction she felt in thinking that George still remembered and felt interested in her, he would have had some reason for fearing, as he occasionally did, that she would never be to him aught save a sister.

CHAPTER XVII.

JEALOUSY.

The day following Mr. Stuart's visit was Saturday, and as there was no school, Mary decided to call upon her sister, whom she had not seen for some months. Mrs. Mason, who had some shopping to do in the village, offered to accompany her, and about two in the afternoon, they set forward in Mr. Knight's covered buggy. The roads were smooth and dry, and in a short time they reached the bridge near the depot. A train of cars bound for Boston was just going out, and from one of the windows Mr. Stuart was looking, and waving his hand towards Mary, who bowed in token of recognition.

The sight and sound of the cars made "old Charlotte," whom Mrs. Mason was driving, prick up her ears, and feet too, and in a few moments she carried her load to the village. Leaving Mrs. Mason at the store, Mary proceeded at once to Mrs. Campbell's. She rang the door-bell a little timidly, for the last time she saw her sister, she had been treated with so much coldness, that she now felt some anxiety with regard to the reception she was likely to meet.

"Is Miss Campbell at home?" she asked of the girl who answered her ring.

"Yes, she's at home," replied the girl, "but is busy dressing for company."

"Tell her her sister is here, if you please. I won't detain her long," said Mary, trying hard to shake off the tremor which always came upon her, when she found herself in Mrs. Campbell's richly furnished house.

Conducting Mary into the parlor, the girl departed with her message to Ella, who, together with the young lady whom Mr. Knight had styled a "white-eyed pucker," but whose real name was Eliza Porter, was dressing in the chamber above. The door of the room was open, and from her position, Mary could hear distinctly every word which was uttered.

"Miss Ella," said the girl, "your sister is in the parlor, and wants to see you."

"My sister," repeated Ella, "oh, forlorn! What brought her here to-day? Why didn't you tell her I wasn't at home?"

"I never told a lie in my life," answered the honest servant girl, while Miss Porter in unfeigned surprise said "Your sister! I didn't know you had one. Why doesn't she live at home?"

Concealment was no longer possible, and in a half vexed, half laughing

111

tone, Ella replied, "Why, I thought you knew that I was an orphan whom Mrs. Campbell adopted years ago."

"You an orphan!" returned Miss Porter. "Well, if I ever! Who adopted your sister?"

"A poor woman in the country," was Ella's answer.

Miss Porter, who was a notorious flatterer, replied, "I must see her, for if she is any thing like you, I shall love her instantly."

"Oh, she isn't like *me*" said Ella, with a curl of her lip. "She's smart enough, I suppose, but she hasn't a bit of polish or refinement. She doesn't come here often, and when she does, I am always in a fidget, for fear some of the city girls will call, and she'll do something *outré*."

"I guess, then, I won't go down, at least not till I'm dressed," answered Miss Porter; and Ella, throwing on a dressing-gown, descended to the parlor, where she met her sister with the ends of her fingers, and a simple, "Ah, Mary, how d'ye do? Are you well?"

After several commonplace remarks, Ella at last asked, "How did you know I was at home?"

"Mr. Knight told me," said Mary.

"Mr. Knight," repeated Ella; "and pray, who is he? I don't believe he's on my list of acquaintances."

"Do you remember the man who carried me to the poor-house?" asked Mary.

"Hush—sh!" said Ella, glancing nervously towards the door. "There is a young lady up stairs, and it isn't necessary for her to know you've been a pauper."

By this time Miss Porter was dressed. She was very fond of display, and wishing to astonish the "country girl" with her silks and satins, came rustling into the parlor.

"My sister," said Ella carelessly.

Miss Porter nodded, and then throwing herself languidly upon the sofa, looked down the street, as if expecting some one. At last, supporting herself on her elbow, she lisped out, "I don't believe that he'th coming, for here 'tis after four!"

"Tisn't likely he'll stay in the graveyard all night," returned Ella. "I wish we'd asked him whose graves he was going to visit, don't you?" Then, by way of saying something more to Mary, she continued, "Oh, you ought to know what an adventure I had yesterday. It was a most miraculous escape, for I should certainly have been killed, if the most magnificent-looking gentleman you ever saw, hadn't caught me just in time to keep Beauty from throwing me. You ought to see his eyes, they were perfectly splendid!"

Mary replied, that she herself thought he had rather handsome eyes.

"*You!* where did you ever see him?" asked Ella.

"He visited my school yesterday afternoon."

"Oh, no, that can't be the one," returned Ella, while Miss Porter, too, said, "Certainly not; our cavalier never thaw the inthide of a district school-houth, I know."

"I am quite sure he saw one yesterday," said Mary, relating the circumstance of Mr. Knight's meeting him at the spot where Ella came so near getting a fall.

"Did he go home with you?" asked Ella, in a tone plainly indicating that a negative answer was expected.

Mary understood the drift of her sister's questioning, and promptly replied, "Yes, he went home with me, and staid to tea."

Ella's countenance lowered, while Miss Porter exclaimed, "I declare, we may as well give up all hope, for your sister, it seems, has the first claim."

"Pshaw!" said Ella, contemptuously, while Miss Porter, again turning to Mary, asked, "Did you learn his name? If you did, you are more fortunate than we were; and he came all the way home with us, too, leading Ella's pony; and besides that, we met him in the street this morning."

"His name," returned Mary, "is Stuart, and he lives in Boston, I believe."

"Stuart,—Stuart,—" repeated Ella; "I never heard Lizzie Upton, or the Lincolns, mention the Stuarts, but perhaps they have recently removed to the city. Any way, this young man is somebody, I know."

Here Miss Porter, again looking down the road, exclaimed, "There, he's coming, I do believe."

Both girls rushed to the window, but Mr. Stuart was not there; and when they were reseated, Mary very gravely remarked, that he was probably ere this in Worcester, as she saw him in the eastern train.

"Why, really," said Ella, "you seem to be well posted in his affairs. Perhaps you can tell us whose graves he wished to find. He said he had some friends buried here, and inquired for the sexton."

Mary knew nothing about it, and Ella, as if thinking aloud, continued, "It must be that he got belated, and went from the graveyard, across the fields, to the depot;—but, oh horror!" she added, "there comes Lizzie Upton and the rest of the Boston girls. Mary, I guess you'll have to go, or rather, I guess you'll have to excuse me, for I must run up and dress. By the way, wouldn't you like some flowers? If you would just go into the kitchen, and ask Bridget to show you the garden."

Mary had flowers enough at home, and so, in spite of Ella's manoeuvre, she went out at the front door, meeting "Lizzie Upton, and the rest of the Boston girls," face to face. Miss Porter, who acted the part of hostess while Ella was dressing, was quickly interrogated by Lizzie Upton, as to who the young lady was they met in the yard.

"That's Ella Campbell's sister," said Miss Porter. Then lowering her voice to a whisper, she continued, "Don't you believe, Ella isn't Mrs. Campbell's own daughter, but an adopted one!"

"I know that," answered Lizzie; "but this sister, where does she live?"

"Oh, in a kind of a heathenish, out-of-the-way place, and teaches school for a living."

"Well," returned Lizzie, "she is a much finer looking girl than Ella."

"How can you say so," exclaimed three or four girls in a breath, and Lizzie replied, "Perhaps she hasn't so much of what is called beauty in her face, but she has a great deal more intellect."

Here the door-bell again rang; and Ella, having made a hasty toilet, came tripping down the stairs in time to welcome Rose Lincoln, whom she embraced as warmly as if a little eternity, instead of three days, had elapsed since they met.

"I had perfectly despaired of your coming," said she "Oh, how sweet you do look! But where's Jenny?"

Rose's lip curled scornfully, as she replied, "Why, she met Mary Howard in the store, and I couldn't drag her away."

"And who is Mary Howard?" asked Lizzie Upton.

Rose glanced at Ella, who said, "Why, she's the girl you met going out of the yard."

"Oh, yes.—I know,—your sister," returned Lizzie. "Isn't she to be here? I have noticed her in church, and should like to get acquainted with her. She has a fine eye and forehead."

Ella dared not tell Lizzie, that Mary was neither polished nor refined, so she answered, that "she could not stay this afternoon, as Mrs. Mason, the lady with whom she lived, was in a hurry to go home."

Miss Porter looked up quickly from her embroidery, and winked slyly at Ella in commendation of her falsehood. Jenny now came bounding in, her cheeks glowing, and her eyes sparkling like diamonds.

"I'm late, I know," said she, "but I met Mary in the store, and I never know when to leave her. I tried to make her come with me, telling her that as you were her sister 'twas no matter if she weren't invited; but she said that Mrs. Mason had accepted an invitation to take tea with Mrs. Johnson, and she was going there too."

Instantly Lizzie Upton's eyes were fixed upon Ella, who colored scarlet; and quickly changing the conversation, she commenced talking about her adventure of the evening before, and again the "magnificent-looking stranger, with his perfectly splendid eyes," was duly described.

"Oh, yes," said Jenny, who generally managed to talk all the time, whether she was heard or not. "Yes, Mary told me about him. He was in her school yesterday, and if I were going to describe George Moreland, I could not do it more accurately than she did, in describing Mr. Stuart. You never saw George, did you?"

"No," said Ella pettishly, "but seems to me Mary is dreadful anxious to have folks know that Mr. Stuart visited her school."

"No, she isn't," answered Jenny. "I told her that I rode past her school-house yesterday, and should have called, had I not seen a big man's head protruding above the window sill. Of course, I asked who he was, and she told me about him, and how he saved you from a broken neck."

Ella's temper, never the best, was fast giving way, and by the time the company were all gone, she was fairly in a fit of the pouts. Running up stairs, and throwing herself upon the bed, she burst into tears, wishing herself dead, and saying she knew no one would care if she were, for every body liked Mary better than they did her.

Miss Porter, who stood by, terribly distressed of course, rightly guessed that the every body, on this occasion, referred merely to Mr. Stuart and Lizzie Upton. Ella was always jealous of any commendation bestowed upon Mary seeming to consider it as so much taken from herself, and consequently, could not bear that Lizzie should even think well of her. The fact, too, that Mr. Stuart had not only visited her school, but also walked home with her, was a sufficient reason why she should he thoroughly angry. Miss Porter knew that the surest method of coaxing her out of her pouting fit, was to flatter her, and accordingly she repeated at least a dozen complimentary speeches, some of which she had really heard, while others were manufactured for the occasion. In this way the cloud was gradually lifted from her face, and erelong she was laughing merrily at the idea, that a girl "so wholly unattractive as Mary, should ever have made her jealous!"

CHAPTER XVIII.

A NEW PLAN.

The summer was drawing to a close, and with it Mary's school. She had succeeded in giving satisfaction to the entire district with the exception of Mrs. Bradley, who "didn't know why Tim should be licked and thrashed round just because his folks wasn't wuth quite so much as some others," this being, in her estimation, the only reason why the notorious Timothy was never much beloved by his teachers. Mr Knight, with whom Mary was a great favorite, offered her the school for the coming winter, but she had decided upon attending school herself, and after modestly declining his offer, told him of her intention.

"But where's the money coming from?" said he.

Mary laughingly asked him how many bags of shoes he supposed she had stitched during the last two years.

"More'n two hundred, I'll bet," said he.

"Not quite as many as that," answered Mary; "but still I have managed to earn my clothes, and thirty dollars besides; and this, together with my school wages, will pay for one term, and part of another."

"Well, go ahead," returned Mr. Knight. "I'd help you if I could. Go ahead, and who knows but you'll one day be the President's wife."

Like the majority of New England farmers, Mr Knight was far from being wealthy. From sunrise until sundown he worked upon the old homestead where his father had dwelt. Spring after spring, he ploughed and planted the sandy soil. Autumn after autumn he gathered in the slender harvest, and still said he would not exchange his home among the hills for all the broad acres of his brother, who at the far West, counted his dollars by the thousands. He would gladly have helped Mary, but around his fireside were six children dependent upon him for food, clothing, and education, and he could only wish his young friend success in whatever she undertook.

When Widow Perkins heard that Mary was going away to school, she forgot to put any yeast in the bread which she was making, and bidding Sally Ann "watch it until it riz," she posted off to Mrs. Mason's to inquire the particulars, reckoning up as she went along how much fourteen weeks' wages would come to at nine shillings (a dollar and a half New England currency) per week.

"'Tain't no great," said she, as simultaneously with her arrival at Mrs. Mason's door, she arrived at the sum of twenty-one dollars. "'Tain't no great, and I wouldn't wonder if Miss Mason fixed over some of her old gowns for her."

But with all her quizzing, and "pumping," as Judith called it, she was unable to ascertain any thing of importance, and mentally styling Mrs. Mason, Mary, Judith and all, "great gumpheads," she returned home, and relieved Sally Ann from her watch over unleavened bread. Both Mrs. Mason and Mary laughed heartily at the widow's curiosity, though, as Mary said, "It was no laughing matter where the money was to come from which she needed for her books and clothing."

Every thing which Mrs. Mason could do for her she did, and even Judith, who was never famous for generosity; brought in one Saturday morning a half-worn merino, which she thought "mebby could be turned and sponged, and made into somethin' decent," adding, in an undertone, that "she'd had it out airin' on the clothes hoss for more'n two hours!"

Sally Furbush, too, brought over the old purple silk which "Willie's father had given her." She was getting on finely with her grammar, she said, and in a few days she should write to Harper, so that he might have time to engage the extra help he would necessarily need, in bringing out a work of that kind!

"I should dedicate it to Mrs. Grundy," said she, "just to show her how forgiving I can be, but here is a difficulty. A person, on seeing the name, '*Mrs. Polly Grundy*,' would naturally be led to inquire for '*Mr.* Polly Grundy,' and this inquiry carried out, might cause the lady some little embarrassment, so I've concluded to have the dedication read thus:—'To Willie's father, who sleeps on the western prairie, this useful work is tremblingly, tearfully, yet joyfully dedicated by his relict, Sarah.'"

Mary warmly approved of this plan, and after a few extra flourishes in the shape of a courtesy, Sally started for home.

A few days afterward, Jenny Lincoln came galloping up to the school-house door, declaring her intention of staying until school was out, and having a good time. "It's for ever and ever since I've seen you," said she, as she gathered up the skirt of her blue riding-dress, and followed Mary into the house, "but I've been so bothered with those city girls. Seems as though they had nothing to do but to get up rides in hay carts, or picnics in the woods and since Henry came home they keep sending for us. This afternoon they have all gone blackberrying in a hay cart, but I'd rather come here."

At this point, happening to think that the class in Colburn who were toeing the mark so squarely, would perhaps like a chance to recite, Jenny seated herself near the window, and throwing off her hat, made fun for herself and some little boys, by tickling their naked toes with the end of her riding-whip. When school was out, and the two girls were alone, Jenny entered at once upon the great object of her visit.

"I hear you are going to Wilbraham," said she, "but I want you to go to Mount Holyoke. We are going, a whole lot of us, that is, if we can pass examination. Rose isn't pleased with the idea, but I am. I think 'twill be fun to wash potatoes and scour knives. I don't believe that mother would ever have sent us there if it were not that Ida Selden is going. Her father and her aunt Martha used to be schoolmates with Miss Lyon, and they have always intended that Ida should graduate at Mount Holyoke. Now, why can't you go, too?"

Instantly Mary thought of Mr. Stuart, and his suggestion. "I wish I could," said she, "but I can't. I haven't money enough, and there is no one to give it to me."

"It wouldn't hurt Mrs. Campbell to help you a little," returned Jenny. "Why, last term Ella spent almost enough for candies, and gutta-percha toys, to pay the expense of half a year's schooling, at Mount Holyoke. It's too bad that she should have every thing, and you nothing."

Here Jenny's remarks were interrupted by the loud rattling of wheels, and the halloo of many voices. Going to the door she and Mary saw coming down the road at a furious rate, the old hay cart, laden with the young people from Chicopee, who had been berrying in Sturbridge, and were now returning home in high glee. The horses were fantastically trimmed with ferns and evergreens, while several of the girls were ornamented in the same way. Conspicuous among the noisy group, was Ella Campbell. Henry Lincoln's broad-brimmed hat was resting on her long curls, while her white sun-bonnet was tied under Henry's chin.

The moment Jenny appeared, the whole party set up a shout so deafening, that the Widow Perkins came out in a trice, to see "if the old Harry was to pay, or what." No sooner did Henry Lincoln get sight of Mary, than springing to his feet, and swinging his arm around his head, he screamed out, "Three cheers for the school ma'am and her handsome lover, Billy! Hurrah!"

In the third and last hurrah, the whole company joined, and when that was finished, Henry struck up on a high key,

"Oh, where have you been, Billy boy, Billy boy,
Oh, where have you been charming Billy?"

but only one voice joined in with his, and that was Ella's! Mary reddened at what she knew was intended as an insult, and when she heard her sister's voice chiming in with Henry, she could not keep back her tears.

"Wasn't that smart?" said Jenny, when at last the hay cart disappeared from view, and the noise and dust had somewhat subsided. Then as she saw the tears in Mary's eyes, she added, "Oh, I wouldn't care if they did teaze me about Billy Bender. I'd as lief be teazed about him as not."

"It isn't that," said Mary, smiling in spite of herself, at Jenny's frankness. "It isn't that. I didn't like to hear Ella sing with your brother, when she must have known he meant to annoy me."

"That certainly was wrong," returned Jenny; "but Ella isn't so much to blame as Henry, who seems to have acquired a great influence over her during the few weeks he has been at home. You know she is easily flattered, and I dare say Henry has fully gratified her vanity in that respect, for he says she is the only decent-looking girl in Chicopee. But see, there comes Mrs. Mason, I guess she wonders what is keeping you so long."

The moment Mrs. Mason entered the school-room, Jenny commenced talking about Mount Holyoke, her tongue running so fast, that it entirely prevented any one else from speaking, until she stopped for a moment to take breath. Then Mrs. Mason very quietly remarked, that if Mary wished to go to Mount Holyoke she could do so. Mary looked up inquiringly, wondering what mine had opened so suddenly at her feet; but she received no explanation until Jenny had bidden her good-bye, and gone. Then she learned that Mrs. Mason had just received $100 from a man in Boston, who had years before owed it to her husband, and was unable to pay it sooner. "And now," said Mrs. Mason, "there is no reason why you should not go to Mount Holyoke, if you wish to."

The glad tears which came to Mary's eyes were a sufficient evidence that she did wish to, and the next day a letter was forwarded to Miss Lyon, who promptly replied, expressing her willingness to receive Mary as a pupil. And now Rice Corner was again thrown into a state of fermentation. Mary was going to Mount Holyoke, and what was more marvellous still, Mrs. Mason had bought her a black silk dress, which cost her a dollar a yard! and more than one good dame declared her intention of "giving up," if paupers came on so fast. This having been a pauper was the thing of which Mary heard frequently, now that her prospects were getting brighter. And even Ella, when told that her sister was going to Mount Holyoke, said to Miss Porter, who was still with her, "Why, isn't she getting along real fast for one who has been on the town?"

Mrs. Lincoln, too, and Rose were greatly provoked, the former declaring she would not send her daughters to a school which was so cheap that paupers and all could go, were it not that Lizzie Upton had been there, and Ida Selden was going. Jenny, however, thought differently. She was delighted, and as often as she possibly could, she came to Mrs. Mason's to talk the matter over, and tell what good times they'd have, "provided they didn't set her to pounding clothes," which she presumed they would, just because she was so fat and healthy. The widow assumed a very resigned air, saying "She never did meddle with other folks' business, and she guessed she shouldn't begin by 'tendin' to Mary's, but 'twas a miracle where all the money came from."

A few more of the neighbors felt worried and troubled but as no attention was paid to their remarks, they gradually ceased, and by the time Mary's preparations were completed, curiosity and gossip seemed to have subsided altogether. She was quite a favorite in the neighborhood, and on the morning when she left home, there was many a kind good-bye, and word of love spoken to her by those who came to see her off. Mr. Knight carried her to the depot, where they found Sally Furbush, accompanied by Tasso, her constant attendant. She knew that Mary was to leave that morning, and had walked all that distance, for the sake of seeing her, and giving her a little parting advice. It was not quite time for the cars, and Mr. Knight, who was always in a hurry, said "he guessed he wouldn't stay," so squeezing both of Mary's hands, he bade her good-bye, telling her "to be a good girl, and not get to running after the sparks."

Scarcely was he gone, when Mary's attention was attracted by the sound of many voices, and looking from the window, she saw a group of the city girls advancing towards the depot. Among them was Ella, talking and laughing very loudly Mary's heart beat very rapidly, for she thought her sister was coming to bid her good-bye, but she was mistaken. Ella had no thought or care for her, and after glancing in at the sitting-room, without seeming to see its inmates, though not to see them was impossible, she turned her back, and looking across the river, which was directly in front, she said in her most drawling tone, "Why don't Rose come? I shan't have time to see her at all, I'm afraid."

Lizzie Upton, who was also there, looked at her in astonishment, and then said, "Why, Ella, isn't that your sister?"

"My sister? I don't know. Where?" returned Ella.

Mary laughed, and then Ella, facing about, exclaimed, "Why, Mary, you here? I forgot that you were going this morning."

Before Mary could reply. Sally Furbush arose, and passed her hand carefully over Ella's head. Partly in fear, and partly in anger, Ella drew back from the crazy woman, who said, "Don't be alarmed, little one, I only wanted to find the cavity which I felt sure was there."

Lizzie Upton's half-smothered laugh was more provoking to Ella, than Sally's insinuation of her want of brains, but she soon recovered her equanimity, for Mr. Lincoln's carriage at that moment drove up. Henry sprang nimbly out, kissing his hand to Ella, who blushed, and then turning to Rose, began wishing she, too, was old enough to go to Mount Holyoke.

"I guess you'd pass about as good an examination now, as some who are going," returned Rose, glancing contemptuously towards Mary, to whom Jenny was eagerly talking.

This directed Henry's attention that way, and simultaneously his own and Mary's eyes met. With a peculiar expression of countenance, he stepped towards her, saying "Good morning, school ma'am. For what part are you bound with all this baggage?" pointing to a huge chest with a feather bed tied over it, the whole the property of a daughter of Erin, who stood near, carefully guarding her treasure.

Had he addressed Mary civilly, she would have replied with her usual politeness, but as it was, she made no reply and he turned to walk away. All this time Tasso lay under the table, winking and blinking at his old enemy, with an expression in his eyes, which Henry would hardly have relished, could he have seen him.

"Hark! Isn't that the cars?" said Jenny, as a low, heavy growl fell on her ear; but she soon ascertained what it was, for as Henry was leaving the room, he kicked aside the blue umbrella, which Sal had brought with her for fear of a shower, and which was lying upon the floor.

In an instant, Tasso's growl changed to a bark, and bristling with anger, he rushed towards Henry, but was stopped by Sal just in time to prevent his doing any mischief. With a muttered oath, which included the "old woman" as well as her dog, the young man was turning away, when Jenny said, "Shame on you, to swear before ladies!"

After assuring himself by a look that Ella and the city girls were all standing upon the platform, Henry replied with a sneer, "I don't see any ladies in the room."

Instantly Sal, now more furious than the dog, clutched her long, bony fingers around his arm, saying, "Take back that insult, sir, or Tasso shall tear you in pieces! What am I, if I am not a lady?"

Henry felt sure that Sal meant what she said, and with an air of assumed deference, he replied as he backed himself out of his uncomfortable quarters,

"I beg your pardon Mrs. Furbush, I forgot that you were present."

The whistle of the cars was now heard, and in a moment the locomotive stood puffing before the depot. From one of the open windows a fair young face looked out, and a voice which thrilled Mary's every nerve, it seemed so familiar, called out, "Oh, Rosa, Jenny, all of you, I'm so glad you are here; I was afraid there would be some mistake, and I'd have to go alone."

"Isn't your father with you?" asked Henry, bowing so low, that he almost pitched headlong from the platform.

"No," answered the young lady, "he couldn't leave, nor George either, so Aunt Martha is my escort. She's fast asleep just opposite me, never dreaming, I dare say, that we've stopped."

"The mischief," said Henry. "What's to be done? The old gent was obliged to be in Southbridge to-day, so he bade me put Rose and Jenny under your father's protection; but as he isn't here I'll have to go myself."

"No you won't either," returned Ida, "Aunt Martha is as good as a man any time, and can look after three as well as one."

"That's Ida Selden! Isn't she handsome?" whispered Jenny to Mary.

But Mary hardly heard her. She was gazing admiringly at Ida's animated face, and tracing in it a strong resemblance to the boyish features, which looked so mischievously out from the golden locket, which at that moment lay next to her heart.

"All aboard," shouted the shrill voice of the conductor and Mary awoke from her reverie, and twining her arms around Sally Furbush's neck, bade her good-bye.

"The Lord be with you," said Sally, "and be sure you pay strict attention to Grammar!"

Mary next looked for Ella, but she stood at a distance jesting lightly with Henry Lincoln, and evidently determined not to see her sister, who was hurrying towards her, when "All aboard" was again shouted in her ear, while at the same moment, the conductor lifted her lightly upon the step where Rose and Jenny were standing.

"This car is brim full," said Rose, looking over her shoulder, "but I guess you can find a good seat in the next one."

The train was already in motion, and as Mary did not care to peril her life or limbs for the sake of pleasing Rose, she followed her into the car, where there was a goodly number of unoccupied seats, notwithstanding Rose's assertion to the contrary. As the train moved rapidly over the long, level meadow, and passed the Chicopee burying-ground, Mary looked out to catch a glimpse of the thorn-apple tree, which overshadowed the graves of her parents, and then, as she thought how cold and estranged was the only one left of all the home circle, she drew her veil over her face and burst into tears.

"Who is that young lady?" asked Ida, who was riding backward and consequently directly opposite to Mary.

"What young lady?" said Rose; and Ida replied, "The one who kissed that queer-looking old woman and then followed you and Jenny into the cars."

"Oh, that was Mary Howard," was Rose's answer.

"Mary Howard!" repeated Ida, as if the name were one she had heard before, "who is she, and what is she?"

"Nobody but a town pauper," answered Rose, "and one of Jenny's protegee's. You see she is sitting by her."

"She doesn't seem like a pauper," said Ida. "I wish she would take off that veil. I want to see how she looks."

"Rough and blowsy, of course, like any other country girl," was Rose's reply.

By this time Mary had dried her tears, and when they reached the station at Warren, she removed her veil, disclosing to view a face, which instead of being "rough and blowsy" was smooth and fair almost as marble.

"That isn't a pauper, I know," said Ida; and Rose replied, "Well, she has been, and what's the difference?"

"But where does she live now?" continued Ida. "I begin to grow interested."

"I suppose you remember Mrs. Mason, who used to live in Boston," answered Rose. "Well, she has adopted her, I believe, but I don't know much about it, and care a good deal less."

"Mrs. Mason!" repeated Ida. "Why, Aunt Martha thinks all the world of her, and I fancy she wouldn't sleep quite so soundly, if she knew her adopted daughter was in the car. I mean to tell her.—Aunt Martha, Aunt Martha!"

But Aunt Martha was too fast asleep to heed Ida's call, and a gentle shake was necessary to rouse her to consciousness. But when she became fully awake, and knew why she was roused, she started up, and going towards Mary, said in her own peculiarly sweet and winning manner, "Ida tells me you are Mrs. Mason's adopted daughter, and Mrs. Mason is the dearest friend I ever had. I am delighted to see you."

Jenny immediately introduced her to Mary, as Miss Selden, whispering in her ear at the same time that she was George's aunt; then rising she gave her seat to Aunt Martha, taking another one for herself near Rose and Ida. Without seeming to be curious at all, Aunt Martha had a peculiar way of drawing people out to talk of themselves, and by the time they reached the station, where they left the cars for Mt. Holyoke, she had learned a good share of Mary's early history, and felt quite as much pleased with the freshness and simplicity of her young friend, as Mary did with her polished and elegant manners.

CHAPTER XIX.

MT. HOLYOKE

"Oh, forlorn what a looking place!" exclaimed Rose Lincoln, as from the windows of the crowded vehicle in which they had come from the cars, she first obtained a view of the not very handsome village of South Hadley.

Rose was in the worst of humors, for by some mischance, Mary was on the same seat with herself, and consequently she was very much distressed, and crowded. She, however, felt a little afraid of Aunt Martha, who she saw was inclined to favor the object of her wrath, so she restrained her fault-finding spirit until she arrived at South Hadley, where every thing came in for a share of her displeasure.

"*That* the Seminary!" said she contemptuously, as they drew up before the building. "Why, it isn't half as large, or handsome as I supposed. Oh, horror! I know I shan't stay here long."

The furniture of the parlor was also very offensive to the young lady, and when Miss Lyon came in to meet them, she, too, was secretly styled, "a prim, fussy, slippery-tongued old maid." Jenny, however, who always saw the bright side of every thing, was completely charmed with the sweet smile, and placid face, so well remembered by all who have seen and known, the founder of Mt. Holyoke Seminary. After some conversation between Miss Lyon and Aunt Martha it was decided that Rose and Jenny should room together, as a matter of course, and that Mary should room with Ida. Rose had fully intended to room with Ida herself, and this decision made her very angry: but there was no help for it and she was obliged to submit.

Our readers are probably aware, that an examination in certain branches is necessary, ere a pupil can be admitted into the school at Mt. Holyoke, where the course of instruction embraces three years, and three classes, Junior, Middle, and Senior. Rose, who had been much flattered on account of her scholarship, confidently expected to enter the Middle class. Jenny, too, had the same desire, though she confessed to some misgivings concerning her knowledge of a goodly number of the necessary branches. Ida was really an excellent scholar, and was prepared to enter the Senior class, while Mary aspired to nothing higher, than admission into the Junior. She was therefore greatly surprised, when Aunt Martha, after questioning her as to what she had studied, proposed that she should be examined for the Middle class.

"Oh, no," said Mary quickly, "I should fail, and I wouldn't do that for the world."

"Have you ever studied Latin?" asked Aunt Martha.

Before Mary could reply, Rose exclaimed, "*She* study Latin! How absurd! Why, she was never away to school in her life."

Aunt Martha silenced her with a peculiar look, while Mary answered, that for more than two years, she had been reading Latin under Mrs. Mason's instruction.

"And you could not have a better teacher," said Aunt Martha. "So try it by all means."

"Yes, do try," said Ida and Jenny, in the same breath; and after a time, Mary rather reluctantly consented.

"I'll warrant she intends to sit by us, so we can tell her every other word," muttered Rose to Jenny, but when the trial came she thought differently.

It would be wearisome to give the examination in detail, so we will only say, that at its close, Rose Lincoln heard with shame and confusion, that she could only be admitted into the Junior Class, her examination having proved a very unsatisfactory one. Poor Jenny, too, who had stumbled over almost every thing, shared the same fate, while Mary, expecting nothing, and hoping nothing, burst into tears when told that she had acquitted herself creditably, in all the branches requisite for an admission into the Middle class.

"Mrs. Mason will be so glad, and Billy, too," was her first thought; and then, as she saw how disappointed Jenny looked, she seized the first opportunity to throw her arms around her neck, and whisper to her how sorry she was that she had failed.

Jenny, however, was of too happy a temperament to remain sad for a long time, and before night her loud, merry laugh had more than once rang out in the upper hall, causing even Miss Lyon to listen, it was so clear and joyous. That afternoon, Aunt Martha, who was going to call upon Mrs. Mason, started for home, leaving the girls alone among strangers. It was a rainy, dreary day, and the moment her aunt was gone, Ida threw herself upon the bed and burst into tears. Jenny, who occupied the next room, was also low spirited, for Rose was terribly cross, calling her a "ninny hammer," and various other dignified names. Among the four girls, Mary was the only cheerful one, and after a time she succeeded in comforting Ida, while Jenny, catching something of her spirit, began to laugh loudly, as she told a group of girls how many ludicrous blunders she made when they undertook to question her about Euclid, which she had never studied in her life!

And now in a few days life at Mt. Holyoke commenced in earnest. Although perfectly healthy, Mary looked rather delicate, and it was for this reason, perhaps, that the sweeping and dusting of several rooms were assigned to her, as her portion of the labor. Ida and Rose fared much worse, and were greatly shocked, when told that they both belonged to the wash circle!

"I declare," said Rose, "it's too bad. I'll walk home before I'll do it;" and she glanced at her white hands, to make sure they were not already discolored by the dreaded soap suds!

Jenny was delighted with her allotment, which was dish-washing.

"I'm glad I took that lesson at the poor-house years ago," said she one day to Rose, who snappishly replied, "I'd shut up about the poor-house, or they'll think you the pauper instead of Madam Howard."

"Pauper? Who's a pauper?" asked Lucy Downs, eager to hear so desirable a piece of news.

Ida Selden's large black eyes rested reprovingly upon Rose, who nodded towards Mary, and forthwith Miss Downs departed with the information, which was not long in reaching Mary's ears.

"Why, Mary, what's the matter?" asked Ida, when towards the close of the day she found her companion weeping in her room. Without lifting her head, Mary replied, "It's foolish in me to cry, I know, but why need I always be reproached with having been a pauper. I couldn't help it. I promised mother I would take care of little Allie as long as she lived, and if she went to the poor-house, I had to go too."

"And who was little Allie?" asked Ida, taking Mary's hot hands between her own.

In few words Mary related her history, omitting her acquaintance with George Moreland, and commencing at the night when her mother died. Ida was warm-hearted and affectionate, and cared but little whether one were rich or poor if she liked them. From the first she had been interested in Mary, and now winding her arms about her neck, and kissing away her tears, she promised to love her, and to be to her as true and faithful a friend as Jenny. This promise, which was never broken, was of great benefit to Mary, drawing to her side many of the best girls in school, who soon learned to love her for herself, and not because the wealthy Miss Selden seemed so fond of her.

Neither Ida nor Rose were as happy in school, as Mary and Jenny. Both of them fretted about the rules, which they were obliged to observe, and both of them disliked and dreaded their portion of the work. Ida, however, was happier than Rose, for she was fonder of study, and one day when particularly interested in her lessons, she said to Mary, that she believed she should be tolerably contented, were it not for the everlasting washing.

Looking up a moment after, she saw that Mary had disappeared. But she soon returned, exclaiming, "I've fixed it. It's all right. I told her I was a great deal stronger than you, that I was used to washing, and you were not, and that it made your side ache; so she consented to have us exchange, and after this you are to dust for me, and I am to wash for you."

Ida disliked washing so much, that she raised no very strong objections to Mary's plan, and then when she found how great a kindness had really been shown her, she tried hard to think of some way in which to repay it. At last, George Moreland, to whom she had written upon the subject, suggested something which met her views exactly. Both Ida and her aunt had told George about Mary, and without hinting that he knew her, he immediately commenced making minute inquiries concerning her, of Ida, who communicated them to Mary, wondering why she always blushed so deeply, and tried to change the conversation. In reply to the letter in which Ida had told him of Mary's kindness, George wrote, "You say Miss Howard is very fond of music, and that there is no teacher connected with the institution. Now why not give her lessons yourself? You can do it as well as not, and it will be a good way of showing your gratitude."

Without waiting to read farther, Ida ran in quest of Mary, to whom she told what George had written. "You don't know," said she, "how much George asks about you. I never saw him so much interested in any one before, and half the girls in Boston are after him, too."

"Poor fellow, I pity him," said Mary; and Ida continued, "Perhaps it seems foolish in me to say so much about him, but if you only knew him, you wouldn't wonder. He's the handsomest young man I ever saw, and then he's so good, so different from other young men, especially Henry Lincoln."

Here the tea bell rang, and the conversation was discontinued.

When Rose heard that Mary was taking music lessons, she exclaimed to a group of girls with whom she was talking, "Well, I declare, beggars taking music lessons! I wonder what'll come next? Why, you've no idea how dreadfully poor she is. Our summer residence is near the alms-house, and when she was there I saw a good deal of her. She had scarcely any thing fit to wear, and I gave her one of my old bonnets, which I do believe she wore for three or four years."

"Why Rose Lincoln," said Jenny, who had overheard all, and now came up to her sister, "how can you tell what you know is not true?"

"Not true?" angrily retorted Rose. "Pray didn't she have my old bonnet?"

"Yes," answered Jenny, "but I bought it of you, and paid you for it with a bracelet Billy Bender gave me,—you know I did."

Rose was cornered, and as she saw noway of extricating herself, she turned on her heel and walked away, muttering about the meanness of doing a charitable deed, and then boasting of it!

The next day Jenny chanced to go for a moment to Mary's room. As she entered it, Mary looked up, saying, "You are just the one I want to see. I've been writing about you to Billy Bender. You can read it if you choose."

When Jenny had finished reading the passage referred to, she said, "Oh, Mary, I didn't suppose you overheard Rose's unkind remarks about that bonnet."

"But I did," answered Mary, "and I am glad, too, for I had always supposed myself indebted to her instead of you. Billy thought so, too, and as you see, I have undeceived him. Did I tell you that he had left Mr. Selden's employment, and gone into a law office?"

"Oh, good, good. I'm so glad," exclaimed Jenny, dancing about the room. "Do you know whose office he is in?"

"Mr. Worthington's," answered Mary, and Jenny continued: "Why, Henry is studying there. Isn't it funny? But Billy will beat him, I know he will,—he's so smart. How I wish he'd write to me! Wouldn't I feel grand to have a gentleman correspondent?"

"Suppose you write to him," said Mary, laughingly. "Here's just room enough," pointing to a vacant spot upon the paper. "He's always asking about you, and you can answer his questions yourself."

"I'll do it," said Jenny, and seizing the pen, she thoughtlessly scribbled off a ludicrous account of her failure, and of the blunders she was constantly committing, while she spoke of Mary as the pattern for the whole school, both in scholarship and behavior.

"There!" said she, wiping her gold pen upon her silk apron (for Jenny still retained some of the habits of her childhood) "I guess he'll think I'm crazy, but I hope he'll answer it, any way."

Mary hoped so too, and when at last Billy's letter came, containing a neatly written note for Jenny, it was difficult telling which of the two girls was the happier.

Soon after Mary went to Mount Holyoke, she had received a letter from Billy, in which he expressed his pleasure that she was at school, but added that the fact of her being there interfered greatly with his plan of educating her himself. "Mother's ill health," said he, "prevented me from doing any thing until now, and just as I am in a fair way to accomplish my object, some one else has stepped in before me. But it is all right, and as you do not seem to need my services at present, I shall next week leave Mr. Selden's employment, go into Mr. Worthington's law office as clerk, hoping that when the proper time arrives, I shall not be defeated in another plan which was formed in boyhood, and which has become the great object of my life."

Mary felt perplexed and troubled. Billy's letters of late had been more like those of a lover than a brother, and she could not help guessing the nature of "the plan formed in boyhood." She knew she should never love him except with a sister's love, and though she could not tell him so, her next letter lacked the tone of affection with which she was accustomed to write, and on the whole a rather formal affair. Billy, who readily perceived the change, attributed it to the right cause, and from that time his letters became far less cheerful than usual.

Mary usually cried over them, wishing more than once that Billy would transfer his affection from herself to Jenny, and it was for this reason, perhaps, that without stopping to consider the propriety of the matter, she first asked Jenny to write to him, and then encouraged her in answering his notes, which (as her own letters grew shorter) became gradually longer and longer, until at last his letters were addressed to Jenny, while the notes they contained were directed to Mary!

CHAPTER XX.

THE CLOSING OF THE YEAR.

Rapidly the days passed on at Mount Holyoke. Autumn faded into winter, whose icy breath floated for a time over the mountain tops, and then melted away at the approach of spring, which, with its swelling buds and early flowers, gave way in its turn to the long bright days of summer. And now only a few weeks remained ere the annual examination at which Ida was to be graduated. Neither Rose nor Jenny were to return the next year, and nothing but Mr. Lincoln's firmness and good sense had prevented their being sent for when their mother first heard that they had failed to enter the Middle class.

Mrs. Lincoln's mortification was undoubtedly greatly increased from the fact that the despised Mary had entered in advance of her daughters. "Things are coming to a pretty pass," said she. "Yes, a pretty pass; but I might have known better than to send my children to such a school."

Mr. Lincoln could not forbear asking her in a laughing way, "if the schools which she attended were of a higher order than Mount Holyoke."

Bursting into tears, Mrs. Lincoln replied that "she didn't think she ought to be *twitted* of her poverty."

"Neither do I," returned her husband. "You were no more to blame for working in the factory, than Mary is for having been a pauper!"

Mrs. Lincoln was silent, for she did not particularly care to hear about her early days, when she had been an operative in the cotton mills of Southbridge. She had possessed just enough beauty to captivate the son of the proprietor, who was fresh from college, and after a few weeks' acquaintance they were married. Fortunately her husband was a man of good sense, and restrained her from the commission of many foolish acts. Thus when she insisted upon sending for Rose and Jenny, he promptly replied that they should not come home! Still, as Rose seemed discontented, complaining that so much exercise made her side and shoulder ache, and as Jenny did not wish to remain another year unless Mary did, he consented that they should leave school at the close of the term, on condition that they went somewhere else.

"I shall never make any thing of Henry," said he, "but my daughters shall receive every advantage, and perhaps one or the other of them will comfort my old age."

He had spoken truly with regard to Henry, who was studying, or pretending to study law in the same office with Billy Bender. But his father heard no favorable accounts of him, and from time to time large bills were presented for the payment of carriage hire, wine, and "drunken sprees" generally. So it is no wonder the disappointed father sighed, and turned to his daughters for the comfort his only son refused to give.

But we have wandered from the examination at Mount Holyoke, for which great preparations were being made. Rose, knowing she was not to return, seemed to think all further effort on her part unnecessary; and numerous were the reprimands, to say nothing of the black marks which she received. Jenny, on the contrary, said she wished to retrieve her reputation for laziness, and leave behind a good impression. So, never before in her whole life had she behaved so well, or studied so hard as she did during the last few weeks of her stay at Mount Holyoke. Ida, who was expecting her father, aunt and cousin to be present at the anniversary, was so engrossed with her studies, that she did not observe how sad and low spirited Mary seemed. She had tasted of knowledge, and now thirsted for more; but it could not be; the funds were exhausted, and she must leave the school, never perhaps to return again.

"How much I shall miss my music, and how much I shall miss you," she said one day to Ida, who was giving her a lesson.

"It's too bad you haven't a piano," returned Ida, "you are so fond of it, and improve so fast!" then after a moment she added, "I have a plan to propose, and may as well do it now as any time. Next winter you must spend with me in Boston. Aunt Martha and I arranged it the last time I was at home, and we even selected your room, which is next to mine, and opposite to Aunt Martha's. Now what does your ladyship say to it?"

"She says she can't go," answered Mary.

"Can't go!" repeated Ida. "Why not? Jenny will be in the city, and you are always happy where she is; besides you will have a rare chance for taking music lessons of our best teachers; and then, too, you will be in the same house with George, and that alone is worth going to Boston for, I think."

Ida little suspected that her last argument was the strongest objection to Mary's going, for much as she wished to meet George again, she felt that she would not on any account go to his own home, lest he should think she came on purpose to see him. There were other reasons, too, why she did not wish to go. Henry and Rose Lincoln would both be in the city, and she knew that neither of them would scruple to do or say any thing which they thought would annoy her. Mrs. Mason, too, missed her, and longed to have her at home; so she resisted all Ida's entreaties, and the next letter which went to

Aunt Martha, carried her refusal.

In a day or two, Mary received two letters, one from Billy and one from Mrs. Mason, the latter of which contained money for the payment of her bills; but on offering it to the Principal, how was she surprised to learn that her bills had not only been regularly paid and receipted, but that ample funds were provided for the defraying of her expenses during the coming year. A faint sickness stole over Mary, for she instantly thought of Billy Bender, and the obligations she would now be under to him for ever. Then it occurred to her how impossible it was that he should have earned so much in so short a time; and as soon as she could trust her voice to speak, she asked who it was that had thus befriended her.

Miss —— was not at liberty to tell, and with a secret suspicion of Aunt Martha, who had seemed much interested in her welfare, Mary returned to her room to read the other letter, which was still unopened. It was some time since Billy had written to her alone, and with more than her usual curiosity, she broke the seal; but her head grew dizzy, and her spirits faint, as she read the passionate outpouring of a heart which had cherished her image for years, and which, though fearful of rejection, would still tell her how much she was beloved. "It is no sudden fancy," said he, "but was conceived years ago, on that dreary afternoon, when in your little room at the poor-house, you laid your head in my lap and wept, as you told me how lonely you were. Do you remember it, Mary? I do; and never now does your image come before me, but I think of you as you were then, when the wild wish that you should one day be mine first entered my heart. Morning, noon, and night have I thought of you, and no plan for the future have I ever formed which had not a direct reference to you. Once, Mary, I believed my affection for you returned, but now you are changed greatly changed. Your letters are brief and cold, and when I look around for the cause, I am led to fear that I was deceived in thinking you ever loved me, as I thought you did. If I am mistaken, tell me so; but if I am not, if you can never be my wife, I will school myself to think of you as a brother would think of an only and darling sister."

This letter produced a strange effect upon Mary. She thought how much she was indebted to one who had stood so faithfully by her when all the world was dark and dreary. She thought, too, of his kindness to the dead, and that appealed more strongly to her sympathy than aught else he had ever done for her. There was no one to advise her, and acting upon the impulse of the moment, she sat down and commenced a letter, the nature of which she did not understand herself, and which if sent, would have given a different coloring to the whole of her after life. She had written but one page, when the study bell rang, and she was obliged to put her letter by till the morrow. For several days she had not been well, and the excitement produced by Billy's letter tended to increase her illness, so that on the following morning when she attempted to rise, she found herself seriously ill. During the hours in which she was alone that day, she had ample time for reflection, and before night she wrote another letter to Billy, in which she told him how impossible it was for her to be the wife of one whom she had always loved as an own, and dear brother. This letter caused Mary so much effort, and so many bitter tears, that for several days she continued worse, and at last gave up all hope of being present at the examination.

"Oh it's too bad," said Ida, "for I *do* want you to see Cousin George, and I know he'll be disappointed too, for I never saw any thing like the interest he seems to take in you."

A few days afterwards as Mary was lying alone, thinking of Billy, and wondering if she had done right in writing to him as she did, Jenny came rushing in wild with delight.

Her father was down stairs, together with Ida's father George, and Aunt Martha. "Most the first thing I did," said she, "was to inquire after Billy Bender! I guess Aunt Martha was shocked, for she looked so *queer*. George laughed, and Mr. Selden said he was doing well, and was one of the finest young men in Boston. But why don't you ask about George? I heard him talking about you to Rose, just as I left the parlor."

Mary felt sure that any information of her which Rose might give would not be very complimentary, and she thought right; for when Rose was questioned concerning "Miss Howard," she at first affected her ignorance of such a person; and then when George explained himself more definitely, she said, "Oh, *that* girl! I'm sure I don't know much about her, except that she's a *charity scholar*, or something of that kind."

At the words "charity scholar," there was a peculiar smile on George's face; but he continued talking, saying, "that if that were the case, she ought to be very studious and he presumed she was."

"As nearly as I can judge of her," returned Rose, "she is not remarkable for brilliant talents; but," she added, as she met Ida's eye, "she has a certain way of showing off, and perhaps I am mistaken with regard to her."

Very different from this was the description given of her by Ida, who now came to her cousin's side, extolling Mary highly, and lamenting the illness which would prevent George from seeing her. Aunt Martha, also, spoke a word in Mary's favor, at the same time endeavoring to stop the unkind remarks of Rose, whom she thoroughly disliked, and who she feared was becoming too much of a favorite with George. Rose was not only very handsome, but she also possessed a peculiar faculty of making herself agreeable whenever she chose, and in Boston she was quite a favorite with a certain class of young men. It was for George Moreland, however, that her prettiest and most coquettish airs were practised. He was the object which she would secure; and when she heard Mary Howard so highly commended in his presence, she could not forbear expressing her contempt, fancying that he, with his high English notions, would feel just as she did, with regard to poverty and low origin. As for George, it was difficult telling whom he did prefer, though the last time Rose was in Boston, rumor had said that he was particularly attentive to her; and Mrs. Lincoln, who was very sanguine, once hinted to Ida, the probability that a relationship would sooner or later exist between the two families.

Rose, too, though careful not to hint at such a thing in Ida's presence, was quite willing that others of her companions at Mount Holyoke should fancy there was an intimacy, if not an engagement between herself and Mr. Moreland. Consequently he had not been in South Hadley twenty-four hours, ere he was pointed out by some of the villagers, as being the future husband of the elder Miss Lincoln, whose haughty, disagreeable manners had become subject of general remark. During the whole of George's stay at Mount Holyoke, Rose managed to keep him at her side, entertaining him occasionally with unkind remarks concerning Mary, who, she said, was undoubtedly feigning her sickness, so as not to appear in her classes, where she knew she could do herself no credit; "but," said she, "as soon as the examination is over, she'll get well fast enough, and bother us with her company to Chicopee."

In this Hose was mistaken, for when the exercises closed Mary was still too ill to ride, and it was decided that she should remain a few days until Mrs. Mason could come for her. With many tears Ida and Jenny bade their young friend good-bye, but Rose, when asked to go up and see her turned away disdainfully, amusing herself during their absence by talking and laughing with George Moreland.

The room in which Mary lay, commanded a view of the yard and gateway; and after Aunt Martha, Ida, and Jenny had left her, she arose, and stealing to the window, looked out upon the company as they departed. She could readily divine which was George Moreland, for Rose Lincoln's shawl and satchel were thrown over his arm, while Rose herself walked close to his elbow, apparently engrossing his whole attention. Once he turned around, but fearful of being herself observed, Mary drew back behind the window curtain, and thus lost a view of his face. He, however, caught a glimpse of her, and asked if that was the room in which Miss Howard was sick.

Rose affected not to hear him, and continued enumerating the many trials which she had endured at school, and congratulating herself upon her escape from the "horrid place." But for once George was not an attentive listener. Notwithstanding his apparent indifference, he was greatly disappointed at not seeing Mary. It was for this he had gone to Mount Holyoke; and in spite of Rose's endeavors to make him talk, he was unusually silent all the way, and when they at last reached Chicopee, he highly offended the young lady by assisting Jenny to alight instead of herself.

"I should like to know what you are thinking about," she said rather pettishly, as she took his offered hand to say good-bye.

With a roguish look in his eye, George replied, "I've been thinking of a young lady. Shall I tell you her name?"

Rose blushed, and looking interestingly embarrassed answered, that of course 'twas no one whom she knew.

"Yes, 'tis," returned George, still holding her hand and as Aunt Martha, who was jealously watching his movements from the window, just then called out to him "to jump in, or he'd be left," he put his face under Rose's bonnet, and whispered, "Mary Howard!"

"Kissed her, upon my word!" said Aunt Martha with a groan, which was rendered inaudible to Ida by the louder noise of the engine.

CHAPTER XXI.

VACATION.

In Mrs. Mason's pleasant little dining parlor, the tea-table was neatly spread for two, while old Judith, in starched gingham dress, white muslin apron, bustled in and out, occasionally changing the position of a curtain or chair, and then stepping backward to witness the effect. The stuffed rocking chair, with two extra cushions, and a pillow, was drawn up to the table, indicating that an invalid was expected to occupy that seat, while near one of the plates was a handsome bouquet, which Lydia Knight had carefully arranged, and brought over as a present for her young teacher. A dozen times had Lydia been told to "clip down to the gate and see if they were comin';" and at last, seating herself resignedly upon the hall stairs, Judith began to wonder "what under the sun and moon had happened."

She had not sat there long, ere the sound of wheels again drew her to the door, and in a moment old Charlotte and the yellow wagon entered the yard. Mary, who was now nearly well, sprang out, and bounding up the steps, seized Judith's hand with a grasp which told how glad she was to see her.

"Why, you ain't dreadful sick, is you?" said Judith peering under her bonnet.

"Oh, no, not sick at all," returned Mary; and then, as she saw the chair, with its cushions and pillows, she burst into a loud laugh, which finally ended in a hearty cry, when she thought how kind was every one to her.

She had been at home but a few days when she was solicited to take charge of a small select school. But Mrs Mason thought it best for her to return to Mount Holyoke, and accordingly she declined Mr. Knight's offer, greatly to his disappointment, and that of many others. Mrs. Bradley, who never on any occasion paid her school bill, was the loudest in her complaints, saying that, "for all Tim never larnt a speck, and stood at the foot all summer long when Mary kept before, he'd got so sassy there was no living with him, and she wanted him out of the way."

Widow Perkins, instead of being sorry was glad, for if Mary didn't teach, there was no reason why Sally Ann shouldn't. "You'll never have a better chance," said she to her daughter, "there's no stifficut needed for a private school, and I'll clap on my things and run over to Mr Knight's before he gets off to his work."

It was amusing to see Mr. Knight's look of astonishment, when the widow made her application. Lydia, who chanced to be present, hastily retreated behind the pantry door, where with her apron over her mouth, she laughed heartily as she thought of a note, which the candidate for teaching had once sent them, and in which "i's" figured conspicuously, while her mother was "*polightly* thanked for those yeast?"

Possibly Mr. Knight thought of the note, too, for he gave the widow no encouragement, and when on her way home she called for a moment at Mrs. Mason's, she "thanked her stars that Sally Ann wasn't obliged to keep school for a livin', for down below where she came from, teachers warn't fust cut!"

One morning about a week after Mary's return, she announced her intention of visiting her mother's grave. "I am accustomed to so much exercise," said she, "that I can easily walk three miles, and perhaps on my way home I shall get a ride."

Mrs Mason made no objection, and Mary was soon on her way. She was a rapid walker, and almost before she was aware of it, reached the village. As she came near Mrs. Campbell's, the wish naturally arose that Ella should accompany her. Looking up she saw her sister in the garden and called to her.

"Wha-a-t?" was the very loud and uncivil answer which came back to her, and in a moment Ella appeared round the corner of the house, carelessly swinging her straw flat, and humming a fashionable song. On seeing her sister she drew back the corners of her mouth into something which she intended for a smile, and said, "Why, I thought it was Bridget calling me, you looked so much like her in that gingham sun-bonnet. Won't you come in?"

"Thank you," returned Mary, "I was going to mother's grave, and thought perhaps you would like to accompany me."

"Oh, no," said Ella, in her usual drawling tone, "I don't know as I want to go. I was there last week and saw the monument."

"What monument?" asked Mary, and Ella replied "Why, didn't you know that Mrs. Mason, or the town, or somebody, had bought a monument, with mother's and father's, and Franky's, and Allie's name on it?"

Mary waited for no more, but turned to leave, while Ella, who was anxious to inquire about Ida Selden, and who could afford to be gracious, now that neither Miss Porter, nor the city girls were there, called after her to stop and rest, when she came back. Mary promised to do so, and then hurrying on, soon reached the graveyard, where, as Ella had said, there stood by her parents' graves a large handsome monument.

William Bender was the first person who came into her mind, and as she thought of all that had passed between them, and of this last proof of his affection, she seated herself among the tall grass and flowers, which grew upon her mother's grave, and burst into tears. She had not sat there long, ere she was roused by the sound of a footstep. Looking up, she saw before her the young gentleman, who the year previous had visited her school in Rice Corner. Seating himself respectfully by her side, he spoke of the three graves, and asked if they were her friends who slept there. There was something so kind and affectionate in his voice and manner, that Mary could not repress her tears, and snatching up her bonnet which she had thrown aside she hid her face in it and again wept.

For a time, Mr. Stuart suffered her to weep, and then gently removed the gingham bonnet, and holding her hand between his, he tried to divert her mind by talking upon other topics, asking her how she had been employed during the year, and appearing greatly pleased, when told that she had been at Mount Holyoke. Observing, at length, that her eyes constantly rested upon the monument, he spoke of that, praising its beauty, and asking if it were her taste.

"No," said she, "I never saw it until to-day, and did not even know it was here."

"Some one wished to surprise you, I dare say," returned Mr. Stuart. "It was manufactured in Boston, I see. Have you friends there?"

Mary replied that she had one, a Mr. Bender, to which Mr. Stuart quickly rejoined, "Is it William Bender? I have heard of him through our mutual friend George Moreland, whom you perhaps have seen."

Mary felt the earnest gaze of the large, dark eyes which were fixed upon her face, and coloring deeply, she replied that they came from England in the same vessel.

"Indeed!" said Mr. Stuart. "When I return to the city shall I refresh his memory a little with regard to you?"

"I'd rather you would not," answered Mary. "Our paths in life are very different; and he of course would feel no interest in me."

"Am I to conclude that you, too, feel no interest in him?" returned Mr. Stuart, and again his large eyes rested on Mary's face, with a curious expression.

But she made no reply, and soon rising up, said it was time for her to go home.

"Allow me to accompany you as far as Mrs. Campbell's," said Mr. Stuart. "I am going to call upon Miss Ella, whose acquaintance I accidentally made last summer. Suppose you call too. You know her, of course?" Mary replied that she did, and was about to speak of the relationship between them, when Mr. Stuart abruptly changed the conversation, and in a moment more they were at Mrs. Campbell's door. Ella was so much delighted at again seeing Mr. Stuart, that she hardly noticed her sister at all, and did not even ask her to remove her bonnet. After conversing a while upon indifferent subjects, Mr. Stuart asked Ella to play, saying he was very fond of music. But Ella, like other fashionable ladies, "couldn't of course play any thing,—was dreadfully out of practice, and besides that her music was all so old-fashioned."

Mr. Stuart had probably seen such cases before, and knew how to manage them, for he continued urging the matter, until Ella arose, and throwing back her curls, sauntered to wards the piano, saying she should be obliged to have some one turn the leases for her. Mr. Stuart of course volunteered his services, and after a violent turning of the music-stool by way of elevating it, and a turning back by way of lowering it, Ella with the air of a martyr, declared herself ready to play whatever Mr. Stuart should select, provided it were not "old."

A choice being made she dashed off into a spirited waltz, skipping a good many notes, and finally ending with a tremendous crash. Fond as Mr. Stuart was of music, he did not call for a repetition from her, but turning to Mary asked if she could play.

Ella laughed aloud at the idea, and when Mary replied that she did play a little, she laughed still louder, saying, "Why, *she* can't play, unless it's 'Days of Absence,' with one hand, or something of that kind."

"Allow me to be the judge," said Mr. Stuart, and leading Mary to the piano, he bade her play any thing she pleased.

Ida had been a faithful teacher, and Mary a persevering pupil, so that whatever she played was played correctly and with good taste; at least Mr. Stuart thought so, for he kept calling for piece after piece, until she laughingly told him her catalogue was nearly exhausted, and she'd soon be obliged to resort to the *scales!*

Ella looked on in amazement, and when Mary had finished playing, demanded of her where she had learned so much, and who was her teacher; adding that her *fingering* was wretched; "but then," said she, "I suppose you can't help it, your fingers are so stiff!"

For a moment Mr. Stuart regarded her with an expression which it seemed to Mary she had seen before, and then consulting his watch, said he must go, as it was nearly car time, After he was gone, Ella asked Mary endless questions as to where she met him, what he said, and if she told him they were sisters. "How elegantly he was dressed," said she, "Didn't you feel dreadfully ashamed of your gingham sun-bonnet and gown?"

"Why, no," said Mary. "I never once thought of them."

"I should, for I know he notices every thing," returned Ella; and then leaning on her elbow so as to bring herself in range of the large mirror opposite, she continued, "seems to me my curls are not arranged becomingly this morning."

Either for mischief, or because she really thought so, Mary replied "that they did not look as well as usual;" whereupon Ella grew red in the face, saying that "she didn't think she looked so very badly."

Just then the first dinner bell rang, and starting up Ella exclaimed, "Why-ee, *I* forgot that ma expected General H. to dine. I must go and dress this minute."

Without ever asking her sister to stay to dinner, she hastily left the room. Upon finding herself so unceremoniously deserted, Mary tied on the despised gingham bonnet and started for home. She had reached the place where Ella the year before met with Mr. Stuart, when she saw a boy, whom she knew was living at the poor-house, coming down the hill as fast as a half blind old horse could bring him. When he got opposite to her he halted, and with eyes projecting like harvest apples, told her to "jump in, for Mrs. Parker was dying, and they had sent for her."

"I've been to your house," said he, "and your marm thought mebby I'd meet you."

Mary immediately sprang in, and by adroitly questioning Mike, whose intellect was not the brightest in the world, managed to ascertain that Mrs. Parker had been much worse for several days, that Sal Furbush had turned nurse; faithfully attending her night and day, and occasionally sharing "her vigils" with a "sleek, fancy-looking girl, who dressed up in meetin' clothes every day, and who had first proposed sending for Mary." Mary readily guessed that the "sleek, fancy-looking" girl was Jenny, and on reaching the poor house she found her suspicions correct, for Jenny came out to meet her, followed by Sally, who exclaimed, "Weep, oh daughter, and lament, for earth has got one woman less and Heaven one female more!"

Passing into the house, Mary followed Jenny to the same room where once her baby sister had lain, and where now upon the same table lay all that was mortal of Mrs. Parker. Miss Grundy, who was standing near the body, bowed with a look of very becoming resignation, and then as if quite overcome, left the room. Just then a neighbor, who seemed to be superintending affairs, came in, and Mary asked what she could do to assist them.

"Nothing until to-morrow, when if you please you can help make the shroud," answered the woman, and Jenny catching Mary around the neck, whispered, "You'll stay all night with me; there's no one at home but Rose, and we'll have such a nice time."

Mary thought of the little room up stairs where Alice had died, and felt a desire to sleep there once more, but upon inquiry she found that it was now occupied by Sally Furbush.

"You must come and see my little parlor," said she to Mary, and taking her hand she led her up to the room, which was greatly improved. A strip of faded, but rich carpeting was before the bed. A low rocking-chair stood near the window, which was shaded with a striped muslin curtain, the end of which was fringed out nearly a quarter of a yard, plainly showing Sally's handiwork. The contents of the old barrel were neatly stowed away in a square box, on the top of which lay a worn portfolio, stuffed to its utmost capacity with manuscript.

"For all this elegance," said Sally, "I am indebted to my worthy and esteemed friend, Miss Lincoln."

But Mary did not hear, for her eyes were riveted upon another piece of furniture. At the foot of the bed stood Alice's cradle, which Billy Bender had brought there on that afternoon now so well remembered by Mary.

"Oh, Sally," said she, "how came this here?"

"Why," returned Sally, hitting it a jog, "I don't sleep any now, and I thought the nights would seem shorter, if I had this to rock and make believe little Willie was in it. So I brought it down from the garret, and it affords me a sight of comfort, I assure you!"

Mary afterwards learned that often during the long winter nights the sound of that cradle could be heard, occasionally drowned by Sally's voice, which sometimes rose almost to a shriek, and then died away in a low, sad wail, as she sang a lullaby to the "Willie who lay sleeping on the prairie at the West."

As there was now no reason why she should not do so, Mary accompanied Jenny home, where, as she had expected, she met with a cool reception from Rose, who merely nodded to her, and then resumed the book she was reading. After tea, Mary stepped for a moment into the yard, and then Rose asked Jenny what she intended doing with her "genteel visitor."

"Put her in the best chamber, and sleep there myself," said Jenny, adding that "they were going to lie awake all night just to see how it seemed."

But in spite of this resolution, as midnight advanced Jenny found that Mary's answers, even when Billy Bender was the topic, became more and more unsatisfactory, and finally ceased altogether. Concluding to let her sleep a few minutes, and then wake her up, Jenny turned on her pillow and when her eyes again opened, the morning sun was shining through the half-closed shutters, and the breakfast bell was jingling in the lower hall.

When Mary returned to the poor-house, she found a new arrival in the person of Mrs. Perkins! The widow had hailed Mike as he passed her house the day before, and on learning how matters stood, offered to accompany him home. Mike, who had an eye for "fancy-looking girls," did not exactly like Mrs. Perkins' appearance. Besides that, his orders were to bring Mary, and he had no idea of taking another as a substitute. Accordingly, when on his return from Mrs. Mason's, he saw the widow standing at her gate, all equipped with parasol and satchel, he whipped up his horse, and making the circuit of the school-house, was some ways down the road ere the widow suspected his intentions. "Thanking her stars" (her common expression) "that she had a good pair of feet," Mrs. Perkins started on foot, reaching the poor-house about sunset. She was now seated in what had been Mrs. Parker's room, and with pursed-up lips, and large square collar very much like the present fashion, was stitching away upon the shroud, heaving occasionally a long-drawn sigh, as she thought how lonely and desolate poor Mr. Parker must feel!

"Will you give me some work?" asked Mary, after depositing her bonnet upon the table.

"There's nothing for you," returned Mrs. Perkins. "I can do all that is necessary, and prefer working alone."

"Yes, she shall help too, if she wants to," snapped out Mrs. Grundy, with one of her old shoulder jerks. "Mary's handy with the needle, for I larnt her myself."

In a short time Mrs. Perkins disappeared from the room, and Sally's little bright eyes, which saw every thing, soon spied her out in the woodshed asking Mr. Parker "if Polly Grundy couldn't be kept in the kitchen where she belonged."

Scarcely had she left the shed when Miss Grundy herself appeared, fretting about "the meddlesome old widow who had come there stickin' round before Mrs. Parker was hardly cold!"

This put a new idea into Sally's head, and the whole household was startled as she broke out singing, "the loss of one is the gain of another," and so forth. Mrs. Perkins proposed that she should be shut up, but Miss Grundy, for once in Sally's favor, declared "she'd fight, before such a thing should be done;" whereupon Mrs. Perkins lamented that the house had now "no head," wondering how poor Mr. Parker would get along with "such an unmanageable crew."

Numerous were the ways with which the widow sought to comfort the widower, assuring him "that she ached for him clear to her heart's core! and I know how to pity you, too," said she, "for when my Hezekiah died I thought I couldn't stand it." Then by way of administering further consolation, she added that "the *wust* was to come, for only them that had tried it knew how lonesome it was to live on day after day, and night after night, week in and week out, without any husband or wife."

Mr. Parker probably appreciated her kindness, for when after the funeral the following day she announced her intention of walking home, he ordered Mike to "tackle up," and carry her. This was hardly in accordance with the widow's wishes, and when all was in readiness, she declared that she was afraid to ride after Mike's driving. Uncle Peter was then proposed as a substitute, but the old man had such a dread of Mrs. Perkins, who Sal (for mischief) had said was in love with him, that at the first intimation he climbed up the scuttle hole, where an hour afterwards he was discovered peeping cautiously out to see if the coast was clear. Mr. Parker was thus compelled to go himself, Miss Grundy sending after him the very Christian-like wish that "she hoped he'd tip over and break the widow's neck!"

CHAPTER XXII.

EDUCATION FINISHED.

Vacation was over, and again in the halls of Mount Holyoke was heard the tread of many feet, and the sound of youthful voices, as one by one the pupils came back to their accustomed places. For a time Mary was undecided whether to return or not, for much as she desired an education, she could not help feeling delicate about receiving it from a stranger; but Mrs. Mason, to whom all her thoughts and feelings were confided, advised her to return, and accordingly the first day of the term found her again at Mount Holyoke, where she was warmly welcomed by her teachers and companions. Still it did not seem like the olden time, for Ida was not there, and Jenny's merry laugh was gone. She had hoped that her sister would accompany her, but in reply to her persuasions, Ella answered that "she didn't want to work,—she wasn't obliged to work,—and she wouldn't work!" quoting Rose Lincoln's "pain in the side, callous on her hand, and cold on her lungs," as a sufficient reason why every body should henceforth and for ever stay away from Mount Holyoke.

Mrs. Lincoln, who forgot that Rose had complained of a pain in her side long before she ever saw South Hadley, advised Mrs. Campbell, by all means, never to send her daughter to such a place. "To be sure it may do well enough," said she, "for a great burly creature like Mary Howard, but your daughter and mine are altogether too delicate and daintily bred to endure it."

Mrs. Campbell of course consented to this, adding that she had secured the services of a highly accomplished lady as governess for Ella, and proposing that Rose and Jenny, instead of accompanying their mother to the city as usual, should remain with her during the winter, and share Ella's advantages. To this proposition, Mrs. Lincoln readily assented, and while Mary, from habitual exercise both indoors and out, was growing more and more healthful and vigorous, Rose Lincoln, who was really delicate, was drooping day by day, and growing paler and paler in the closely heated school-room, where a breath of fresh air rarely found entrance, as the "accomplished governess" could not endure it. Daily were her pupils lectured upon the necessity of shielding themselves from the winter winds, which were sure "to impart such a rough, blowzy appearance to their complexion."

Rose profited well by this advice, and hardly any thing could tempt her into the open air, unless it were absolutely necessary. All day long she half reclined upon a small sofa, which at her request was drawn close to the stove, and even then complaining of being chilly she sometimes sat with her shawl thrown over her shoulders. Jenny, on the contrary, fanned herself furiously at the farthest corner of the room, frequently managing to open the window slyly, and regale herself with the snow which lay upon the sill. Often, too, when her lessons were over for the day, she would bound away, and after a walk of a mile or so, would return to the house with her cheeks glowing, and her eyes sparkling like stars. Burnishing a striking contrast to her pale, sickly sister, who hovered over the stove, shivering if a window were raised, or a door thrown open.

In the course of the winter Mrs. Lincoln came up to visit her daughters, expressing herself much pleased with Rose's improved looks and manners. "Her complexion was so pure" she said, "so different from what it was when she came from Mount Holyoke."

Poor Jenny, who, full of life and spirits came rushing in to see her mother, was cut short in her expression of joy by being called "a perfect bunch of fat!"

"Why, Jenny, what does make you so red and coarse?" said the distressed mother. "I know you eat too much," and before Mrs. Lincoln went home, she gave her daughter numerous lectures concerning her diet; but it only made matters worse; and when six weeks after, Mrs. Lincoln came again she found that Jenny had not only gained five pounds, but that hardly one of her dresses would meet!

"Mercy me!" said she, the moment her eye fell upon Jenny's round, plump cheeks, and fat shoulders, "you are as broad as you are long. What a figure you would cut in Boston!"

For once the merry Jenny cried, wondering how she could help being healthy and fat. Before Mrs. Lincoln left Chicopee, she made a discovery, which resulted in the removal of Jenny to Boston. With the exception of the year at Mount Holyoke, Jenny had never before passed a winter in the country, and now everything delighted her. In spite of her governess's remonstrance, all her leisure moments were spent in the open air, and besides her long walks, she frequently joined the scholars, who from the district school came over at recess to slide down the long hill in the rear of Mrs. Campbell's barns and stables. For Jenny to ride down hill at all was bad enough, "but to do so with *district school* girls, and then be drawn up by coarse, vulgar boys, was far worse;" and the offender was told to be in readiness to accompany her mother home, for she could not stay in Chicopee another week.

"Oh, I'm so glad," said Rose, "for now I shan't freeze to death nights."

Mrs. Lincoln demanded what she meant, and was told that Jenny insisted upon having the window down from the top, let the weather be what it might; "and," added Rose 'when the wind blows hard I am positively obliged to hold on to the sheets to keep myself in bed!"

"A Mount Holyoke freak," said Mrs. Lincoln. "I wish to mercy neither of you had ever gone there."

Rose answered by a low cough, which her mother did not hear, or at least did not notice. Jenny, who loved the country and the country people, was not much pleased with her mother's plan. But for once Mrs. Lincoln was determined, and after stealing one more sled-ride down the long hill, and bidding farewell to the old desk in the school-house, sacred for the name carved three years before with Billy Bender's jack-knife, Jenny went back with her mother to Boston, leaving Rose to droop and fade in the hot, unwholesome atmosphere of Miss Hinton's school-room.

Not long after Jenny's return to the city, she wrote to Mary an amusing account of her mother's reason for removing her from Chicopee. "But on the whole, I am glad to be at home," said she, "for I see Billy Bender almost every day. I first met him coming down Washington Street, and he walked with me clear to our gate. Ida Selden had a party last week, and owing to George Moreland's influence, Billy was there. He was very attentive to me, though Henry says 'twas right the other way. But it wasn't. I didn't ask him to go out to supper with me. I only told him I'd introduce him to somebody who would go, and he immediately offered me his arm. Oh, how mother scolded, and how angry she got when she asked me if I wasn't ashamed, and I told her I wasn't!

"Billy doesn't appear just as he used to. Seems as though something troubled him; and what is very strange, he never speaks of you, unless I do first. You've no idea how handsome he is. To be sure, he hasn't the air of George Moreland, and doesn't dress as elegantly, but I think he's finer looking. Ever so many girls at Ida's party asked who he was, and said 'twas a pity he wasn't rich, but that wouldn't make any difference with me,—I'd have him just as soon as though he was wealthy.

"How mother would go on if she should see this! But I don't care,—I like Billy Bender, and I can't help it, and *entre nous*, I believe he likes me better than he did! But I must stop now, for Lizzie Upton has called for me to go with her and see a poor blind woman in one of the back alleys."

From this extract it will be seen that Jenny, though seventeen years of age, was the same open-hearted, childlike creature as ever. She loved Billy Bender, and she didn't care who knew it. She loved, too, to seek out and befriend the poor, with which Boston, like all other large cities, abounded. Almost daily her mother lectured her upon her bad taste in the choice of her associates, but Jenny was incorrigible, and the very next hour might perhaps be seen either walking with Billy Bender, or mounting the rickety stairs of some crazy old building, where a palsied old woman or decrepit old man watched for her coming, and blessed her when she came.

Early in the spring Mr. Lincoln went up to Chicopee to make some changes in his house, preparatory to his family's removal thither. When he called at Mrs. Campbell's to see Rose, he was greatly shocked at her altered and languid appearance. The cough, which her mother had not observed fell ominously on his ear; for he thought of a young sister who many years before in the bloom of girlhood had passed away from his side. A physician was immediately called and after an examination Rose's lungs were pronounced diseased, though not as yet beyond cure. She was of course taken from school; and with the utmost care, and skilful nursing, she gradually grew better.

Jenny, who had never been guilty of any great love for books, was also told that her school days were over, and congratulated herself upon being a "full grown young lady," which fact no one would dispute, who saw her somewhat large dimensions.

When Ella learned that Jenny as well as Rose was emancipated from the school-room, she immediately petitioned her mother for a similar privilege, saying that she knew all that was necessary for her to know. Miss Hinton, too, being weary of one pupil, and desiring a change for herself, threw her influence in Ella's favor, so that at last Mrs. Campbell yielded; and Ella, piling up her books, carried them away, never again referring to them on any occasion, but spending her time in anticipating the happiness she should enjoy the following winter; when she was to be first introduced to Boston society.

Unlike this was the closing of Mary's school days. Patiently and perseveringly, through the year she had studied, storing her mind with useful knowledge; and when at last the annual examination came, not one in the senior class stood higher, or was graduated with more honor than herself. Mrs. Mason, who was there, listened with all a parent's pride and fondness to her adopted child, as she promptly responded to every question. But it was not Mrs. Mason's presence alone which incited Mary to do so well. Among the crowd of spectators she caught a glimpse of a face which twice before she had seen, once in the school-room at Rice Corner, and once in the graveyard at Chicopee. Turn which way she would, she felt, rather than saw, how intently Mr. Stuart watched her, and when at last the exercises were over, and she with others arose to receive her Diploma, she involuntarily glanced in the direction where she knew he sat. For an instant their eyes met, and in the expression of his, she read an approval warmer than words could have expressed.

That night Mary sat alone in her room, listening almost nervously to the sound of every footstep, and half starting up if it came near her door. But for certain reasons Mr. Stuart did not think proper to call, and while Mary was confidently expecting him, he was several miles on his way home.

In a day or two Mary returned to Chicopee, but did not, like Ella, lay her books aside and consider her education finished. Two or three hours each morning were devoted to study, or reading of some kind. For several weeks nothing was allowed to interfere with this arrangement, but at the end of that time, the quiet of Mrs. Mason's house was disturbed by the unexpected arrival of Aunt Martha and Ida, who came up to Chicopee for the purpose of inducing Mrs. Mason and Mary to spend the coming winter in Boston. At first Mrs. Mason hesitated, but every objection which either she or Mary raised was so easily put aside, that she finally consented, saying she would be ready to go about the middle of November. Aunt Martha, who was a bustling, active little woman, and fancied that her brother's household always went wrong without her, soon brought her visit to a close, and within the week went back to Boston, together with Ida.

The day following their departure, Mrs. Perkins came over to inquire who "them stuck up folks was, and if the youngest wasn't some kin to the man that visited Mary's school two years before;" saying "they favored each other enough to be brother and sister."

"Why, so they do," returned Mary. "I have often tried to think who it was that Ida resembled; but they are not at all related, I presume."

Mrs. Mason said nothing, and soon changing the conversation, told Mrs. Perkins of her projected visit.

"Wall, if it don't beat all what curis' things turn up!" said the widow. "You are going to Boston, and mercy knows what'll become of me,—but laws, I ain't a goin' to worry; I shall be provided for some way."

"Why, what is the matter?" asked Mrs. Mason, noticing for the first time that her visitor seemed troubled.

After walking to the window to hide her emotions, and then again resuming her rocking chair, the widow communicated to them the startling information that Sally Ann was going to be married!

"Married! To whom?" asked Mrs. Mason and Mary in the same breath, but the widow said they must "guess;" so after guessing every marriageable man or boy in town they gave it up, and were told that it was no more nor less than Mr. Parker!

"Mr. Parker!" repeated Mary. "Why, he's old enough to be her father, ain't he?"

"Oh, no," returned Mrs. Perkins; "Sally Ann will be thirty if she lives till the first day of next January."

"You have kept the matter very quiet," said Mrs. Mason; and the widow, exacting from each a promise never to tell as long as they lived, commenced the story of her wrongs.

It seems that not long after Mrs. Parker's demise, Mr. Parker began to call at the cottage of the widow, sometime to inquire after her health, but oftener to ask about a *red heifer* which he understood Mrs. Perkins had for sale! On these occasions Sally Ann was usually invisible, so week after week Mr. Parker continued to call, talking always about the "red heifer," and whether he'd better buy her or not.

"At last," said the widow, "I got sick on't, and one day after he'd sat more'n two hours, says I, 'Ebenezer, if you want that red heifer, say so, and that'll end it.' Up he jumps, and says he, 'I'll let you know in a few days;' then pullin' from his trowsers pocket two little nurly apples, he laid 'em on the table as a present for Sally Ann! Wall, the next time he come I was sick, and Sally Ann let him in. I don't know what possessed me, but thinks to me I'll listen, and as I'm a livin' woman, instead of ever mentioning the heifer, he asked as fair and square as ever a man could, if she'd have him! and Sally Ann, scart nigh about to death, up and said 'Yes.'"

Here the widow, unable to proceed further, stopped, but soon regaining breath continued, "Nobody but them that's passed through it can guess how I felt. My head swam, and when I come to I was lyin' on the broad stair."

"Are they to be married soon?" asked Mrs. Mason, and Mrs. Perkins answered, "Of course. Was there ever an old fool of a widower who wasn't in a hurry? Next Thursday is the day sot, and I've come to invite you, and see if you'd lend me your spoons and dishes, and them little towels you use on the table, and your *astor* lamps, and some flowers if there's any fit, and let Judy come over to help about cookin' the turkey and sperrib!"

Mrs. Mason promised the loan of all these things, and then the widow arose to go. Mary, who accompanied her to the door, could not help asking whether Mr. Parker had finally bought her red heifer.

The calico sun-bonnet trembled, and the little gray eyes flashed indignantly as she said, "That man never wanted my red heifer a bit more than he wanted me!"

True to her promise, Mrs. Mason the next Thursday sent Judith over to the cottage with her "spoons, dishes, little towels, and *astor* lamp," while she herself carried over the best and fairest flowers which had escaped the frosts of autumn. Mary was chosen to dress the bride, who, spite of her red hair, would have looked quite well, had her skirt been a trifle longer and wider. Mrs. Perkins had insisted that five breadths of silk was sufficient, consequently Sally Ann looked as Sal Furbush said, "not wholly unlike a long tallow candle, with a red wick."

Mrs. Perkins, who flourished in a lace cap and scarlet ribbons, greeted her son-in-law with a burst of tears, saying she little thought when they were young that she should ever be his mother!

For the sake of peace Mr. Parker had invited Miss Grundy to be present at the wedding, but as this was the first intimation that Miss Grundy had received of the matter, she fell into a violent fit of anger, bidding him to "go to grass with his invitations," and adding very emphatically, that "she'd have him to know she never yet saw the day when she'd marry *him*, or any other living man."

Mr. Parker of course couldn't dispute her, so he turned away, wondering within himself "what made *wimmen* so queer!"

The day following the wedding, the bride went to her new home, where she was received by Miss Grundy with a grunt which was probably intended for a "how d'ye do." Uncle Peter expressed his pleasure at making the acquaintance of one more of the "fair sect," but hoped that "estimable lady her mother, wouldn't feel like visiting her often, as mothers were very apt to make mischief." Sally Furbush was the only cool and collected one present, and she did the honors of the house so gracefully and well, that but for the wildness of her eyes and an occasional whispering to herself, the bride would never have suspected her of insanity.

CHAPTER XXIII.

LIFE IN BOSTON.

"Come this way, Mary. I'll show you your chamber. It's right here next to mine," said Ida Selden, as on the evening of her friend's arrival she led her up to a handsomely furnished apartment, which for many weeks had borne the title of "Mary's room."

"Oh, how pleasant!" was Mary's exclamation, as she surveyed the room in which every thing was arranged with such perfect taste.

A cheerful coal fire was blazing in the grate, for no murderous stove was ever suffered to invade the premises where Aunt Martha ruled. The design of the Brussels carpet was exquisitely beautiful, and the roses upon it looked as if freshly plucked from the parent stalk. At one end of the room, and just opposite the grate, were two bay windows, overlooking Mr. Selden's fine, large garden, and shaded by curtains of richly embroidered lace. In front of the fire was a large easy chair, covered with crimson damask; and scattered about the room were ottomans, divans, books, pictures, and every thing which could in any way conduce to a young lady's comfort or happiness. On the marble mantel there stood two costly vases, filled with rare flowers, among which Mary recognized her favorites. But ere she had time to speak of it, Ida opened a side door, disclosing to view a cosy little bedroom, with a large closet and bathing room adjoining.

"Here," said she, "you are to sleep; but you needn't expect to be entirely exclusive, for every night when I feel cold or fidgety, I shall run in here and sleep with you. Is it a bargain?"

Mary was too happy to speak, and dropping into the easy chair she burst into tears. In a moment Ida, too, was seated in the same chair, and with her arm around Mary's neck was wondering why she wept. Then as her own eyes chanced to fall upon the vases, she brought one of them to Mary, saying, "See, these are for you,—a present from one, who bade me present them with his compliments to the little girl who nursed him on board the Windermere, and who cried because he called her ugly!"

Mary's heart was almost audible in its beatings, and her cheeks took the hue of the cushions on which she reclined. Returning the vase to the mantel-piece, Ida came back to her side, and bending closer to her face, whispered, "Cousin

George told me of you years ago when he first came here, but I forgot all about it, and when we were at Mount Holyoke, I never suspected that you were the little girl he used to talk so much about. But a few days before he went away he reminded me of it again, and then I understood why he was so much interested in you. I wonder you never told me you knew him, for of course you like him. You can't help it."

Mary only heard a part of what Ida said. "Just before he went away.—" Was he then gone, and should she not see him after all? A cloud gathered upon her brow, and Ida readily divining its cause, replied, "Yes, George is gone. Either he or father must go to New Orleans, and so George of course went. Isn't it too bad? I cried and fretted, but he only pulled my ears, and said he should think I'd be glad for he knew we wouldn't want a great six-footer domineering over us, and following us every where, as he would surely do were he at home."

Mary felt more disappointed than she was willing to acknowledge, and for a moment she half wished herself back in Chicopee, but soon recovering her equanimity, she ventured to ask how long George was to be gone.

"Until April, I believe," said Ida; "but any way you are to stay until he comes, for Aunt Martha promised to keep you. I don't know exactly what George said to her about you, but they talked together more than two hours, and she says you are to take music lessons and drawing lessons, and all that. George is very fond of music."

Here thinking she was telling too much, Ida suddenly stopped, and as the tea bell just then rang, she started up, saying, "Oh, I forgot that father was waiting in the parlor to see you. I've said so much about you that his curiosity is quite roused, but I can introduce you at the table just as well." Our lady readers will pardon Mary if before meeting Mr. Selden she gave herself a slight inspection in the long mirror, which hung in her dressing room. Passing the brush several times through her glossy hair, and smoothing down the folds of her neatly fitting merino, she concluded that she looked well enough for a traveller, and with slightly heightened color, followed Ida into the supper room, where she found assembled Mrs. Mason, Aunt Martha, and Mr. Selden. The moment her eye fell upon the latter, she recognized the same kindly beaming eye and pleasant smile, which had won her childish heart, when on board the Windermere he patted her head, as George told how kind she had been to him.

"We have met before, I believe," said he, and warmly shaking her hand he bade her welcome to Boston.

Then seating her by his side at the table he managed by his kind attentions to make both her and Mrs. Mason feel perfectly at home. Aunt Martha, too, was exceedingly polite, but after what Ida had told her, Mary could not help feeling somewhat embarrassed in her presence. This, however, gradually wore away, and before the evening was over she began to feel very much at home, and to converse with Aunt Martha as freely and familiarly as with Ida.

The next morning between ten and eleven the door bell rang, and in a moment Jenny Lincoln, whose father's house was just opposite, came tripping into the parlor. She had lost in a measure that rotundity of person so offensive to her mother, and it seemed to Mary that there was a thoughtful expression on her face never seen there before, but in all other respects, she was the same affectionate, merry-hearted Jenny.

"I just this minute heard you were here, and came over just as I was," said she, glancing at the same time at her rich, though rather untidy morning wrapper. After asking Mary if she wasn't sorry George had gone, and if she expected to find Mr. Stuart, she said, "I suppose you know Ella is here, and breaking every body's heart, of course. She went to a concert with us last evening, and looked perfectly beautiful. Henry says she is the handsomest girl he ever saw, and I do hope she'll make something of him, but I'm afraid he is only trifling with her, just as he tries to do with every body."

"I am afraid so too," said Ida, "but now Mary has come perhaps he'll divide his attentions between the two."

If there was a person in the world whom Mary thoroughly detested, it was Henry Lincoln, and the idea of his trifling with *her*, made her eyes sparkle and flash so indignantly that Ida noticed it, and secretly thought that Henry Lincoln would for once find his match. After a time Mary turned to Jenny, saying, "You haven't told me a word about,—about William Bender. Is he well?"

Jenny blushed deeply, and hastily replying that he was the last time she saw him, started up, whispering in Mary's ear, "Oh, I've got so much to tell you, —but I must go now."

Ida accompanied her to the door, and asked why Rose too did not call. In her usual frank, open way, Jenny answered, "You know why. Rose is so queer."

Ida understood her and replied, "Very well; but tell her that if she doesn't see fit to notice my visitors, I certainly shall not be polite to hers."

This message had the desired effect; for Rose, who was daily expecting a Miss King, from Philadelphia, felt that nothing would mortify her more than to be neglected by Ida, who was rather a leader among the young fashionables. Accordingly after a long consultation with her mother, she concluded it best to call upon Mary. In the course of the afternoon, chancing to be near the front window, she saw Mr. Selden's carriage drive away from his door, with Ida and her visitor.

"Now is my time," thought she; and without a word to her mother or Jenny, she threw on her bonnet and shawl, and in her thin French slippers, stepped across the street and rang Mr. Selden's door bell. Of course she was "so disappointed not to find the young ladies at home," and leaving her card for them, tripped back, highly pleased with her own cleverness.

Meantime Ida and Mary were enjoying their ride about the city, until coming suddenly upon an organ-grinder and monkey, the spirited horses became frightened and ran, upsetting the carriage, and dragging it some distance. Fortunately Ida was only bruised, but Mary received a severe cut upon her head, which, with the fright, caused her to faint. A young man, who was passing down the street and saw the accident, immediately came to the rescue; and when Mary awoke to consciousness, Billy Bender was supporting her, and gently pushing back from her face the thick braids of her long hair. At first she thought she was not much hurt, but when she attempted to lift her head she uttered a cry of pain, and laid it heavily back upon his bosom.

"Who is she?—Who is she?" asked the eager voices of the group around, but no one answered, until a young gentleman, issuing from one of the fashionable drinking saloons, came blustering up, demanding "what the row was."

Upon seeing Ida, his manner instantly changed, and after learning that she, with another young lady, had been upset, he ordered the crowd "to stand back," at the same time forcing his way forward until he caught a sight of Mary's face.

"Whew, Bill," said he, "your old flame the pauper, isn't it?"

It was fortunate for Henry Lincoln that Billy Bender's arms were both in use, otherwise he might have measured his length upon the side walk, which exercise he would hardly have relished in the presence of Ida. As it was, Billy frowned angrily upon him, and in a fierce whisper bade him beware how he used Miss Howard's name. By this time the horses were caught, anther carriage procured, and Mary, still supported by Billy Bender, was carefully lifted into it, and borne back to Mr. Selden's house. Henry Lincoln also accompanying her, and giving out numerous orders as to "what ought to be done!"

Many of Ida's friends, hearing of the accident, flocked in to see her, and to inquire after the young lady who was injured. Among the first who called was

Lizzie Upton, whom the reader has once met in Chicopee. On her way home she stopped at Mrs. Campbell's, where she was immediately beset by Ella, to know "who the beautiful young lady was that Henry Lincoln had so heroically saved from a violent death,—dragging her out from under the horses' heels!"

Lizzie looked at her a moment in surprise, and then replied, "Why, Miss Campbell, is it possible you don't know it was your own sister!"

It was Henry Lincoln himself who had given Ella her information, without, however, telling the lady's name; and now, when she learned that 'twas Mary, she was too much surprised to answer, and Lizzie continued, "I think you are laboring under a mistake. It was not Mr. Lincoln, who saved your sister's life, but a young law student, whom you perhaps have seen walking with George Moreland."

Ella replied that she never saw George Moreland, as he left Boston before she came; and then as she did not seem at all anxious to know whether Mary was much injured or not, Lizzie soon took her leave. Long after she was gone, Ella sat alone in the parlor, wondering why Henry should tell her such a falsehood, and if he really thought Mary beautiful. Poor simple Ella,—she was fast learning to live on Henry Lincoln's smile, to believe each word that he said, to watch nervously for his coming and to weep if he stayed away. There were other young men in Boston, who, attracted by her pretty face, and the wealth of which she was reputed to be heiress, came fawningly around her, but with most strange infatuation, she turned from them all, caring only for Henry Lincoln. He, on the contrary, merely sought her society for the sake of passing away an idle hour, boasting among his male acquaintances of the influence had acquired over her, by complimenting her curls and pretty face! He knew that she was jealous of any praise or attention bestowed by him upon another, and had purposely told her what he did of Mary, exulting within himself as he saw the pain his words inflicted.

"I know he was only trying to tease me," was the conclusion to which Ella finally came, and then there arose in her mind a debate as to whether, under the circumstances, it were not best to treat her sister with rather more respect than she was wont to do. "The Seldens," thought she, "are among the first. If they notice her others will, and why should not I?"

This question was at last decided in the affirmative, and towards the close of the afternoon, she started for Mr. Selden's, on her way meeting with Henry, who asked "where she was going?"

"To see that *beautiful* young lady," returned Ella, rather pettishly; whereupon Henry laughed aloud, and asked "if it were not a little the richest joke he had ever put upon her."

Ella saw no joke at all, but as Henry had turned about, and was walking back with her, she could not feel angry, and prattled on, drinking in his words of flattery, as he told her how charmingly she looked at the concert, and how jealous he felt when he saw so many admiring eyes gazing upon what he considered his own exclusive property! The very expressive look which accompanied this remark made Ella's heart beat rapidly, for Henry had never before said any thing quite so pointed, and the cloud, which for a time had rested on her brow, disappeared.

When they reached Mr. Selden's house, Henry announced his intention of calling also to inquire after Mary whom he respected on her sister's account! "But," said he, "I am in something of a hurry, and as you girls have a thousand things to talk about, I hardly think I can wait for you."

"Oh, pray, don't wait," returned Ella, hoping in her heart that he would.

Upon asking for Mary, she was taken immediately to her room, where she found her reclining upon a sofa, attired in a tasteful crimson morning gown, which gave a delicate tint to her cheeks. She was paler than usual, and her thick shining hair was combed up from her forehead in a manner highly becoming to her style of beauty. Until that day Ella had never heard her sister called handsome—never even thought such a thing possible; but now, as she looked upon her, she acknowledged to herself that Henry was more than half right, and she felt a pang of jealousy,—a fear that Mary might prove her rival. Still she tried to be agreeable, telling her how fortunate she was in being at Mr. Selden's, "for," said she, "I dare say some of our first people will notice you just because you are here!"

Ida hastily walked to the window, standing with her back towards Ella, who continued. "I think it's so funny. I've inquired and inquired about Mr. Stuart, but no one knows him, and I've come to the conclusion he was an impostor, —or a country schoolmaster, one or the other."

There was a suppressed laugh behind the lace curtain where Ida stood, and when Mary began to defend Mr. Stuart, she came out, and with great apparent interest asked who he was, and where they had seen him. Afterwards Mary remembered the mischief which shone in Ida's eyes as they described Mr. Stuart, but she thought nothing of it then.

After asking Mary who paid for her music lessons,—how many new dresses she'd got, and who cut them, Ella started to go, carelessly saying as she left the room, that when Mary was able she should expect to see her at Mrs. Campbell's.

In the mean time Henry had become so much engaged in a conversation with Mr. Selden, that he forgot the lapse of time until he heard Ella coming down the stairs. Then impelled by a mean curiosity to see what she would do, he sat still, affecting not to notice her. She heard his voice, and knew that he was still in the parlor. So for a long time she lingered at the outer door, talking very loudly to Ida, and finally, when there was no longer any excuse for tarrying, she suddenly turned back, and shaking out her cloak and tippet, exclaimed, "Why, where can my other glove be? I must have dropped it in the parlor, for I do not remember of having had it up stairs!"

The parlor was of course entered and searched, and though no missing glove was found, the company of Henry Lincoln was thus secured. Have my readers never seen a Henry Lincoln, or an Ella Campbell?

CHAPTER XXIV.

A CHANGE OF OPINION.

"Oh, mother won't you take this pillow from my head, and put another blanket on my feet, and fix the fire, and give me some water, or something? Oh, dear, dear!—" groaned poor Rose Lincoln, as with aching head and lungs, she did penance for her imprudence in crossing the wet, slippery street in thin slippers and silken hose.

Mrs. Lincoln, who knew nothing of this exposure, loudly lamented the extreme delicacy of her daughter's constitution, imputing it wholly to Mount Holyoke discipline, and wishing, as she had often done before, that "she'd been wise and kept her at home." Jenny would have wished so, too, if by this means Rose's illness could have been avoided, for it was not a very agreeable task to stay in that close sick room, listening to the complaints of her fault-finding sister, who tossed and turned and fretted, from morning until night, sometimes wishing herself dead, and then crying because she "wanted something, and didn't know what."

"Oh, dear," said she, one evening several days after the commencement of her illness, "how provoking to be obliged to lie here moping with the dullest of all dull company, when there's Mrs. Russell's party next week, and I've such a lovely dress to wear. Why ain't I as strong and healthy as you? though I wouldn't be so fat for any thing."

Jenny knew that whatever answer she could make would not be the right one, so she said nothing, and after a moment Rose again, spoke.

"I'll go to that party sick or well. I wouldn't miss of it for any thing."

This time Jenny looked up in surprise, asking why her sister was so particularly anxious to attend the party.

"Because," returned Rose, "Mary Howard will be there, and you know as well as I how awkward she'll appear,—never was in any kind of society in her life."

"I don't see what inducement that can be for you to expose your health," said Jenny, and Rose continued: "I want to see Ida mortified once, for she might know better than to bring a green, country girl here, setting her up as something wonderful, and expecting every body to believe it just because

Miss Selden said so. Didn't you tell me there was some one continually going to inquire after Mary?"

"Yes," answered Jenny; whereupon Rose got very angry, complaining that no one called upon her except that little simpleton Ella, who only came, when she thought there was a chance of seeing Henry!

"Seems to me you've changed your mind with regard to Ella," said Jenny.

"No I hain't either," answered Rose, "I always thought her silly, and now she hangs round Henry so much I'm thoroughly disgusted. But see,—there's Henry now, at Mr. Selden's gate,—with another gentleman."

The moon was shining brightly, and looking out, Jenny saw Billy Bender and her brother mounting the steps which led to Mr. Selden's door.

"It's funny that they should be together," thought she, while Rose continued, "Nothing will surprise me now, if Henry has got to running after her. I am glad George Moreland is away, though I fancy he's too much good sense to swallow a person, just because Ida and his old maid aunt say he must."

Here the conversation was interrupted by the entrance of Mr. Lincoln, who came as usual to see his daughter. In the mean time the two young men, who accidentally met at the gate, had entered Mr. Selden's parlor, and inquired for the young ladies.

"Come, you must go down," said Ida to Mary, when the message was delivered. This is the third time Mr. Bender has called, and you have no excuse for not now seeing him. "By the way," she continued, as Mary said something about 'Billy,' "don't call him Billy; we know him as *Mr.* Bender and Billy is so,—so,—"

"So countrified," suggested Mary.

"Yes, countrified if you please," returned Ida. "So after this he is *William.* Haven't you noticed that Jenny calls him so? But come," she added mischievously, "never mind brushing your hair. Mr. Stuart isn't down there!"

With the exception of the time when she was hurt, Mary had not seen William for more than two years and a half and now when she met him, she was so much embarrassed that she greeted him with a reserve, amounting almost to coldness. He on the contrary, was perfectly self-possessed, but after a few commonplace remarks, he seated himself on the opposite side of the room, and entered into conversation with Mrs. Mason concerning Chicopee and its inhabitants. Frequently Mary's eyes rested upon him, and she felt a thrill of pride when she saw how much his residence in Boston had improved him, and how handsome he really was. But any attempt to converse with him was rendered impossible by Henry Lincoln, who, toady as he was, thought proper to be exceedingly polite to Mary, now that the Seldens noticed her so much. Seating himself by her side with all the familiarity of an old friend, and laying his arm across the back of the sofa, so that to William it looked as if thrown around her shoulders, he commenced a tirade of nonsense as meaningless as it was disagreeable. More than once, too, he managed to let fall a very pointed compliment, feeling greatly surprised to see with what indifference it was received.

"Confound the girl!" thought he, beginning to feel piqued at her coldness. "Is she made of ice, or what?"

And then he redoubled his efforts at flattery, until Mary, quite disgusted, begged leave to change her seat, saying by way of apology that she was getting too warm. In the course of the evening George Moreland was mentioned. Involuntarily Mary blushed, and Henry, who was watching her proposed that she resume her former seat, "for," said he, "you look quite as warm and red where you are."

"The nearest I ever knew him come to any thing witty," whispered Ida, from behind a fire screen. "I do believe you've rubbed up his ideas, and I predict that you win him instead of Ella."

Mary did not even smile, for to her there was something revolting in the idea of being even teased about Henry, who was conceited enough to attribute her reserve to the awe which he fancied his "elegant presence" inspired! If Ella with all her wealth and beauty placed an invaluable estimate upon his attentions, why should not her unpretending sister be equally in love with him? And the young dandy stroked his mustache with his white fingers, and wondered what Ella Campbell would say if she knew how much her sister admired him, and how very nearly his admiration was returned!

At length William arose to go, and advancing towards Mary, he took her hand, saying in a low tone with marked emphasis on the word *sister*, "I find my sister greatly changed and improved since I last saw her."

"And you too are changed," returned Mary, her eyes filling with tears, for William's manner was not as of old.

"Yes, in more respects than one," said he, "but I shall see you again. Do you attend Mrs. Russell's party?"

Mary replied in the affirmative, and the next moment he was gone. Half an hour after, Henry, too, departed, saying to Mary as he went out, "You musn't fail to be at Mrs. Russell's, for I shall only go for the sake of seeing you.—

Truth, upon my honor, what little I have," he continued, as Mary's eyes flashed forth her entire disbelief of what he said. "I am in earnest now, if I never was before."

Ida laughed aloud at the mystified picture which Mary's face presented as the door closed upon Henry. "You are too much of a novice to see through every thing, but you'll learn in time that opinions frequently change with circumstances," said she.

That night in his chamber, with his heels upon the marble mantel, and his box of cigars and bottle of brandy at his side, the man of fashion soliloquized as follows: "Zounds! How that girl has improved. Never saw the like in my life.—Talk about family and rank, and all that stuff. Why, there isn't a lady in Boston that begins to have the *air distingué* which Mary Howard has. Of course she'll be all the go. Every thing the Seldens take up is. Ain't I glad Moreland is in New Orleans; for with his notions he wouldn't hesitate to marry her if he liked her, poor as she is. Now if she only had the chink, I'd walk up to her quick. I don't see why the deuce the old man need to have got so involved just now, as to make it necessary for me either to work or have a rich wife. Such eyes too, as Mary's got! Black and fiery one minute, blue and soft the next. Well, any way I'll have a good time flirting with her, just for the sake of seeing Ella wince and whimper, if nothing more. Bah! What a simpleton she is, compared with Mary. I wonder how much Mrs. Campbell *is* worth, and if Ella will have it all."

And the young man retired to dream of debts liquidated by the gold which a marriage with Ella Campbell would bring him.

———

163

CHAPTER XXV.

THE PARTY.

"Bring me my new dress, Jenny; I want to see if the Honiton lace on the caps is as wide as Ida Selden's."

"What do you mean?" asked Jenny, turning quickly towards her sister, whose white, wasted face looked fitter for a shroud than a gay party dress.

"I mean what I say," returned Rose; "I'm not going to be cooped up here any longer. I'm going to the party to-morrow night, if I never go again!"

"Why, Rose Lincoln, are you crazy?" asked Jenny. "You haven't been in the street yet, and how do you expect to go to-morrow night? Mother wouldn't let you, if she were here."

"Well, thank fortune, she and father both are in Southbridge; and besides that, I'm a great deal better; so hand me my dress."

Jenny complied, and reclining on pillows scarcely whiter than herself, Rose Lincoln examined and found fault with a thin gossamer fabric, none suited for any one to wear in a cold wintry night, and much less for her.

"There, I knew it wasn't as wide as Ida's into an eighth of an inch," said she, measuring with her finger the expensive lace. "I'll have some new. Come, Jenny, suppose you go down street and get it, for I'm bent upon going;" and the thoughtless girl sprang lightly upon the floor, and *chasséd* half way across the room to show how well and strong she was.

Jenny knew that further expostulation from her was useless, but she refused to go for the lace, and Sarah, the servant girl, was sent with a note from Rose saying she wanted a nice article, 8 or 10 dollars per yard.

"I don't believe father would like to have you make such a bill," said Jenny when Sarah was gone. "Mother didn't dare tell him about your new dress, for he told her she mustn't get any thing charged, and he said, too, something about hard times. Perhaps he's going to fail. Wouldn't it be dreadful?"

If Rose heard the last part of this sentence she did not need it, for to her the idea of her father's failing was preposterous. When the dinner bell rang she threw on a heavy shawl, and descending to the dining parlor, remained below stairs all the afternoon, forcing back her cough, and chatting merrily with a group of young girls who had called to see her, and congratulated her upon

164

her improved health, for excitement lent a deep glow to her cheek, which would easily deceive the inexperienced. The next day, owing to overexertion, Rose's temples were throbbing with pain, and more than once, she half determined not to go; but her passion for society was strong, and Mrs. Russell's party had so long been anticipated and talked about that she felt she would not miss it for the world, and as she had confessed to Jenny, there was also a mean curiosity to see how Mary Howard would appear at a fashionable party.

"Saturate my handkerchief with cologne, and put the vinaigrette where I can reach it while you arrange my hair," said she to Sarah, who at the usual hour came up to dress her young mistress for the evening. "There, be careful and not brush so hard, for that ugly pain isn't quite gone—now bring me the glass and let me see if I do look like a ghost."

"Pale, delicate folks is always more interesting than red, hearty ones," said the flattering servant, as she obeyed.

"Mercy, how white I am!" exclaimed Rose, glancing at the ashen face reflected by the mirror. "Rub my cheeks with cologne, Sarah, and see if that won't bring some color into them. There, that'll do. Now hand me my dress. Oh, isn't it beautiful?" she continued, as she threw aside the thickly wadded double gown, and assumed a light, thin dress, which fell in soft, fleecy folds around her slight figure.

"Faith, an ye looks sweet, God bless you," said Sarah as she clasped the diamond bracelet around the snowy arms and fastened the costly ornaments in the delicate ears.

When her toilet was completed, Rose stood up before the long mirror, and a glow of pride came to her cheeks, as she saw how lovely she really was.

"You's enough sight handsomer than Miss Jenny," whispered Sarah, as the door opened and Jenny appeared, more simply arrayed than her sister, but looking as fresh and blooming as a rose-bud.

"How beautiful you are, Rosa," said she, "only it makes me shiver to look at your neck and arms. You'll wear your woollen sack, besides your shawl and cloak, won't you?"

"Nonsense, I'm not going to be bundled up this way, for don't you see it musses the lace," said Rose, refusing the warm sack which Jenny brought her.

A rap at the door and a call from Henry that the carriage was waiting, ended the conversation, and throwing on their cloaks and hoods, the girls descended to the hall, where with unusual tenderness Henry caught up his invalid sister, and drawing her veil closely over her face, carried her to the covered sleigh, so that her feet might not touch the *icy walk.*

"What! Rose Lincoln here!" exclaimed half a dozen voices as Rose bounded into the dressing-room.

"Yes, Rose Lincoln *is* here," she replied, gayly divesting herself of her wrapping. "I'm not going to die just yet, I guess, neither am I going to be housed up all winter. The fresh air has done me good already,—see," and she pointed to a bright round spot which burnt upon her cheeks.

A young girl, whose family had one by one fallen victims to the great New England plague, consumption, shuddered and turned way, for to her eye the glow which Rose called health was but the hectic bloom of death.

"How beautiful she is!" said more than one, as with her accustomed grace Rose entered the brilliant drawing-room. And truly Rose was beautiful that night, but like the gorgeous foliage of the fading autumn 'twas the beauty of decay, for death was written on her blue-veined brow, and lurked amid the roses on her cheek. But little thought she of that, as with smiling lip and beaming eye she received the homage of the admiring throng.

"Upon my word, you do look very well," said Henry, coming for a moment to his sister's side. "Why, you'd be the star of the evening, were it not for *ma belle* Ella. See, there she comes," and he pointed to a group just entering the room.

An expression of contempt curled Rose's lip, as she glanced at Ella, and thought of being outshone by her dollish figure and face. "I'm in no danger, unless a more formidable rival than that silly thing appears," thought she; and she drew up her slender form with a more queenly grace, and bowed somewhat haughtily to Ella, who came up to greet her. There was a world of affection in Ella's soft hazel ayes, as they looked eagerly up to Henry, who for the sake of torturing the young girl feigned not to see her until she had stood near him some minutes. Then offering her his hand he said, with the utmost nonchalance, "Why, Ella, are you here? I was watching so anxiously for your sister that I did not notice your entrance."

Ella had dressed herself for the party with more than usual care, and as she smoothed down the folds of her delicate pink silk, and shook back her long glossy curls, she thought, "He cannot think Mary handsomer than I am to-night;" and now when the first remark he addressed to her was concerning her sister, she replied rather pettishly, "I believe you are always thinking about Mary."

"Now, don't be jealous," returned Henry, "I only wish to see the contrast between you."

166

Ella fancied that the preference would of course be in her favor, and casting aside all unpleasant feelings, she exerted herself to the utmost to keep Henry at her side, asking him numberless questions, and suddenly recollecting something which she wished to tell him, if he made a movement towards leaving her.

"Confound it. How tight she sticks to a fellow," thought he, "but I'll get away from her yet."

Just then Ida and Mary were announced. Both Aunt Martha and Ida had taken great pains to have their young friend becomingly dressed, and she looked unusually well in the embroidered muslin skirt, satin waist, and blonde bertha which Aunt Martha had insisted upon her accepting as a present. The rich silken braids of her luxuriant hair were confined at the back of her finely formed head with a golden arrow, which, with the exception of a plain band of gold on each wrist, was the only ornament she wore. This was her first introduction to the gay world, but so keen was her perception of what was polite and proper, that none would ever have suspected it and yet there was about her something so fresh and unstudied, that she had hardly entered the room ere many were struck with her easy, unaffected manners, so different from the practised airs of the city belles.

Ella watched her narrowly, whispering aside to Henry how sorry she felt for poor Mary, she was so *verdant*, and really hoping she wouldn't do any thing very awkward, for 'twould mortify her to death! "but, look," she added, "and see how many people Ida is introducing her to."

"Of course, why shouldn't she?" asked Henry; and Ella replied, "I don't know,—it seems so funny to see Mary here, don't it?"

Before Henry could answer, a young man of his acquaintance touched his shoulder, saying, "Lincoln, who is that splendid-looking girl with Miss Selden? I haven't seen a finer face in Boston, for many a day."

"That? Oh, that's Miss Howard, from Chicopee. An intimate friend of our family. Allow me the pleasure of introducing you," and Henry walked away, leaving Ella to the tender mercies of Rose, who, as one after another quitted her side, and went over to the "enemy," grew very angry, wondering if folks were bewitched, and hoping Ida Selden "felt better, now that she'd *made* so many notice her protegée."

Later in the evening, William Bender came, and immediately Jenny began to talk to him of Mary, and the impression she was making. Placing her hand familiarly upon his arm, as though that were its natural resting place, she led him towards a group, of which Mary seemed the centre of attraction. Near her stood Henry Lincoln, bending so low as to threaten serious injury to his fashionable pants, and redoubling his flattering compliments, in proportion as Mary grew colder, and more reserved in her manner towards him. Silly and conceited as he was, he could not help noticing how differently she received William Bender from what she had himself. But all in good time, thought he, glancing at Ella, to see how she was affected by his desertion of her, and his flirtation with her sister. She was standing a little apart from any one, and with her elbow resting upon a marble stand, her cheeks flushed, and her eyelashes moist with the tears she dared not shed, she was watching him with feelings in which more of real pain than jealousy was mingled; for Ella was weak and simple-hearted, and loved Henry Lincoln far better than such as he deserved to be loved.

"Of what are you thinking, Ella?" asked Rose, who finding herself nearly alone, felt willing to converse with almost any one.

At the sound of her voice Ella looked up, and coming quickly to her side, said, "It's so dull and lonesome here, I wish I'd staid at home."

In her heart Rose wished so too, but she was too proud to acknowledge it, and feeling unusually kind towards Ella, whose uneasiness she readily understood, she replied, "Oh, I see you are jealous of Henry, but he's only trying to teaze you, for he can't be interested in that awkward thing."

"But he is. I 'most *know* he is," returned Ella, with a trembling of the voice she tried in vain to subdue; and then, fearing she could not longer restrain her emotion, she suddenly broke away from Rose, and ran hastily up to the dressing-room.

Nothing of all this escaped Henry's quick eye, and as sundry unpaid bills for wine, brandy, oyster suppers, and livery, came looming up before his mind, he thought proper to make some amends for his neglect. Accordingly when Ella returned to the drawing-room, he offered her his arm, asking "what made her eyes so red," and slyly pressing her hand, when she averted her face saying, "Nothing,—they weren't red."

Meantime William Bender, having managed to drop Jenny from his arm, had asked Mary to accompany him to a small conservatory, which was separated from the reception rooms by a long and brilliantly lighted gallery. As they stood together, admiring a rare exotic, William's manner suddenly changed, and drawing Mary closer to his side, he said distinctly, though hurriedly, "I notice, Mary, that you seem embarrassed in my presence, and I have, therefore, sought this opportunity to assure you that I shall not again distress you by a declaration of love, which, if returned, would now give me more pain than pleasure, for as I told you at Mr. Selden's, I am changed in more respects than one. It cost me a bitter struggle to give you up, but reason and judgment finally conquered, and now I can calmly think of you, as some time belonging to another, and with all a brother's confidence, can tell you that I, too, love another,—not as once I loved you, for that would be impossible but with a calmer, more rational love."

All this time Mary had not spoken, though the hand which William had taken in his trembled like an imprisoned bird; but when he came to speak of loving another, she involuntarily raised his hand to her lips, exclaiming, "It's Jenny, it's Jenny."

"You have guessed rightly," returned William, smiling at the earnestness of her manner. "It is Jenny, though how such a state of things ever came about, is more than I can tell."

Mary thought of the old saying, "Love begets love," but she said nothing, for just then Jenny herself joined them. Looking first at William, then at Mary, and finally passing her arm around the latter, she whispered, "I know he's told you, and I'm glad, for somehow I couldn't tell you myself."

Wisely thinking that his company could be dispensed with, William walked away, leaving the two girls alone. In her usual frank way, Jenny rattled on, telling Mary how happy she was, and how funny it seemed to be engaged, and how frightened she was when William asked her to marry him.

Fearing that they might be missed, they at last returned to the parlor, where they found Ella seated at the piano, and playing a very spirited polka. Henry, who boasted that he "could wind her around his little finger," had succeeded in coaxing her into good humor, but not at all desiring her company for the rest of the evening, he asked her to play, as the easiest way to be rid of her. She played unusually well, but when, at the close of the piece, she looked around for commendation, from the one for whose ear alone she had played, she saw him across the room, so wholly engrossed with her sister that he probably did not even know when the sound of the piano ceased.

Poor Ella; it was with the saddest heartache she had ever known that she returned from a party which had promised her so much pleasure, and which had given her so much pain. Rose, too, was bitterly disappointed. One by one her old admirers had left her for the society of the "pauper," as she secretly styled Mary, and more than once during the evening had she heard the "beauty" and "grace" of her rival extolled by those for whose opinion she cared the most; and when, at one o'clock in the morning, she threw herself exhausted upon the sofa, she declared "'twas the last party she'd ever attend."

Alas, for thee, Rosa, that declaration proved too true!

CHAPTER XXVI.

MAKING UP HIS MIND.

For more than an hour there had been unbroken silence in the dingy old law office of Mr. Worthington, where Henry Lincoln and William Bender still remained, the one as a practising lawyer and junior partner of the firm, and the other as a student still, for he had not yet dared to offer himself for examination. Study was something which Henry particularly disliked; and as his mother had trained him with the idea, that labor for him was wholly unnecessary, he had never bestowed a thought on the future, or made an exertion of any kind.

Now, however, a different phase of affairs was appearing. His father's fortune was threatened with ruin; and as, on a morning several weeks subsequent to Mrs. Russell's party, he sat in the office with his heels upon the window sill, and his arms folded over his head, he debated the all-important question, whether it were better to marry Ella Campbell, for the money which would save him from poverty, or to rouse himself to action for the sake of Mary Howard, whom he really fancied he loved!

Frequently since the party had he met her, each time becoming more and more convinced of her superiority over the other young ladies of his acquaintance. He was undoubtedly greatly assisted in this decision by the manner with which she was received by the fashionables of Boston, but aside from that, as far as he was capable of doing so, he liked her, and was now making up his mind whether to tell her so or not.

At last, breaking the silence, he exclaimed, "Hang me if I don't believe she's bewitched me, or else I'm in love.—Bender, how does a chap feel when he's in love?"

"Very foolish, judging from yourself," returned William; and Henry replied, "I hope you mean nothing personal, for I'm bound to avenge my honor, and t'would be a deuced scrape for you and me to fight about 'your sister,' as you call her, for 'tis she who has inspired me, or made a fool of me, one or the other."

"You've changed your mind, haven't you?" asked William, a little sarcastically.

"Hanged if I have," said Henry. "I was interested in her years ago, when she was the ugliest little vixen a man ever looked upon, and that's why I teazed her so,—I don't believe she's handsome now, but she's something, and that something has raised the mischief with me. Come, Bender, you are better acquainted with her than I am, so tell me honestly if you think I'd better marry her."

The expression of William's face was a sufficient answer, and with something of his old insolence, Henry continued, "You needn't feel jealous, for I tell you Mary Howard looks higher than you. Why, she'd wear the crown of England, as a matter of course, any day."

With a haughty frown, William replied, "You have my permission, sir, to propose as soon as you please. I rather wish you would," then taking his hat, he left the office, while Henry continued his soliloquy, as follows:—"I wonder what the old folks would say to a penniless bride. Wouldn't mother and Rose raise a row? I'd soon quiet the old woman, though, by threatening to tell that she was once a factory girl,—yes, a factory girl. But if dad smashes up I'll have to work, for I haven't brains enough to earn my living by my wit. I guess on the whole, I'll go and call on Ella, she's handsome, and besides that, has the rhino too, but, Lord, how shallow!" and the young man broke the blade of his knife as he struck it into the hard wood table, by way of emphasizing his last words.

Ella chanced to be out, and as Henry was returning, he overtook Ida Selden and Mary Howard, who were taking their accustomed walk. Since her conversation with William a weight seemed lifted from Mary's spirits, and she now was happier far than she ever remembered of having been before. She was a general favorite in Boston, where all of her acquaintances vied with each other in making her stay among them as agreeable as possible. Her facilities for improvement, too, were great, and what was better than all the rest, George Moreland was to return much sooner than he at first intended. While she was so happy herself, Mary could not find it in her heart to be uncourteous to Henry, and her manner towards him that morning was so kind and affable that it completely upset him; and when he parted with her at Mr. Selden's gate, his mind was quite made up to offer her his heart and hand.

"I shall have to work," thought he, as he entered his room to decide upon the best means by which to make his intentions known. "I shall have to work, I know, but for her sake I'd do any thing."

There was a bottle of Madeira standing upon the table and as he announced his determination of "doing any thing for the sake of Mary Howard," his eye fell upon his favorite beverage. A deep blush mounted to his brow, and a fierce struggle between his love for Mary and his love for the wine-cup ensued. The former conquered, and seizing the bottle he hurled it against the marble fire jamb, exclaiming, "I'll be a *man*, a sober man, and never shall the light of Mary's eyes grow dim with tears wept for a drunken husband!"

Henry was growing eloquent, and lest the inspiration should leave him, he sat down and wrote to Mary, on paper what he could not tell her face to face. Had there been a lingering doubt of her acceptance, he would undoubtedly have wasted at least a dozen sheets of the tiny gilt-edged paper, but as it was, one would suffice, for *she* would not scrutinize his handwriting,—*she* would not count the blots, or mark the omission of punctuating pauses. She would almost say *yes* before she read it. So the letter, which contained a sincere apology for his uncivil treatment of her in former years, and an ardent declaration of love for her now, was written sealed, and directed, and then there was a gentle rap upon the door. Jenny wished to come in for a book which was lying upon the table.

Henry had resolved to keep his family ignorant of his intentions, but at the sight of Jenny he changed his mind,—Jenny loved Mary, too. Jenny would be delighted at the prospect of having her for a sister, and would help him brave the storm of his mother's displeasure.

"Jenny," said he, grasping at her dress, as she passed him on her way from the room, "Jenny, sit down here. I want to tell you something." Jenny glanced at the fragments of the wine bottle, then at her brother's flushed face, and instantly conjecturing that he had been drinking, said reproachfully, as she laid her soft, white hand on his brow "Oh, brother, brother!"

He understood her meaning, and drawing her so closely to him that his warm breath floated over her cheek, replied, "I'm not drunk, for see, there is no scent of alcohol in my breath, for I have sworn to reform,—sworn that no drop of ardent spirits shall ever again pass my lips."

The sudden exclamation of joy, the arms thrown so affectionately around his neck, the hot tears upon her cheek, and the kisses that warm-hearted sister imprinted upon his lips should have helped him to ratify that vow. But not for her sake had it been made, and shaking her off, he said, "Don't make a fool of yourself, Jenny, I wasn't in any danger of disgracing you, for I was only a moderate drinker. But really, I do want to talk with you on a very important subject. I want to ask who of all your acquaintances you would prefer to have for a sister, for I am going to be married."

"To Ella?" asked Jenny, and Henry replied scornfully, "No, ma'am! my wife must have a soul, a heart, and a mind, to make up for my deficiency on those points. To be plain, how would you like to have me marry Mary Howard?"

"Not at all—Not at all," was Jenny's quick reply, while her brother said angrily, "And why not? Are you, too, proud as Lucifer, like the rest of us? I could tell you something, Miss, that would bring your pride down a peg or two. But answer me, why are you unwilling for me to marry Mary?"

Jenny's spirit was roused too, and looking her brother fully in his face, she unhesitatingly replied, "You are not worthy of her; neither would she have you."

"And this from my own sister?" said Henry, hardly able to control his wrath. "Leave the room, instantly,—But stay," he added, "and let me hear the reasons for what you have asserted."

"You know as well as I," answered Jenny, "that one as pure and gentle as Mary Howard, should never be associated with you, who would trample upon a woman's better nature and feelings, for the sake of gratifying your own wishes. Whenever it suits your purpose, you flatter and caress Ella Campbell, to whom your slightest wish is a law, and then when your mood changes, you treat her with neglect; and think you, that knowing all this, Mary Howard would look favorably upon you, even if there were no stronger reason why she should refuse you?"

"If you mean the brandy bottle," said Henry, growing more and more excited, "have I not sworn to quit it, and is it for you to goad me on to madness, until I break that vow?"

"Forgive me if I have been too harsh," said Jenny, taking Henry's hand. "You are my brother, and Mary my dearest friend, and when I say I would not see her wedded to you, 'tis not because I love you less, but her the more. You are wholly unlike, and would not be happy together. But oh, if her love would win you back to virtue, I would almost beg her, on my bended knees, not to turn away from you."

"And I tell you her love *can* win me back, when nothing else in the kingdom will," said Henry, snatching up the note and hurrying away.

For a time after he left the room, Jenny sat in a kind of stupefied maze. That Mary would refuse her brother, she was certain, and she trembled for the effect that refusal would produce upon him. Other thoughts, too, crowded upon the young girl's mind, and made her tears flow fast. Henry had hinted of something which he could tell her if he would, and her heart too well foreboded what that something was. The heavy sound of her father's footsteps, which sometimes kept her awake the livelong night, his pale haggard face in the morning, and her mother's nervous, anxious manner, told her that ruin was hanging over them.

In the midst of her reverie, Henry returned. He had delivered the letter, and now, restless and unquiet, he sat down to await its answer. It came at last,— his rejection, yet couched in language so kind and conciliatory, that he could not feel angry. Twice,—three times he read it over, hoping to find some intimation that possibly she might relent; but no, it was firm and decided, and while she thanked him for the honor he conferred upon her, she respectfully declined accepting it, assuring him that his secret should be kept inviolate.

"There's some comfort in that," thought he, "for I wouldn't like to have it known that I had been refused by a poor unknown girl," and then, as the conviction came over him that she would never he his, he laid his head upon the table, and wept such tears as a spoiled child might weep when refused a toy, too costly and delicate to be trusted in its rude grasp.

Erelong, there was another knock at the door, and, hastily wiping away all traces of his emotion, Henry admitted his father, who had come to talk of their future prospects, which were even worse than he had feared. But he did not reproach his wayward son, nor hint that his reckless extravagance had hastened the calamity which otherwise might possibly have been avoided. Calmly he stated the extent to which they were involved, adding that though an entire failure might be prevented a short time, it would come at last; and that an honorable payment of his debts would leave them beggars.

"For myself I do not care," said the wretched man, pressing hard his aching temples, where the gray hairs had thickened within a few short weeks. "For myself I do not care but for my wife and children,—for Rose, and that she must miss her accustomed comforts, is the keenest pang of all."

All this time, Henry had not spoken, but thought was busily at work. He could not bestir himself; he had no energy for that now; but he could marry Ella Campbell, whose wealth would keep him in the position he now occupied, besides supplying many of Rose's wants.

Cursing the fate which had reduced him to such an extremity, towards the dusk of evening, Henry started again for Mrs. Campbell's. Lights were burning in the parlor and as the curtains were drawn back, he could see through the partially opened shutter, that Ella was alone. Reclining in a large sofa chair, she sat, leaning upon her elbow, the soft curls of her brown hair falling over her white arm, which the full blue cashmere sleeve exposed to view. She seemed deeply engaged in thought, and never before had she looked so lovely to Henry, who, as he gazed upon her, felt a glow of pride, in thinking that fair young girl could be his for the asking.

"I wish she was not so confounded flat," thought he, hastily ringing the door-bell.

Instantly divining who it was, Ella sprang up, and when Henry entered the

175

parlor, he found her standing in the centre of the room, where the full blaze of the chandelier fell upon her childish features, lighting them up with radiant beauty.

"And so my little pet is alone," said he, coming forward, and raising to his lips the dainty fingers which Ella extended towards him. "I hope the old aunty is out," he continued, "for I want to see you on special business."

Ella noticed how excited he appeared, and always on the alert for something when he was with her, she began to tremble, and without knowing what she said, asked him "what he wanted of her?"

"Zounds!" thought Henry, "she meets me more than half-way;" and then, lest his resolution should fail, he reseated her in the chair she had left, and drawing an ottoman to her side, hastily told her of his love, ending his declaration, by saying that from the first time he ever saw her, he had determined that she should be his wife! And Ella, wholly deceived, allowed her head to droop upon his shoulder, while she whispered to him her answer. Thus they were betrothed,—Henry Lincoln and Ella Campbell.

"Glad am I to be out of that atmosphere," thought the newly engaged young man, as he reached the open air, and began to breathe more freely. "Goodness me, won't I lead a glorious life, with that jar of tomato sweetmeats! Now, if she'd only hung back a little,—but no, she said yes before I fairly got the words out; but money covereth a multitude of sins,—I beg your pardon, ma'am," said he quickly, as he became conscious of having rudely jostled a young lady, who was turning the corner.

Looking up, he met Mary Howard's large, dark eyes fixed rather inquiringly upon him. She was accompanied by one of Mr. Selden's servants, and he felt sure she was going to visit her sister. Of course, Ella would tell her all, and what must Mary think of one who could so soon repeat his vows of love to another? In all the world there was not an individual for whose good opinion Henry Lincoln cared one half so much as for Mary Howard's; and the thought that he should now surely lose it maddened him. The resolution of the morning was forgotten, and that night a fond father watched and wept over his inebriate son, for never before had Henry Lincoln been so beastly intoxicated.

CHAPTER XXVII.

THE SHADOWS DEEPEN.

From one of the luxuriously furnished chambers of her father's elegant mansion, Jenny Lincoln looked mournfully out upon the thick angry clouds, which, the livelong day, had obscured the winter sky. Dreamily for a while she listened to the patter of the rain as it fell upon the deserted pavement below, and then, with a long, deep sigh, she turned away and wept. Poor Jenny!—the day was rainy, and dark, and dreary, but darker far were the shadows stealing over her pathway. Turn which way she would, there was not one ray of sunshine, which even her buoyant spirits could gather from the surrounding gloom. Her only sister was slowly, but surely dying, and when Jenny thought of this she felt that if Rose could only live, she'd try and bear the rest; try to forget how much she loved William Bender, who that morning had honorably and manfully asked her of her parents, and been spurned with contempt,—not by her father, for could he have followed the dictates of his better judgment, he would willingly have given his daughter to the care of one who he knew would carefully shield her from the storms of life. It was not he, but the cold, proud mother, who so haughtily refused William's request, accusing him of taking underhanded means to win her daughter's affections.

"I had rather see you dead!" said the stony-hearted woman, when Jenny knelt at her feet, and pleaded for her to take back the words she had spoken —"I had rather see you dead, than married to such as *he*. I mean what I have said, and you will never be his."

Jenny knew William too well to think he would ever sanction an act of disobedience to her mother, and her heart grew faint, and her eyes dim with tears, as she thought of conquering the love which had grown with her growth, and strengthened with her strength. There was another reason, too, why Jenny should weep as she sat there alone in her room. From her father she had heard of all that was to happen. The luxuries to which all her life she had been accustomed, were to be hers no longer. The pleasant country house in Chicopee, dearer far than her city home, must be sold, and nowhere in the wide world, was there a place for them to rest.

It was of all this that Jenny was thinking that dreary afternoon; and when at last she turned away from the window, her thoughts went back again to her sister, and she murmured, "If *she* could only live."

But it could not be;—the fiat had gone forth, and Rose, like the fair summer flower whose name she bore, must fade and pass away. For several days after Mrs. Russell's party she tried to keep up, but the laws of nature had been outraged, and now she lay all day in a darkened room, moaning with pain, and wondering why the faces of those around her were so sad and mournful.

"Jenny," said she one day when the physician, as usual, had left the room without a word of encouragement—"Jenny, what does make you look so blue and forlorn. I hope you don't fancy I'm going to die? Of course I'm not."

Here a coughing fit ensued, and after it was over, she continued, "Isn't George Moreland expected soon?"

Jenny nodded, and Rose proceeded, "I must, and *will* be well before he comes, for 'twill never do to yield the field to that Howard girl, who they say is contriving every way to get him,—coaxing round old Aunt Martha, and all that. But how ridiculous! George Moreland, with his fastidious, taste, marry a pauper!" and the sick girl's fading cheek glowed, and her eyes grew brighter at the absurd idea!

Just then Mr. Lincoln entered the room. He had been consulting with his wife the propriety of taking Rose to her grandmother's in the country. She would thus be saved the knowledge of his failure, which could not much longer be kept a secret; and besides that, they all, sooner or later, must leave the house in which they were living; and he judged it best to remove his daughter while she was able to endure the journey. At first Mrs. Lincoln wept bitterly for if Rose went to Glenwood, she, too, must of course go and the old brown house, with its oaken floor and wainscoted ceiling, had now no charms for the gay woman of fashion who turned with disdain from the humble roof which had sheltered her childhood.

Lifting her tearful eyes to her husband's face, she said "Oh, I can't go there. Why not engage rooms at the hotel in Glenwood village. Mother is so odd and peculiar in her ways of living, that I never can endure it," and again Mrs. Lincoln buried her face in the folds of her fine linen cambric, thinking there was never in the world a woman as wretched as herself.

"Don't, Hatty, don't; it distresses me to see you feel thus. Rooms and board at the hotel would cost far more than I can afford to pay, and then, too,—" here he paused, as if to gather courage for what he was next to say; "and then, too, your mother will care for Rose's *soul* as well as body."

Mrs. Lincoln looked up quickly, and her husband continued, "Yes, Hatty, we need not deceive ourselves longer. Rose must die, and you know as well as I whether our training has been such as will best fit her for another world."

For a time Mrs. Lincoln was silent, and then in a more subdued tone, she said, "Do as you like, only you must tell Rose. *I* never can."

Half an hour after, Mr. Lincoln entered his daughter's room, and bending affectionately over her pillow, said, "How is my darling to-day?"

"Better, better,—almost well," returned Rose, raising herself in bed to prove what she had said. "I shall be out in a few days, and then you'll buy me one of those elegant plaid silks, won't you? All the girls are wearing them, and I haven't had a new dress this winter, and here 'tis almost March."

Oh, how the father longed to tell his dying child that her next dress would be a shroud. But he could not. He was too much a man of the world to speak to her of death,—he would leave that for her grandmother; so without answering her question, he said, "Rose, do you think you are able to be moved into the country?"

"What, to Chicopee? that horrid dull place! I thought we were not going there this summer."

"No, not to Chicopee, but to your grandma Howland's, in Glenwood. The physician thinks you will be more quiet there, and the pure air will do you good."

Rose looked earnestly in her father's face to see if he meant what he said, and then replied, "I'd rather go any where in the world than to Glenwood. You've no idea how, I hate to stay there. Grandma is so queer, and the things in the house so fussy and countrified,—and cooks by a *fireplace*, and washes in a tin basin, and wipes on a crash towel that hangs on a roller!"

Mr. Lincoln could hardly repress a smile at Rose's reasoning, but perceiving that he must be decided, he said, "We think it best for you to go, and shall accordingly make arrangements to take you in the course of a week or two. Your mother will stay with you, and Jenny, too, will be there a part of the time;" then, not wishing to witness the effect of his words, he hastily left the room, pausing in the hall to wipe away the tears which involuntarily came to his eyes, as he overheard Rose angrily wonder, "why she should be turned out of doors when she wasn't able to sit up!"

"I never can bear the scent of those great tallow candles, never," said she; "and then to think of the coarse sheets and patchwork bedquilts—oh, it's dreadful!"

Jenny's heart, too, was well-nigh bursting, but she forced down her own sorrow, while she strove to comfort her sister, telling her how strong and well the bracing air of the country would make her, and how refreshing when her fever was on would be the clear, cold water which gushed from the spring near the thorn-apple tree, where in childhood they so oft had played. Then she spoke of the miniature waterfall, which not far from their grandmother's door, made "fairy-like music;" all the day long, and at last, as if soothed by the sound of that far-off falling water, Rose forgot her trouble, and sank into a sweet, refreshing slumber, in which she dreamed that the joyous summer-time had come, and that she, well and strong as Jenny had predicted, was the happy bride of George Moreland, who led her to a grass-grown grave,—the grave of Mary Howard, who had died of consumption and been buried in Glenwood!

While Rose was sleeping, Jenny stole softly down the stairs, and throwing on her shawl and bonnet, went across the street, to confide her troubles with Mary Howard; who, while she sympathized deeply with her young friend, was not surprised, for, from her slight acquaintance with Mrs Lincoln, she could readily believe that one so ambitious and haughty, would seek for her daughter a wealthier alliance than a poor lawyer. All that she could say to comfort Jenny she did, bidding her to wait patiently, and hope for the best.

"You are blue and dispirited," said she, "and a little fresh air will do you good. Suppose we walk round a square or two; for see, the rain is over now."

Jenny consented, and they had hardly gone half the length of a street when William himself joined them. Rightly guessing that her absence would not be noticed, Mary turned suddenly into a side street, leaving William and Jenny to themselves. From that walk Jenny returned to her home much happier than she left it. She had seen William,—had talked with him of the past, present, and future,—had caught from his hopeful spirit the belief that all would be well in time, and in a far more cheerful frame of mind, she re-entered her sister's room; and when Rose, who was awake, and noticed the change in her appearance, asked what had happened, she could not forbear telling her.

Rose heard her through, and then very kindly informed her that "she was a fool to care for such a rough-scuff."

In a few days, preparations were commenced for moving Rose to Glenwood, and in the excitement of getting ready, she in a measure forgot the tallow candles and patchwork bedquilt, the thoughts of which had so much shocked her at first.

"Put in my embroidered merino morning gown," said she to Jenny, who was packing her trunk, "and the blue cashmere one faced with white satin; and don't forget my best cambric skirt, the one with so much work on it, for when George Moreland comes to Glenwood I shall want to look as well as possible; and then, too, I like to see the country folks open their mouths, and stare at city fashions.'

"What makes you think George will come to Glenwood?" asked Jenny, as she packed away dresses her sister would never wear.

"I know, and that's enough," answered Rose; "and now, before you forget it, put in my leghorn flat, for if I stay long, I shall want it; and see how nicely you can fold the dress I wore at Mrs. Russell's party!"

"Why, Rose, what can you possibly want of that?" asked Jenny, and Rose replied, "Oh, I want to show it to grandma, just to hear her groan over our extravagance, and predict that we'll yet come to ruin!"

Jenny thought that if Rose could have seen her father that morning, when the bill for the dress and its costly trimmings was presented, she would have wished it removed for ever from her sight. Early in the winter Mr. Lincoln had seen that all such matters were settled, and of this bill, more recently made, he knew nothing.

"I can't pay it now," said he promptly to the boy who brought it. "Tell Mr. Holton I will see him in a day or two."

The boy took the paper with an insolent grin, for he had heard the fast circulating rumor, "that one of the *big bugs* was about to smash up;" and now, eager to confirm the report, he ran swiftly back to his employer, who muttered, "Just as I expected. I'll draw on him for what I lent him, and that'll tell the story. My daughters can't afford to wear such things, and I'm not going to furnish money for his."

Of all this Rose did not dream, for in her estimation there was no end to her father's wealth, and the possibility of his failing had never entered her mind. Henry indeed had once hinted it to her on the occasion of her asking him "how he could fancy Ella Campbell enough to marry her."

"I'm not marrying *her*, but her *money*" was his prompt answer; "and I assure you, young lady, we are more in need of that article than you imagine."

Rose paid no attention to this speech, and when she found that her favorite Sarah was not to accompany her, she almost wept herself into convulsions, declaring that her father, to whom the mother imputed the blame, was cruel and hard-hearted, and that if it was Jenny instead of herself who was sick, she guessed "she'd have forty waiting-maids if she wanted them."

"I should like to know who is to take care of me?" said she. "Jenny isn't going, and grandma would think it an unpardonable extravagance to hire a servant. I will not go, and that ends it! If you want to be rid of me, I can die fast enough here."

Mrs. Lincoln had nothing to say, for she well knew she had trained her daughter to despise every thing pertaining to the old brown house, once her childhood home, and where even now the kind-hearted grandmother was busy in preparing for the reception of the invalid. From morning until night did the little active form of Grandma Howland flit from room to room, washing windows which needed no washing, dusting tables on which no dust was lying, and doing a thousand things which she thought would add to the comfort of Rose. On one room in particular did the good old lady bestow more than usual care. 'Twas the "spare chamber," at whose windows Rose, when a little girl, had stood for hours, watching the thin, blue mist and fleecy clouds, as they floated around the tall green mountains, which at no great distance seemed to tower upward, and upward, until their tops were lost in the sky above. At the foot of the mountain and nearer Glenwood, was a small sheet of water which now in the spring time was plainly discernible from the windows of Rose's chamber, and with careful forethought Mrs. Howland arranged the bed so that the sick girl could look out upon the tiny lake and the mountains beyond. Snowy white, and fragrant with the leaves of rose and geranium which had been pressed within their folds, were the sheets which covered the bed, the last Rose Lincoln would ever rest upon. Soft and downy were the pillows, and the patchwork quilt, Rose's particular aversion, was removed, and its place supplied by one of more modern make.

Once Mrs. Howland thought to shade the windows with the Venetian blinds which hung in the parlor below; but they shut out so much sunlight, and made the room so gloomy, that she carried them back, substituting in their place plain white muslin curtains. The best rocking chair, and the old-fashioned carved mirror, were brought up from the parlor; and then when all was done, Mrs. Howland gave a sigh of satisfaction that it was so well done, and closed the room until Rose should arrive.

CHAPTER XXVIII.

GLENWOOD.

Through the rich crimson curtains which shaded Rose Lincoln's sleeping room, the golden beams of a warm March sun wore stealing, lighting up the thin features of the sick girl with a glow so nearly resembling health, that Jenny, when she came to wish her sister good morning, started with surprise at seeing her look so well.

"Why, Rose, you are better," said she, kissing the fair cheek on which the ray of sunlight was resting.

Rose had just awoke from her deep morning slumber, and now remembering that this was the day appointed for her dreaded journey to Glenwood, she burst into tears, wondering "why they would persist in dragging her from home."

"It's only a pretence to get me away, I know," said she, "and you may as well confess it at once. You are tired of waiting upon me."

Mr. Lincoln now came in to see his daughter, but all his attempts to soothe her were in vain. She only replied, "Let me stay at home, here in this room, my own room;" adding more in anger than sorrow, "I'll try to die as soon as I can; and be out of the way, if that's what you want!"

"Oh, Rose, Rose! poor father don't deserve that," said Jenny, raising her hand as if to stay her sister's thoughtless words while Mr Lincoln, laying his face upon the pillow so that his silvered locks mingled with the dark tresses of his child, wept bitterly,—bitterly.

And still he could not tell her *why* she must leave her home. He would rather bear her unjust reproaches, than have her know that they were beggars; for a sudden shock the physician said, might at any time end her life. Thoroughly selfish as she was, Rose still loved her father dearly, and when she saw him thus moved, and knew that she was the cause, she repented of her hasty words, and laying her long white arm across his neck, asked forgiveness for what she had said.

"I will go to Glenwood," said she; "but must I stay there long?"

"Not long, not long, my child," was the father's reply, and Jenny brushed away a tear as she too thought, "not long."

And so, with the belief that her stay was to be short, Rose passively suffered them to dress her for the journey, which was to be performed partly by railway and partly in a carriage. For the first time since the night of his engagement with Ella Campbell, Henry was this morning free from intoxicating drinks. He had heard them say that Rose must die, but it had seemed to him like an unpleasant dream, from which he now awoke to find it a reality. They had brought her down from her chamber, and laid her upon the sofa in the parlor, where Henry came unexpectedly upon her. He had not seen her for several days, and when he found her lying there so pale and still, her long eyelashes resting heavily upon her colorless cheek, and her small white hands hanging listlessly by her side, he softly approached her thinking her asleep, kissed her brow, cheek and lips, whispering as he did so, "Poor girl! poor Rosa! so young and beautiful."

Rose started, and wiping from her forehead the tear her brother had left there, she looked anxiously around. Henry was gone, but his words had awakened in her mind a new and startling idea. Was she going to die? Did they think so, and was this the reason of Henry's unwonted tenderness? and sinking back upon her pillows, she wept as only those weep to whom, in the full flush of youth and beauty, death comes a dreaded and unwelcome guest.

"I cannot die,—I will not die," said she at last, rousing herself with sudden energy; "I feel that within me which says I shall not die. The air of Glenwood will do me good, and grandma's skill in nursing is wonderful."

Consoled by these reflections, she became more calm, and had her father now given his consent for her to remain in Boston, she would of her own accord have gone to Glenwood.

The morning train bound for Albany stood in the depot, waiting the signal to start; and just before the final "all aboard" was sounded, a handsome equipage drove slowly up, and from it alighted Mr. Lincoln, bearing in his arms his daughter, whose head rested wearily upon his shoulder. Accompanying him were his wife, Jenny, and a gray-haired man, the family physician. Together they entered the rear car, and instantly there was a hasty turning of heads, a shaking of curls, and low whispers, as each noticed and commented upon the unearthly beauty of Rose, who in her father's arms, lay as if wholly exhausted with the effort she had made.

The sight of her, so young, so fair, and apparently so low, hushed all selfish feelings, and a gay bridal party who had taken possession of the ladies' saloon, immediately came forward, offering it to Mr. Lincoln, who readily accepted it, and laying Rose upon the long settee, he made her as comfortable as possible with the numerous pillows and cushions he had brought with him. As the creaking engine moved slowly out of Boston, Rose asked that the window might be raised, and leaning upon her elbow, she looked out upon her native city, which she was leaving for ever. Some such idea came to her mind; but quickly repressing it, she turned towards her father, saying with a smile, "I shall be better when I see Boston again."

Mr. Lincoln turned away to hide a tear, for he had no hope that she would ever return. Towards nightfall of the next day they reached Glenwood, and Rose, more fatigued than she was willing to acknowledge, now that she was so determined to get well, was lifted from the carriage and carried into the house. Mrs. Howland hastened forward to receive her, and for once Rose forgot to notice whether the cut of her cap was of this year's fashion or last.

"I am weary," she said. "Lay me where I can rest." And with the grandmother leading the way, the father carried his child to the chamber prepared for her with so much care.

"It's worse than I thought 'twas," said Mrs. Howland, returning to the parlor below, where her daughter, after looking in vain for the big rocking-chair, had thrown herself with a sigh upon the chintz-covered lounge. "It's a deal worse than I thought 'twas. Hasn't she catched cold, or been exposed some way?"

"Not in the least," returned Mrs. Lincoln, twirling the golden stopper of her smelling bottle. "The foundation of her sickness was laid at Mount Holyoke, and the whole faculty ought to be indicted for manslaughter."

Jenny's clear, truthful eyes turned towards her mother, who frowned darkly, and continued: "She was as well as any one until she went there, and I consider it my duty to warn all parents against sending their daughters to a place where neither health, manners, nor any thing else is attended to, except religion and housework."

Jenny had not quite got over her childish habit of occasionally setting her mother right on some points, and she could not forbear saying that Dr. Kleber thought Rose injured herself by attending Mrs. Russell's party.

"Dr. Kleber doesn't know any more about it than I do," returned her mother. "He's always minding other folks' business, and so are you. I guess you'd better go up stairs, and see if Rose doesn't want something."

Jenny obeyed, and as she entered her sister's chamber, Rose lifted her head languidly from her pillow, and pointing to a window, which had been opened that she might breathe more freely, said, "Just listen; don't you hear that horrid croaking?"

Jenny laughed aloud, for she knew Rose had heard "that horrid croaking" move than a hundred times in Chicopee, but in Glenwood every thing must necessarily assume a goblin form and sound. Seating herself upon the foot of the bed, she said, "Why, that's the frogs. I love to hear them dearly. It makes me feel both sad and happy, just as the crickets do that sing under the hearth in our old home at Chicopee."

Jenny's whole heart was in the country, and she could not so well sympathize with her nervous, sensitive sister, who shrank from country sights and country sounds. Accidentally spying some tall locust branches swinging in the evening breeze before the east window, she again spoke to Jenny, telling her to look and see if the tree leaned against the house, "for if it does," said she, "and creaks I shan't sleep a wink to-night."

After assuring her that the tree was all right, Jenny added, "I love to hear the wind howl through these old trees, and were it not for you, I should wish it might blow so that I could lie awake and hear it."

When it grew darker, and the stars began to come out. Jenny was told "to close the shutters."

"Now, Rose," said she, "you are making half of this, for you know as well as I, that grandma's house hasn't got any shutters."

"Oh, mercy, no more it hasn't. What *shall* I do?" said Rose, half crying with vexation. "That coarse muslin stuff is worse than nothing, and everybody'll be looking in to see me."

"They'll have to climb to the top of the trees, then," said Jenny, "for the ground descends in every direction, and the road, too, is so far away. Besides that, who is there that wants to see you?"

Rose didn't know. She was sure there was somebody, and when Mrs. Howland came up with one of the nicest little suppers on a small tea-tray, how was she shocked to find the window covered with her best blankets, which were safely packed away in the closet adjoining.

"Rose was afraid somebody would look in and see her," said Jenny, as she read her grandmother's astonishment in her face.

"Look in and see her!" repeated Mrs. Howland. "I've undressed without curtains there forty years, and I'll be bound nobody ever peeked at me. But come," she added, "set up, and see if you can't eat a mouthful or so. Here's some broiled chicken, a slice of toast, some currant jelly that I made myself, and the swimminest cup of black tea you ever see. It'll eenamost bear up an egg."

"Sweetened with brown sugar, ain't it?" said Rose sipping a little of the tea.

In great distress the good old lady replied that she was out of white sugar, but some folks loved brown just as well.

"Ugh! Take it away," said Rose. "It makes me sick and I don't believe I can eat another mite," but in spite of her belief the food rapidly disappeared, while she alternately made fun of the little silver spoons, her grandmother's bridal gift, and found fault because the jelly was not put up in porcelain jars, instead of the old blue earthen tea-cup, tied over with a piece of paper!

Until a late hour that night, did Rose keep the whole household (her mother excepted) on the alert, doing the thousand useless things which her nervous fancy prompted. First the front door, usually secured with a bit of whittled shingle, must be *nailed*, "or somebody would break in." Next, the windows, which in the rising wind began to rattle, must be made fast with divers knives, scissors, combs and keys; and lastly, the old clock must be stopped, for Rose was not accustomed to its striking, and it would keep her awake.

"Dear me!" said the tired old grandmother, when, at about midnight, she repaired to her own cosy little bedroom, "how fidgety she is. I should of s'posed that livin' in the city so, she'd got used to noises."

In a day or two Mr. Lincoln and Jenny went back to Boston, bearing with them a long list of articles which Rose must and would have. As they were leaving the house Mrs Howland brought out her black leathern wallet, and forcing two ten dollar bills into Jenny's hand, whispered, "Take it to pay for them things. Your pa has need enough for his money, and this is some I've earned along, knitting, and selling butter. At first I thought I would get a new chamber carpet, but the old one answers my turn very well, so take it and buy Rose every thing she wants."

And all this time the thankless girl up stairs was fretting and muttering about her grandmother's *stinginess*, in not having a better carpet "than the old faded thing which looked as if manufactured before the flood!"

CHAPTER XXIX.

A NEW DISCOVERY.

On the same day when Rose Lincoln left Boston for Glenwood, Mrs. Campbell sat in her own room, gloomy and depressed. For several days she had not been well, and besides that, Ella's engagement with Henry Lincoln filled her heart with dark forebodings, for rumor said that he was unprincipled, and dissipated, and before giving her consent Mrs. Campbell had labored long with Ella, who insisted "that he was no worse than other young men,—most of them drank occasionally, and Henry did nothing more!"

On this afternoon she had again conversed with Ella, who angrily declared, that she would marry him even if she knew he'd be a drunkard, adding, "But he won't be. He loves me better than all the world, and I shall help him to reform."

"I don't believe your sister would marry him," continued Mrs. Campbell, who was becoming much attached to Mary.

"I don't believe she would, either, and for a very good reason, too," returned Ella, pettishly jerking her long curls. "But I can't see why you should bring her up, for he has never been more than polite to her, and that he assured me was wholly on my account."

"She isn't pleased with your engagement!" said Mrs. Campbell; and Ella replied, "Well, what of that? It's nothing to her, and I didn't mean she should know it; but Jenny, like a little tattler, must needs tell her, and so she has read me a two hours' sermon on the subject. She acted so queer, too, I didn't know what to think of her, and when she and Henry are together, they look so funny, that I almost believe she wants him herself, but she can't have him,—no, she can't have him,"—and secure in the belief that *she* was the first and only object of Henry's affection, Ella danced out of the room to attend to the seamstress who was doing her plain sewing.

After she was gone, Mrs. Campbell fell asleep, and for the first time in many a long year dreamed of her old home in England. She did not remember it herself, but she had so often heard it described by the aunt who adopted her, that now it came up vividly before her mind, with its dark stone walls, its spacious grounds, terraced gardens, running vines and creeping roses. Something about it, too, reminded her of what Ella had once said of her mother's early home, and when she awoke, she wondered that she had never questioned the child more concerning her parents. She was just lying back again upon her pillow, when there was a gentle rap at the door, and Mary Howard's soft voice asked permission to come in.

"Yes, do," said Mrs. Campbell. "Perhaps you can charm away my headache, which is dreadful."

"I'll try," answered Mary. "Shall I read to you?"

"If you please; but first give me my salts. You'll find them there in that drawer."

Mary obeyed, but started as she opened the drawer, for there, on the top, lay a small, old-fashioned miniature, of a fair young child, so nearly resembling Franky, that the tears instantly came to her eyes.

"What is it?" asked Mrs Campbell, and Mary replied, "This picture,—so much like brother Franky. May I look at it?"

"Certainly," said Mrs. Campbell. "That is a picture of my sister."

For a long time Mary gazed at the sweet childish face, which, with its clustering curls, and soft brown eyes, looked to her so much like Franky. At last, turning to Mrs. Campbell, she said, "You must have loved her very much. What was her name?"

"Ella Temple," was Mrs. Campbell's reply, and Mary instantly exclaimed, "Why, *that was my mother's name!*"

"Your mother, Mary!—your mother!" said Mrs. Campbell, starting up from her pillow. "But no; it cannot be. Your mother is lying in Chicopee, and Ella, my sister, died in England."

Every particle of color had left Mary's face, and her eyes, now black as midnight, stared wildly at Mrs. Campbell. The sad story, which her mother had once told her, came back to her mind, bringing with it the thought, which had so agitated her companion.

"Yes," she continued, without noticing what Mrs. Campbell had said, "my mother was Ella Temple, and she had two sisters, one her own, and the other, a half sister,—Sarah Fletcher and Jane Temple,—both of whom came to America many years ago."

"Tell me more,—tell me all you know!" whispered Mrs. Campbell, grasping Mary's hand; "and how it came bout that I thought she was dead,—my sister."

Upon this point Mary could throw no light, but of all that she had heard from her mother she told, and then Mrs Campbell, pointing to her writing desk, said, "Bring it to me. I must read that letter again."

Mary obeyed, and taking out a much soiled, blotted letter, Mrs. Campbell asked her to read it aloud. It was as follows—"Daughter Jane,—I now take this opportunity of informing you, that I've lost your sister Ella, and have now no child saving yourself, who, if you behave well, will be my only heir. Sometimes I wish you were here, for it's lonesome living alone, but, I suppose you're better off where you are. Do you know any thing of that girl Sarah? Her cross-grained uncle has never written me a word since he left England. If I live three years longer I shall come to America, and until that time, adieu. Your father,—Henry Temple Esq. M.P."

"How short and cold!" was Mary's first exclamation, for her impressions of her grandfather were not very agreeable.

"It is like all his letters," answered Mrs. Campbell "But it was cruel to make me think Ella was dead, for how else could I suppose he had lost her? and when I asked the particulars of her death, he sent me no answer; but at this I did not so much wonder, for he never wrote oftener than once in two or three years, and the next that I heard, he was dead, and I was heiress of all his wealth."

Then, as the conviction came over her that Mary was indeed the child of her own sister, she wound her arms about her neck, and kissing her lips, murmured, "My child,—my Mary. Oh, had I known this sooner, you should not have been so cruelly deserted, and little Allie should never have died in the alms-house. But you'll never leave me now, for all that I have is yours— yours and Ella's."

The thought of Ella touched a new chord, and Mrs Campbell's tears were rendered less bitter, by the knowledge that she had cared for, and been a mother, to one of her sister's orphan children.

"I know now," said she, "why, from the first, I felt so drawn towards Ella, and why her clear, large eyes, are so much like my own lost darling's, and even you, Mary—"

Here Mrs. Campbell paused, for proud as she now was of Mary, there had been a time when the haughty lady turned away from the sober, homely little child, who begged so piteously "to go with Ella" where there was room and to spare. All this came up in sad review, before Mrs. Campbell, and as she recalled the incidents of her sister's death, and thought of the noble little Frank, who often went hungry and cold that his mother and sisters might be warmed and fed, she felt that her heart would burst with its weight of sorrow.

"Oh, my God!" said she, "to die so near me,—my only sister, and *I* never know it,—never go near her. *I* with all my wealth, as much hers as mine,—and she dying of starvation."

Wiping the hot tears from her own eyes, Mary strove to comfort her aunt by telling her how affectionately her mother had always remembered her. "And even on the night of her death," said she, "she spoke of you, and bade me, if I ever found you, love you for her sake."

"Will you, do you love me?" asked Mrs. Campbell.

Mary's warm kiss upon her cheek, and the loving clasp of her arms around her aunt's neck, was a sufficient answer.

"Do you know aught of my Aunt Sarah?" Mary asked at last; and Mrs. Campbell replied, "Nothing definite. From father we first heard that she was in New York, and then Aunt Morris wrote to her uncle, making inquiries concerning her. I think the Fletchers were rather peculiar in their dispositions, and were probably jealous of our family for the letter was long unanswered, and when at last Sarah's uncle wrote, he said, that 'independent of *old Temple's* aid she had received a good education;' adding further, that she had married and gone west, and that he was intending soon to follow her. He neither gave the name of her husband, or the place to which they were going, and as all our subsequent letters were unanswered, I know not whether she is dead or alive; but often when I think how alone I am, without a relative in the world, I have prayed and wept that she might come back; for though I never knew her,—never saw her that I remember, she was my mother's child, and I should love her for that."

Just then Ella came singing into the room, but started when she saw how excited Mrs. Campbell appeared, and how swollen her eyelids were.

"Why, what's the matter?" said she. "I never saw you cry before, excepting that time when I told you I was going to marry Henry," and Ella laughed a little spiteful laugh, for she had not yet recovered from her anger at what Mrs. Campbell had said when she was in there before.

"Hush—sh," said Mary softly; and Mrs. Campbell, drawing Ella to her side, told her of the strange discovery she had made; then beckoning Mary to approach, she laid a hand upon each of the young girls' heads, and blessing them, called them "her own dear children."

It would be hard telling what Ella's emotions were. One moment she was glad, and the next she was sorry, for she was so supremely selfish, that the fact of Mary's being now in every respect her equal, gave her more pain than pleasure. Of course, Mrs. Campbell would love her best,—every body did who knew her,—every body but Henry. And when Mrs. Campbell asked why she did not speak, she replied, "Why, what shall I say? shall I go into ecstasies about it? To be sure I'm glad,—very glad that you are my aunt. Will Mary live here now?"

"Yes, always," answered Mrs. Campbell; and "No never," thought Mary.

Her sister's manner chilled her to the heart. She thoroughly understood her, and felt sure they could not be happy together, for Ella was to live at home even after her marriage. There was also another, and stronger reason, why Mary should not remain with her aunt. Mrs. Mason had the first, best claim upon her. She it was who had befriended her when a lonely, neglected orphan, taking her from the alms-house, and giving her a pleasant, happy home. She it was, too, who in sickness and health had cared for her with all a mother's love, and Mary would not leave her now. So when Mrs. Campbell began to make plans for the future, each one of which had a direct reference to herself, she modestly said she should never desert Mrs. Mason, stating her reasons with so much delicacy, and yet so firmly, that Mrs. Campbell was compelled to acknowledge she was right, while at the same time she secretly wondered whether Ella for *her* sake would refuse a more elegant home were it offered her.

All that afternoon the contrast between the two girls grew upon her so painfully, that she would almost gladly have exchanged her selfish, spoilt Ella, for the once despised and neglected orphan; and when at evening Mary came to say "Good night," she embraced her with a fervency which seemed to say she could not give her up.

Scarcely had the door closed upon Mary, ere there was a violent bell ring, and Henry Lincoln was ushered into the parlor, where Ella, radiant with smiles, sat awaiting him. They were invited that evening to a little sociable, and Ella had bestowed more than usual time and attention upon her toilet, for Henry was very observant of ladies' dresses, and now that "he had a right," was constantly dictating, as to what she should wear, and what she should not. On this evening every thing seemed fated to go wrong. Ella had heard Henry say that he was partial to mazarine blue, and not suspecting that his preference arose from the fact of his having frequently seen her sister in a neatly fitting blue merino she determined to surprise him with his favorite color. Accordingly, when Henry entered the parlor, he found her arrayed in a rich blue silk, made low in the neck with loose, full sleeves, and flounced to the waist. The young man had just met Mary at the gate, and as usual after seeing her was in the worst of humors.

His first salutation to Ella was "Well, Mother Bunch, you look pretty, don't you?"

"I don't know. Do I?" said Ella, taking him literally.

"Do you?" he repeated, with an impatient toss of his head. "All but the pretty. I advise you to take off that thing" (pointing to the dress), "I never saw you look worse."

Since Ella's engagement she had cried half the time, and now, as usual, the tears came to her eyes, provoking Henry still more.

"Now make your eyes red," said he. "I declare, I wonder if there's any thing of you but tears."

"Please don't talk so," said Ella, laying her hand on his arm. "I had this dress made on purpose to please you, for you once said you liked dark blue."

"And so I do on your sister, but your complexion is different from hers, and then those *ruffles* and bag sleeves make you look like a little barrel!"

"You told me you admired flounces, and these sleeves are all the fashion," said Ella, the tears again flowing in spite of herself.

"Well, I do think Mary looks well in flounces," returned Henry, "but she is almost a head taller than you, and better proportioned every way."

Ella longed to remind him of a time when he called her sister "a hay pole," while he likened herself to "a little sylph, fairy;" &c., but she dared not; and Henry, bent on finding fault, touched her white bare shoulder, saying "I wish you wouldn't wear such dresses. Mary don't except at parties, and I heard a gentleman say that she displayed better taste than any young lady of his acquaintance."

Ella was thoroughly angry, and amid a fresh shower of tears exclaimed, "*Mary,—Mary,*—I'm sick of the name. It's nothing but Mary,—Mary all day long with Mrs. Campbell, and now *you* must thrust her in my face. If you think her so perfect, why don't you marry her, instead of me?"

"Simply because she won't have me," returned Henry, and then not wishing to provoke Ella too far, he playfully threw his arm around her waist, adding "But come, my little beauty, don't let's quarrel any more about her. I ought to like *my sister*, and you shouldn't be jealous. So throw on your cloak, and let's be off."

"Oh, no, not yet. It's too early" answered Ella, nothing loth to have an hour alone with him.

So they sat down together upon the sofa, and after asking about Rose, and how long Jenny was to remain in Glenwood, Ella, chancing to think of the strange discovery that day made with regard to herself and Mary, mentioned it to Henry, who seemed much more excited about it than she had been.

"Mrs. Campbell, your mother's sister!" said he. "And Mary's aunt too? Why didn't you tell me before?"

"Because I didn't think of it," returned Ella. "And it's nothing so very marvellous either, or at least it does not affect *me* in the least." Henry did not reply, but there was that passing through his mind which might affect Ella not a little. As the reader knows, he was marrying her for her money; and now if that money was to be shared with another, the bride lost half her value! But such thoughts must not be expressed, and when Henry next spoke, he said very calmly, "Well, I'm glad on Mary's account, for your aunt will undoubtedly share her fortune with her;" and Henry's eyes turned upon Ella with a deeper meaning than she could divine.

It was so long since Ella had felt the need of money that she had almost ceased to know its value, and besides this, she had no suspicion of Henry's motive in questioning her; so she carelessly replied that nothing had been said on the subject, though she presumed her aunt would make Mary heiress with herself, as she had recently taken a violent fancy to her. Here the conversation flagged, and Henry fell into a musing mood, from which Ella was forced to rouse him when it was time to go. As if their thoughts were flowing in the same channel, Mrs. Campbell that evening was thinking of Mary, and trying to devise some means by which to atone for neglecting her so long. Suddenly a new idea occurred to her, upon which she determined immediately to act, and the next morning Mr. Worthington was sent for, to draw up a new will, in which Mary Howard was to share equally with her sister.

"Half of all I own is theirs by right," said she, "and what I want is, that on their 21st birth-day they shall come into possession of the portion which ought to have been their mother's, while at my death the remainder shall be equally divided between them."

The will was accordingly drawn up, signed and sealed, Mr. Worthington keeping a rough draft of it, which was thrown among some loose papers in his office. A few afterwards Henry coming accidentally upon it, read it without any hesitation.

"*That* settles it at once," said he, "and I can't say I'm sorry, for I was getting horribly sick of her. Now I'd willingly marry Mary without a penny, but Ella, with only one quarter as much as I expected, and that not until she's twenty-one, is a different matter entirely. But what am I to do? I wish Moreland was here, for though he don't like me (and I wonder who does), he wouldn't mind lending me a few thousand. Well, there's no help for it; and the sooner the old man breaks now, the better. It'll help me out of a deuced mean scrape, for of course I shall be *magnanimous*, and release Ella at once from her engagement with a *ruined man*."

The news that Mary was Mrs. Campbell's niece spread rapidly, and among those who came to congratulate her, none was more sincere than William Bender. Mary was very dear to him, and whatever conduced to her happiness added also to his. Together with her he had heard the rumor of Mr. Lincoln's downfall, and while he felt sorry for the family, he could not help hoping that it would bring Jenny nearer to him. Of this he told Mary, who hardly dared trust herself to reply, lest she should divulge a darling secret, which she had cherished ever since Mrs. Campbell had told her that, in little more than a year, she was to be the rightful owner of a sum of money much larger than she had ever dreamed it possible for her to possess. Wholly unselfish, her thoughts instantly turned towards her adopted brother. A part of that sum should be his, and with that for a stepping stone to future wealth, Mrs. Lincoln, when poor and destitute, could no longer refuse him her daughter Mrs Campbell, to whom alone she confided her wishes, gave her consent, though she could not understand the self-denying love which prompted this act of generosity to a stranger.

And now Mary was very happy in thinking how much good she could do. Mrs. Mason, her benefactress, should never want again. Sally Furbush, the kind-hearted old crazy woman who had stood by her so long and so faithfully, should share her home wherever that home might be; while better than all the rest, William Bender, the truest, best friend she ever had, should be repaid for his kindness to her when a little, unknown pauper. And still the world, knowing nothing of the hidden causes which made Mary's laugh so merry and her manner so gay, said that "the prospect of being an heiress had turned her head, just as it always did those who were suddenly elevated to wealth."

CHAPTER XXX.

THE CRISIS.

Mr. Lincoln had failed. At the corners of the streets, groups of men stood together, talking over the matter, and ascribing it, some to his carelessness, some to his extreme good nature in indorsing for any one who asked, and others, the knowing ones, winking slyly as they said "they guessed he knew what he was about,—they'd known before of such things as failing rich;" but the mouths of these last were stopped when they heard that the household furniture, every thing, was given up for the benefit of his creditors, and was to be sold at auction during the coming week.

In their parlors at home wives and daughters also discussed the matter, always ending by accusing Mrs. Lincoln of unwarrantable extravagance, and wondering how the proud Rose would bear it, and suggesting that "she could work in the factory just as her mother did!". It was strange how suddenly Mrs. Lincoln's most intimate friends discovered that she had once been a poor factory girl, remembering too that they had often noticed an air of vulgarity about her! Even Mrs. Campbell was astonished that she should have been so deceived, though she pitied the daughters, "who were really refined and lady-like, considering—" and then she thought of Henry, hoping that Ella would be now willing to give him up.

But with a devotion worthy of a better object, Ella replied, that he was dearer to her than ever. "I have not loved him for his wealth," said she, "and I shall not forsake him now" And then she wondered why he staid so long away, as day after day went by, and still he came not. It was in vain that Mary, who visited the house frequently, told her of many things which might detain him. Ella saw but one. He fancied she, too, would desert him, like the cold unfeeling world. And then she begged so imploringly of her sister to go to him, and ask him to come, that Mary, loth as she was to do so, finally complied. She found him in his office, and fortunately alone. He was looking very pale and haggard, the result of last night's debauch, but Mary did not know of this. She only saw grief for his misfortune, and her voice and manner were far more cordial than usual as she bade him good afternoon.

"It is kind in you, Miss Howard, to come here," said he, nervously pressing the hand she offered. "I knew *you* would not forsake me, and I'd rather have your sympathy than that of the whole world."

Wishing to end such conversation, Mary replied, "I came here, Mr. Lincoln, at Ella's request. Ever since your father's failure she has waited anxiously for you—"

She was prevented from saying more by Henry, who, with a feigned bitterness of manner, exclaimed, "Ella need not feel troubled, for I am too honorable to insist upon her keeping an engagement, which I would to Heaven had never been made. Tell her she is free to do as she pleases."

"You are mistaken, sir," answered Mary; "Ella does not wish to be free. But come with me; I promised to bring you."

With an air of desperation, Henry took his hat, and started with Mary for Mrs. Campbell's. Oh, how eagerly Ella sprang forward to meet him, and burying her face in his bosom, she sobbed like a child.

"Hush, Ella, this is foolish," said he; and then seating her in a chair, he asked, "why he was sent for."

"I was afraid,—afraid you might think I did not love you now," answered Ella.

"I could not blame you if you did not," said Henry. "Matters have changed since we last met, and I am not mean enough to expect you to keep your engagement."

"But if *I* expect it,—If *I* wish it?" asked Ella, raising her tear-wet eyes to his face.

"You are excited now," said he, "but in a few days you'll thank me for my decision. An alliance with poverty could be productive of nothing but unhappiness to you; and while I thank you for your unselfish love, I cannot accept it, for I am determined that, so long as I am poor, I shall never marry; and the sooner you forget me, the better, for, Ella, I am not deserving of your love."

Then, with a cold adieu, he left her; and when, half an hour afterwards, Mary entered the parlor, she found her sister lying upon the sofa, perfectly motionless, except when a tremor of anguish shook her slight frame. A few words explained all, and taking her head in her lap, Mary tried to soothe her. But Ella refused to be comforted; and as she seemed to prefer being alone, Mary ere long left her, and bent her steps towards Mr. Lincoln's dwelling, which presented a scene of strange confusion. The next day was the auction, and many people of both sexes had assembled to examine, and find fault with, the numerous articles of furniture, which were being removed to the auction room.

"Where's them silver candlesticks, and that cake-basket that cost up'ards of a hundred dollars?" asked one fussy, vulgar-looking old woman, peering into closets and cupboards, and even lifting trunk lids in her search. "I want some such things, and if they go for half price or less, mebby Israel will bid; but I don't see 'em. I'll warrant they've hid 'em."

Mary was just in time to hear this remark, and she modestly replied, that Mr. Lincoln's creditors had generously presented him with all the silver, which was now at Mr. Selden's.

The woman stared impudently at her a moment, and then said, "Now, that's what I call downright cheatin'? What business has poor folks with so much silver. Better pay their debts fust. That's my creed."

Mary turned away in disgust, but not until she heard the woman's daughter whisper, "Don't, mother,—that's Miss Howard,—Mrs. Campbell's niece," to which the mother replied, "Wall, who cares for that? Glad I gin her a good one. Upper crust ain't no better than I be."

Passing through the hall, where several other women were examining and depreciating Mrs. Lincoln's costly carpets, pronouncing them "half cotton," &c., Mary made her way up the stairs, where in a chamber as yet untouched, she found Jenny and with her William Bender. Mrs. Lincoln's cold, scrutinizing eyes were away, and Mr. Lincoln had cordially welcomed William to his house, telling him of his own accord where his daughter could be found. Many a time in his life for Mary's sake had William wished that he was rich, but never had he felt so intense a longing for money, as he did when Jenny sat weeping at his side, and starting at each new sound which came up from the rabble below.

"Oh, Mary, Mary!" she said, as the latter entered the room, "to-morrow every thing will be sold, and I shall have no home. It's dreadful to be poor."

Mary knew that from bitter experience, and sitting down by her young friend, her tears flowed as freely as Jenny's had often flowed for her, in the gray old woods near Chicopee poor-house. Just then there was an unusual movement in the yard below, and looking from the window, Jenny saw that they were carrying the piano away.

"This is worse than all," said she. "If they only knew how dear that is to me, or how dear it will be when—"

She could not finish, but Mary knew what she would say. The piano belonged to Rose, whose name was engraved upon its front, and when she was dead, it would from that fact be doubly dear to the sister. A stylish-looking carriage now drew up before the house, from which Mrs. Campbell alighted and holding up her long skirts, ascended the stairs, and knocked at Jenny's door.

"Permeely," called out the old lady who had been disappointed in her search for the silver candlesticks, "wasn't that Miss Campbell? Wall, she's gone right into one of them rooms where t'other gal went. I shouldn't wonder if Mr. Lincoln's best things was hid there, for they keep the door locked."

Accidentally Mr. Lincoln overheard this remark, and in his heart he felt that his choicest treasure was indeed there. His wife, from whom he naturally expected sympathy, had met him with desponding looks and bitter words, reproaching him with carelessness, and saying, as in similar circumstances ladies too often do, that "she had forseen it from the first, and that had he followed her advice, 'twould not have happened."

Henry, too, seemed callous and indifferent, and the father alone found comfort in Jenny's words of love and encouragement. From the first she had stood bravely by him refusing to leave the house until all was over; and many a weary night, when the great city was hushed and still, a light had gleamed from the apartment where, with her father, she sat looking over his papers, and trying to ascertain as far as possible, to what extent he was involved. It was she who first suggested the giving up of every thing; and when Henry, less upright than his noble sister, proposed the withholding of a part, she firmly answered, "No, father don't do it. You have lost your property, but do not lose your self-respect."

Always cheerful, and sometimes even gay in his presence, she had succeeded in imbuing him with a portion of her own hopeful spirit, and he passed through the storm far better than he could otherwise have done. Mrs. Campbell's visit to the house was prompted partly from curiosity, and partly from a desire to take away Jenny, who was quite a favorite with her.

"Come, my dear," said she, pushing back the short, thick curls which clustered around Jenny's forehead, "you must go home with me. This is no place for you. Mary will go too," she continued; and then on an "aside" to Mary, she added, "I want you to cheer up Ella; she sits alone in her room, without speaking or noticing me in any way."

At first Jenny hesitated, but when William whispered that she had better go; and Mrs. Campbell, as the surest way of bringing her to a decision, said, "Mr. Bender will oblige me by coming to tea," she consented, and closely veiled, passed through the crowd below, who instinctively drew back, and ceased speaking, for wherever she was known, Jenny was beloved. Arrived at Mrs. Campbell's, they found Ella, as her mother had said, sitting alone in her room, not weeping, but gazing fixedly down the street, as if expecting some one who did not come!

In reply to Jenny's anxious inquiries as to what was the matter, Mary frankly told all, and then Jenny, folding her arms around the young girl, longed to tell her how unworthy was the object of such love. But Henry was her brother, and she could not. Softly caressing Ella's cheek, she whispered to her of brighter days which perhaps would come. The fact that it was *his* sister —Henry's sister—opened anew the fountain of Ella's tears, and she wept for a long time; but it did her good, and for the remainder of the afternoon she seemed more cheerful, and inclined to converse.

The next day was the auction, and it required the persuasion of both Mrs. Campbell and Mary to keep Jenny from going, she knew not whither herself, but any where, to be near and take one more look at the dear old furniture as it passed into the hands of strangers. At last Mrs. Campbell promised that black Ezra, who had accompanied her from Chicopee, should go and report faithfully all the proceedings, and then Jenny consented to remain at home, though all the day she seemed restless and impatient, wondering how long before Uncle Ezra would return, and then weeping as in fancy she saw article after article disposed of to those who would know little how to prize it.

About five o'clock Uncle Ezra came home, bringing a note from Ida, saying that the carriage would soon be round for Mary and Jenny, both of whom must surely come, as there was a pleasant surprise awaiting them. While Mary was reading this, Jenny was eagerly questioning Uncle Ezra with regard to the sale, which, he said, "went off uncommon well," owing chiefly, he reckoned, "to a tall, and mighty good-lookin' chap, who kept bidding up and up, till he got 'em about where they should be. Then he'd stop for someone else to bid."

"Who was he?" asked Mary, coming forward, and joining Jenny.

"Dun know, Miss; never seen him afore," said Uncle Ezra, "but he's got heaps of money, for when he paid for the pianner, he took out a roll of bills near about big as my two fists!"

"Then the piano is gone," said Jenny sadly, while Mary asked how much it brought.

"Three hundred dollars was the last bid I heard from that young feller, and somebody who was biddin' agin him said, 'twas more'n 'twas wuth."

"It wasn't either," spoke up Jenny, rather spiritedly, "It cost five hundred, and it's never been hurt a bit."

"Mr. Bender bought that *little fiddle* of your'n," continued Uncle Ezra, with a peculiar wink, which brought the color to Jenny's cheeks; while Mary exclaimed, "Oh, I'm so glad you can have your guitar again."

Here the conversation was interrupted by the arrival of the carriage, which came for the young ladies, who were soon on their way to Mr. Selden's, Mary wondering what the surprise was, and Jenny hoping William would call in the evening. At the door they met Ida, who was unusually merry,—almost too much so for the occasion, it seemed to Mary, as she glanced at Jenny's pale, dispirited face. Aunt Martha, too, who chanced to cross the hall, shook Mary's hand as warmly as if she had not seen her for a year, and then with her broad, white cap-strings flying back, she repaired to the kitchen to give orders concerning the supper.

Mary did not notice it then, but she afterwards remembered, that Ida seemed quite anxious about her appearance, for following her to her room, she said, "You look tired, Mary. Sit down and rest you awhile. Here, take my vinaigrette,—that will revive you." Then as Mary was arranging her hair, she said, "Just puff out this side a little more;—there, that's right. Now turn round, I want to see how you look."

"Well, how do I?" asked Mary, facing about as Ida directed.

"I guess you'll do," returned Ida. "I believe Henry Lincoln was right, when he said that this blue merino, and linen collar, was the most becoming dress you could wear: but you look well in every thing, you have so fine a form."

"Don't believe all her flattery," said Jenny, laughingly "She's only comparing your tall, slender figure with little dumpy me; but I'm growing thin,—see," and she lapped her dress two or three inches in front.

"Come, now let's go down," said Ida, "and I'll introduce you, to Jenny's surprise, first."

With Ida leading the way, they entered the music room, where in one corner stood Rose's piano, open, and apparently inviting Jenny to its side. With a joyful cry, she sprang forward, exclaiming, "Oh, how kind in your father; I almost know we can redeem it some time. I'll teach school,—any thing to get it again."

"Don't thank father too much," answered Ida, "for he has nothing to do with it, except giving it house room, and one quarter's teaching will pay that bill!"

"Who *did* buy it, then?" asked Jenny; and Ida replied, "Can't tell you just yet. I must have some music first. Come, Mary, you like to play. Give me my favorite, 'Rosa Lee,' with variations."

Mary was passionately fond of music, and, for the time she had taken lessons, played uncommonly well. Seating herself at the piano, she became oblivious to all else around her, and when a tall figure for a moment darkened the doorway, while Jenny uttered a suppressed exclamation of surprise, she paid no heed, nor did she become conscious of a third person's presence until the group advanced towards her, Ida and Jenny leaning upon the piano, and the other standing at her right, a little in the rear. Thinking, if she thought at all, that it was William Bender, Mary played on until the piece was finished, and then, observing that her companions had left the room, she turned and met the dark, handsome eyes,—not of William Bender, but of one who, with a peculiar smile, offered her his hand, saying, "I believe I need no introduction to Miss Howard, except a slight change in the name, which instead of being *Stuart* is Moreland!"

Mary never knew what she said or did. She only remembered a dizzy sensation in her head, a strong arm passed round her, and a voice which fully aroused her as it called her "Mary," and asked if she were faint. Just then Ida entered the room, announcing tea, and asking her if she found "Mr. Stuart" much changed? At the tea-table Mary sat opposite George, and every time she raised her eyes, she met his fixed upon her, with an expression so like that of the picture in the golden locket which she still wore, that she wondered she had not before recognized George Moreland in the Mr. Stuart who had so puzzled and mystified her. After supper she had an opportunity of seeing why George was so much beloved at home. Possessing rare powers of conversation, he seemed to know exactly what to say, and when to say it, and with a kind word and pleasant smile for all, he generally managed to make himself a favorite, notwithstanding his propensity to tease, which would occasionally show itself in some way or other. During the evening William Bender called, and soon after Henry Lincoln also came in, frowning gloomily when he saw how near to each other were William and his sister, while he jealously watched them, still keeping an eye upon George and Mary, the latter of whom remembered her young sister, and treated him with unusual coldness. At last, complaining of feeling *blue*, he asked Ida to play, at the same time sauntering towards the music room, where stood his sister's piano. "Upon my word," said he, "this looks natural. Who bought it?" and he drummed a few notes of a song.

"Mr. Moreland bought it. Wasn't he kind?" said Jenny, who all the evening had been trying for a chance to thank George, but now when she attempted to do so he prevented her by saying, "Oh don't—don't—I can imagine all you wish to say, and I hate to be thanked. Rose and I are particular friends, and it afforded me a great deal of pleasure to purchase it for her—but," he added, glancing at his watch, "I must be excused now, as I promised to call upon my ward."

"Who's that?" asked Jenny, and George replied that it was a Miss Herndon, who had accompanied him from New Orleans to visit her aunt, Mrs. Russell.

"He says she's an heiress, and very beautiful," rejoined Ida, seating herself at the piano.

Instantly catching at the words "heiress" and "beautiful," Henry started up, asking "if it would be against all the rules of propriety for him to call upon her thus early."

"I think it would," was George's brief answer, while Mary's eyes flashed scornfully upon the young man, who, rather crestfallen, announced himself ready to listen to Ida whom he secretly styled "an old maid," because since his first remembrance she had treated him with perfect indifference.

That night before retiring the three girls sat down by the cheerful fire in Mary's room to talk over the events of the day, when Mary suddenly asked Ida to tell her truly, if it were not George who had paid her bills at Mount Holyoke.

"What bills?" said Jenny, to whom the idea was new while Ida replied, "And suppose it was?"

"I am sorry," answered Mary, laying her head upon the table.

"What a silly girl," said Ida. "He was perfectly able, and more than willing, so why do you care?"

"I do not like being so much indebted to any one," was Mary's reply, and yet in her secret heart there was a strange feeling of pleasure in the idea that George had thus cared for her, for would he have done so, if—. She dared not finish that question even to herself,—dared not ask if she hoped that George Moreland loved her one half as well as she began to think she had always loved him. Why should he, with his handsome person and princely fortune, love one so unworthy, and so much beneath him? And then, for the first time, she thought of her changed position since last they met. Then she was a poor, obscure schoolmistress,—now, flattered, caressed, and an heiress. Years before, when a little pauper at Chicopee, she had felt unwilling that George should know how destitute she was, and now in the time of her prosperity she was equally desirous that he should, for a time at least, remain ignorant of her present condition.

"Ida," said she, lifting her head from the table "does George know that I am Mrs. Campbell's niece?"

"No," answered Ida, "I wanted to tell him, but Aunt Martha said I'd better not."

"Don't then," returned Mary, and resuming her former position she fell into a deep reverie, from which she was at last aroused, by Jenny's asking "if she intended to sit up all night?"

The news that George Moreland had returned, and bought Rose Lincoln's piano, besides several other articles, spread rapidly, and the day following his arrival Mary and Ida were stopped in the street by a group of their companions, who were eager to know how George bore the news that his betrothed was so ill, and if it was not that which had brought him home so soon, and then the conversation turned upon Miss Herndon, the New Orleans lady who had that morning appeared in the street; "And don't you think," said one of the girls, "that Henry Lincoln was dancing attendance upon her? If I were you," turning to Mary, "I'd caution my sister to be a little wary of him. But let me see, their marriage is to take place soon?"

Mary replied that the marriage was postponed indefinitely, whereupon the girls exchanged meaning glances and passed on. In less than twenty-four hours, half of Ella's acquaintances were talking of her discarding Henry on account of his father's failure, and saying "that they expected it, 'twas like her."

Erelong the report, in the shape of a condolence, reached Henry, who caring but little what reason was assigned for the broken engagement, so that he got well out of it assumed a much injured air, but said "he reckoned he should manage to survive;" then pulling his sharp-pointed collar up another story, and brushing his pet mustache, wherein lay most of his mind, he walked up street, and ringing at Mrs. Russell's door, asked for Miss Herndon, who vain as beautiful, suffered his attentions, not because she liked him in the least, but because she was fond of flattery, and there was something exceedingly gratifying in the fact that at the North, where she fancied the gentlemen to be icicles, she had so soon made a conquest. It mattered not that Mrs. Russell told her his vows were plighted to another. She cared nothing for that. Her life had been one long series of conquests, until now at twenty-five there was not in the whole world a more finished or heartless coquette than Evren Herndon.

Days passed on, and at last rumors reached Ella, that Henry was constant in his attendance upon the proud southern beauty, whose fortune was valued by hundreds of thousands. At first she refused to believe it, but when Mary and Jenny both assured her it was true, and when she her self had ocular demonstration of the fact, she gave way to one long fit of weeping; and then, drying her eyes, declared that Henry Lincoln should see "that she would not die for him."

Still a minute observer could easily have seen that her gayety was feigned, for she had loved Henry Lincoln as sincerely as she was capable of loving, and not even George Moreland, who treated her with his old boyish familiarity could make her for a moment forget one who now passed her coldly by, or listened passively while the sarcastic Evren Herndon likened her to a waxen image, fit only for a glass case!

CHAPTER XXXI.

A QUESTION

Towards the last of April, Mrs. Mason and Mary returned to their old home in the country. On Ella's account, Mrs. Campbell had decided to remain in the city during a part of the summer, and she labored hard to keep Mary also, offering as a last inducement to give Mrs. Mason a home too. But Mrs. Mason preferred her own house in Chicopee, and thither Mary accompanied her, promising, however, to spend the next winter with her aunt, who wept at parting with her more than she would probably have done had it been Ella.

Mary had partially engaged to teach the school in Rice Corner, but George, assuming a kind of authority over her, declared she should not.

"I don't want your eyes to grow dim and your cheeks pale, in that little pent-up room," said he. "You know I've been there and seen for myself."

Mary colored, for George's manner of late had puzzled her, and Jenny had more than once whispered in her ear "I know George loves you, for he looks at you just as William does at me, only a little more so!"

Ida, too, had once mischievously addressed her as "Cousin," adding that there was no one among her acquaintances whom she would as willingly call by that name. "When I was a little girl," said she, "they used to tease me about George, but I'd as soon think of marrying my brother. You never saw Mr. Elwood, George's classmate, for he's in Europe now. Between you and me, I like him and—"

A loud call from Aunt Martha prevented Ida from finishing, and the conversation was not again resumed. The next morning Mary was to leave, and as she stood in the parlor talking with Ida, George came in with a travelling satchel in his hand, and a shawl thrown carelessly over his arm.

"Where are you going?" asked Ida.

"To Springfield. I have business there," said George.

"And when will you return?" continued Ida, feeling that it would be doubly lonely at home.

"That depends on circumstances," said he. "I shall stop at Chicopee on my way back, provided Mary is willing."

Mary answered that she was always glad to see her friends, and as the carriage just then drove up, they started together for the depot. Mary never remembered of having had a more pleasant ride than that from Boston to Chicopee George was a most agreeable companion, and with him at her side she seemed to discover new beauties in every object which they passed, and felt rather sorry when the winding river, and the blue waters of Pordunk Pond warned her that Chicopee Station was near at hand.

"I shall see you next week," said George, as he handed her from the cars, which the next moment rolled over the long meadow, and disappeared through the deep cut in the sandy hillside.

For a week or more Judith had been at Mrs. Mason's house, putting things to rights, and when the travellers arrived they found every thing in order. A cheerful fire was blazing in the little parlor, and before it stood the tea-table nicely arranged, while two beautiful Malta kittens, which during the winter had been Judith's special care, lay upon the hearth-rug asleep, with their soft velvet paws locked lovingly around each other's neck.

"Oh, how pleasant to be at home once more, and alone," said Mrs. Mason, but Mary did not reply. Her thoughts were elsewhere, and much as she liked being alone, the presence of a certain individual would not probably have marred her happiness to any great extent. But *he* was coming soon, and with that in anticipation, she appeared cheerful and gay as usual.

Among the first to call upon them was Mrs. Perkins who came early in the morning, bringing her knitting work and staying all day. She had taken to dressmaking, she said, and thought may-be she could get some new ideas from Mary's dresses, which she very coolly asked to see. With the utmost good humor, Mary opened her entire wardrobe to the inspection of the widow, who, having recently forsaken the Unitarian faith, and gone over to the new Methodist church in River street, turned conscientiously away from the gay party dresses, wondering how sensible people, to say nothing of Christian people, could find pleasure in such vanities!

"But then," said she, "I hear you've joined the Episcopals, and that accounts for it, for they allow of most any thing, and in my opinion ain't a whit better than the Catholics."

"Why, we are Catholic. Ain't you?" asked Mary.

The knitting work dropped, and with a short ejaculatory prayer of "Good Lord," Mrs. Perkins exclaimed, "Well, I'm glad you've owned up. Half on 'em deny it,—but there 'tis in black and white in the Prayer Book, 'I believe in the Holy Catholic Church.'"

It was in vain that Mary referred her to the Dictionary for a definition of the word 'Catholic.' She knew all she wanted to know, and she shouldn't wonder, bein' 'twas Friday, if Miss Mason didn't have no meat for dinner.

The appearance of a nicely roasted bit of veal quieted her fears on that subject, and as the effects of the strong green tea became apparent, she said, "like enough she'd been too hard on the Episcopals, for to tell the truth, she never felt so solemn in her life as she did the time she went to one of their meetins'; but," she added, "I do object to them two gowns, and I can't help it!"

At last the day was over, and with it the visit of the widow, who had gathered enough gossiping materials to last her until the Monday following, when the arrival in the neighborhood of George Moreland, threw her upon a fresh theme, causing her to wonder "if 'twan't Mary's beau, and if he hadn't been kinder courtin' her ever since the time he visited her school."

She felt sure of it when, towards evening, she saw them enter the school-house, and nothing but the presence of a visitor prevented her from stealing across the road, and listening under the window. She would undoubtedly have been highly edified, could she have heard their conversation. The interest which George had felt in Mary when a little child, was greatly increased when he visited her school in Rice Corner, and saw how much she was improved in her manners and appearance; and it was then that he conceived the idea of educating her, determining to marry her if she proved to be all he hoped she would.

That she did meet his expectations, was evident from the fact that his object in stopping at Chicopee, was to settle a question which she alone could decide. He had asked her to accompany him to the school-house, because it was there his resolution had been formed, and it was there he would make it known. Mary, too, had something which she wished to say to him. She would thank him for his kindness to her and her parents' memory; but the moment she commenced talking upon the subject, George stopped her, and for the first time since they were children, placed his arm around her waist, and kissing her smooth white brow, said, "Shall I tell you, Mary, how you can repay it?"

She did not reply, and he continued, "Give me a husband's right to care for you, and I shall be repaid a thousand fold."

Whatever Mary's answer might have been, and indeed we are not sure that she answered at all, George was satisfied; and when he told her how dear she was to him, how long he had loved her, and asked if he might not hope that he, too, had been remembered, the little golden locket which she placed in his hand was a sufficient reply. Without Ida's aid he had heard of the relationship existing between Mrs. Campbell and Mary, but it made no difference with him. His mind had long been made up, and in taking Mary for his wife, he felt that he was receiving the best of Heaven's blessings.

Until the shadows of evening fell around them they sat there, talking of the future, which George said should be all one bright dream of happiness to the young girl at his side, who from the very fulness of her joy wept as she thought how strange it was that she should be the wife of George Moreland, whom many a dashing belle had tried in vain to win. The next morning George went back to Boston, promising to return in a week or two, when he should expect Mary to accompany him to Glenwood, as he wished to see Rose once more before she died.

CHAPTER XXXII.

GOING HOME.

The windows of Rose Lincoln's chamber were open, and the balmy air of May came in, kissing the white brow of the sick girl, and whispering to her of swelling buds and fair young blossoms, which its breath had wakened into life, and which she would never see.

"Has Henry come?" she asked of her father, and in the tones of her voice there was an unusual gentleness, for just as she was dying Rose was learning to live.

For a time she had seemed so indifferent and obstinate, that Mrs. Howland had almost despaired. But night after night, when her daughter thought she slept, she prayed for the young girl, that she might not die until she had first learned the way of eternal life. And, as if in answer to her prayers, Rose gradually began to listen, and as she listened, she wept, wondering though why her grandmother thought her so much more wicked than any one else. Again, in a sudden burst of passion, she would send her from the room, saying, "she had heard preaching enough, for she wasn't going to die,—she wouldn't die any way."

But at last such feelings passed away, and as the sun of her short life was setting, the sun of righteousness shone more and more brightly over her pathway, lighting her through the dark valley of death. She no longer asked to be taken home, for she knew that could not be, but she wondered why her brother stayed so long from Glenwood, when he knew that she was dying.

On her return from the city, Jenny had told her as gently as possible of his conduct towards Ella, and of her fears that he was becoming more dissipated than ever. For a time Rose lay perfectly still, and Jenny, thinking she was asleep, was about to leave the room, when her sister called her back, and bidding her sit down by her side, said, "Tell me, Jenny, do you think Henry has any love for me?"

"He would be an unnatural brother if he had not," answered Jenny, her own heart yearning more tenderly towards her sister, whose gentle manner she could not understand.

"Then," resumed Rose, "if he loves me, he will be sorry when I am dead, and perhaps it may save him from ruin."

The tears dropped slowly from her long eyelashes, while Jenny, laying her round rosy cheek against the thin pale face near her, sobbed out, "You must not die,—dear Rose. You must not die, and leave us."

From that time the failure was visible and rapid, and though letters went frequently to Henry, telling him of his sister's danger, he still lingered by the side of the brilliant beauty, while each morning Rose asked, "Will he come to-day?" and each night she wept that he was not there.

Calmly and without a murmur she had heard the story of their ruin from her father, who could not let her die without undeceiving her. Before that time she had asked to be taken back to Mount Auburn, designating the spot where she would be buried, but now she insisted upon being laid by the running brook at the foot of her grandmother's garden, and near a green mossy bank where the spring blossoms were earliest found, and where the flowers of autumn lingered longest. The music of the falling water, she said would soothe her as she slept, and its cool moisture keep the grass green and fresh upon her early grave.

One day, when Mrs. Lincoln was sitting by her daughter and, as she frequently did, uttering invectives against Mount Holyoke, &c., Rose said, "Don't talk so, mother. Mount Holyoke Seminary had nothing to do with hastening my death. I have done it myself by my own carelessness;" and then she confessed how many times she had deceived her mother, and thoughtlessly exposed her health, even when her lungs and side were throbbing with pain. "I know you will forgive me," said she, "for most severely have I been punished."

Then, as she heard Jenny's voice in the room below, she added, "There is one other thing which I would say to you Ere I die, you must promise that Jenny shall marry William Bender. He is poor, I know, and so are we, but he has a noble heart, and now for my sake, mother, take back the bitter words you once spoke to Jenny, and say that she may wed him. She will soon be your only daughter, and why should you destroy her happiness? Promise me, mother, promise that she shall marry him."

Mrs. Lincoln, though poor, was proud and haughty still, and the struggle in her bosom was long and severe, but love for her dying child conquered at last, and to the oft-repeated question, "Promise me, mother, will you not?" she answered, "Yes, Rose, yes, for your sake I give my consent though nothing else could ever have wrung it from me."

"And, mother," continued Rose, "may he not be sent for now? I cannot be here long, and once more I would see him, and tell him that I gladly claim him as a brother."

A brother! How heavily those words smote upon the heart of the sick girl. Henry was yet away, and though in Jenny's letter Rose herself had once feebly traced the words, "Come, brother,—do come," he still lingered, as if bound by a spell he could not break. And so days went by and night succeeded night, until the bright May morning dawned, the last Rose could ever see. Slowly up the eastern horizon came the warm spring sun, and as its red beams danced for a time upon the wall of Rose's chamber, she gazed wistfully upon it, murmuring, "It is the last,—the last that will ever rise for me."

William Bender was there. He had come the night before, bringing word that Henry would follow the next day. There was a gay party to which he had promised to attend Miss Herndon, and he deemed that a sufficient reason why he should neglect his dying sister, who every few minutes asked eagerly if he had come. Strong was the agony at work in the father's heart, and still he nerved himself to support his daughter while he watched the shadows of death as one by one they crept over her face. The mother, wholly overcome, declared she could not remain in the room, and on the lounge below she kept two of the neighbors constantly moving in quest of the restoratives which she fancied she needed. Poor Jenny, weary and pale with watching and tears, leaned heavily against William; and Rose, as often as her eyes unclosed and rested upon her, would whisper, "Jenny,—dear Jenny, I wish I had loved you more."

Grandma Howland had laid many a dear one in the grave, and as she saw another leaving her, she thought, "how grew her store in Heaven," and still her heart was quivering with anguish, for Rose had grown strongly into her affection. But for the sake of the other stricken ones she hushed her own grief, knowing it would not be long ere she met her child again. And truly it seemed more meet that she with her gray hair and dim eyes should die even then, than that Rose, with the dew of youth still glistening upon her brow, should thus early be laid low.

"If Henry does not come," said Rose, "tell him it was my last request that he turn away from the wine-cup, and say, that the bitterest pang I felt in dying, was a fear that my only brother should fill a drunkard's grave. He cannot look upon me dead, and feel angry that I wished him to reform. And as he stands over my coffin, tell him to promise never again to touch the deadly poison."

Here she became too much exhausted to say more, and soon after fell into a quiet sleep. When she awoke, her father was sitting across the room, with his head resting upon the window sill, while her own was pillowed upon the strong arm of George Moreland, who bent tenderly over her, and soothed her as he would a child. Quickly her fading cheek glowed, and her eye sparkled with something of its olden light; but "George,—George," was all she had strength to say, and when Mary, who had accompanied him, approached her, she only knew that she was recognized by the pressure of the little blue-veined hand, which soon dropped heavily upon the counterpane, while the eyelids closed languidly, and with the words, "He will not come," she again slept, but this time 'twas the long, deep sleep, from which she would never awaken.

Slowly the shades of night fell around the cottage where death had so lately left its impress. Softly the kind-hearted neighbors passed up and down the narrow staircase, ministering first to the dead, and then turning aside to weep as they looked upon the bowed man, who with his head upon the window sill, still sat just as he did when they told him she was dead. At his feet on a little stool was Jenny, pressing his hands, and covering them with the tears she for his sake tried in vain to repress.

At last, when it was dark without, and lights were burning upon the table, there was the sound of some one at the gate, and in a moment Henry stepped across the threshold, but started and turned pale when he saw his mother in violent hysterics upon the lounge, and Mary Howard bathing her head and trying to soothe her. Before he had time to ask a question, Jenny's arms were wound around his neck, and she whispered, "Rose is dead.—Why were you so late?"

He could not answer. He had nothing to say, and mechanically following his sister he entered the room where Rose had died. Very beautiful had she been in life; and now, far more beautiful in death, she looked like a piece of sculptured marble; as she lay there so cold, and still, and all unconscious of the scalding tears which fell upon her face, as Henry bent over her, kissing her lips, and calling upon her to awake and speak to him once more.

When she thought he could bear it, Jenny told him of all Rose had said, and by the side of her coffin, with his hand resting upon her white forehead, the conscience-stricken young man swore, that never again should ardent spirits of any kind pass his lips, and the father who stood by and heard that vow, felt that if it were kept, his daughter had not died in vain.

The day following the burial. George and Mary returned to Chicopee, and as the next day was the one appointed for the sale of Mr. Lincoln's farm and country house, he also accompanied them.

"Suppose you buy it," said he to George as they rode over the premises. "I'd rather you'd own it than to see it in the hands of strangers."

"I intended doing so," answered George, and when at night he was the owner of the farm, house and furniture, he generously offered it to Mr. Lincoln rent free, with the privilege of redeeming it whenever he could.

This was so unexpected, that Mr. Lincoln at first could hardly find words to express his thanks, but when he did he accepted the offer, saying, however, that he could pay the rent, and adding that he hoped two or three years of hard labor in California, whither he intended going, would enable him to purchase it back. On his return to Glenwood, he asked William, who was still there, "how he would like to turn farmer for a while."

Jenny looked up in surprise, while William asked what he meant.

Briefly then Mr. Lincoln told of George's generosity, and stating his own intentions of going to California, said that in his absence somebody must look after the farm, and he knew of no one whom he would as soon trust as William.

"Oh, that'll be nice," said Jenny, whose love for the country was as strong as ever. "And then, Willie, when pa comes back we'll go to Boston again and practise law, you and I!"

William pressed the little fat hand which had slid into his, and replied, that much as he would like to oblige Mr. Lincoln, he could not willingly abandon his profession, in which he was succeeding even beyond his most sanguine hopes. "But," said he, "I think I can find a good substitute in Mr. Parker, who is anxious to leave the poor-house. He is an honest, thorough-going man, and his wife, who is an excellent housekeeper, will relieve Mrs. Lincoln entirely from care."

"Mercy!" exclaimed the last-mentioned lady, "I can never endure that vulgar creature round me. First, I'd know she'd want to be eating at the same table, and I couldn't survive that!"

Mr. Lincoln looked sad. Jenny smiled, and William replied, that he presumed Mrs. Parker herself would greatly prefer taking her meals quietly with her husband in the kitchen.

"We can at least try it," said Mr. Lincoln, in a manner so decided that his wife ventured no farther remonstrance, though she cried and fretted all the time, seemingly lamenting their fallen fortune, more than the vacancy which death had so recently made in their midst.

Mr. Parker, who was weary of the poor-house, gladly consented to take charge of Mr. Lincoln's farm, and in the course of a week or two Jenny and her mother went out to their old home, where every thing seemed just as they had left it the autumn before. The furniture was untouched, and in the front parlor stood Rose's piano and Jenny's guitar, which had been forwarded from Boston. Mr. Lincoln urged his mother-in-law to accompany them, but she shook her head, saying, "the old bees never left their hives," and she preferred remaining in Glenwood.

Contrary to Mrs. Lincoln's fears, Sally Ann made no advances whatever towards an intimate acquaintance, and frequently days and even weeks would elapse without her ever seeing her mistress, who spent nearly all her time in her chamber, musing upon her past greatness, and scolding Jenny, because she was not more exclusive. While the family were making arrangements to move from Glenwood to Chicopee. Henry for the first time in his life began to see of how little use he was to himself or any one else. Nothing was expected of him, consequently nothing was asked of him, and as his father made plans for the future, he began to wonder how he himself was henceforth to exist. His father would be in California, and he had too much pride to lounge around the old homestead, which had come to them through George Moreland's generosity.

Suddenly it occurred to him that he too would go with his father,—he would help him repair their fortune,—he would not be in the way of so much temptation as at home,—he would be a man, and when he returned home, hope painted a joyful meeting with his mother and Jenny, who should be proud to acknowledge him as a son and brother. Mr. Lincoln warmly seconded his resolution, which possibly would have never been carried out, had not Henry heard of Miss Herndon's engagement with a rich old bachelor whom he had often heard her ridicule. Cursing the fickleness of the fair lady, and half wishing that he had not broken with Ella, whose fortune, though not what he had expected, was considerable, he bade adieu to his native sky, and two weeks after the family removed to Chicopee, he sailed with his father for the land of gold.

But alas! The tempter was there before him, and in an unguarded moment he fell. The newly-made grave, the narrow coffin, the pale, dead sister, and the solemn vow were all forgotten, and a debauch of three weeks was followed by a violent fever, which in a few days cut short his mortal career. He died alone, with none but his father to witness his wild ravings, in which he talked of his distant home, of Jenny and Rose, Mary Howard, and Ella, the last of whom he seemed now to love with a madness amounting almost to frenzy. Tearing out handfuls of his rich brown hair, he thrust it into his father's hand, bidding him to carry it to Ella, and tell her that the heart she had so earnestly coveted was hers in death. And the father, far more wretched now than when his first-born daughter died, promised every thing, and when his only son was dead, he laid him down to sleep beneath the blue sky of

California, where not one of the many bitter tears shed for him in his far off home could fall upon his lonely grave.

CHAPTER XXXIII

CONCLUSION.

Great was the excitement in Rice Corner when it was known that on the evening of the tenth of September a grand wedding would take place, at the house of Mrs. Mason. Mary was to be married to the "richest man in Boston," so the story ran, and what was better yet, many of the neighbors were to be invited. Almost every day, whether pleasant or not, Jenny Lincoln came over to discuss the matter, and to ask if it were not time to send for William, who was to be one of the groomsmen, while she, together with Ida, were to officiate as bridesmaids. In this last capacity Ella had been requested to act, but the tears came quickly to her large mournful eyes, and turning away she wondered how Mary could thus mock her grief!

From one fashionable watering place to another Mrs. Campbell had taken her, and finding that nothing there had power to rouse her drooping energies, she had, towards the close of the summer, brought her back to Chicopee, hoping that old scenes and familiar faces would effect what novelty and excitement had failed to do. All unworthy as Henry Lincoln had been, his sad death had cast a dark shadow across Ella's pathway. Hour after hour would she sit, gazing upon the locks of shining hair, which over land and sea had come to her in a letter from the father, who told her of the closing scene, when Henry called for her, to cool the heat of his fevered brow. Every word and look of tenderness was treasured up, and the belief fondly cherished that he had always loved her thus, else why in the last fearful struggle was she alone remembered of all the dear ones in his distant home?

Not even the excitement of her sister's approaching marriage could awaken in her the least interest, and if it were mentioned in her presence she would weep, wondering what she had done that Mary should be so much happier than herself, and Mrs. Campbell remembering the past, could but answer in her heart that it was just. Sometimes Ella accused her sister of neglect, saying she had no thought for any one, except George Moreland, and his elegant house in Boston. It was in vain that Mary strove to convince her of her mistake. She only shook her head, hoping her sister would never know what it was to be wretched and desolate as she was. Mary could have told her of many weary days and sleepless nights, when there shone no star of hope in her dark sky, and when even her only sister turned from her in scorn; but she would not, and wiping away the tears which Ella's unkindness had called forth, she went back to her home, where busy preparations were making for her bridal.

Never before had Mrs. Perkins, or the neighborhood generally, had so much upon their hands at one time. Two dressmakers were sewing for Mary. A colored cook, with a flaming red turban, came up from Worcester to superintend the culinary department, and a week before the wedding Aunt Martha also arrived, bringing with her a quantity of cut glass of all sizes and dimensions, the uses of which could not even be guessed, though the widow declared upon her honor, a virtue by which she always swore, that two of them were called "cellar dishes," adding that the "Lord only knew what that was!"

With all her quizzing, prying, and peeking, Mrs. Perkins was unable to learn any thing definite with regard to the wedding dress, and as a last resort, she appealed to Jenny, "who of course ought to know, seein' she was goin' to stand up with 'em."

"O, yes, I know," said Jenny, mischievously, and pulling from her pocket a bit of brown and white plaid silk,—Mary's travelling dress,—she passed it to the widow, who straightway wondered at Mary's taste in selecting "that gingham-looking thing!"

Occasionally the widow felt some doubt as she heard rumors of pink brocades, India muslins, heavy silks, and embroidered merino morning-gowns; "but law," thought she "them are for the city. Any thing 'll do for the country, though I should s'pose she'd want to look decent before all the Boston top-knots that are comin'."

Three days before the wedding, the widow's heart was made glad with a card of invitation, though she wondered why Mrs. Mason should say she would be "at home." "Of course she'd be to hum,—where else should she be!"

It was amusing to see the airs which Mrs. Perkins took upon herself, when conversing with some of her neighbors, who were not fortunate enough to be invited. "They couldn't ask every body, and 'twas natural for them to select from the best families."

Her pride, however, received a fall when she learned that Sally Furbush had not only been invited, and presented with a black silk dress for the occasion, but that George Moreland, who arrived the day preceding the wedding, had gone for her himself, treating her with all the deference that he would the most distinguished lady. And truly for once Sally acquitted herself with a great deal of credit, and remembering Miss Grundy's parting advice, to "keep her tongue between her teeth," she so far restrained her loquacity, that a stranger would never have thought of her being crazy.

The bridal day was bright, beautiful, and balmy, as the first days of September often are, and when the sun went down, the full silvery moon came softly up, as if to shower her blessings upon the nuptials about to be celebrated. Many and brilliant lights were flashing from the windows of Mrs. Mason's cottage, which seemed to enlarge its dimensions as one after another the guests came in. First and foremost was the widow with her rustling silk of silver gray, and the red ribbons which she had sported at Sally Ann's wedding. After a series of manoeuvres she had succeeded in gaining a view of the supper table, and now in a corner of the room she was detailing the particulars to an attentive group of listeners.

"The queerest things I ever see," said she, "and the queerest names, too. Why, at one end of the table is a *muslin de laine puddin'—*"

"A what?" asked three or four ladies in the same breath, and the widow replied,—"May-be I didn't get the name right,—let me see:—No, come to think, it's a *Charlotte* somebody puddin' instead of a muslin de laine. And then at t'other end of the table is what I should call a dish of *hash*, but Judith says it's 'chicken Sally,' and it took the white meat of six or seven chickens to make it. Now what in the world they'll ever do with all them legs and backs and things, is more'n I can tell, but, land sake there come some of the *puckers*. Is my cap on straight?" she continued, as Mrs. Campbell entered the room, together with Ella, and a number of Boston ladies.

Being assured that her cap was all right, she resumed the conversation by directing the attention of those nearest her to Ella, and saying in a whisper, "If she hain't faded in a year, then I don't know; but, poor thing, she's been disappointed, so it's no wonder!" and thinking of her own experience with Mr. Parker, the widow's heart warmed toward the young girl, who, pale and languid, dropped into the nearest seat, while her eyes moved listlessly about the room. The rich, showy dresses of the city people also, came in for observation, and while the widow marvelled at their taste in wearing "collars as big as capes," she guessed that Mary'd feel flat in her checkered silk, when she came to see every body so dressed up.

And now guest after guest flitted down the narrow staircase and entered the parlor, which with the bedroom adjoining was soon filled. Erelong Mr. Selden, who seemed to be master of ceremonies appeared, and whispered something to those nearest the door. Immediately the crowd fell back, leaving a vacant space in front of the mirror. The busy hum of voices died away, and only a few suppressed whispers of, "There!—Look!—See!—Oh, my!" were heard, as the bridal party took their places.

The widow, being in the rear, and rather short, slipped off her shoes, and mounted into a chair, for a better view, and when Mary appeared, she was very nearly guilty of an exclamation of surprise, for in place of the "checkered silk" was an elegant *moire antique*, and an expensive bertha of point lace, while the costly bridal veil, which swept the floor, and fell in soft folds on either side of her head, was confined to the heavy braids of her hair by diamond fastenings. A diamond necklace encircled her slender throat, and bracelets of the same shone upon her round white arms. The whole was the gift of George Moreland, who had claimed the privilege of selecting and presenting the bridal dress, and who felt a pardonable pride when he saw how well it became Mary's graceful and rather queenly form.

At her left stood her bridesmaids, Ida and Jenny, while at George's right, were Mr. Elwood and William Bender the latter of whom looked on calmly while the solemn words were spoken which gave the idol of his boyhood to another and if he felt a momentary pang when he saw how fondly the newly made husband bent over his young bride, it passed away as his eye fell upon Jenny, who was now dearer to him, if possible, than Mary had ever been.

Among the first to congratulate "Mrs. Moreland," was Sally Furbush, followed by Mrs. Perkins, who whispered to George that "she kinder had a notion how 'twoud end when she first saw him in the school-house; but I'm glad you've got him," turning to Mary, "for it must be easier livin' in the city than keepin' school. You'll have a hired girl, I s'pose?"

When supper was announced, the widow made herself very useful in waiting upon the table, and asking some of the Boston ladies "if they'd be helped to any thing in them dishes," pointing to the *finger glasses*, which now for the first time appeared in Rice Corner! The half suppressed mirth of the ladies convinced the widow that she'd made a blunder, and perfectly disgusted with "new-fangled fashions" she retreated into the kitchen, were she found things more to her taste, and "thanked her stars, she could, if she liked, eat with her fingers, and wipe them on her pocket handkerchief!"

Soon after her engagement, Mary had asked that Sally should go with her to her city home. To this George willingly consented, and it was decided that she should remain with Mrs. Mason until the bridal party returned from the western tour they were intending to take. Sally knew nothing of this arrangement until the morning following the wedding, when she was told that she was not to return to the poor-house again.

"And verily, I have this day met with a great deliverance," said she, and tears, the first shed in many a year mingled with the old creature's thanks for this unexpected happiness. As Mary was leaving, she whispered in her ear "If your travels lead you near Willie's grave, drop a tear on it for my sake. You'll find it under the buckeye tree, where the tall grass and wild flowers grow."

George had relatives in Chicago, and after spending a short time in that city, Mary, remembering Sally's request, expressed a desire to visit the spot renowned as the burial place of "Willie and Willie's father." Ever ready to gratify her slightest wish, George consented, and towards the close of a mild autumnal day, they stopped at a small public house on the border of a vast prairie. The arrival of so distinguished looking people caused quite a commotion, and after duly inspecting Mary's handsome travelling dress, and calculating its probable cost, the hostess departed to prepare the evening meal, which was soon forthcoming.

When supper was over, and the family had gathered into the pleasant sitting room, George asked if there was ever a man in those parts by the name of "Furbush."

"What! Bill Furbush?" asked the landlord.

George did not know, but thought likely that might have seen his name, as his son was called William.

"Lud, yes," returned the landlord. "I knowed Bill Furbush well,—he came here about the same time I did, he from Massachusetts, and I from Varmount; but, poor feller, he was too weakly to bear much, and the first fever he took finished him up. His old woman was as clever a creature as ever was, but she had some high notions."

"Did she die too?" asked George.

Filling his mouth with an enormous quid of tobacco, the landlord continued, "No, but it's a pity she didn't, for when Bill and the boy died, she went ravin' mad, and I never felt so like cryin' as I did when I see her a tearin' her hair an goin' on so. We kept her a spell, and then her old man' brother's girl came for her and took her off; and the last I heard, the girl was dead, and she was in the poor-house somewhere east. She was born there, I b'lieve."

"No she warn't, either," said the landlady, who for some minutes had been aching to speak. "No she warn't, either. I know all about it. She was born in England, and got to be quite a girl before she came over. Her name was Sarah Fletcher, and Peter Fletcher, who died with the cholera, was her own uncle, and all the connection she had in this country;—but goodness suz, what ails you?" she added, as Mary turned deathly white, while George passed his arm around her to keep her from falling. "Here, Sophrony, fetch the camphire; she's goin' to faint."

But Mary did not faint, and after smelling the camphor, she said, "Go on, madam, and tell me more of Sarah Fletcher."

"She can do it," whispered the landlord with a sly wink. "She knows every body's history from Dan to Beersheby."

This intimation was wholly lost on the good-humored hostess, who continued, "Mr. Fletcher died when Sarah was small, and her mother married a Mr. ——, I don't justly remember his name"

"Temple?" suggested Mary.

"Yes, Temple, that's it. He was rich and cross, and broke her heart by the time she had her second baby. Sarah was adopted by her Grandmother Fletcher who died, and she came with her uncle to America."

"Did she ever speak of her sisters?" asked Mary, and the woman replied, "Before she got crazy, she did. One of 'em, she said, was in this country somewhere, and t'other the one she remembered the best, and talked the most about, lived in England. She said she wanted to write to 'em, but her uncle, he hated the Temples, so he wouldn't let her, and as time went on she kinder forgot 'em, and didn't know where to direct, and after she took crazy she never would speak of her sisters, or own that she had any."

"Is Mr. Furbush buried near here?" asked George; and the landlord answered, "Little better than a stone's throw. I can see the very tree from here, and may-be your younger eyes can make out the graves. He ought to have a grave stun, for he was a good feller."

The new moon was shining, and Mary, who came to her husband's side, could plainly discern the buckeye tree and the two graves where "Willie and Willie's father" had long been sleeping. The next morning before the sun was up, Mary stood by the mounds where often in years gone by Sally Furbush had seen the moon go down, and the stars grow pale in the coming day, as she kept her tireless watch over her loved and lost.

"Willie was my cousin—your cousin," said Mary, resting her foot upon the bit of board which stood at the head of the little graves. George understood her wishes, and when they left the place, a handsome marble slab marked the spot where the father and his infant son were buried.

Bewildered, and unable to comprehend a word, Sally listened while Mary told her of the relationship between them; but the mists which for years had shrouded her reason were too dense to be suddenly cleared away; and when Mary wept, winding her arms around her neck and calling her "Aunt;" and when the elegant Mrs. Campbell, scarcely less bewildered than Sally herself, came forward addressing her as "sister," she turned aside to Mrs. Mason, asking in a whisper "what had made them crazy."

But when Mary spoke of little Willie's grave, and the tree which overshadowed it, of the green prairie and cottage by the brook, once her western home, Sally listened, and at last one day, a week or two after her arrival in Boston, she suddenly clasped her hands closely over her temples, exclaiming, "It's come! It's come! I remember now,—the large garden,—the cross old man,—the dead mother,—the rosy-cheeked Ella I loved so well—"

"That was my mother,—my mother," interrupted Mary.

For a moment Sally regarded her intently, and then catching her in her arms, cried over her, calling her, "her precious child," and wondering she had never noticed how much she was like Ella.

"And don't you remember the baby Jane?" asked Mrs Campbell, who was present.

"Perfectly,—perfectly," answered Sally. "He died, and you came in a carriage; but didn't cry,—nobody cried but Mary."

It was in vain that Mary tried to explain to her that Mrs. Campbell was her sister,—once the baby Jane. Sally was not to be convinced. To her Jane and the little Alice were the same. There was none of her blood in Mrs. Campbell's veins, "or why," said she, "did she leave us so long in obscurity, me and my niece, *Mrs. George Moreland, Esq.!*"

This was the title which she always gave Mary when speaking of her, while to Ella, who occasionally spent a week in her sister's pleasant home, she gave the name of "little cipher," as expressing exactly her opinion of her. Nothing so much excited Sally, or threw her into so violent a passion, as to have Ella call her aunt.

"If I wasn't her kin when I wore a sixpenny calico," said she, "I certainly am not now that I dress in purple and fine linen."

When Sally first went to Boston, George procured for her the best possible medical advice, but her case was of so long standing that but little hope was entertained of her entire recovery. Still every thing was done for her that could be done, and after a time she became far less boisterous than formerly, and sometimes appeared perfectly rational for days. She still retained her taste for literature, and nothing but George's firmness and decision prevented her from sending off the manuscript of her grammar, which was now finished. It was in vain that he told her she was not now obliged to write for a living, as he had more than enough for her support.

She replied it was not *money* she coveted, but *reputation*,—a name,—to be pointed at as Mrs. Sarah Furbush, authoress of "Furbush's Grammar," &c., —*this* was her aim!

"You may write all you choose for the entertainment of ourselves and our friends," said George, "but I cannot allow you to send any thing to a publisher,"

Sally saw he was in earnest, and at last yielded the point, telling Mary in confidence that "she never saw any one in her life she feared as she did Esquire Moreland when he set his foot down!"

And George did seem to have a wonderful influence over her, for a single look from him would quiet her when in her wildest moods. In spite of the desire she once expressed of finding her sister, Mrs. Campbell's pride at first shrank from acknowledging a relationship between herself and Sally Furbush, but the fact that George Moreland brought her to his home, treating her in every respect as his equal, and always introducing her to his fashionable friends as his aunt, gradually reconciled her to the matter, and she herself became at last very attentive to her, frequently urging her to spend a part of the time with her. But Sal always refused, saying that "for the sake of her niece she must be very particular in the choice of her associates!"

True to her promise, on Mary's twenty-first birth-day, Mrs Campbell made over to her one fourth of her property, and Mary, remembering her intentions towards William Bender, immediately offered him one half of it. But he declined accepting it, saying that his profession was sufficient to support both himself and Jenny, for in a few weeks Jenny, whose father had returned from California, was coming, and already a neat little cottage, a mile from, the city, was being prepared for her reception. Mary did not urge the matter, but many an article of furniture more costly than William was able to purchase found its way into the cottage, which with its overhanging vines, climbing roses, and profusion of flowers, seemed just the home for Jenny Lincoln.

And when the flowers were in full bloom, when the birds sung amid the trees, and the summer sky was bright and blue, Jenny came to the cottage, a joyous, loving bride, believing her own husband the best in the world, and wondering if there was ever any one as happy as herself. And Jenny was very happy. Blithe as a bee she flitted about the house and garden, and if in the morning a tear glistened in her laughing eyes as William bade her adieu, it was quickly dried, and all day long she busied herself in her household matters, studying some agreeable surprise for her husband, and trying for his sake to be very neat and orderly. Then when the clock pointed the hour for his return, she would station herself at the gate, and William, as he kissed the moisture from her rosy cheek, thought her a perfect enigma to weep when he went away, and weep when he came home.

There was no place which Ella loved so well to visit, of where she seemed so happy, as at the "Cottage," and as she was of but little use at home, she frequently spent whole weeks with Jenny, becoming gradually more cheerful, —more like herself, but always insisting that she should never be married.

The spring following Mary's removal to Boston, Mrs. Mason came down to the city to live with her adopted daughter, greatly to the delight of Aunt Martha, whose home was lonelier than it was wont to be, for George was gone, and Ida too had recently been married to Mr. Elwood, and removed to Lexington, Kentucky.

And now a glance at Chicopee, and our story is done. Mr. Lincoln's California adventure had been a successful one, and not long after his return he received from George Moreland a conveyance of the farm, which, under Mr. Parker's efficient management, was in a high state of cultivation. Among the inmates of the poor-house but few changes have taken place. Miss Grundy, who continues at the helm, has grown somewhat older and crosser; while Uncle Peter labors industriously at his new fiddle, the gift of Mary, who is still remembered with much affection.

Lydia Knight, now a young lady of sixteen, is a pupil at Mount Holyoke, and Mrs. Perkins, after wondering and wondering where the money came from, has finally concluded that "some of *George's folks* must have sent it!"

THE END.